You're so Basic

Finding You

Angela Casella

ac

Also by Angela Casella

Babes of Brewing

Best Served Cold

Worst Nanny Ever

Unlucky in Love

The Love Fixers

The Love Bandits

The Love Losers

The Love Destroyers

The Thief Who Saved Christmas

Finding You

You're so Extra

You're so Bad

You're so Basic

You're so Vain

Fairy Godmother Agency

A Borrowed Boyfriend

A Stolen Suit

A Brooding Bodyguard

A Reluctant Roommate

Bringing Down the House (Nicole and Damien's story)

Highland Hills

(co-written with Denise Grover Swank)

Matchmaking a Billionaire

Matchmaking a Single Dad

Matchmaking a Grump

Matchmaking a Roommate

Bad Luck Club

(co-written with Denise Grover Swank)

Love at First Hate

Jingle Bell Hell

Fraudulently Ever After

Matchmaking Mischief

Asheville Brewing

(co-written with Denise Grover Swank)

Any Luck at All

Better Luck Next Time

Getting Lucky

Bad Luck Club

Luck of the Draw (novella)

All the Luck You Need (prequel novella) by Angela Casella

To the leaf peepers. May we all find that perfect leaf.

Chapter One

Danny

My safe space has been commandeered by a hungover pirate. If that sounds overly dramatic, then let me assure you: it's mostly true.

It's November first, and my new roommate, Mira, rolled up in her moving truck at around noon, still dressed in her Halloween costume from last night and smelling like the bar she owns. She overslept, and her movers were on a tight schedule, so they couldn't wait for her to get changed.

I'd told Mira it wasn't necessary for her to hire movers. I work from home, so I would have helped her. I know my friend Burke offered to help too. He's marrying Mira's sister, Delia, which is why she's joining me in my nepotism apartment. She needed a place to live after breaking up with her ex, and Burke had already decided to move out of the apartment we'd shared for over a decade. He owns it, and he's been letting me live here rent free for years out of generosity.

Sure, I got groceries and cooked and helped Burke with tech support, but those favors were nothing next to what he was doing for me, and I knew it. So I couldn't exactly complain when he told me his fiancée's sister was moving in with me. Instead, I finally put my foot down and insisted that if he wasn't here to benefit from my cooking and tech expertise, I would be paying him a fair rent or I would be moving out.

He agreed, but he set the rent.

It's not fair—to him, to be clear. The apartment is a penthouse loft in downtown Asheville, and if he sold it, he'd be able to add more millions to his trust fund.

Then again, I have to live with *her*.

I haven't spent much time with Mira, but she's loud and outspoken and has every mark of someone who's going to destroy my peace. My life might not be exciting, but it's comfortable. It follows a familiar rhythm that helps me anticipate what will happen and when. I depend on that, but I sense it is about to be pulled out from under my feet.

That's why my other friend Leonard, Burke's business partner, put forth a third offer of moving help—he wanted to see the way my face looked when a hurricane of a woman moved into my space.

But Mira turned down all of our offers and hired a couple of guys to do what we would have done for free. She's "a woman who takes care of her own business," she insisted. Being as my little sister Ruthie's the same way, I knew it would do no good to keep arguing.

So I sat at my desk, feeling like one lazy asshole as I watched the movers lug her stuff upstairs and into Burke's empty room. There wasn't much of it, thank God, just some boxes and a few suitcases.

It's funny how a person's life can be to condensed to so little.

If I had to move out of this apartment tomorrow, and maybe I will, I wouldn't even have that much. It's enough to humble a man.

Now, she's in her room, presumably unpacking, and I'm sitting at my desk in the corner of the living room. Staring at my computer without actually working on anything, my headphones on.

Footsteps pad down the hall. I don't have a dog, so there's only one person it could be. A throat clears. I stare at my computer screen for a second, hoping she just has allergies. But it happens again. Sighing, I turn to look at her.

She changed out of her pirate costume and is wearing animal-print leggings and an oversized shirt a shade of pink that makes my eyes want to close. Her hair is black, her eyes the color of a glass of whiskey, and she wears eye makeup that reminds me of a cat. She's hot, which doesn't make her presence more welcome. If anything, the opposite is true.

It's been long enough since I've been with a woman that it doesn't take much to make me feel sexually frustrated, and the way those leggings curve over her thighs and ass is making me...uncomfortable.

"It's a little dark out here, don't you think?" she asks, and her voice has the audacity to be sexy too, a little low and throaty. "Can I put my SAD lamp over there?"

She points to the corner where my favorite armchair sits. It doesn't know what indignities lie in store for it.

"What's a SAD lamp?" More importantly, does this mean she plans on claiming the armchair?

"It's for Seasonal Affective Disorder." She strolls over to the corner in question and lowers into my armchair with a loud oomph, as if she can't even sit quietly. I try not to flinch, but I'm filled with the awareness that my chair's going to smell like her.

"The light's already starting to change. I can't take it when it's only bright for five hours of the day." She waves at one of the large plate glass windows overlooking Asheville as if it has offended her. "Makes me go nuts."

"You wake up late," I tell her, feeling compelled to speak the obvious. "If you want it to stay bright for longer, try getting up in the morning."

She looks at me like I'm an idiot. "Where's the fun in that?"

I could tell her it's plenty fun to bike up to a mountain peak and watch the sun come up in a sea of colors...especially if you can manage it on a day when there isn't anyone else around. Or to be the first to arrive at a coffee shop and grab a table by the window. But that would lead to a conversation, which is exactly what I'm trying to avoid. I've decided the less we have to do with each other, the better. For my own sanity.

"Yeah, the lamp is fine." I prefer low lighting at home, but I'll give her the lamp if it'll make her happy. Especially if it'll make her step off.

"Thanks for being so cool about everything, Danny," she says with a broad, red-lipped smile, which immediately makes me feel guilty. She doesn't know her presence is making my skin itch. It's also not her fault. Normal people don't get agitated by the presence of strangers. Especially strangers who are hot women. I could tell her to call me Daniel, but she knows me through a few of the only people who still call me Danny. It would make me seem rude.

I *am* rude, but I'd prefer to give people time to figure that out.

I nod and slide the earphones back into place.

"Say, Danny…"

I lower the earphones, then take my blue-light-filtering glasses off and rub my eyes.

"What's up?"

She bounces a little in the chair, and I try not to notice the way it makes her breasts sway under her shirt. "I'm getting a record table delivered. It's this really rad, vintage-looking piece. A little *I finally moved out of my ex-boyfriend's apartment* gift to myself. I was thinking I'd put in my room, but if you want it out here…"

I don't. I listen to podcasts while I work. Then again, I'm probably going to have to move my desk into my bedroom, aren't I? I'm in the second, much smaller bedroom, so I'll be squeezed up against my bed if I move my two-screen set up in there, but that's a small price to pay for peace.

"Sure," I say tightly. "Do whatever you like."

She tips her head to the side, her dark hair swaying with the movement. My eyes follow it against my will. "Are you one of those people who says things you don't mean? Because we'll have to cure you of that. I prefer a more straightforward approach."

"I'm trying to be polite," I say through clenched teeth. The words came out a little sharper than intended. They're not polite at all, honestly, and Ruthie would be ashamed of me. Hell, her daughter Izzy would probably say she was ashamed of me, too, and she'd do it with a pushed-out lower lip that would make it ten times more effective.

Mira's eyes light up with something like humor. "Ah-ha, so there's someone in there after all. I've been trying to tease you out."

"What's *that* supposed to mean?" I grind out.

"That you're more boarded up than a murder house."

I can actually feel my jaw ticking. "You don't know me well enough to make that assessment."

"And it's obvious you don't want me to get to know you," she accuses, lifting her eyebrows.

There she goes, naming the elephant in the room and inviting it to be her pet.

I have my reasons for not wanting her here. Many of them, in fact. I'd prefer to keep them to myself.

"I seriously doubt we enjoy the same music," I tell her. It's a dickish thing to say, but I'm starting to feel like a dick.

Her eyebrows hike up higher, practically meeting her hair line. Her face is expressive in its disdain. "So that's a no to listening to sweet, sweet tunes in the living room. Gotcha. I can tell you're going to be a barrel of laughs."

The buzzer rings, and she jumps up out of my favorite chair. I look away, trying not to give off Gollum vibes, then sigh again and get to my feet. "Let me help—"

A slash of her hand attempts to shut me down. "I've got this, Danny. It's just a box. I'm going to have to build it up here."

She'll probably refuse to let me help with that, too.

"I *insist*," I say tightly.

"Well, I can't prevent you from following me," she says as she makes her way to and then out of the door. I *do* follow her, because now that I've decided I'm helping, I won't be put off. "Men do like to follow me around."

"Is that why your boyfriend asked you to move out?" I ask before my mind can catch up with my mouth. Fuck. I don't usually let that happen anymore. I feel a flash of remorse, but once words are released into the ether, they can't be reclaimed.

She looks back at me, clearly surprised, and stops walking so abruptly I almost barrel into her. "Is it weird that I like you more when you're a dick than when you're being quiet and agreeing to everything?"

"Yes, probably. I'm sorry. I shouldn't have said that. Either thing, actually."

Her lips curve upward in a smile that's so bright it feels like it unhinges something inside of me. I want to reach out and touch it.

I can practically hear one of my friends telling me this is what happens when a man lets himself go too long without sex.

"What?" she asks, lifting her fingers to her lips and taking what I wanted for herself. "Did I fuck up my lipstick? I did it without a mirror."

"No," I say woodenly, my mind hitched on that image of her painting her lips that bright shade of red without a mirror. "It's great. Perfect."

"Ah." She grins. "We're back to the monosyllabic words."

"Perfect has two syllables." Damn my inability to let a logical fallacy slide.

"And there's my grump." Her eyes are dancing with amusement —amusement at me—but for some reason I find myself smiling.

"Maybe I like to keep people guessing."

"That's one of us, then," she says. She gives her lips another tap, then says, "Living with Bryon made me realize that he was a shallow, dumb dick on legs. *I'm* the one who broke up with *him*."

"Oh," I say, which is as much intelligence as I'm capable of at the moment.

Then she heads toward the stairs. She goes down ahead of me, and it would take the will of a man who's had sex more recently than a year and nine months ago to avoid watching her swaying ass as she descends the steps.

When we get to the bottom, there's a gigantic box waiting outside the plate glass door of the building—and no deliveryman in sight.

"Are you kidding me?" Mira mutters as she opens the door and glances left and right. "Someone could have stolen my baby."

"I thought you said this was a record table?" I ask. Because it looks big enough to build a dining room table for the army of men who apparently follow her around.

She shrugs. "I have a lot of records, and I also took a lot of Byron's."

"Let's get it inside," I say, grabbing one end of the box.

She picks up the other, and we back it through the door.

"Elevator," I say, nodding to the elevator at the other end of the lobby, past the mailboxes. It's an old claptrap kind of thing, with a heavy door you need to pull open yourself, and an accordion style door beyond it that opens when you press the button. It's charming in the way old things are—and every time I see it, I think about the people who lived here forty years ago. Fifty.

"No way." She shakes her head for emphasis. "That thing wigs me out. Getting stuck on an elevator is my idea of hell."

"Why don't you let me take it up, then?" I say. "I like the elevator."

"Of course you do," she scoffs, but there's some merriment in her eyes. "It's a fossil."

"I can't be much older than you," I comment, hoisting my end of the box a little higher, because dammit if it's not starting to seem like we'll be carrying it up a few flights of stairs.

"I may be thirty, but I have the soul of a much younger person. You have the soul of an old guy whose balls are hanging down to his knees."

Her eyes are glimmering as she says it, and it's obvious she's having fun, or near enough.

"I'll go at the bottom," I volunteer, because the weight will settle on whoever's in that position. I'm taller and bigger, and therefore the weight should settle on me.

"No, I will," she insists. "I don't like walking backward. That wigs me out too."

"So no elevators and no moonwalking. Got it."

"See!" she says, her voice louder than it has any reason to be. "You're so old."

In my head I can hear another woman telling me something similar.

We don't fit together anymore, Danny. You're too...well...basic. Shit. I didn't mean that. I guess it's just that we want different things. You want...this life. I want something more.

It was my ex-girlfriend Daphne who said that, and it still burns. Daphne, who fate is flinging back at me like a boomerang after all these years. She works at Big Bear Games, the company that's interested in buying the computer game that my buddy Drew and I made over the last several years in our free time. I have a meeting there in a few weeks. I'll be seeing her again. I'll finally have a chance to—

"Come on, dude, this is heavy!" Mira says, jostling the box.

"I strongly object to you taking the bottom position."

She gives me a wicked look with those cat eyes. "That's what she said."

Damn. This woman is going to kill me.

"Okay, just remember you're the one who made the decision."

We back it up to the staircase, and I start up the steps. I try to take as much of the weight as I can, even though gravity has different ideas.

"You doing okay down there?" I ask, because the box has hidden most of Mira from me. I can just see a flash of her black hair, her whiskey eyes.

"Never better," she says. Then she starts humming some infernal pop song under her breath as if to prove she's comfortable with the situation.

But we're still on the first set of stairs.

I make her pause when we get to the second floor landing. She rolls her eyes and calls me a grandfather, but I can tell she's feeling it. It's there in the bead of sweat falling down her hairline.

"I can probably carry this up by myself," I offer.

What I'd really do, is carry it over to the elevator opening on the second floor, but if I get her to agree, I figure I can lug it up any way I choose.

"No way. I need to get some exercise."

So we start up the next set of stairs.

That's when it happens. A tiny furry creature that looks like a mouse comes scurrying down the side of the steps. It runs over *my foot*. I flinch but keep hold of the box.

"Pumpkin," shouts a mournful voice from the next landing, and I get a glimpse of a small round face and curly hair before I hear a screech from down below.

I grab the end of the box for all I'm worth, because I can feel Mira losing her grip on it. Her side falls with a bang, a slew of swearing that probably educated that child more than any fifth grader could, and then she falls down the four or five steps to the landing below.

Shit, shit, shit. I still have the enormous box on the steps, and I can't let it slide down, because it'd slide right into her.

"What have you done to Pumpkin?!" the little girl on the landing screams, as if her rodent didn't cause this mess to begin with.

Without knowing what else to do, I start lugging the box up as fast as I can, knowing the faster I'm done, the faster I can get back to Mira. The kid sees me coming and screams again, slamming the door as if she thinks I'm some kind of weirdo. I finally get to the top and set the box down, then practically vault down the steps to get to Mira. She's not screaming now, but her face is pale.

"Are you okay?" I ask.

I'm scared to touch her, to hurt her, but I reach out and tuck her hair behind her ear, then cup her cheek. "Where does it hurt?"

She gives a pained laugh. "Fucking everywhere. I think I broke my left foot when I dropped the box on it, and then I *definitely* broke my ankle when I fell. But on the plus side..." She lifts up her hand, showing me the furry little rodent. It's orange with spots. "I'm kind of a hero, you know."

"The city will hold a parade in your honor." I realize I'm still touching her, like an asshole, so I take my hand away and pull out my phone.

"What are you doing?" she hisses.

"Calling an ambulance."

"No way. I have really shitty insurance. I can't pay for an ambulance. Can you drive me to the emergency room?"

I eye her ankle, which is twisted at an abnormal angle.

"It's not a good idea."

"Please, Danny." I'm taken aback by the way she's looking at me. I may be good at the mechanics of poker, but I can't usually detect the feelings that are running beneath someone's face like currents in a river. Still, even I can see vulnerability in her face. The need. This is a woman who won't ask anyone for anything—even moving help that's freely offered. So I can only say yes. I think I'd probably do anything she asked me to at that moment.

I nod. "What do you want to do about your baby?"

She curses again, then asks, "Do you have a pen?"

"No."

"Ask Pumpkin's people for a pen after the kid gets done screaming bloody murder, then this is what I want you to write on it."

She tells me, then hands over the little creature, which promptly bites me. The door to the landing swings open again, and a big guy is standing in it. He's wide and beefy with a buzzed head and a face that's probably red no matter what he does with it.

"You the folks who are terrorizing children?"

I stand up, my back straightening, and lift up the squirming rodent. "This yours? It ran down the stairs and made my friend drop her box and fall. Looks like she broke her ankle."

He loses some of his swagger. "Yes, that's Pumpkin." He lifts a hand to his stubbled jaw. "Your friend okay?"

"No," I say slowly, then repeat, "She *broke her ankle*. You have a pen we can borrow?"

I could ask him to keep the box for us, of course, or bring it upstairs. But this is what Mira asked me to do, and I really would give her anything right now.

"Uh, sure," he says.

"Stay put," I tell Mira, mostly because I want to amuse her.

"Asshole," she says with a small smile.

Then I head upstairs. By the time I get to the landing, the big guy's back. I exchange Pumpkin for the pen.

"My name's Big Mike."

Well, that's accurate, anyway.

"When you're ready to give the pen back—"

I interrupt him. "I'm not going to pay you a visit to give it back, buddy. She has a broken ankle. That your pet caused. You're lucky I don't call my lawyer friend."

Not that Shane would bother with such a small case, even though he's my best friend. Even so, the threat's always a good one to keep in your back pocket.

"Right, right," he says, but he gives the pen a longing look before he backs through the door, Pumpkin hanging on to his hand with her teeth, the little devil. I'm not sure what he likes about the pen so much, it looks like a promotional giveaway from someplace called The Treasure Club.

"Danny?" Mira calls. "Can we hurry this up?"

I scrawl the message as quickly as I can onto the surface of the box, then push it up against the wall by the door so it's out of the way.

If you steal this box, you'll be cursed to have seven years of bad sex. So don't steal it.

Then I hurry back down the stairs, nearly tripping in my haste.

"This might hurt," I say, worry twining through me. I don't want to hurt her. I might not want her to live in my apartment or sit in my chair, but suddenly it seems very important for nothing else to hurt her.

"I'm sure it absolutely will," she says.

Then I scoop her up, taking care not to touch her ankle.

I know she's in pain. I know it from the way she buries her head into my shirt, her head tucked beneath mine, and wraps her arms around my neck, her fingers brushing the hair in a way that sends pleasant sensations through me. But she doesn't cry out or make any kind of sound at all.

Sometimes it makes me uncomfortable to touch people I don't know. The awkwardness of it. Their skin might feel strange against mine, their scent unwelcome. But I don't feel that way with her. Her body seems to fit against mine, and her scent fits her in a way that meets my sense of order—spicy and confident, cloves with a hint of vanilla. A feeling of protectiveness fills me, demanding that I make it all right, even though I know it's impossible to rewind time. Cradling her against my chest, I start down the stairs.

"I guess we should have taken the elevator," she says in a small voice, her voice muffled by my shirt.

"Yes," I say, "I thought that was obvious."

Chapter Two

Mira

"Eight weeks?" I sputter, repeating the words the doctor just said to me. Wasn't hearing about the surgery bad enough?

I mean, seriously, why should an ankle injury require surgery *and* two months to recuperate? If a guy falls down on the football field, they give him a few minutes to shake it off and then send him back in with a probable concussion.

Okay, probably not the best example.

Still. This news is unacceptable.

I can't be off my feet for that long. I run a bar, for God's sake, and I run it well.

Besides, there's the cost to think of. My deductible is ten thousand dollars. *Ten thousand dollars.* The bar is doing great, but it's not doing the kind of great where I can fork over ten grand without it feeling like someone shivved me.

For a fleeting second, I wish Danny were here, and not in the waiting room, so I could give him a *can you believe this guy?* look. Then again, he'd probably side with the doctor.

"Can't you just, I don't know, prescribe me crutches? I can hobble around and keep the cast off the ground. I'll be golden."

The doctor frowns at me, his face creasing handsomely. He's

attractive in a completely generic way—the kind of person my mother would rave about, ending her tirade of praise with *and he's a doctor*. But I could care less about snagging a man, much less a man in scrubs. The only man I'm thinking about at the moment is my new roommate.

Danny surprised me today. First, by having a personality. Second, by being surprisingly good looking after he took off those ugly glasses, like in one of those movies where the girl removes the glasses that took up half her face and reveals she's been a stone-cold fox all along. Or maybe I didn't notice the stealthy fox thing he had going on because the other couple of times I've briefly interacted with him he's shown no glimmer of personality whatsoever. But he's got these intense dark brown eyes, surrounded by eyelashes I'd need to use Black as Night mascara to achieve, and thick, wavy dark hair that's just asking to get tousled.

Oh, and he also surprised me by saving my ass.

As a rule, I'd rather not be saved, but I couldn't think of any smarter way to get to the hospital without the use of one leg. So I let him scoop me up into his arms. He's surprisingly sturdy for such a tall, lanky guy, and it felt...nice, being held against his chest. Like maybe I could rest for a moment.

And I can't deny it was pretty sweet, the way he didn't try to mansplain the need for an ambulance to me—or convince me that I should let Lucas Burke, my sister's fiancé, cover the bill, which he's definitely going to try to do. Hell, Danny even took the trouble to leave that stupid note on the record table box, just like I asked him to. Earlier, in the apartment, he'd obviously been trying to appease me by saying yes to everything I asked, but he wasn't doing that in the stairwell. And when we got to the ER, he kept up a steady stream of conversation, even though he looked worn out. He also refrained from asking me five hundred times if I was all right. Maybe that's because I obviously wasn't, but I was grateful. It felt like he was being good to me because he genuinely cared, like a prince in one of those dumb movies my little sister loved as a kid...

If the prince were a grumpy computer programmer with a stick up his ass and staggeringly ugly reading glasses. I mean, seriously, those things are—

"Of course you'll have crutches," Hot Doc says, giving me a mental shake. "But you told me you're on your feet for most of your shift. You're not going to heal like that."

"Are you going to run my bar?" I ask pointedly. "Because I worked way too hard to let that shit slide."

"You don't have employees?"

I do. My co-bartender Azalea is fan-fucking-tastic, and we just hired a fill-in bartender so we can have actual lives, but we'll need someone else to cover for me. The bar's successful enough, so I could hire someone. It's just...

It's *my bar*.

Glitterati is my brainchild. Someone once wrote in a review that walking inside immediately gave him a headache, which I took as a compliment. It's not easy to give a person an immediate headache. But apparently two parts glitter, thirty parts color, and four parts Britney Spears will do the job. Every piece of that bar carries something of me inside of it, from the resin bar top that I poured myself to the ever-changing drink list. I don't know what Glitterati would be without me.

Maybe you don't know what you'd be without Glitterati.

The voice in my head is clearly stupid, though. So I ignore it and tell the doctor with a straight face that I'm indispensable.

The doctor gives me a look that I'm familiar with, one that has nothing to do with busted ankles and sprained feet. "I can see that," he says, a corner of his mouth hitching up, his blue-gray eyes sparkling.

It does less than nothing for me. I might as well be watching a commercial for foot fungus cream. What this charmer doesn't know is that I'm charmed out. I'm not going to fall for any B.S. from another man who knows how to talk the talk, no thank you. My ex Byron wasn't my first mistake, but moving in with him after two weeks of dating was a piece of idiocy I won't be repeating—and living with him for two months after we broke up was a hell I'll never live in again.

I'd much rather interfere with other people's romantic lives than bother with my own. My sister and my friend Shauna are taken and my co-bartender, Azalea, has no interest in humans with penises, otherwise I might try to hurl the hot doc at one of them.

"So you can understand the problem," I tell him, using the clicker attached to the bed to raise it up higher. My ankle is a constant throbbing pain, and I'm about five seconds away from begging him for some sweet, sweet drugs. "Can't I get, like, a steroid shot or something?"

"At least a month and a half off your feet," he says sternly. "You don't want to walk with a limp for the rest of your life."

"Shit, I guess I don't," I admit.

My last thought before tuning out is that Danny isn't going to like this news one bit. I think both of us were banking on the fact that our schedules don't align, but now we're going to be seeing a lot more of each other than either of us bargained for. He wanted to come back here with me after the triage team finally decided a very clearly broken ankle was worthy of medical attention, but I wouldn't let him. I told him it was because the nurse might want to disrobe me, and he gave me a scandalized look that reminded me of the way my grandfather used to heave a sigh whenever a "heavy petting" scene came on TV. Then he clenched his jaw and said he'd stay in the waiting room if it made me more comfortable.

Teasing him might become a new hobby.

"Well, I'll *need* new hobbies," I muse aloud.

"Or you can find a boyfriend." The doctor's so sure of himself he doesn't even seem to realize he's breaking rules. I'm pretty sure it's frowned upon to try to pick up patients high on pain meds. Not that I've had anything but some expired Tylenol Danny had in his car.

"Yeah, that's a no from me," I say with a laugh. "I want to be entertained, not bored."

The crease between his eyes suggests I'm the only person who's turned him down recently. Or maybe ever. He opens his pretty mouth to say something, but a knock lands on the door. The way he jolts away suggests he *does* know he was doing something wrong.

Busted, Hot Doc.

"Can I come in?" I hear my sister saying. "They said she was allowed visitors."

Damn Danny and his big mouth. He must have called her as soon as they took me back, even though I very clearly told him not to contact anyone until I'd spoken to a doctor.

"Certainly," the doctor says, and then my sister opens the door, revealing herself in all of her vava-voom hot redhead splendor. I can tell from the way Hot Doc lets his gaze linger on her curvy figure that he's immediately switched camps, the traitor. But when his gaze dips to the huge-ass engagement ring on her ring finger, he droops like a daisy left out of the water. "You must be..."

Engaged to a hot millionaire, is what she is.

"Her sister," Delia says, hurrying to my bedside.

"Oh, I'm fine." I wave a hand at her. "Nothing a little surgery and four weeks off my feet won't cure."

"Eight," Hot Doc interjects. "Six at the bare minimum." I'm starting to think he just likes the sound of his own voice.

I glower at him, but he ignores me, making his way toward the door and muttering something about admissions paperwork and stubborn women.

I'm about to say something to Delia, but when Hot Doc leaves, I catch a glimpse of Danny leaning against the opposite wall of the hallway, poring over his phone. He's holding it close to his face, most likely because he took off those hideous glasses earlier. I'll bet the Judas is busy texting everyone else I know. Hell, maybe he even made a Facebook post.

"What the fuck?" I say to Delia in a furious undertone the second before the door swings shut. "Why'd you let Danny come back here?"

She glances around the small but serviceable room and pulls up one of the two visitor chairs. "Mira," she says as she sits, looking wildly out of place in her bright blue and yellow dress in this room of muted whites and blues. "The poor man was beside himself. He was acting like this was all his fault."

"Oh, he knows it was entirely my fault."

She gives me a stern look no one should ever have to get from their little sister. "You really should have taken the elevator."

Seriously? Did he have to tell her *everything*? For someone who's so closed-lipped half the time, he can certainly be chatty.

"Danny," I call out. There are probably rules about shouting in a hospital, but I'm realistic enough to know I can't hop over to the door on my one good leg and then miraculously kick him in the ass with it.

The door cracks open, and his face appears in the narrow space. He's back to that neutral expression of earlier, before he revealed his surly personality.

"Yes, you," I say, because he's paused mid-opening of the door. "I don't know multiple grown men who go by the name of Danny."

"I don't go by it either," he says, annoyance flashing in his eyes as he pushes the door the rest of the way open and steps in. The feeling of victory that flushes through me from getting a reaction, even a bad one, probably says something about my emotional health.

"No?" I ask as the door closes behind him. "That's not what I've heard."

"Me either," Delia says, sounding concerned. "Is there something else you'd like us to call you?"

"Yeah," I add. "How about *narc*? I thought you and I had an understanding."

"Calling her was the right thing to do," he says, running his fingers across the top of the pocket of his jeans. Shit, I probably shouldn't be looking in the vicinity of his pockets. He might get the wrong idea. But the thought makes my gaze wander to the place between his pockets. I abruptly look up to meet his eyes, but he looks away. A guilty conscience at work, clearly. But he sighs and says, "You and I barely know each other, and you had a medical emergency. If something happened to me at the apartment, I wouldn't be pissed off if you called *my* sister."

So, he has a sister, huh?

I'm suddenly deeply curious about her. "What's her name? I need to know who to look for after I push you out of the window. We both know it's going to happen."

He gives me a half smile, one corner of his mouth lifting above the other, and I can't help but marvel, again, about how smiling—really smiling—changes his face. "Ruthie. But I don't think she'd take kindly to you pushing me out the window. She likes me most of the time."

I want to ask more questions, but my own sister is staring at me, worried, and I can't have that.

"I wouldn't call it an emergency," I say, but the words lack conviction, because my leg is propped up, and I was just told I need surgery. I keep trying to sugarcoat the whole thing in my mind, but it's not making the medicine go down easier.

"You just told me you need surgery, Mira," Delia says, her expression worried as she leans forward in her chair to check out my fucked-up foot. They took off my shoe and wrapped it up.

"*Surgery?*" Danny asks, looking a little pale.

"They said it was no big deal," I insist. "A little chop-chop, thirty minutes at the most. They're doing it tomorrow, and they said I'd only be in here for a couple of days afterward."

Delia puts a hand on my shoulder. "Please come and stay with us when you get out, Mira. I don't like the thought of you being alone."

Laughter snorts out of me. "That's not much of a compliment to Danny, or whatever-his-name-is over there." I wave in his direction.

"Oh, that's okay," he says awkwardly, shifting on his feet. "I know she didn't mean it like that. But you don't have to go anywhere." He swallows, as if it's incredibly difficult for him to say all of this out loud and with anything resembling conviction. My eyes follow the motion. "I'll help you."

"As you just said, we barely know each other," I feel the need to point out, even though I am *absolutely* not going to move in with Delia and Lucas. They're in the phase of being in love that is sickening to outside people. I'm happy for them, obviously, but I'd prefer to be happy for them from a distance. Shaking off the thought, I add, "I don't even know what your preferred name is."

"I shouldn't have said that. Danny's fine," he says, his gaze darting to the door like he's considering a sudden and abrupt escape. "My friends call me Danny."

"So we're friends now?"

He grins at me then, and to my shock, I feel...something. It's the way it makes his whole face brightens up. His eyes gleam, creasing at the corners in a way that tells me that when he laughs, he gives it his everything, and his whole body seems to hum. Without knowing how I know, I'm certain this is a man who smiles when he means to and only then. "You know what? All things considered, I guess we'd better be friends."

"Does this mean you won't make a Facebook post about my ankle?"

His brow furrows in that familiar frown. "I don't use Facebook.

Everyone knows their security is a joke. You probably shouldn't use it either."

Honestly, it was a rookie mistake for me to think otherwise. The man's a Boomer trapped in the body of a surprisingly attractive thirty-something.

"It's like I always say." I point a finger at him. "I don't have any secrets."

From the look on his face—his intensely dark eyes narrowed, his brow furrowed—the same can't be said for Danny.

Eeen-teresting.

Chapter Three

Danny

CONVERSATION WITH RUTHIE

So, she was there for less than a day before she broke her ankle? That's one way to get rid of an unwanted roommate. Maybe you've been listening to too many of those true crime podcasts.

No such thing. And I didn't push her.

That's your story, and you're sticking to it. ;-) ;-) ;-)

Very funny. One winky face would have done the job. Why haven't I seen you in a week? What are you plotting?

…

It doesn't have the same effect when you actually send the ellipsis.

It shall all be revealed in good time. Try not to kill your roommate.

I'll take that into consideration. If she doesn't kill me first.

. . .

"**R**uthie's up to something," I comment.

My buddies Leonard and Shane came over to help me out with a special project. We're all sitting on the floor of my apartment, circled around the bright pink contents of the box that still says *If you steal this box, you'll be cursed to have seven years of bad sex. So don't steal it.*

Well, shit. I guess I cursed myself, because I'm the one who brought it up here. Then again, I'm already almost two years in, since jacking off isn't exactly good sex.

Shane laughs, grounding me back in the moment. "When isn't your sister up to something?"

Ruthie would say he's being condescending. She'd be right. There's always been this push-pull between them, like they knew they needed to share me and didn't care to.

At the same time, he does have a point. My sister's twenty-eight years old, and she's always trying to reach up and grab a star—to find the one business idea that'll be lucrative enough that she can quit her waitressing job. It hasn't happened yet, but I believe in her. Always have.

So I shrug. "Maybe this is the one."

"And maybe it's another waste of money."

"Sick burn," Leonard comments.

Leonard and I are dressed casually, like usual. Shane's wearing a suit, but he's done us the favor of taking off his tie. When we were kids, Shane used to make fun of suits, and now he's become one. If only he'd been a shark back when I got into legal trouble ten years ago. But he wasn't, and I was a kid who couldn't afford anything but a public defender, and the rest is history.

Anyway, suits and swagger aside, Shane's the same kid who used to wear pocket protectors and insisted on being the Bard in our Dungeons and Dragons games because he liked playing the recorder. He's been my best friend since the second grade, years before we met Burke and Drew, and well over a decade before we met Leonard, so I guess we're stuck with each other. It seems like all five of us are, actually, even though Drew surprised us all by moving to Puerto Rico with his girlfriend and her grandmother. Temporarily, he said, but it's already been months.

He could be gone a decade, and we'd still consider him family. That's how it's always been with Shane, Burke, Drew, Leonard, and me.

Mira and I are kind of stuck together too.

I keep thinking about that moment when she fell—the sinking panic that filled my gut. There wasn't a damn thing I could do to stop it from happening. Other than convincing her not to take the bottom position in the first place. I should have, obviously. If I had even a fourth of Leonard's swagger and Burke's charm, maybe I could have.

I didn't like seeing that powerhouse of a woman brought down by the heavy box of poorly labelled parts that are now spread out in front of us.

While we were waiting in the emergency room, Mira was quiet and almost contrite, probably because the expired Tylenol in my car wouldn't dull a toothache, let alone a broken ankle. I tried to distract her by talking. I'm not supposed to tell anyone the details of my actual job, the one I'm shackled to by the private legal agreement I made with my boss, so I told her about the game instead.

My buddy Drew and I made True Colors together—I did the coding, and he handled the design. It took us years to finish it. For me, it started as a distraction, something I did to take the bad taste of work out of my mouth. For him, as a full-time game designer who spent most of his days designing zombie clowns, it was a chance to design a game he actually liked. Only later did it occur to me that it could give both of us an escape from our shitty jobs.

It's a survival game, of which there are plenty, but ours is special. My friends and I have always loved hiking in the Blue Ridge Mountains. We go for a two-week camping trip every year, and our game is an offshoot of that. But we're also kids who grew up on Dungeons and Dragons, so it's set in a fantasy world, the elements of which slowly unfold during gameplay.

When I told Mira about that part in the ER, she asked, "If I play it, will I get to ride a dragon?"

"No dragons."

"What's fantasy without dragons?" she asked.

Her pout was pretty, and I had to dig my nails into my palm to distract myself from it. It's not cool to want to fuck a woman who has a broken ankle, but my libido has taken a liking to Mira. Maybe it would take a liking to any sexy woman who gets close right now. Or maybe—

"Hey, you're a lawyer," Leonard says, snapping his fingers and pointing at Shane, as if there might be any disagreement about which of us is the lawyer.

"When'd you notice I was a lawyer?" Shane asks him with a smirk, tugging me back to the moment. To the guys sitting next to me and the box on the floor in front of us. To the smell of chemicals and the uncomfortable squeak of Styrofoam as Shane shifts the pieces around. I itch for my earphones. But it's a familiar itch, and I'm used to ignoring it. With them, it doesn't really cost me. "Was it when I bailed you out of jail?" Shane continues.

Leonard snaps his fingers, grinning. "That must've been it. Now, whaddya say? Will you bail me out again if I kill whoever wrote these instructions? They must've done it just to fuck with us. None of the parts match." He folds the inadequate directions into a paper airplane and sails it at my head before grabbing his beer up off the floor.

I catch the airplane before it hits my nose, then examine it.

"Nicely done." A half-second later, I shake my head in disgust. "One page. One page for all of this." I wave at the mess of wood and screws and other parts from the box. "That's not efficient, it's just stupid."

"Beer me," Leonard says.

"I'm guessing we're all going to need one," Shane agrees.

I nod and head into the kitchen to get us some cold ones.

It's Wednesday night. Mira's not coming home until tomorrow, but I figured it would be a nice gesture if I put the record table together for her.

Okay, maybe I figured she's stubborn enough to try building it herself with her cast propped up on a pile of my books. I'd prefer not to have to stand by like an asshole and watch her do that. And if the finished record table is sitting in the living room with a conciliatory bow on top of it when she gets home, I won't have to.

I don't have any bows, obviously, but Delia probably has a collection of them.

She and Burke are at the hospital visiting Mira. The surgery went well yesterday, I guess. When Mira comes home, she'll be on pain meds and crutches, and she'll have to spend a lot of time on the couch. Delia told me, again, that Mira should come stay with her, but I get the feeling her sister won't go for it. I may not have known Mira long, but it's obvious she's the kind of woman who doesn't like to be told what to do. Or to rely on other people. I've never found that easy myself, so I can't hold it against her.

I'm going to make sure she's okay. I feel a bone-deep need to, because she got hurt on my watch. It may not have been my fault, per se. But it *is* my responsibility. I asked Delia what would make her comfortable, and she helped me unpack a few of Mira's personal things. There are now throw pillows on my couch and a print of a squirrel smoking a pipe on the wall. I don't hate them.

Then there's the record table. I *do* hate that. The color reminds me of the Pepto my mother always forced on me when I made the mistake of admitting to a stomach ache. Still, Mira broke her ankle for it—the least I can do is build it.

When I come back with the beers, Leonard's laughing and waving a stick around like it's a sword. "This one's labeled Z. It jumps from G to fucking Z. You think the person who put this together was high? One time when I was high, I thought I'd solved all the mysteries of the universe, but then I couldn't remember any of the brilliant shit after I woke up."

I hand over the beers. Leonard takes his with his free hand, still gripping that random thin rod.

I have no idea how that stick could possibly be part of a record table.

"This is going to be a long night, isn't it?" I ask with a sigh.

"Don't underestimate the power of beer," Leonard says, waving his bottle at me.

"Or overestimate it," Shane puts in.

"I can rebuild houses, I'll figure this shit out, no problem," Leonard says. It's true enough—he and Burke run a house flipping business, L&L Restoration, that they started a few months back, after Burke left his family's empire. Lucky for him, he still has plenty to fall back on, from this apartment to his trust fund. I don't say this with any bitterness. If there's anyone who deserves such a gift, it's him.

"And you're supposed to be brilliant," Leonard adds, pointing to me. "Didn't you get into MENSA?"

"I only applied because you dared me. Those people are fucking weird, and coming from me, that's saying something. Besides, putting together poorly labelled furniture isn't one of my few talents," I say. I could add that if I were really brilliant, I would have figured out a way to get out of my agreement with my boss that didn't entail spending years making a complicated computer game. But even though my friends know the basic story about how I came to work at a company I hate for a man I abhor, I haven't shared all of the shitty details.

"Lucky for you, the word impossible doesn't exist in my vocabulary," Leonard continues. "I'm a god of small things."

Shane gives him an incredulous look. "Buddy, you walked right into this, so I've got to do it. That's what your girlfriend told me last week."

Leonard laughs the loudest of any of us.

We work on the record table for a while, shooting the shit while Leonard tells us what goes where. He's surprisingly good at figuring out the for-shit directions. He claims it's because his mind works in mysterious ways too. We're toward the end when he looks me in the eye and asks, "You give any more thought to what Josie said?"

"No," I bluster.

I'm lying, and from the expression on his face, he knows it. Josie the Great is a psychic who Leonard and Burke know. Don't ask me how. I'm sure they've explained at some point, but that's the kind of don't-need-to-know information that goes in one ear and out the other.

I've only met her once. She took one look at me and told me that I've already met my soulmate and made a bad impression on her... the same day I found out my ex-girlfriend works for the company that's interested in buying the game that may very well save my life.

I'm not the kind of guy who believes in that sort of thing.

Computers make sense. They operate according to logic. People do not. They say one thing and mean another. They ask to be left alone and then expect you to show up with flowers. They tell you they like you just as you are, and the next minute they get upset because you haven't changed. Some people, like Josie, claim they can communicate with the other side when by its very nature, death is unknowable. Any sort of greater power would also, per force, be unknowable and beyond understanding.

So I don't really believe Josie the Great is either great or psychic, but...

There's no denying that what she said, foolish and vapid or not, has been on my mind.

"My boy's much too logical to believe in that bullshit," Shane says. "Right, buddy?"

Leonard laughs. "Right. You're just saying that because after he falls, you're gonna be next on the chopping block."

"So you feel like something got chopped off, huh, Leonard?" Shane says with a grin.

"Laugh all you want, brother," he says with a know-it-all smile, "you'll see what it's like on the other side soon enough."

Leonard's in a relationship with Shauna, one of Mira and Delia's friends. She's a sarcastic potter with purple hair, and I honestly couldn't think of anyone better equipped to keep up with him.

"When's the meeting?" Shane asks, watching me.

"A little over two weeks from now," I say, trying to sound off-handed, like I haven't been thinking of it steadily. I haven't seen Daphne in years, but her words stuck with me long after I stopped thinking about our failed relationship.

Too basic.

Basic means boring—any fool knows that.

It shouldn't bother me, being boring, and in some ways it's an aspiration of mine. The world can be too much for me—too loud, too bright, too demanding—so I like taking in little pieces of it at a time. Picking up a latte and sitting in the park. Working on the balcony in the afternoon or evening, when the sun's not too bright. Drinking a beer with my buddies at one of their houses, or in a bar that's so bad it's not flocked with tourists. Spending quality time with my sister and my niece. Biking in the mountains and watching the sun rise above them and wrap them up with gold. Those little pleasures might sound small, but sew them together, and you get something good.

Except for Safe-T Net. I'd give my day job away in a fucking heartbeat, if I could afford to.

That's where my long game with the computer game comes in. If we make good money off it, and I've convinced myself it's worth good money, I might finally be able to quit.

Drew had some money saved up, so he's already quit his job. Of course, he didn't have the same shitty reasons to stay. I don't blame him for moving, but I wish he'd come back to take this meeting with me. I'm going into the unknown alone, and that's never been something I'm good at in real life. Online, it's different.

"You determined to remind her there's nothing basic about your schlong?" Leonard asks with a grin, lifting his beer as if to...I don't know, salute my dick. I lift my beer to salute back.

"I don't know, man," I say. "Maybe." But my mind summons up an image of Mira after that box dropped on her foot, cuddled in a ball at the junction in the middle of the stairs. I feel a hollowness in my chest. Maybe I can't shake that memory because I feel like a dick for not doing more to prevent her accident. I guess I also admire her for being brave and tough and—

I'm supposed to be thinking about Daphne.

I shrug self-consciously, trying to scrub my mind. But it's not so easily scrubbed. Sometimes when images come into my head, they stick as surely as if they were covered in glue. "She's the one who got away, I guess," I say mechanically. "I was in love with her."

"She didn't get away so much as she stepped out on you," Leonard says, giving me a pointed look.

"Yes, Leonard," I say flatly. "You've made it very clear how you feel about Daphne."

He shrugs. "I'm not going to get in the way of you getting your freak on, brother, but I think she did you dirty. We all did."

I glance at Shane, who inclines his head in agreement.

"She got a job in Paris," I tell them, a little annoyed. "Who wouldn't have taken it?"

"You," Shane says. "You wouldn't have left her."

He's right, but for some reason I say, "I could have gone with her. She asked me."

I couldn't have gone, actually. My agreement with Safe-T Net stipulates that I can't take any international trips longer than two weeks. She didn't know about that, though, because I never told her about the agreement.

I'd thought about it.

I'd danced around it.

But for some reason I'd never shared that part of my life with her. My sister would probably say it was because I subconsciously didn't trust her, but I saw it as simple compartmentalization. The Safe-T Net situation happened before Daphne and I met, therefore it was unnecessary to tell her about it. And, indeed, I wasn't *supposed* to tell anyone.

My friends knew, and so did Ruthie, who'd been at the middle of the whole thing in some ways, but that's because they'd all been there while it was going down.

"No doubt," Leonard says, but it lacks conviction. "Well, I'm sure y'all will have a lot to talk about."

She will, anyway. Daphne lived in Paris for a few years, and now she's back in Asheville. I'm still where I was eight years ago, back when she called me basic. Living in an apartment I don't own. Working at a job that I hate but can't yet quit.

If my life seemed boring to her back then, it sure as shit won't be interesting now. I'm still not the kind of guy who enjoys networking events and cocktail hours with strangers who'd like to be impressed. I'll never be.

When I first found out about her connection to Big Bear Games, in a scheduling email sent by an assistant, I promised myself I would change her impression of me. It had seemed important, because it had been years since I'd met a woman who'd made me feel anything but the most...well, basic sort of interest. Maybe there was a reason for that, I'd speculated, and Daphne could be that reason. I've thought about emailing her directly, asking her to get a drink to 'clear the air,' but every time I sit down to write the message, I seem to find something else to do. And she hasn't reached out to contact me either. In the chaos of the last few days, I haven't really thought about it.

"Didn't Mira say she wanted to give you a makeover?" Leonard asks offhandedly, his lips twitching like they want to smile.

My friends being the loudmouths they are, Mira has heard all about Daphne and our past. Before she moved in she offered, with an enthusiasm that made me want to lock myself in my room, to give me a makeover like in some eighties movie I've heretofore avoided watching. I'd like to keep up that trend.

It was embarrassing for obvious reasons, and also because I, like most people, would prefer for the people I find attractive not to think I'm unattractive.

"She's got the use of one leg," I tell him. "I don't think she'll be keen on the idea anymore."

He snorts and runs a hand back through his hair. "I wouldn't be too sure about that, brother. She seems like the kind of woman who gets something into her mind and won't let go. Like a pitbull."

"I wouldn't call her that to her face," Shane says with a whistle. "I once called Ruthie that to her face, and she tried to hit me in the balls."

"She was ten," I say with a smirk.

"I took the threat seriously," he says, straightening up as best as he can seeing as we're sitting on the floor around the half-built record table, which looks more like a tank, if you ask me.

Leonard scoffs. "Do I look stupid to you? I'd never say that to a woman. Ten years old or a hundred and ten."

They get into a discussion of whether Leonard does, in fact, look stupid, but my mind isn't anchored in this room anymore. It's moved on to thinking about Mira coming back.

Here's an unexpected truth: I actually want her to. She was only here for a matter of hours on Monday, and I spent most of that time wanting her gone, but the apartment feels strangely empty without her. She has a certain frankness about her that I find appealing—a talent for cutting through the bullshit most people layer on like it's whipped cream.

After the guys leave, I stay up late poking at the code for a local bank. There are so many ins getting inside would be as easy as pushing a pin into a cushion. I send them an email with the details from one of my junk accounts. If they try to figure out who I am, they'll run up against a wall. I can't help them, not right now, but someone else can.

Then an email comes in from Daphne:

Daniel—

I couldn't believe it when they told me who was behind True Colors. It's brilliant, Daniel. Everything we're looking for in a survival game.

I very much look forward to seeing you again and catching up. There's so much for us to discuss. Actually, I was wondering if you'd be willing to meet up outside of the office before the meeting. I'm traveling for the next two weeks, but what do you say we meet at Glitterati at 5:00 p.m. on Wednesday, November 17?

xx Daphne

MY FIRST THOUGHT ISN'T EXCITEMENT, EVEN THOUGH SHE just reached out to me directly for the first time in eight years and sent me the same invitation I'd thought about making to her.

It's that she's asking me to meet at Mira's bar.

Still, I reply to the email and tell her yes.

Chapter Four

Mira

My leg is stretched out in front of me on the backseat of Burke's car. I stare it down like the traitor it is, and it doesn't even do me the decency of staring back. My sister and her man picked me up from the hospital this morning. Thanks to Delia, who brought me toiletries and a long-sleeved red dress. I'm not wearing the outfit I came in with on Monday. This is also probably for the best because they scissored my favorite leggings off of me. If not for Delia, I would have been going home in nothing but a shirt. A statement, to be sure, but not one I'm in the mood to make.

I'm grateful for her help, but not grateful enough to agree to her final, heartfelt pitch for me to spend the next several weeks at their house.

"No means no, Delia," I sigh out.

"You heard her, Sunshine," Burke says, and takes a turn toward the apartment building. Thank goodness someone's ears are working.

"I'm just worried," my sister says, glancing back at me.

"Yes," I agree. "We all know you're worried."

When Burke finally pulls up to the apartment building, miraculously finding a close space on the street, I glance out the window and straighten a little in my seat. Danny's waiting out front, hands in his pocket, leaned up against the wall like a rangy James Dean. If James Dean only wore brown and taupe with his jeans. Something warms inside of me, seeing him standing against the side of the building, watching the road and completely missing the location of his friend's car. He may be directionally challenged, but it's sweet that he wants to be out here.

Well...presuming he's not just waiting for delivery food.

"You ready?" Delia asks, looking back at me again.

"Yes, for the love of God." I shake a finger at her and do my best to ignore the throbbing of my ankle. "And you are not to check in on me every five minutes. I'm going to be just fine."

"You told Azalea you're taking the next week off, right? No going in at all?"

I'd had a healthy negotiation with my doctor. After next week, he admitted it should be okay if I go in during the day to help with prep and talk strategy—seated, of course. But I won't be able to pull a full shift for another month and a half—at least. He keeps throwing around that two month figure, which I don't appreciate.

Azalea is already looking for another temporary staffer to carry some of the weight, and in the meantime, Delia will be filling in. She's helped out off and on since I first opened, and since her career is an eclectic assortment of part-time jobs, she has the ability to be flexible. I'm not confident we're going to find a magical unicorn of a staffer, to be honest. The skyrocketing rents and mortgages in this town have priced out people who work in bars and restaurants, and the Wendy's on Merrimon Ave has had a Help Wanted - $15/hr sign in its window for so long it has gone dusty—probably because no one is there to clean it. That's why I lived with Byron for months after things went sour. And then more sour. And then so toxic it felt like we were chugging bleach every morning.

"Well?" Delia prompts.

"Yup," I say, reaching for the door handle. "Not going anywhere. Not doing anything."

"Wait, let me do that," Burke says as if I've suddenly lost the ability to operate a door handle. He gets out of the car as I swing the door open, and I almost spear him with one of my crutches.

He shakes his head ruefully, amused, because he's gotten to know me a bit. "You won't let your future brother-in-law help you?"

"Nope. No can do," I say, awkwardly lifting myself out with one leg. "And no treating me like I'm Delia's decrepit spinster sister."

"No one called you a spinster," he says with a sparkle in his eyes. He's a handsome man—a real prince charming type—but I don't hold it against him. He's a good one. He's the kind of guy who'll take care of my sister when she needs it and back off when she doesn't. That's a rare quality in a person.

"Ha. Ha. Very funny. You're lucky I mostly like you."

Delia's already made it around the car by the time I managed to get out, and the worry in her eyes makes me desperate to get upstairs. It's unseasonably warm, the kind of day that makes me want to stroll around downtown and soak up the energy. But I'm not in fine strolling form.

"I'm okay," I tell her for what feels like the five hundredth time. I don't hold it against her, honestly. Her best friend died eight years ago, and she's understandably protective of the people she has left, but I need to pretend my body's not broken. I'm not used to standing still, and I can already feel this whole situation throwing me off my game.

This girl's game will not be thrown. I'm already clinging to the prospect of going into Glitterati for a planning sesh about our holiday drinks and events. A week and a half isn't so long. I've talked to Azalea a few times, and the last time I called, she texted back:

I love you, babe, but you've got to leave me the fuck alone. I've got this. Focus on figuring out what else you want to do for the holiday line.

So, I have left her alone. Even if my fingers are itching to send texts asking for photos of the bar and stories about what happened last night and the night before. We're closed on Mondays, so I've only missed two nights. Still, I can't think of the last time I missed two nights in a row at the bar.

I said as much to Delia earlier, and she gave me a sad look, like I was a dog the shelter was talking about putting down, and said, "Are you listening to yourself?"

To be fair, I've been living with my ex for months, so staying at the bar was preferable to being home, but I guess she's not wrong. Work's been my life ever since I got the bar off the ground. And I like it that way. When I think about spending the next week at the apartment, with nothing to do, I want to crawl out of my skin. The last few days at the hospital, even though I was doped up, have been excruciating, with nothing to do except watch TV and read and look out the damn window. The view was pretty nice, not gonna lie, but I didn't have any desire to stare at it repeatedly.

I used to love reading, especially the spicy stuff, but I've gotten out of the habit. It's hard to sit still. To keep my mind focused on anything that isn't related to the bar.

I'm still a little doped up right now, but I've promised myself I'm cutting out the hard stuff and only taking extra-strength Tylenol when I need it. I had a friend who got addicted to pain pills a few years back, and I'm not going there. No thank you.

"Look," I tell Delia now, my voice a little pitchy. I point to Danny, who has only now caught on to our presence.

He's making his way over to us, and my pulse picks up because I recognize my chance to escape from my little sister's mother-henning.

"Danny came down to meet us," I add, "so he'll help me if I need any assistance. No need for you guys to give me an in-person escort." I make a scooting gesture. "Go on and get to work. Or whatever it is you crazy kids have in mind."

Danny gives me a long up and down look, taking me in, and although I'm sure he's just checking out my pink cast, I feel every bit of his perusal. It's those eyes of his, so intense and probing, behind his hideous glasses.

"I have a face, you know," I tell him, and his eyes lift sharply to mine. Is he...blushing?

"You have a pink cast," he comments factually. "It's unusual. I figure people wear bright things because they want other people to notice them."

"Or they just like pink," I say, lifting my eyebrows. "*I* like pink."

His lips lift into a small smile, not quite the kind that lights up his face, but there's a glimmer of amusement in his eyes. Something inside of me responds to it. "You don't say."

Burke claps Danny on the back in that whole not-a-hug thing guys do, and my sister hugs me carefully with one arm, as if she's still afraid I might break. Or break worse, I guess.

"Call me if you need me," she says, her voice soft. "Or even if you don't and you're just going crazy from being stuck inside."

No one can say she doesn't understand me.

"I will," I lie.

I'm the big sister here, and it should be my job to take care of her, not the other way around. If I were to tell her so, she would undoubtedly insist it's our job to take care of each other. Fine. But I'm not going to bottle up her sunshine. She's newly engaged and happy, and I don't want to do anything to screw that up.

Besides, other than the Byron mess and my ankle, I'm fine. My bar is doing better than ever, and if I'm having a bit of a crisis because I have trouble handing over the reins, then that's my own problem. Most people would kill for a vacation. Admittedly, they probably wouldn't choose to spend it in pain and on the couch, but so be it.

"I'm going to call you," she threatens.

"If it's before tomorrow, there's a very low chance I'll answer," I tell her honestly.

There are more goodbyes, more reassurances, and then Danny and I are left awkwardly standing on the sidewalk, him with his two perfectly good legs and ankles and me with my cast and crutches.

"Shall we?" he says.

I start laughing without really knowing why, armpits balanced on my crutches. Despite the fresh outfit, there's a very good chance I smell, and it's only now I'm realizing that it won't be easy taking a shower without any assistance.

"What?" he asks, self-consciously, shifting his weight between his feet. For some reason, it only makes me laugh harder.

"It's just…you sound like a dude in some regency movie. *Shall we*, like you're going to hook your arm around mine and take me for a walkabout."

"It would work better if you weren't on crutches," he says, then nods to the door of the building. I can tell without knowing why that he's itchy to get back inside. The traffic's busy out here, and farther down the road a siren is going off. Admittedly, it's not a pleasant spot for a chat.

I'm still chuckling as we approach the building.

"You enjoy laughing at me, don't you?" he asks as he opens the door. His eyes land on me again, but there's no annoyance in them this time, just slight amusement.

"I like laughing as a rule," I tell him.

"It's a good thing you have a nice laugh," he says, entering the building after I swing my way through.

It's a compliment no one's ever given me, and I turn my head to glance at him as the door closes behind him. He's looking at me, and he gives a small smile, as if to say he means it but won't be repeating it. I'll bet that's true. He doesn't seem like the sort of man who throws out compliments like they're candy in a parade. That makes the ones he gives actually mean something.

"You know we're going to have to take the elevator, right?" he says.

"You and that elevator." I shake my head at him. "I'm beginning to think you should move into it."

"You're not going to get me out of the apartment so easily," he says with a nearly-there smile.

I start swinging my way down the hall on the crutches, and he walks along beside me companionably. He's close enough that my shoulder brushes his arm, and I have a flashback to what it felt like to have his arms around me in that stairwell. It gives me a flush of goodwill toward him that's not at all reflected in what I say next. "Does this bring me back to the necessity of pushing you out of the window?"

"Probably," he says easily, "but Burke might have questions for you."

"He's an easy mark," I tease, giving him a slight bump with my shoulder. It's obvious he misunderstands, because he touches my arm to steady me. "He's so fond of my sister, he'll overlook a lot of bad behavior on my part. Possibly even outright murder."

"This means I'm not leaving you my record collection in my will," he reports as we come to a stop in front of the death trap elevator.

"It's a good thing we probably don't have the same taste in music," I say wryly, giving him a sidelong look.

He glances at me, still standing there.

I stare back at him.

"You want to press the button?" he finally asks.

"What am I, a five-year-old?" Truthfully, yes, I desperately want to press the button. I don't want to go on the elevator, mind you, but pressing buttons is an inherently fun thing to do.

"Sure. My niece likes doing it too."

So a niece and a sister. I want to ask him more questions, but I'm annoyed by the offer—and the way I want to take him up on it. So I glower at him as I balance on the crutches and reach out and press the button, enjoying the tactile feel of it.

"How many times have you ridden on this thing, anyway?" I ask.

"Dozens. Maybe hundreds." He nods as if he's agreeing with himself. "It's perfectly safe."

"Perfect. So it just *looks* like it's going to break down at any minute."

"Precisely," he says, adjusting the bridge of the glasses. "The way it's engineered is actually sturdier and longer-lasting than many of the elevators that are made today. People have been riding on it for over a hundred years."

"Your mansplaining isn't making me feel any better about this," I tell him as I listen to the squeak of the elevator descending to us.

"I wasn't..." He gives a pained sigh, then scuffs the floor with his shoe and says, "My sister Ruthie accuses me of that all the time."

I shoot him a look. "So stop doing it. Problem solved for me *and* for Ruthie. She sounds like a very smart woman, by the way."

"She is, but that's not...it's just...I did some research on the elevator after your accident. I was trying to make you feel better. I'm not the best at expressing myself."

"Oh," I say, at a loss. There's a gooey feeling inside of me that's trying to make itself known, like that time in third grade when I ended up eating half of the brownies before they made it into the pan. That didn't end well for my stomach, and this won't end well for the rest of me if I let it take over. "Thank you."

The elevator arrives, and Danny pulls back the heavy door. The sight of it makes me shudder. It's so heavy and large, it's easy to imagine being stuck in here. When I was a little kid, I watched a wildly inappropriate horror movie about being buried alive, and I had nightmares about it for weeks. It was my worst nightmare, being cooped up in a small space, unable to move, stuck.

Of course, that's about to be my life for the next several weeks, more or less, but at least the apartment is bigger than this box.

"It's okay," Danny says. "It—"

He clearly wants to mention something else about the engineering, but he swallows it, so he's a man who can listen. Good to know.

I step into it slowly, still thinking about backing out, and he follows me inside. It's a small space for the two of us, and I realize he's bigger than I'd thought. Probably six-two or six-three, and not skin and bones. He's rangy but fit. I'm standing perpendicular to the doors, and he stops opposite me.

I swallow, then roll my eyes as he nods toward the button pad. "I'm really not five."

"Never said you were," he says. "But I figured you'd appreciate feeling in control of something right now. Even something small. That's how I feel when I'm scared."

It's another nice thing, so I don't comment. I just reach out and press the button, my stomach lurching as the elevator starts to move.

"Kind of cool, isn't it?" he asks, his eyes glimmering as he watches me.

"Yeah," I say, because it actually *is* kind of cool. I like the accordion door on the inside, and there's an antique light in a brass fixture above our heads. But then there's a lurching motion that sways me right off my one foot and crutches. "Fuck!" I scream as I start to fall.

Chapter Five

Mira

One of my crutches goes flying—the one I need less, thankfully—and Danny catches me, his hands sturdy against my arms. For the second time this week, I find myself being held to his chest. It's a nice chest, warm and hard, but I don't particularly want to be there. Because I was promised this elevator would reach its destination, and after that awful lurching feeling, it stopped moving. Something tells me it's not because we're on our floor.

Jesus, what is with my life lately? Did someone curse me? Maybe Byron did it because I put lemon juice in his milk. Or that dude I told off at the bar the other night.

"What's going on?"

For a man who seems to have a logical explanation for everything, he's temporarily speechless, but his lips open, so hopefully an explanation will be forthcoming.

I figured the situation was dire enough, but then the light flickers out, instantly making things two hundred times worse.

I lift my head up to look at him, although I'm not sure why, because it's impossible to see. Panic twists my guts into knots. *"Danny."*

"It's okay," he says in an even voice, then surprises me by running a hand over my hair. "We'll figure this out."

He helps me balance on the crutch and my one good foot, but my heart is racing, and I'm not sure I can stay upright. I plant a palm on his chest and am surprised to feel his heart is racing too, so maybe he's not as immune to threat of possible death-by-elevator as he seems.

"It's going to be okay," he says evenly, placing his hand over mine. It's warm and large, and for a split second something very strange happens. I feel a pulse of awareness of him—of his body in the dark and his hand layered over mine and the feeling of his fast-beating heart. Of his scent too—nothing special, just a clean soap smell. Practical, like Danny, but also manly. Tingles shoot through my hand, layered under his, and zip around my body like they're soda bubbles, and I feel myself leaning in closer. Maybe it's just because he's another person, and it feels like we've been dropped into a void where only the two of us exist.

I should hobble back, but I can't bring myself too. It feels like I'd fall off the edge of the world. "Danny, I'm scared," I hear myself admitting.

Surely it must be someone else saying those words, because I can't remember ever saying anything like that to anyone before.

"I am too." It's not exactly reassuring, but at least he's honest.

"Can you feel for the call button?"

He lifts his hand from mine, and in my panic, I almost snatch it back before realizing he's doing exactly what I asked.

A second later, he says, "I pressed all of them."

"*All of them?*"

I can practically feel him giving me that half smile, almost patronizing but not. "There are only four buttons. Nothing happened."

"Yes, I can see that nothing happened. *What are we going to do now?*"

"I'm going to try the door to see if we're close to the nearest opening. Maybe I can climb out."

"No," I hiss, fisting my hand in the fabric of his shirt. "You're not climbing out. What if the elevator falls while you're halfway out, and you get cut in half? I'll be left in here with half a body."

"That's what would upset you most about that scenario?" he asks, almost amused but not quite, like he's working his way up to doing something heroic and stupid. No thank you, I'm keeping ahold of that shirt.

"Your eyes staring blindly up at me from your severed torso? Yes."

"Look on the bright side," he says. He's leaning down, so his voice is close to my ear, rumbling through my body. I get that strange feeling again, like I'm both terrified and a little turned on. "If I got chopped in half, you'd be left with my bottom half."

"Great. A dick without a brain. You'd think I'd be used to that, but no thanks."

He swallows, which I feel because I still have my hand pressed to his chest like some kind of freak. "Do you have your phone?"

"Holy shit, why didn't I think of that?" I say.

"Because you're full of adrenaline. It dulls your ability to think clearly."

"Okay, Dr. Phil."

"You know he's not actually—"

"Yes, goddammit." Leaving one hand wrapped around his shirt to make sure he doesn't magically leave me alone in here, and also so I don't fall. I reach into my right pocket with the other and take out the phone, immediately turning on the flashlight.

"Shit," Danny says, flinching and turning his head from the light like he's a vampire. But he doesn't move away from me, probably because I've still got a death grip on his shirt. "You got it directly in my eye."

"Sorry," I say, switching it off. It's too bright anyway. We've been in here long enough that we're becoming used to the dark, which only adds to my terror.

What if we're stuck here all day? What if we're stuck here for *several* days?

"You wouldn't eat me, would you?" I muse.

"What the fuck?" he asks, suddenly swear happy. I guess I bring it out in people. I can't say I'm sorry for it.

"I mean, if we're stuck in here for a week."

"We'd die of thirst before we did hunger, and why would we be in here for a week? Your sister would get worried way before then. And people would start wondering why the elevator's not working. There are more lazy people in the world than you'd think."

He's right. A sigh of relief escapes me, and then I realize I'm holding the phone like an idiot, not doing anything with it.

"Who should I call?"

"Burke," he says. "He's the owner of the unit."

"Don't you know the building staff?" I ask, surprised. He's lived here for something like ten years.

"Sure. But he's the one who matters."

"Oh," I say, loosening my grip on his shirt a little. "Don't—"

"*To them.* He's rich. People try not to piss rich people off."

"Good point."

The battery's almost dead, but there's more than enough for a phone call. I dial in Burke's number, press the call button, and... nothing happens.

"It's not working," I say in horror.

He curses. "Sometimes they don't work in elevators. It's the metal. The radio waves—"

"I seriously don't care why it's happening, just that it is." I press the call button again, then shove the phone at Danny. "Crouch down on the floor and see if it works. I can't do it because of my leg."

He makes sure I'm balanced, then gets down and hands me the crutch I dropped. Then he crouches down again, the phone clutched in his hand, the slight glow illuminating him. I watch as he gets up, lifting it as high as it will go and tries again. From his expression, it's obvious nothing is happening. Then he lowers it to the bottom corner. Up again, his mouth still a flat line.

"Help," I screech at the top of my lungs. My phone drops, and I hear a crack as it lands on the floor. That's what I get for taking my case off so I could decorate it, then promptly forgetting I intended to do any such thing.

"Sorry," he says, swearing a few more times as he stoops to get it. "But you could have given me a heads up. I'm sensitive to—"

"Heads up," I say, and he barely gets his ears covered before I shout again. "We're stuck in here. We need help. *Help!*"

Crickets. Seriously...does no one live in this building? I remember the big guy from the stairwell, who surely owes us a few favors, so I shout out, "Big Mike! Pumpkin!"

"You're really desperate if you're calling for Pumpkin," Danny says with a soft laugh.

"Of course I'm desperate." He stands back up, the soft glow from my phone showing me where to find him. I lean toward him, feeling myself teetering on the crutches, and he must notice, because he immediately steps forward. My palm touches his chest, finding its spot. It wraps around the fabric and grips. I feel sturdier when I have my hands on him. I don't feel like I'm the only person left on the planet.

"Someone will find us soon," he tells me. "Mira, I think we should sit down. We may be here for a while."

It's exactly what I don't want to hear.

"*Danny.*"

"I know," he says, his hand finding mine again. I'm clutching his shirt so hard, he'll probably have a hole in it. "We'll keep trying the phone and calling out. Every five minutes. That way we won't wear ourselves out. Someone will hear us."

I feel tears pricking at my eyes, my breath coming out funny, like my chest has stopped working. My legs feel weak, my ankle is a constant ache, and my sweaty hands are slipping on the crutches. I'm panicking, but I don't want him to know. He'll think less of me if he does. Men always do. "I don't like small spaces. They make me feel like my skin's too tight."

My voice is small and frightened, and I hate it. I add, "I don't want you to think I'm someone who cries easily."

"I know you're not," he says softly, his voice firm, "and even if you were, that would be okay. There's nothing wrong with crying. I cry when I need to."

I'm floored by him. Actually floored by him. This man is so much more than I'd thought. Every time I have an expectation, he exceeds it.

"Here," he says. "Keep holding on to me."

As if I were about to let go.

He takes my crutches from me, one at a time, and props them in the corner. There's a muted thump when they hit. One of his hands is still holding the phone, so there's a soft glow saving me from complete blindness. Then he shocks me by moving in close, his space crowding mine. And then, once again, he lifts me into a princess hold, one arm beneath my thighs, the other at my back. My awareness of him pulses back to life. I'm aware of the heat of his hands through the bottom of my dress, the sturdy warmth of him and his clean soap smell enveloping me.

Something is most definitely wrong with me.

"You keep doing that, I'm going to start thinking you like touching me," I say, my voice still shaky.

He doesn't comment on it though, he just lowers down to the floor, bringing me with him, then sets me down beside him. We both edge back until we're pressed against the back wall of the elevator. It continues to not work.

"You're a beautiful woman, why wouldn't I like touching you?" he finally comments. "Anyone would like touching you."

"You're not so bad either," I say. I've never been known for having a filter, but any glimmer of one I might have had is gone at the moment, so I add, "But those glasses are really hideous."

His laughter rumbles through me, because our sides are pressed together, every inch of us, like he doesn't want to feel like he's alone in a void either. Like maybe he does enjoy touching me as much as I'm starting to enjoy touching him—in this elevator, at least. This place out of time. My phone is still nestled in his hand, although I'm certain the screen probably broke. At least we have that soft glow to light up our faces.

"I don't like them either."

"So why do you wear them?" I ask, warming to the topic. It's helping me forget that we're stuck here in a little box. Maybe we'll run out of oxygen. Except, no, it's not an airtight space in here.

"Because my sister gave them to me for a Christmas present. I like *her*."

"So stick them in a drawer and take them out whenever she comes over."

"I could do that, I guess," he acknowledges, sounding bemused by the idea.

"You *should*, especially if you're trying to impress that Daphne woman."

I'm not sure why I'm bringing it up now, except maybe I need the reminder. There's someone Danny wants to impress, and it's not me. So, the awareness I'm feeling in between bouts of terror needs to be tucked into a drawer just like those glasses.

"I guess," he says noncommittally. "My friends talk more than they should. I don't know what they told you, but Daphne and I broke up years ago. I shouldn't care about impressing her."

"Still. Even if you're not sure you're interested, you'll want to show her what she's missing. We should find some different shirts for you."

"You want me to be your project, Mira?" he asks turning his

head toward me. He didn't mean it in a sexual way, obviously, but a shock of awareness shivers through me, especially from his closeness and the sound of my name from his lips. It's almost musical the way he says it. His side is still pressed against me—warm and firm—and I feel a deep, almost primal awareness of him.

He's your roommate, I remind myself. *The friend of your future brother-in-law. You know how bad it is to sleep with someone and then get stuck with them.*

It was like that with Byron. It was exciting at first, living together. We had sex everywhere in the apartment, even out on the balcony after everyone was asleep. We lived and breathed each other. But it didn't take long for me to realize that what I thought was love was just a sexual high.

It would be a very bad idea to have sex with Danny. Besides, he's not my type, or at least I didn't think he was. I usually go for artistic types. The kind of guys who are in bands or pretend to be.

Douches, I can hear my Azalea say. *I think that's the word you're looking for.*

I clear my throat and try to prune the intrusive thoughts from my brain. "It'd be easy to give you a makeover. Like in that movie *Can't Buy Me Love*, when she tells Patrick Dempsey she's going to give him a makeover, but he's Patrick Dempsey, so she doesn't really have to do anything, and suddenly he's more popular than she is. Except you look more like Lee Pace than Patrick Dempsey."

"Who's Patrick Dempsey?"

I mean, really...

I nudge his shoulder slightly. "Do you know anything about pop culture?"

I can almost feel him smiling, that real genuine smile that takes over his whole being. "I try to keep it to a bare minimum, but I *do* have a younger sister and a five-year-old niece. I probably know more about Numberblocks than you do. It's a pretty clever show, actually. There are these—"

"I know I should be polite and listen," I say, "but I don't really care, and I'm too keyed up to pretend. I'd like to hear more about your sister and your niece, though." When he speaks about them, there's a warm affection in his voice that's frankly adorable.

"What would you like to know?" he says softly, and I find myself leaning into him a little more, wanting his voice in my ear, the reassuring press of him against me.

"Everything. I'm greedy."

His laughter makes me feel warmer, more present. It pushes the fear back. "Ruthie's five years younger. I took care of her a lot when I was a kid. I felt responsible for her. Still do, I guess. She got married six years ago for all of four months, and then she had Izzy after they split."

"Shit," I say. "Is Izzy's dad involved?"

"No."

"I'm sorry."

"I'm not," he says, his voice hard. "They're better off without him. I only wish things weren't so hard for Ruthie. I help out when she'll let me, but she usually doesn't let me."

"Do your parents help out?"

"No," he adds. "They split up a while back, and they're just as dysfunctional alone as they were together. They can barely help themselves. I used to have to do their taxes when I was a teenager."

"My dad's like that," I say wistfully. "A big kid who just happens to be in his late fifties. My mom's the asshole."

"It happens. I don't much like either of my parents. I don't see them anymore. Haven't for years."

"What about this woman you might or might not want to impress? What does *she* do?"

"Why do you ask?" He turns his head as he says this, and suddenly our faces are very close together. I can feel his breath warm my skin, and it's as if every nerve ending lights up. There's a tension between my legs that makes me want to squirm—or perform a feat that is currently beyond me and climb onto his lap.

This is *crazy*. A week ago, I was convinced he had the personality of an encyclopedia—and not even a good one, like the Encyclopedia Britannica.

I swallow and take a beat to gather myself. To try to become immune to the feeling of his arm against mine. "I need to know who we're trying to impress."

"She broke up with me because she thought I was boring, and she's right. *You* think I'm boring too."

The accusation has bite, because he's not wrong. I *did* think he was boring. But I don't anymore.

"No," I say, honestly. "That was only when you were doing your silent agreeable act. You're much more interesting than you want anyone else to know."

He's quiet for a moment, then says, "I like Pumpkin Spice candles. I bought one a few years back, and the guys still give me shit about it. I have ten brown shirts. No, eleven."

"So you like some boring things, that doesn't make *you* boring. Anyway, I doubt she finds you boring. Maybe she was just testing you. Trying to convince you to get your freak on."

"I don't want to talk about Daphne right now."

My body feels fizzy again, carbonated and charged. Because I'd like to know *why* he doesn't want to talk about her. Is it because he's feeling this crazy urge to touch me too? Or is it because this Daphne woman still has such a hold on him, he doesn't even know where to begin? I know what I want the answer to be...

I breathe in deep and then let it out slowly. "So what are we going to talk about? Your favorite drink? I enjoy figuring out everyone's favorite drink. I'd like to think each person has a signature cocktail, one that can be tweaked depending on mood."

"That's another thing you should know about me, I prefer beer," he says in a wry voice. "I'll bet you get disappointed when people order beer at your bar."

Yes.

"Nah. You just think you prefer it because no one's made you your cocktail yet. We're going to figure it out."

"We are?" he asks. He sounds amused...and interested, maybe.

"You've thrown down the gauntlet now," I say. "I love it when someone doubts me."

"I don't doubt you. Only a fool would doubt you." There's no hesitation behind the words, nothing that marks them as a lie or partial truth. He believes it, and again, I find myself drawn in by him, by this man who seemed so forgettable to me only a few days ago.

It's maybe the first time in my life that I'm grateful to have been wrong about something.

That's when the phone blinks off, leaving us again in pitch black darkness. We're both quiet for a second, and then he leans over and takes my hand, weaving his fingers through mine, as if he knows I need that anchor in the darkness. His hand is large and warm and capable—and I find myself trying to remember the last time a man held my hand like this. Because he wanted to comfort me. Because he cared. I can't remember, and for an instant, my heart pounds for a different reason. I'm confused and scared and turned on, and I don't know what to do with all of the emotions beating at my chest.

Then I warn him, "Danny, I'm going to shout."

I do, and nothing happens. Then I start crying for real before his arms wrap around me and pull me close.

Chapter Six

Danny

It's been maybe an hour a half since the phone guttered out. Mira's sitting in front of me now, her back pushed into me and my arms wrapped around her, and I'm fighting a hard-on. I feel like an asshole for being turned on when she's both terrified and injured, but it's like we're in a sensory deprivation chamber, and all of my senses are focused on *her*. I feel the soft curve of her ass, the dip of her hip, the tickle of her hair. I smell her spicy perfume and the toothpaste she used this morning. I hear her voice, soft but a bit throaty, as she tells me about her father's band. I've been trying to keep her talking to prevent her from falling into the fear and getting lost in it. To keep myself from doing something I shouldn't.

"Has your dad's band ever played at your bar?" I ask. She's already told me about opening the bar—about the years she spent saving money and planning while managing other people's bars and restaurants, about securing the loans and managing to pay them off in record time. Despite myself, I pull her a little closer. It's helping me too, being anchored to her. Feeling her against me—alive and safe, or safe enough, given the situation.

"Yes," she says, laughing softly, her body shaking a little with it.

Everything she does is big—laughing, smiling, calling out for Pumpkin like a damn hamster could save us from this clusterfuck of a situation. At first that made her an intimidating person to be around, but I like it. She's genuine in a way most people are not, which is helpful to a person who has a tendency to be too literal.

Logic suggests we won't be in here much longer. Most of the people in this building are rich. Rich people are used to getting what they want, so if they call for the elevator and it doesn't come, they'll complain. The matter will be investigated, and we'll be saved. The fact that the light guttered out suggests there might be a problem with the power in the building, which might distract everyone for a while. Still, management will get to us eventually.

I haven't told Mira, but I suspect the elevator shaft and doors are thick enough that her screams aren't being heard. I won't take that bit of hope from her, even if I'd prefer not to hear Big Mike's and Pumpkin's names screamed at what sounds like a hundred decibels.

"How'd it go?" I ask.

"I asked him to play cover songs, and he covered the Beatles' 'Revolution' as a bluegrass song. It was pretty sweet, actually. They aired it as a live track on the River."

"The River?"

"Do you never get out?" she asks, some amusement in her voice. "It's a radio station that plays local bands."

"Oh," I say. "I listen to podcasts while I'm working. I've gotten really into a few true crime ones."

"You'll have to tell me which ones you like," she says. "I've been told I'm supposed to stay off my feet."

"Okay," I agree. "My favorite one is *The Murderer Next Door*. Maybe we can listen to it together while I'm working."

One of the things I did while she was gone was move my desk into my bedroom, wedging it in there, but maybe I can move it back out. Or work on my laptop in my favorite armchair. Sure, the bright as fuck SAD lamp is out there now, but maybe I can wear sunglasses. Right now, in this moment, I can't imagine choosing to be away from Mira, for any reason.

"Sounds ominous," she comments.

"We don't have any next-door neighbors," I point out. Our unit is the only one on the floor."

"Well, in that case, I'd like that." She's quiet for a second, then asks, "How come you've never come by the bar with your friends?"

"Would you have noticed if I had?" I ask with some amusement. Because we'd only had a single one-on-one conversation before she moved in with me, right after Burke told me she needed a place to stay. It was as dry as toast without butter, mostly because I don't know how to talk to people I don't know—a problem, because in order to get to know someone you have to go through the motions of meaningless small talk.

"You haven't," she says seriously.

"No. I told you, I have a thing about noise. Crowded places too. I've never gotten diagnosed, but Ruthie thinks I might be on the autism spectrum. I've done some research on it, and it feels right."

I feel her looking back at me again, and I have a stupid urge to trace her cheek, to weave my hand into that soft black hair that's been teasing my face and draw her in for a kiss.

"If you say you've done some research on it, I'm guessing you've done a lot."

I smile at that, even if I'm just smiling into the darkness. "Sure. Some self-testing too."

"If I do something that bothers you," she says, "you have to tell me. I'm not always the best at picking up on hints."

"Me neither. But I've been pretty good about telling you things, haven't I?"

She laughs a little. "Now, maybe. Not in the beginning."

"It only took me about an hour or two to be brutally honest with you."

"Thank you for that," she says softly. "And thank you for telling me about this. I'm guessing you don't tell everyone."

"No," I admit. "I guess I think most things aren't anyone else's business."

I only realize I've been tracing circles on her upper thigh when the dress rides up slightly, and the texture I'm touching changes from her soft dress to her softer skin.

It's...mesmerizing. Her breathing hitches and she layers her hand on top of mine, the soft touch sending a powerful punch of need straight where it doesn't need to go.

"Shit, sorry," I say, stopping. I slide the material back over her legs, even though it's the last thing I want to do. "I didn't mean to overstep...I just...when I'm nervous, it helps me to touch something."

"No." She leans back as if to look at me, but there's not enough light for us to see each other, only to feel, a thought that makes—

Shit. This is an untenable situation. I have a sexy woman in my lap—one who is fast becoming both sexy *and* alluring—and her ass is pressed up against my dick.

"Sorry," I repeat like an idiot.

"I didn't want you to stop," she says, her voice breathy in a way that's not doing my don't-get-hard campaign any favors. "It's helping anchor me in my body. Sitting here in the dark, without any sound except for us...it's like I've stopped existing."

"You're afraid of death," I say like an even bigger idiot, although at least it does me the favor of deflating the desire that was flooding me.

"Of course. Isn't everyone?"

"No. Not actively." I start stroking her upper thigh again, because she said she liked it, and I definitely like it. "I think it's fascinating. It's one of the Big Unknowns."

"Big Unknowns?" She shifts a little against me, and just like that, my cock is letting me know it likes her. As if there were any doubt.

"The things in life that are unknowable. So many things are governed by logic and the rules of science, but there are some Big Unknowns. There's no way anyone can *prove* what happens after death. Science suggests nothing happens, obviously, but there are things that can't be explained. Pulses of energy. Lights flickering on and off when there aren't any power surges. Even the birth of the universe, we know how it happened, but for such a thing to happen...it's...Well, I guess you could call it a miracle."

"I like that you believe in miracles. You don't seem like the kind of man who would." She looks back again and then laughs. "I don't know why I keep turning to look at you. I can't see you."

"It's habit. When we do the same things every day, our body comes to rely on them. To think they're going to happen, even if we're across the world, with something completely different in mind."

"So I think I'm going to see you even though I know I'm not."

"Sure."

She leans back a little, pushing her body into me and giving a jolt to my half-hard dick, then says, her voice low and throaty, "Well, I *know* I feel you."

"Shit, I'm really sorry, Mira. It's been a while, and..."

She leans back further, and now I'm no longer partially hard. I'm made of stone. "It feels good. How long has it been for you?"

Shock radiates through me, because I thought...

Despite a few of the things she's said and done here on the elevator, I figured she didn't see me that way. When a woman insists you need a makeover, it's usually because she doesn't think you're attractive.

So this is good news—confusing but very, very good.

I clear my throat, trying not to think with my dick. "I'd rather not say."

"That long, huh?" she says, amusement in her tone. She leans her ass into me, grinding it slightly against my hard dick. My hand lifts from her leg to her stomach, my fingers fanning out to make it wider, and I hold her there. My mind isn't functioning, so I'm not sure whether I'm holding her there to keep her from moving or because she's exactly where I want her.

"Are you trying to drive me crazy?" I ask, my voice gruff.

"It's been a few months for me too. Maybe I'm trying to drive myself crazy."

I laugh a little at the "few months" remark. "It's been longer than that for me."

"Why?" she asks, still leaning into my dick and making it very hard to form a coherent thought.

The truth is, I'd had a lot of short relationships that led nowhere. Daphne's prognosis of my life—*basic*—had lodged into my head. Everything seemed trite. The small talk, the dinners, the seduction. None of the women I met excited me, and I'm pretty damn sure I didn't excite them either. I'd had a few one night stands, and while they scratched an itch, there are few things more depressing than waking up beside a stranger. Feeling the bone-deep awkwardness of wanting them to leave but not wanting to sound like an asshole. So I'd promised myself that the next time I fucked a woman it would mean something. That I wasn't going to go through the same dance again and again, feeling the lack of profundity at every step of the way except for that one moment of pleasure that was all too likely to spill into sadness—the emptiness of a life half lived. Of something that looked like love but didn't feel like it.

"I got sick of the dance," I say. It's probably the kind of comment that doesn't mean anything to the person hearing it. I do that a lot, say things that make sense in my head and nowhere else, but Mira surprises me by leaning her whole body back into me and sighing.

"I know exactly what you mean."

And I really think she does.

We're silent for a moment, Mira leaning into my hard dick, my hand pressing her closer. I can feel the fabric sliding against her skin and can't help but imagine what it would feel like if my fingers were skating across her soft, hot flesh instead. I could reach under her dress and touch her. Slide her panties to one side. Something tells me she'd invite it right now, and I can almost feel her clenching around my fingers, soft and wet and hungry for my—

She moves against me again, and a groan escapes my lips.

"Danny." She says my name on a whisper, and the sound of it weaves through me. "Are you hard because it's been a long time, or because you want me?"

"Both," I say, blood beating hot in my veins, to my dick. The thought of feeling her slick around my fingers is stuck in my mind, not just with masking tape but glue. Nails, maybe. "Definitely both. I want to touch you. I want to reach under your dress and feel you. I've been imagining it for a while now."

She shifts in my lap so she's sideways. I can't see her in the dark, but I *feel* her. I'm attuned to her every movement, to the sound and feel and scent of her. Especially to the needy ache of my dick, which feels every single shift and sigh she makes. I can sense her head tipping up to me more than I can see it.

"I don't know what this means," I tell her, because honesty is the best policy.

"It doesn't have to mean anything," she says. "We can pretend it never happened after we get out of here, but I think I need you to touch me. I *have* to feel something, Danny. Otherwise I'm going to be lost in here."

"Your ankle, does it hurt?"

"Like hell, but I want to feel something other than pain. I think I need to. I mean it, we don't need to talk about this ever again. This is...a place out of time...a Big Unknown."

In some ways she's right, in some ways she's wrong. But I'm not in the mood for a discussion of the Big Unknowns. She just gave me a green light to touch her, and I want to touch her. Truthfully, I can't think of when I last wanted something so badly.

I dip my head closer to her, so I can feel her breath on my face, the soft puffs of air, the feeling of warmth. I dip closer, and I feel her skin against my lips—her cheek, so soft and warm. I nuzzle it with my lips, feeling more than thinking, and a sound escapes her as she swivels a little more in my lap, her good and bad leg both on one side of my body now, angled toward the back wall so she can face me. Her lips find mine, and I'm lost. They're soft and eager and demanding, and her mouth opens for me, our tongues finding each other. Pausing to suck on her bottom lip, I weave my hand into her silky hair—a deep black that blends in perfectly with the darkness swallowing us—to bring her closer. It feels like I need her everywhere, wrapped around me. I need it with a deep ache I don't understand.

The pitch black of the elevator makes me experience everything else so much more—the warm weight of her on my lap, squirming against my dick, those soft lips consuming and wanting to be consumed by me. I can't take it anymore, and I flip up the skirt of her dress with my free hand and then seek her wet heat while my mouth moves over hers.

She gasps into my mouth, then bites my lip, wringing a sound out of me while my fingers reach under her panties—thin and lacy, I can feel them under my fingers, and find her. She's wet for me, just like I'd hoped she would be, and the sensation of stroking her there, of finding the spot where she buds like a flower and making her squirm harder against me, is better than figuring out a way to break into a system after weeks of trying. It's better than watching the sunrise over the mountains. It's—

"Oh, *Danny*—"

Her mouth has pulled away from mine, which feels unacceptable. Then she shocks me into laughter when she pulls off my glasses.

"You figured this was your big opportunity, huh? Distract me so you could give me your glasses makeover." I circle her clit again and then curl a finger inside of her, needing to feel her clamping around me. My mind is fixed on it, fixed on bringing her pleasure and making her forget the shit-show of this elevator. I want her to remember this moment even if she's determined to forget about it the instant we're free. I want her to wake up at night whispering my name, wet with wanting.

I'm sure I'll question my sanity later, but right now, this is what matters. It's the only thing that matters.

"I'm not giving them back," she says, her voice breathy. She lifts her hips a little as I stroke her, fucking her with my fingers, and I'm so hard that my brain is living in my dick for what is probably the first time in my life. "I'm going to hide them, and I'll only give them back when Ruthie visits. It's for your own good."

I lean in and kiss her neck, sucking in her hot, perfumed flesh as I keep moving my fingers. She presses back into my dick, and there's a very real chance I'm going to come in my pants like a teenager.

"This doesn't feel fair," she says. "You're not getting anything out of it."

"Oh, I definitely wouldn't say that," I tell her before placing a kiss over the damp place I just sucked. "I was imagining what it would feel like for you to clench around my fingers, but sometimes a person's imagination is just too small to comprehend the reality. But that's not to say I'll stop trying. When we get out of here, I'm going to stroke my dick and pretend it's sinking into your sweet, sucking heat."

"Jesus," she says. I hear her swallow, I feel her move her hips. I feel it in my hand, in my dick, and in the mouth that wants to kiss her everywhere. Finding her mouth, I suck on her lip, then move down to her jaw, her long, fragrant neck, and then the swell of her breasts. I noticed earlier the way her dress rides low, showing them off like a present ready to be opened, freed. I dip my head to kiss across them, loving how soft they are against my lips, how it makes her writhe even harder against me.

There's no way I'm removing my hand from between her legs, but I have one perfectly good hand left. I use it to tug down the soft fabric of her dress and the lace of her bra, lowering them enough that I can claim her nipple in my mouth and suck on it while I curl my fingers up inside of her and grind the heel of my palm against her clit. I feel her clenching around me, getting closer, and it's almost enough to make me come myself.

"That feels so damn good," she says, her voice tight. And then she's bucking her hips against my hand, getting my fingers where she wants them, and if possible, I get harder. I'm harder, I think, than I've ever been in my life. It's the darkness, I think. It's this woman.

I shift to her other nipple, still moving my hand inside of her, feeling her clenching around my fingers, soft and wet and tight. Everything is by feel, not sight, but I can see her in my head—dress pushed up at the bottom and down on top, splayed in my lap and riding my hand, her nipple in my mouth.

"Danny," she says, and I decide I have nothing at all against my nickname. Child's name or not, I like it perfectly fine when she says it with that thread of longing and wonder. "*Danny.*"

I release her nipple and kiss her, because I need to claim her lips too. She kisses me back with intention, her lips moving against mine in a dance that isn't the slightest bit boring. I pull back, unmoored.

"You're beautiful when you fall apart," I say into her ear as she clenches around my fingers one last time. Then I pull back and adjust her dress up top. Because I don't like the thought of anyone seeing her like that if the elevator should unexpectedly decide to work again.

"How do you know I look beautiful?" she asks with a laugh. "You can't see me."

"*I know.*"

I lift my fingers to my lips and suck them, because I need to taste her, and right now, this is the only way.

"Did you just...?" Her voice is breathy and soft, still turned on.

"Yeah. If I hadn't, I would have kept thinking about it. It's what you'd call an intrusive thought."

I sense movement, and then her hands are in my hair, stroking it while she wiggles on my lap. "I want to do something for you, too."

"Keep moving like that, it'll happen without you having to do much at all."

"It's not going to be easy to forget this," she says. No one would ever say reading between the lines is my strength, but she sounds a little sad about it.

"But you think we have to."

"Yes, I do," she says. "We're going to live together. I just got out of that horrible situation with Byron, and I can't go through that again."

"That makes sense," I say, even as I cup my hands around her hips, guiding her as she presses down on me. We're dry-humping like a couple of teenagers, her legs off to the side because she has that cast on, but I couldn't give a shit about anything right now except touching her and having her touch me.

I already know I'm not going to be able to forget about this or turn it off. I've probably just guaranteed that my life is going to be hell for the next however-long we live together, because every time I see her, I'm going to think about the way she tastes, the way she clenched around my hand and whispered my name like a prayer. Right now, what comes after doesn't matter, but it will. It definitely will. The future's like a guillotine blade, hanging over my head or maybe my dick.

"What about Daphne?" she asks.

A grunt escapes me, because I don't want to think about Daphne. Quite frankly, I don't really care about her. I'm starting to realize that her words stuck with me more than the end of our relationship did. I guess there's something enlightening about giving a woman an orgasm in an elevator. "You're riding my dick and you're asking about my ex-girlfriend?"

"I'm not riding your dick," she says, her voice sly as she leans in close, her words a whisper against the side of my neck, like the wind on a cool fall morning. "If I were riding your dick, you'd know."

"You're already driving me crazy. I'm not sure I want to know."

It's a lie. It's maybe the most blatant lie I've told in my whole damn life. But here's a truth: if she were riding my dick, I'd want to see it. I'd want to memorize every second and replay it at night when I can't sleep, when my mind is as busy as a hive of bees.

"You'll care about her later," she says. "We're just letting off some steam. It's only because we're stuck in here."

I don't like that she said that. I like it even less that she seems to believe it.

But it's then that the light sizzles back to life. I have a half second to soak her in—her hair a mess from my hands, a pink spot on her neck from where I sucked her in, and her red dress rustled and in disarray. Surprise lights her eyes, followed by something else I'm much too inept to read, and then she's shoving off my lap and away from my needy dick.

There's a crunching sound, and her eyes get wider. She lifts her fingers to her lips.

"Let me guess," I say. "Did you just sit on my glasses?"

"Will you believe me if I say it was an accident?"

Yes, because I don't think she'd ruin them after I told her Ruthie got them for me. Don't ask me how I know, but I'm sure of it.

"I believe you. But I'm guessing you're not sorry it happened."

She laughs, her eyes darting to the doors. "No, I guess I'm not." She pulls them out from under her ass, and it's a stupid thought, but for a second I'm jealous of my messed-up glasses for having been stuck under her sweet, rounded ass. They're mangled, irreparably broken, but she hands them to me anyway.

"Thanks," I say flatly, taking them and shoving them into my pocket. My pants are tented, *obviously* tented, and her gaze lingers there. Her pink tongue darts out and licks her lips, and everything in me follows it.

"Do you—"

But I'll never know what she was about to say. The elevator makes a sudden movement that scares a sound out of Mira. I grab her hand and squeeze it, and seconds later, the elevator finishes the upward trip and jerks to a stop.

"You think we're at our floor?" she asks, staring at the door.

"Who cares?" I say, getting up and lifting her to her one working foot. She places her hand on my chest again—in the place I've come to think of as hers. "I'd get off anywhere." Except that's not quite true. Part of me wouldn't have minded staying inside that elevator with her for the rest of the day, caught inside with nothing to do but learn about each other. I shake off the thought, remembering what she said—this, whatever it's been, is over the second we leave the elevator—then I hand her phone to her.

The screen is cracked, so I grimace and tell her I'll replace it.

"It's fine," she says, "I'm due for an upgrade soon."

Then I help her with the crutches.

When I open the elevator door, we're exactly where we're supposed to be, only Big Mike is standing at the end of the hall, near the apartment. It's strange, him being up here. Our apartment is the only one on this floor—the penthouse, because Burke is the kind of guy who can afford the best.

Mike's wearing a brick red shirt that makes his complexion look even pinker. Mira would have picked out something different for him, too, no doubt. He does a doubletake when we step off the elevator.

"Power was out," he says, as if that explains anything.

"What are you doing up here?" I ask.

He lifts a squirming little body. The escape artist hamster.

"Got myself a Houdini here. Like you guessed, he's my little girl's pet. My ex-wife has primary custody, so I try to keep my daughter happy, you know? What my precious little Pansy wants, she gets. Hey—" He motions to Mira's leg. "Sorry again about what happened with your ankle. Glad to see it worked out."

"It didn't, though," I say flatly, annoyed by his presence, and not just because I'm still partially hard, my thoughts fixed on the slick, hot feeling of Mira around my fingers, her sweet mouth on mine. It's his hamster's fault Mira broke her ankle. "They don't typically give casts to people who don't need them. How'd he get through the fire door?"

Escape artist or not, I struggle to believe such a thing is possible. Then again, I saw the little hamster scurry down the side of the stairs, so the laws of physics might have made an exception for him.

"I couldn't tell you," Mike says gruffly. "All I know is that I looked all over the building for him, and this is where I found him. Say, can we have you over for dinner some night? An apology for..." He gestures to the pink cast on Mira's leg.

"No," I say. Maybe I should have consulted her first, but I can think of few things I'd like less than going over to Big Mike's to have dinner with him and his rodent friend. There's something...off about him. Besides, my whole body is pulsing to get into my apartment so I can take care of the need pounding through my veins, and he's standing in the way of that. Still, I can tell my answer was too blunt, so I add, "No need."

He clears his throat and rocks a little on his feet, the little hamster squirming in his fist.

"Well, have a blessed day," Mira says, pushing past him. "And I'd suggest giving the elevator a pass. We just got stuck in it for two hours, so you can understand why we're not feeling chatty. I'm guessing you didn't hear me calling for you and Pumpkin?"

He opens his mouth to say something and then shuts it. If I had to guess, she caught him off guard. He strikes me as a man who doesn't like feeling that way, although I imagine few people would.

"Huh. Pity," she adds. "We could have used the assist. Well, anyway, we'll see you around."

I'm only too happy to go open the door for her. I don't like this guy, and I'm not too fond of the hamster either, considering all the problems it has caused. Still, it's strange, going through the usual routine of unlocking the door. Stepping inside. There's a weird feeling, like maybe none of this happened except in my head, because for anyone outside of that elevator, it *didn't* happen. It's like Mira and I are once again two housemates who barely know each other. Two people who, on the surface, couldn't be more different. But in my head, things have changed so utterly it's a different landscape than it was before. A different movie.

Still. The magic moment may have ended, but the way it made me feel hasn't. The blood is starting to pound through my veins again—to move south.

"So it's just over?" she asks as I close the door behind us.

The last thing I see is Big Mike giving a wave with his non-hamster hand.

"I'll get Burke to call the super," I say. "Make sure someone takes a look at it, but if I had to guess, it happened because of the electricity going out in the building."

"I'm never going back on that elevator, Danny. I'll learn how to go down the stairs with crutches."

"I'll carry you," I say before I can stop myself.

She licks her lips. I've been too intense—I can tell before she says a word. That's something I've been accused of before, and it'll undoubtedly happen again.

"I'll learn to do it on the crutches," she insists.

I nod. I don't deny her. She's setting boundaries, and it's her right. But there's something I need to do before I can think or function or do anything resembling being a person.

"Danny?" she asks as I make straight for my room.

"I'll be right out." It comes out too loud, almost strangled, but I don't apologize. And I don't turn to look at her. I can't. Because if I did, I'd have to touch her, to pull her into my arms and ask if I could fuck her and not my hand.

Chapter Seven

Mira

Is he...*touching himself* in there?

Danny burst through the apartment so quickly, his gaze intent on the door to his room. It was like the quiet, sedate man I'd met weeks ago had been transformed into a beast, and even though he just made me come—hard—I feel a wild pulsing between my legs. My mind is hooked on the image of him wrapping his big hand around his dick, stroking himself up and down. I want to rip that door open and demand that I'm the only one who gets to touch his cock, which is insane. After all, I meant what I said—what happened on the elevator was beautiful and strange and confusing, but we can't let it change anything.

For one thing, we're living together. If things went south, we'd be stuck with each other. Been there, done that. In my experience, it only leads to resentment. Fun, while you're squeezing lemon juice into the gallon of milk he labeled with his name—not so fun when you forget what you did and drink some of it yourself.

I'm not going through that again, even if being the subject of Danny's intense focus feels amazing. For another, I very much doubt any kind of relationship between us would work. He can't function well around loud noises and bright lights, and the majority of my life—the part that matters most to me—takes place in a bar with a disco ball hanging from its ceiling.

I *am* a loud noise.

The voice in my head whispers that I'd be like a wrecking ball to his peace.

That he'd be an anchor pinning me down.

That I'm not his type at all, and he's also not mine.

Still, the thought of him needing to do that because of me has me almost frantic. So it takes me a while to notice the record table, set up in its pink glory in the corner of the room, where his desk used to be. The reviews all suggested it would be a bitch to build, but it looks sturdy and strong. Then my focus shifts to the throw pillows arranged neatly on the couch. The squirrel, whom I've nick-named Bob, smoking his pipe from his little patch of wall.

Danny did all of this for me.

For a second, the thought fills me with light, like I'm the prism hung up in the corner of the bar's window, bright only at the times of day no one but me and Azalea are there. No one has ever really taken care of me before, other than Delia in one of her mother-hen moods. To my mother, I was a box in which she could stow her resentments. To my father, I was a friend. To every man I've ever been with, I've been a sturdy post they could link themselves to so they don't get carried away by the breeze.

Then consternation floods in, because *he did all of this for me*—and he did it before the elevator. I can't let him, or myself, think this is something it's not. And yet...

And yet, every part of me is attuned to his room, to the possibility of what's going on behind that door. The pervy part of me wants to creep up close to see if I can hear the sound of smacking flesh, of his hand moving over the hard dick I felt nudging at me earlier. He's thinking of me while he's doing it...he *must* be.

I'm also worried about what he did with his desk. He shouldn't have displaced himself for me.

"This is bad," I mutter to myself as I swing my way to my bedroom to grab a phone charger. I plug in the piece of shit phone, nearly tumbling a couple of times since I'm still not used to the crutches. "Really, really stupid."

I shouldn't have called him out on his hard-on. I should have just quietly enjoyed the sensation of it nudging at me. The feeling of liquid heat between my legs while he traced shapes on my thigh and cradled me against his hardness in the dark.

He said it had been a while for him, longer than a few months, so maybe he would've touched anyone that way. Maybe he regrets having his hands on me because he's been saving his bone for this Daphne woman.

I want to growl at the thought, even though it's my own mind that created it, my own mind that's insisting he'd be much better off with someone like her—the kind of woman who probably thinks before she speaks. I don't know much about Danny's ex, other than that she's some computer genius. According to Burke, Danny's one too.

My subconscious doesn't respond with any bright ideas for fixing the problems I've made for myself, so I do what I always do when I find myself thrown. I sink into work mode.

Using my crutches, I hobble over to the kitchen. Danny left my bottles of booze and mixers out on the counter, probably because he didn't know where to stow them. Knowing him, he's aware that they shouldn't go over the refrigerator, where a lot of people put them, since fridges give off heat to keep their insides cool. It's the kind of thing he would have looked up.

Trying not to fixate on the possibility of what's happening behind that door, on the image of his big capable palm stroking his cock, I think about what drink might convince him he's not just a beer man. I set out the things I need on the marble kitchen island and start pouring ingredients into my drink mixer.

A few minutes later, after I've finish making the drink and

tasting it, he emerges from his room. I can see a puckered spot on his shirt where my hand fisted it, and it unleashes something inside of me—a memory of Danny telling me to hold onto him, followed by a memory of his fingers inside of me.

Maybe that's what makes me continue with the trend of saying things I shouldn't—or it might be my truculent nature that does it for me. "Did you just run in there to fuck your hand?"

His pupils dilate, and he lifts his eyebrows as he comes to a stop by the narrower side of the kitchen island, right next to me. He grips the edge of it. "What do you think?"

"I think you did. Did it feel good?" I ask.

"Not as good as you would have."

I clear my throat and shove the glass at him across the island. The drink almost sloshes over the side, which is bad bartender etiquette, but I'm barely functional at the moment. I'll forgive myself.

"A little early for alcohol isn't it?"

"Doesn't feel like it."

"Maybe not, but it's only 11:30 a.m.," he says.

"Shit, is it?" I ask, searching the kitchen area for a wall clock that doesn't exist. "It feels like midnight."

His lips twitch, his eyes landing on mine for just a moment—the irises nearly as black as the pupils. "Being stuck in the elevator with me for two and a half hours made you feel like it was midnight? Or was it our run in with the hamster who broke your ankle that did it?"

A smile fights to break free. "It's just...it felt like a lot happened. Two and half hours barely covers it."

He nods. "A Big Unknown, maybe. A pocket out of time."

"Yeah, I guess."

"Why'd you say no to Big Mike's dinner invitation?" I blurt. I'm not sure why that's the question that comes out, other than that my mind is stuck on the way Danny made me feel, and Big Mike is the least sexy subject I can think of.

He squints at me. "Did you *want* me to say yes?" Something dark passes over his face, settling in deep, like a shadow seeping into his skin. "Oh, do you think it was his roundabout way of asking you out on a date? If you're interested, I can let him know. I mean, sure, he likes strip clubs and doesn't seem like a very good pet owner, but if you don't mind, I suppose—"

"What?" I practically shriek. "No. I would sooner go on a date with Pumpkin. And how do you know about the strip clubs? Did you *see* him at one?"

His mouth twitches. "No, it was that pen he was so hot and bothered about. I looked it up. It turns out the Treasure Club is about a very specific type of treasure."

I shudder dramatically. "Well, I'm glad you turned him down. He kind of wigs me out."

"Good."

"Good that he wigs me out?" I ask incredulously.

"Good that you don't want to go out with him. I don't like him much either, and I'm not good at pretending to like people."

"The way you used to pretend to like me," I say, not sure whether it's an accusation, or even how I want him to respond. "Yes, and you picked up on it very quickly. But I don't have to pretend anymore." Something shifts on his face, and he looks away, padding a thumb against the side of the sweating drink. "I can't drink on the job, Mira. I've got to get back to work."

"Where's your desk?" I blurt.

That didn't sound right. It almost came out as an accusation. I gesture to the record table. "I mean, thank you for building my record table. I wasn't actually looking forward to doing that with one leg, so I'm not even going to tell you I could have done it myself. But you shouldn't have moved your desk for me."

"I think it's for the best," he says, his gaze pinging to the record table and then the cocktail. "It might be distracting for me to work out here."

"You won't bother me," I insist. "I'm just going to be listening to murder podcasts and fucking around on the internet."

He's silent for a second, his eyebrows raised, and then I say, "Oh, you were saying I'd be distracting for you. Fair point. I remember what you said about noise. My mother used to say Delia and I could wake the dead. I've been told I even walk loud."

"That's not why you'd be distracting," he says, his eyebrows still raised.

Oh, for God's sake. Might as well address this directly. We can't go around lusting after each other like a couple of horny zoo animals caught in the same cage. We need to become immune to each other.

"What happened on the elevator was..." I search for words and come up empty, so I'm compromise with "very good. But it's like I said, we're living here together, and I just got out of a relationship, and—"

"I understand," he says with a nod. "What you're saying makes perfect logical sense. I know how to listen, but you asked what I was doing in there and I told you."

"Well, you can work out here if you'd like," I say brightly. He made it pretty clear that he *doesn't* like, but...

I guess I don't love the idea of being alone out here. The space is hardly cavernous, but it's empty and boring and...

When did I last spend a day by myself, with nothing productive to do?

I honestly can't remember. It didn't used to be that way, but it's been long enough that it's hard to remember what it was like before.

"Maybe we could listen to some music or one of those podcasts together," I continue. "I thought you did something like data entry. That's what Burke told Delia."

He's quiet for a second before he tells me, "That's not precisely true. But I had to sign an NDA, so I can't really say much about my work."

Um, hello, interesting.

He couldn't have said anything more certain to make me want to know *exactly* what he's doing in there.

"Huh. Okay. Do you like it?"

"No," he says without hesitation, then pauses and squeezes the side of the kitchen island again. "The work is fine. It's the kind of work I prefer, actually, but my boss is a prick. It's hard to want to succeed when it means creating success for someone you loathe."

I nod. "Been there. I was the night manager for this restaurant, and the owner was a real douchebag. He always told all the women to smile. Like, he'd expect us to smile while we were cleaning up puke. But do you really want to work in your bedroom? Delia showed me the whole apartment the first time I swung by, and no offense, but your room is teensy-tiny. It's like…"

"Like the elevator?" he says with a wry twist of his mouth. "It just so happens that I like that elevator. Maybe even more now."

I ignore the way his words quake through me. "To each their own. You know, I should have said so earlier, but we can totally switch rooms. It doesn't make sense for me to get the big one."

He shifts a little on his feet. "It's like I said earlier. Routine is a powerful thing. I've lived in that room for ten years. I'm not going to leave it now."

"Even for something better?" I ask in disbelief.

His lips curve, commanding my attention, and he plants his big palms on the kitchen island, leaning on it. "Bigger, not better. Not that anyone else has ever needed to tell me this, but they're not always the same. I can see the mountains from my room. The trees. Yours looks out on the city."

"Which suits me," I say with a smile. "Let me guess. Are you one of those leaf peepers? You've already admitted you like pumpkin spice. I'll bet you even have binoculars."

"Guilty as charged. The leaves changed late this year, and they're still out. There's something about all those trees covered in red and orange and yellow. It's amazing to see all colors that appear in nature. It fills me with a sense of wonder I'll never get sick of."

He's intense about the things he likes, and I can't help but appreciate him for that too.

"How about you?" He smiles as he says it. "Something tells me you like the summer."

I smile back, but I'm disarmed. He's right. I live for the sun on my neck and the smell of sea salt in the breeze—maybe a funny thing for someone to say when they've spent their whole life in the mountains, but I'm not the only one who's ever wanted something I can't have. "Try your drink, already. It's like fall in a cup. This has to be your signature."

"Okay," he says in the way of someone who's only humoring me. He lifts it to his lips, and I find myself watching as he presses it to them, remembering the way those lips felt on mine. He sets the cup down with a mute clink. "It's good."

But again, he's obviously humoring me. "Good, but you like beer better."

One corner of his mouth lifts, and his dark eyes meet mine again before focusing lower, on my mouth. "But I like beer better."

"Pumpkin spice beer?"

His smile widens. "Sure, when the mood strikes."

"I'm not giving up. We'll get there."

"Sure. But not today, okay? I need a little time to reset."

"Not today," I agree. "But I *am* going to get you a new pair of glasses to replace the ones my ass destroyed."

His mouth twitches. "Do I get a say in what they look like?"

"Nope. You're my Patrick Dempsey."

"This is like with Ruthie all over again," he informs me.

We're falling into a rhythm that feels natural and seductive, so I purposefully ruin it by asking, "When's your meeting with Daphne?"

His face clears of expression, like a chalkboard rubbed clean. "The guys really did tell you everything, huh?"

"No, but Burke and Leonard tell their girlfriends everything, and my sister and Shauna told me."

"It's in a couple of weeks." He rubs his forehead. "But she asked me to meet up beforehand. That Wednesday." His forehead creases. "Actually, she wants me to meet her at Glitterati."

A little shiver skates down my spine. Firstly, because that's no business meeting. She's interested in seeing the man she threw away. The one she famously, at least in Danny's group of friends, called "basic." Probably because she's had eight years to realize there's more to him than his pumpkin spice addiction.

Secondly, because it feels weird that she chose my bar. I mean, my bar is banging, don't get me wrong, but it feels...overly coincidental.

Also, why would she bring *Danny* there? Doesn't she know him at all?

Glitterati is my favorite place on earth, but I've designed it, purposefully, to be loud and bold and colorful—an assault on the senses.

Maybe she's testing him. If so, it's kind of a shitty test, which suggests she's a shitty person. Danny deserves better than to settle for someone like that.

Or do you just want to believe that because he made you come with his hand and then sucked his fingers?

I swallow hard. "Looks like you're all set up for a reunion, Romeo. There's nothing professional about meeting at a bar. She wants to scope you out."

He shrugs it away. "I'm guessing she wants to clear the air, make sure the meeting goes well."

I doubt it. But I give him a sunny smile. "I'm going to get you some new shirts too. What size are you?"

"I can do my own shopping, Mira."

"You like going to stores?" Because I can't imagine he would, what with the snapping fluorescents and strangers pushing each other for prime placement in line.

"That's what the internet's for."

"I want to do it. Call it a Housewarming present. And I might as well tell you right now that I'm going to keep insisting until you cave." I wave to the pink record table and all the little things he put out for me to help it feel like home. My throat feels slightly clogged as I add, "You gave me something."

He studies me for a second and then gives a decisive nod. "I don't like buttoned shirts. I'm Large."

My mind is a gutter. I choke on my own spit, and he pushes the drink toward me. I probably shouldn't be drinking alcohol at 11:30 am either, but my thoughts are driving me to it. I take a shallow sip.

Huh. It *is* pretty bland.

"I can do better than this. I'm off my game."

"We'll try again later." He grabs a massive water bottle from the counter behind him, fills it up, then lifts it to me as if in a cheers.

"Wait," I say, suddenly desperate, although I have no idea for what.

He pauses. My eyes take in the long line of him, the slight curl of the longer hair at the top of his head and where it's grown out a little at the nape of his neck.

"You're going to call the super?"

"I said I would," he tells me, some grumpiness creeping back into his voice. It must be perversion that makes me want to smile.

"Any other podcasts I should listen to in addition to the murdering neighbor one?"

He lists off a few, then says, "Is there something you need? Something that would make you more comfortable?"

"Do you have any books?"

He looks taken aback by this. "You want to read my books?"

Yes. I want to understand more about how his mind works. He's interesting and inaccessible to me. Like Wordle. I try it every damn morning, and I only crack it once a week. But that feeling of cracking it, boy—it's like finding someone's signature drink on the first go-round.

"Sure. I mean, I'm not so good at keeping still, but I guess I don't have a choice, huh?"

"There's always a choice," he tells me. "It's just that one of them might end with you having a limp. So at least you know you're making the good one." He shrugs. "That's what I tell myself when I'm feeling that way, anyway. It's always better to feel like there are options."

I wonder why he feels trapped, but I don't ask.

It feels like anything I ask will only wind us closer, and it's already been such a strange morning.

He disappears into his room, then returns to the kitchen island with a couple of paperbacks. There's a slight self-consciousness to him as he lowers them in front of me, his finger brushing my hand.

Shit. I'm in trouble if his finger brushing across mine is making me feel like I'm going to internally combust.

"It's okay if you don't like them," he says.

"They're only choices you made from deep down in your soul."

"Exactly." And then, with a smile that would put Mona Lisa to shame, he disappears into his room.

I hope he's enjoying that view of his.

Sighing, I take a slug from the subpar drink. I can practically hear my mother making some disparaging comment about women who day drink, but the mercurial part of me revels in it. Yes, I'm a classless woman. No, I don't care. I prefer myself this way.

Then I grab the books and go park myself on the armchair by the SAD light. Something about it drew me to it from the first moment I walked in here. For one thing, it's directly by a window. For another, it looks...loved, I guess. Like it's the kind of chair that anyone would want to sit in on a rainy day.

These days are going to be metaphorically rainy. It's 11:30, and I've already had all my excitement for the day. Sighing, I prop my cast on an ottoman and turn the chair a little to peer out the window.

To my shock, I can see right into the apartment across the alley. The woman inside of it, who's blonde or maybe white-haired, is staring directly back at me. I wave, and she ducks out of view. Huh, that's weird. Then again, maybe she thinks *I'm* weird for breaking the unwritten rule that we're supposed to pretend the people in the buildings around us don't exist.

My gaze pivots to the next set of windows, maybe a different apartment, and I see a woman feeding a baby in a high chair. She's too far away for me to see her expression, but weariness is apparent in her every moment. I feel you, sister.

Sighing, I set the books down on the coffee table and grab the first one.

John Dies at the End.

I set it down again, because I've already come close enough to the void for one day, thank you very much, and go grab my phone to turn on one of the podcasts Danny recommended. Even doing something as simple as that is taxing with the cast. It's hard not to feel down. I like moving. Being. *Doing*. Normally I run in the afternoons, but I won't be running anywhere anytime soon. The doctor said the only thing I can really do to keep in shape is some arm and chair exercises.

I settle back in the chair and plug the phone into a nearby outlet, but the battery's already charged enough that I'm able to turn it on.

I can practically feel the frown dragging my face down as I see a text from Byron on the home screen.

How's it going. Have any accidents.

Um. Creepy much?
I text back:

You know this is part of my official phone record, right? If I die, PEOPLE WILL KNOW.

Oh, for God's sake. You're so fuckin overdramatic. That's why it would never have worked.

No, it would never have worked because you suck, and I broke up with you.

You deserve what's coming to you, Mira. Karma comes for all of us.

That final line is the title of his latest attempt at a single, which makes it more annoying but no less creepy. My judgment really is shit when it comes to men—and the fact that I spent months sleeping with Byron is proof that chemistry means nothing. We had plenty of chemistry. But he's self-involved and lazy and kind of dumb. I'd feel mean for saying that last bit, especially because people have been making me feel dumb my whole life, but it's true. He's really, genuinely pretty stupid.

Go drink some of your sour milk, you psychopath.

Aw, shit, you got to this one too?

No, but I don't mind him having to pour it out just in case, the jerk.

I send another text.

Goodbye, forever.

So why do I have a sinking feeling it won't be?

Sure enough, three dots appear on the phone a second later.

> I felt bad for hexing you, but now I don't. You mutherfuckin deserve it.

What's this now?

> I don't want to fuck your mother, no, but thanks for asking. What are you talking about with the hex???

> Byron?

> I told you, payback's a bitch.

An uncomfortable feeling skitters down my spine. I don't believe in hexes, obviously, but he's acting erratic. Unreasonable. Kind of...scary.

And when I try to text him back three question marks and the middle finger emoji, it says message undelivered, so the asshole blocked me.

"He's just trying to wig you out," I say, and the sound of my own voice wigs *me* out. It doesn't help that I've been sitting around all day with nothing to do but overthink everything.

Sighing, I enter my group chat with Delia and Shauna. It's still titled the Evans Sisters Want the Goods from when Shauna first started her relationship with Leonard.

I tap my finger on the side of the phone, then tell them about Byron's weird-ass messages.

Me: *You think he really tried to curse me?*
Me: *Danny and I DID just get stuck in an elevator for two hours. And there's the whole ankle thing to consider.*
Shauna: *I want more details about the elevator. Stat.*
Shauna: *Also, I know a psychic we can ask about the hex.*
Me: *Yes, please.*

Shauna: *I'll see if I can get us an appointment. We can also get one of the guys to pay this dude a visit. Show him you're well protected. Hell, I can pay him a visit if you'd like. I know at least fifteen different ways to make a man cry.*
Me: *Tempting, but no. I don't want him to think he rattled me.*
Delia: *OMG. I just saw this. Are you okay? Is Danny okay?*
Me: *Aren't you going to ask if the elevator's okay?*
Delia: *That was coming last.*

We fill her in on everything, including our perspective visit to the psychic. When I set my phone down a few minutes later, I notice the woman across the way is staring at me again. This time she holds my gaze for a solid thirty seconds before looking away.

Fuck, did I just become paranoid?

Chapter Eight

Danny

The day passes in a blur.

I can still smell Mira, taste her. See that image of her from after the lights blinked on inside the box we were stuck in.

When I found out that she was moving in, I figured life as I knew it was over. I was right, just not in the way I thought, and now I'm confused, wrapped up in my mind like a pretzel.

I called Burke earlier and informed him of what happened. He's going to call the building management, but he agrees the incident was probably caused by an electrical short, which also left every clock in our apartment blinking.

He ended our conversation by asking, "Is there something you're not telling me?"

I told him no, and he acted like he believed me. I hadn't felt like I was being obvious, but I guess when you've known someone for most of your life you're at risk of being an open book to them. If only it were vice versa. If only I could read *her* signals. I have no idea what she's thinking. All I know is that she's out there, doing God knows what, and I'm in here at my cramped desk, which barely fits between the window and the bed, thinking about how she tastes.

She made it very clear there can be nothing between us, so I need to put that out of my head. Reset, like I told her I would. But something about her keeps pulling me back in. Earlier, when I left to use the bathroom, she was sitting in my chair, her legs propped up, staring out the window while she listened to *The Murderer Next Door*.

I should have been agitated to see her in my chair, especially since she was eating a damn chocolate bar in it, but I *liked* that she was making herself comfortable. Liked it even more that she was listening to something I'd recommended. I made her some tea since I was making some for myself, and the smile she gave me has stuck with me all afternoon, popping up between lines of code.

It's late now, and I skipped lunch without meaning to.

Shit, should I have offered to make her something? I got used to making food when Burke was around, same as I did when Ruthie was a kid, but he moved out over a week before Mira moved in. I've gotten used to a new routine, and routines help me stay regulated.

I slide my earphones down to my chest, still debating whether I should make dinner, when I hear her calling out, "Danny!"

My heart starts racing. Fuck, how long has she been calling me? Is something wrong? What if she's bleeding out on the floor out there?

I throw the earphones onto my desk and race out into the living room. No sign of her. Adrenaline floods me as I search the kitchen area for her and find nothing.

"Danny?" she calls again, and I realize she's in the bathroom.

I barge through the door and realize several things simultaneously.

One, she's completely naked.

Two, she's in the bathtub.

Three, there's a plastic bag taped around her cast.

It's obvious she was able to climb in and even bathe on her own, only to realize she had no way out without either getting her leg wet or putting pressure on it.

"Danny!" she shouts.

Because I've frozen in the doorway, my eyes taking her in.

"Oh shit," I glance at the wall, trying to count the tiles. Anything to stop myself from thinking of the sight of her in that tub, the water kissing her pink nipples and showing me everything I've been fantasizing about all day. My dick went from terrified to hard in an instant. "Uh, I'm guessing you need help getting out."

"Yeah," she says. "I didn't really think this through. I should have let Delia help."

I laugh, still trying to count those tiles. Twenty. Twenty-two. "I'm surprised she didn't insist on coming over after the elevator incident."

"She did," she says, probably giving me a strange look. I'd know if I weren't looking anywhere else. "She was here for a couple of hours earlier. I updated her about the whole elevator shebang over text, but apparently that wasn't enough. You didn't notice?"

"I had my earphones on." Thirty-five. Thirty-six. "They're noise cancelling, and I get..." How to explain this. "I get in the zone when I'm working on a problem. Sometimes it's hard to notice anything else, or at least it takes a lot. Shit. I'm sorry. What should we do? Maybe you can start by draining the water?"

"That's a good idea," she says. I hear some splashing and then the water starts to drain, a sound I've never liked.

"How about I put a towel over you, and I can lift you out?" I say, my blood beating uncomfortably through my veins, both because I'm terrified I'll hurt her, and because I'm about to hold her naked body with nothing but a towel between us. This isn't the reset I needed, that's for damn sure.

"Yeah," she says, her voice thick. "Yeah, that sounds good."

I walk in, my eyes still on those tiles—fifty-one, fifty-two—and close the door so I can grab the fluffy guest towel I keep hanging there.

"Don't worry," I say. "It's the guest towel. I haven't used it."

"I'm not thinking about the cleanliness of the towel right now, Danny."

Neither am I, damn it.

"Has all of the water drained?"

"Yes," she says, sounding breathy and nervous.

"I would never hurt you on purpose, Mira."

"No, I know you wouldn't. I was being stupid. I shouldn't have tried it by myself."

No, but she feels the need to do everything alone.

"I'm going to walk toward the tub now." I approach the tub with the towel held out in front of me like a shield, but I already saw her. I'm already thinking about the way her body looked under that water—the generous swell of her hips, her breasts with their rosy nipples, and the apex of her legs, opened to my gaze because her cast was propped over the side of the tub.

"Are you ready?" I ask thickly.

"Give it to me," she says, and God help me, I'd like to give her something else. How am I supposed to live with this woman without going insane?

I settle the towel over her and look down to see her peering up to me. I can't read the look on her face. Maybe I'm lucky I can't. "I'm going to pick you up now," I say through a dry throat, because there's no towel over her ass, and I'm going to have my hands on it, or close enough.

"Okay," she says thickly, her eyes on mine.

"Tell me if it hurts."

I crouch down and slide an arm behind her shoulders, another beneath her knees, then lift. Her skin is wet and soft and slippery. "Hang on to me."

She wordlessly wraps her arms around my neck, her grip strong and solid, and the trust in that gesture—and in her request for help —floors me.

"Are you okay?" I ask. Her cast hasn't gotten knocked against anything, so I hope the answer is yes, but I need to hear her say it.

"I'm okay," she confirms.

I carry her to her room like that, her arms linked around my neck while mine are wrapped around her mostly bare body.

Don't think about her ass. Don't think about her ass.

But *of course* I'm thinking about her ass. It would take a stronger man than me not to think about it when it's a few inches away from my hand, pressing against my shirt, which is wet from her skin. I shift my hold on her, lifting her higher, because I don't want her to know I'm the kind of pervert who's turned on by helping an injured woman.

I am that kind of pervert, apparently, because I want to carry her into *my* room.

I don't, though. Let it never be said I'm a man who can't listen. I stride over to her room and kick the door open. After I do, I feel her hands flex around my neck.

"Sorry," I mutter, although I'm not sure what for. Maybe the hard-on she hopefully can't feel.

"Don't you be sorry," she says. "*I'm* sorry. I'm useless. I can't even take a fucking bath by myself."

The frustration in her voice is one I've felt myself. I've walked away from a grocery store before because it was too crowded—from a bar because the music made me feel like it was digging into my skull with a blunt spoon. Those are things people are supposed to be able to do, and sometimes I can't do them.

"You're not useless," I tell her. "If you weren't around, who'd make me alcoholic drinks before noon?" I lower her onto the bed, decorated with pink embroidery that makes me smile. Even in sleep, she wants everything to be a production. The towel is covering her mostly, but she's stretched out naked on her bed, her hair a tangled mess, her gaze on me.

Fuck. She's going to notice.

I try to sidestep behind a pile of boxes and trip over something on the floor. Seconds later, I'm on my ass, sitting next to the curling iron that tried to take me out.

"Are you okay?" Mira asks as she leans forward to see. Her breasts are pushing at the towel, and I have to rip my gaze away.

"Yes," I say, getting to my feet. "Only my dignity is injured. If I'd ended up hurting myself worse, I would have had to tell the emergency room staff that a curling iron did it."

It strikes me that she's probably cold beneath that towel. "Shit, I'm sorry. I'll leave you alone now."

"I like talking to you," she says, sitting up in bed and holding the towel to her chest. It doesn't leave much to the imagination. I can see the swell of her breasts and flashes of the skin the towel isn't covering on her legs. Her hips. I'd like to wrap my hands around them. I'd like to spread her legs open and taste her again.

I turn away and head back through the door before turning around, the door mostly closed behind me so it can hide the bulge in my pants.

"Would you like something to eat?" I ask, pained.

"You don't have to feed me, Danny. I'm only mostly an invalid. I'm going to get something delivered. You want in?"

"No, that's okay," I say. "I think I'm going out."

I hadn't planned on it, but I'm not sure I can spend the rest of the evening here. Maybe one of the guys will grab a drink with me. Or maybe I'll just go for a walk on the greenway. Ruthie made me promise I'd stop biking at night.

I still need a reset, or maybe ten of them.

This is all confusing. Baffling, even. I wasn't happy about Mira encroaching on my space a week ago, but now I feel a powerful draw to her. Maybe I was lonely, the way Ruthie says.

"Hey," Mira says, just as I'm about to turn around and lean into my mind storm.

"Yeah?"

"Have you ever noticed the woman in the apartment across from us? You know, the window on the side of the living room that looks across that alley?"

"A big burly dude used to live there," I tell her, my mind summoning an image of him that I would have preferred to keep in the vault. "He liked to walk around naked. I stopped looking."

"Oh," she says thoughtfully, looking off. "There's a woman in there now—a blonde woman. Or maybe white hair. I can't tell. She was watching me. Isn't that weird?"

"I don't know, were you staring at her?"

"Well, yeah."

"So maybe she thought you were being weird. That happens to me all the time."

"Do you really have binoculars for checking out leaves?"

I lean against the door jam, staring at the little jewelry box on top of her dresser—shaped like a horseshoe—so I don't have to look at her.

No. So I don't stare at her in a way that's bound to make her uncomfortable.

"I see. You've been cooped up for one day, and you're already resorting to watching the neighbors with binoculars?"

"Huh. When you put it that way, it does sound weird. Still..."

"Against my better judgment, I'll put them out for you, Jimmy Stewart."

"Jimmy Stewart?"

"You know." I gesture with my hand. "*Rear Window*. Broken leg. Peeping on the neighbors."

"Does that make you Grace Kelly?" she asks.

Is she smiling? I'd like to know, but I don't look. I can't.

"I guess it must."

"Must be that podcast you got me hooked on. I keep letting the next episode auto play."

I pause, really checking out that jewelry box. Trying hard not to think about the fact that she likes old movies, or at least this one old movie, and has spent all day listening to my favorite podcast. "Goodnight, Mira. I'll see you tomorrow. If you need any help, don't resort to calling out for Big Mike or Pumpkin. Text me. I'll come home."

"You would, wouldn't you?"

My gaze finally finds her, giving into the need to look. Maybe I'm imagining it, but she seems surprised. Maybe even bewildered. I don't like what that suggests about her ex-boyfriend, not that I thought very well of him a few minutes ago.

"Of course," I say firmly.

Then, because I can't help myself, I let my gaze dip, taking in the delightful, infuriating inadequacy of that towel. Her hips, flaring outward from the towel as if they're asking for me to hang onto them. Swallowing, I look away and say, "Have a good night."

I leave. I text Ruthie, asking her if she needs anything and then my buddies, all of whom agree to the drink except for Shane, who's staying at the office late, but there's something I have to do before I go...

Mira would *definitely* feel better than my hand.

Later, when I come back home, there's a whiskey glass waiting on the counter for me. I'm smiling despite myself as I take a sip. I don't know how long it's been sitting out, so maybe the melted ice isn't helping, but the balance of tart and sweet isn't to my liking.

I grab some post-it notes from my desk and leave her a message.

Good. But I still like beer better.

Chapter Nine

Mira

It's Friday.

A week of captivity has passed.

A week of captivity that's made me feel new sympathy for zoo animals, stuck in their tiny cages. Except most animals in captivity were born that way, and I was born with a taste for running across roads and dipping my toes in the ocean and eating cookie dough without giving a second thought to raw eggs. I'm not the sort of person who savors sitting and staring, whether that staring is at a book or a screen or out a window.

Captivity has changed me...and yes, I know that sounds melodramatic. I *am* melodramatic, and captivity has amped that up too. Danny left the binoculars for me out on the kitchen island after our talk last week, along with a note:

Enjoy the peeping. Also, I use them for birds, not leaves. Is that worse? Now that I'm writing it down, it seems worse.

I thought it was cute, which is probably a further sign that captivity is altering my brain chemistry in alarming ways.

I have used those binoculars more shamelessly than sweet, debonair Jimmy Stewart ever would have, God rest his soul. Mostly, I've checked out the apartment across the way. The only furniture I can see from the window is a single folding chair and the kind of portable table a person would usually only set out on a porch. It's not the sort of decorating scheme you'd expect from someone so severe looking. The blond or white-haired woman also appears at the window at strange times of day—sometimes early in the morning, sometimes late at night, sometimes in the middle of the day— meaning her schedule is unpredictable or she's as much of a loser as I currently am. As of yet, she's caught me watching her a couple of times, but never with the 'nocs. Occasionally she knits in there. I'm pretty certain she's up to something. I've said as much to Danny, my sister, and anyone who's inclined to listen.

Most people aren't inclined to listen, and Shauna threatened to steal the binoculars before I got myself arrested for being a peeping Tom. Delia has pointed out that therapy has been very helpful to both to her boyfriend and Shauna's boyfriend—and that therapists can now communicate with their patients online, so "I wouldn't even need to go anywhere."

Speaking of Shauna: apparently her good friend Josie the psychic has been out of town for some sort of dance retreat and thus couldn't fit us in until this afternoon. I'm looking forward to our outing more than any rational person should look forward to visiting a psychic.

There have been only two bright spots of this past week.

Bright Spot One: Visiting Glitterati and figuring out a staggered schedule for my return. I wasn't supposed to do anything this week, but the binoculars must have really thrown Delia for a loop, because she agreed to go with me yesterday afternoon. She insisted on coming because, and I quote, "you need someone to advocate for yourself, and you're obviously not going to do it."

Delia and Azalea both agreed that I should only work before opening for the next five weeks, but after that, it's on. Well, it's on from 5-9, because they have also insisted that I put in another two weeks of half shifts since I "really shouldn't be on my feet that soon anyway."

Honestly. Don't they know what this is doing to my sanity?

I could have pulled rank, but I had a sinking feeling they were right.

Bright Spot Two: Danny.

Danny, who leaves notes and sometimes little offerings for me on the kitchen island every morning. A scone one morning, and a hot chocolate another day. A stone he found in the woods and thinks might have emerald in it.

Danny, who's been taste-testing fall and holiday drinks for me like a champ, even though I still haven't managed to concoct one he likes more than beer, the Philistine. He did give top marks to Santa's Ho, however, so that one's definitely getting added to the menu.

Danny, who's gotten me fully into *The Murderer Next Door*, which, I'll admit, might be fueling my obsession with the woman across the way. He's already listened to all of them, but he's surprisingly cool with me spouting theories at him every night. And yes, he does give me these knowing looks that could drive a woman mad, but the corners of his lips always lift just slightly—and amusing this man is something I savor.

Danny, who's been marathon-watching shows with me, too, even *Bridgerton*, which he admits "isn't his favorite." Since it's only fair, I have been watching shows with him, including *Star Trek: The Next Generation*, which he claims is the best Star Trek.

Danny, who rigged up the bathroom so I could take showers or baths without having to be rescued by him every time. It's less of a relief than it should be, because I'm rather fond of the memory of having his hands firmly wrapped around my wet body...

His glasses haven't arrived yet because they were on backorder, but the shirts I ordered for him did come. He folded them into his wardrobe without any fanfare despite having told me that, "I really, really shouldn't have." Because I went a little crazy—big surprise—and got him a dozen.

They're red and blue and striped and flannel, and I like seeing which one he walks out in each morning. It's like a little gift to the eyeballs, and I like running bets with myself about which one it'll be.

I'd be lying if I didn't admit that each morning, I want him a little more too. Every time he touches me—to hand me mail or a drink or even the remote control, I feel a little electric zing, like I've been rubbing my skin against balloons and am super charged.

Needless to say, I've been thinking about that morning we spent in the elevator a lot—every time I pass it to make my way inexpertly down the stairs, something Danny insists on helping me with whenever he hears me opening the door. I guess he's stopped wearing his headphones so he can be prepared to jump into action every time I take a near plunge down the stairs.

Since he always goes out of his way to help me and make my life easier, I've tried to do the same for him. I know a few other neurodivergent people, but I've heard the old axiom that no two autistic people experience autism the same way. So I researched ways to make people with sensory differences more comfortable. I've started giving myself only one spray of perfume, rather than two. Turning the TV down. I only use the SAD lamp when his door is closed.

We've fallen into a routine that I like, but I know it can't last. I'll go back to my life—to the vampire hours of the bar, and it'll immerse me the way it always does. And Danny won't want to follow me there. We'll be like ships in the night, our only communication relegated to those notes we pass back and forth.

Truthfully, I depend on those notes. And when I got up this morning, a week and five days after I broke my ankle—yes, I'm counting, dammit—the first thing I do is head out to the kitchen to check for one.

It's there on the kitchen island, beneath a latte in a paper cup.

It may be basic, but it has caffeine. Come on. Tell me you don't enjoy pumpkin spice.

I take a sip before realizing the drink is cold, probably because Danny wakes up hours before I do. He's the kind of insane super person who gets up early to work out. I've learned he usually bikes for an hour or so before coming back to shower and start his workday. I like watching him walk in sweaty, when I'm up in time to see it. It's a nice sight to start *my* day.

I have also, in my captivity, become a pervert, because I think of licking the sweat off his arm. Of asking if I can watch him take a shower. Of stripping off those tight shorts he wears, which leave very little to the imagination—not that I'm only working with imagination...

I've felt his hard dick, pressed up against me, and I think about it at night, when I'm alone. When I know that all I'd have to do is hobble the several feet from my room to his to claim what I want.

I've been telling myself the captivity is to blame, and also that I wouldn't feel this way if I'd gotten any action recently. But I know better than to fully believe it. Danny's intense and funny and smart and good, and I *like* him. I can't remember the last time I actually liked someone I was also attracted to.

Sighing, I nuke the coffee in a mug, then blow on it and take a sip.

Dammit, when it's not as cold as the arctic tundra, it *is* delicious.

I write an A- on the note, on the off-chance that I might miss Danny if he leaves his office-slash-closet room, and promise myself I'll impress him with the drink I concoct tonight.

I make my way to the couch, where I do some seated exercises and listen to the last few episodes of the third season of *The Murderer Next Door*. And, fine, I do something that's become a bit of a habit and is arguably creepier than using those binoculars—

I Google Daphne Elliot.

According to social media, Daphne is at a conference in Copenhagen this week, because she's the kind of woman who gets sent on business trips to Copenhagen. She's sleek and auburn-haired and very...well, adult looking, with these little wire glasses that make her look like a Math-a-lete. A *sexy* Math-a-lete.

The first time I Googled her, I had a good reason—or at least I assured myself it was one. She'd asked Danny to meet at Glitterati, so it seemed feasible that I might recognize her. But I haven't seen her before, or at least I don't remember her. So I sent a screenshot of her photo to Azalea and asked, *Do you recognize her?*

Three dots popped up, and my heart beat a little faster until the message came through from my friend.

> Do I ever. She's a triple threat. Good job, hotttt,
> and also friendly. But she's sadly heterosexual.
> (Plays tiny violin.) Why?

I told her, acting like it was no big deal to me if Danny decided he wanted to be with her again, and she responded, *lucky guy*, which didn't elevate my mood. Truthfully, I'd been hoping Azalea was going to tell me that Daphne is one of those people who asks for five substitutions in a drink and still sends it back. Of course, just because she was nice to Azalea doesn't mean she's a nice person.

I'll bet those conference attendees in Copenhagen have nothing good to say about her, even if they're all grinning at her in the photographs like she's the second coming and they'd like her to autograph their mousepads.

With another sigh, I toss my phone across the couch. I try to tell myself it would be a good thing if Danny and Daphne decide to embark on a little second chance romance. If he's with someone else, I'll have to stop noticing him. He can just be my roommate, the way he's supposed to be.

By early afternoon, I'm so bored that I'd voluntarily go anywhere—the DMV, the post office, or even the gynecologist. Hell, I'd go to an aging white male gynecologist who says things like "getting up there in years, girl" and asks intrusive questions about my sex life while rooting around in my vagina. So I'm relieved as hell when Shauna texts to confirm we're still on for our four o'clock appointment to see Josie the Great. Delia says she's coming too, probably because it gives her a way to check on me without seeming like she's checking on me.

By the time the buzzer rings, I've exhausted everything I could possibly do in the apartment—with the exception of Danny.

"Oh, thank the sweet lord," I mutter, climbing to my feet with the crutches. "I'll be right down!" I say into the buzzer, better at balancing now that I've been on these suckers for a while. I manage to get my coat on, then grab my bag from the hook Danny mounted for it on the wall by the door and leave the apartment. I make it down a couple of steps before it happens—I plant one of the crutches badly, and I don't know if I'll be able to course correct. Panic pounds through my veins as I feel myself teetering dangerously, and I'm sure I'm going to fall and break the other ankle. I'm going to—

I hear the door slamming open. Danny swears, then seconds later his arm is wrapping around my back. It's a black sweater today. I figured it would make his eyes even more intense and sexy.

A sidelong glance confirms that it does, dammit.

"I don't need help," I lie, mostly because I'm disconcerted by how much of a relief it is that he's offering. Again. He keeps offering me things I didn't know I needed, and I keep taking them. Usually, when people offer me help, I deny them, but it's different with Danny. Maybe it's because he offers help in the way I want it, and he's so unobtrusive about it, it feels natural. Like giving someone a cookie after you've made a tray of them.

"Yup, that's obvious, tough guy. I could carry you down like last time, or we could walk like this. What'll it be?"

"Walk like this," I say, because it somehow feels like there's more dignity to it.

Or because the last time he carried you like that, you nearly broke and asked him to carry you up to his bedroom, an intrusive voice whispers.

The intrusive voice is rude, and I tell it to shut the hell up.

"Okay," he says, his strong arm encircling my back.

He doesn't tell me I'm an idiot, possibly because we both know I'm an idiot.

"Don't you need to wear your headphones for concentration?" I ask as we slowly make our way down, Danny's strong grip making me feel secure.

"They help, but no I don't. Anyway, maybe I care less about fucking up. I'm hoping to quit soon."

"Because of the game?" I ask, curious. I'm more familiar with the game now, because I've spent hours of my free time playing it on my laptop over the last week. At first I didn't get the appeal...why spend time pretending to do chores while ignoring the chores I could be doing in my real life?

But then I got addicted. Mostly because a little fantasy creature that looks like a rainbow-colored puffball started following me around, and I got off on having a fantasy creature sidekick.

That, and Danny and his buddy Drew started playing it with me. It's not available to the public yet, but they play it all the time to search for bugs, and Danny assured me I was fulfilling a very essential role by helping them too.

"Yeah," Danny says, easing me down a step. "We'll see. I'm hoping to get a decent offer."

I give him a sidelong look. "So your makeover is important on multiple levels."

He smiles unintentionally—I can tell because of the small crease in his forehead, as if he's unclear on why he's smiling. We take another step down. "You really think they're going to give me a better deal if Daphne thinks I look like Patrick Dozey?"

"Dempsey," I correct. "And no, you don't look like him in a literal sense. But you *can* get a glow up like he did."

"I don't know whether to be insulted."

I lean into him a little. Maybe I should cool it on the makeover stuff, but wearing clothes that suit me always gives me a confidence boost, so I figured the same would be true for him. It's also become something of a running joke between us. "Choose not to be. It'll go easier on both of us that way. Your new glasses are going to arrive later today."

"Oh good, I'll be able to see again."

I think he's joking. I'm mostly sure of it. He's already told me he's far-sighted, and they help him on the computer. He has a pair of reading glasses from the supermarket that make him look like someone's grandfather, though, so he hasn't been that hard-up.

"Don't you want to know what they look like?" I ask.

I feel him watching me as we descend another step. "So long as they're not bright pink, I think we'll be fine. Where are you going, anyway?"

I puff out air. "Byron told me that he put a hex on me, so Shauna suggested we pay a visit to her psychic friend and find out. I don't really believe in any of that shit, but you never know."

His arm stiffens around me. "He did what?" he says in a rough voice.

"Oh, it's fine." I give him a sidelong glance and find his gaze pinned on me. He looks...pissed. Maybe even dangerous, although not to me.

"It's *not* fine. And you're going to go see *Josie*?"

"You know this person?" I ask, caught off guard.

"Yeah," he says distantly. "I met her on one pretty memorable occasion."

"That's all you're going to say about it? We need to work on your gossip skills."

"No thanks."

We take another couple of steps, and then he pulls me back suddenly, his hand encircling my hip. A jolt of appreciation shoots through me before I realize why he did it. It's not because he's suddenly decided we should get busy in the stairwell. That damn hamster is sitting on the trim at the side of the stairs, staring up at us through beady black eyes.

Chapter Ten

Mira

"I've recently formed a case of paranoia, but I'm starting to think this animal has it out for us," I say. "Do you believe hamsters are capable of evil?"

"Can you grab the banister?" he asks, dodging the question. So maybe I'm not the only one who's a little bit scared of Pumpkin. "I'll pick him up."

I do as he asks, and he does as he said he would. Except the little rodent sinks its teeth into his hand. I see it happening, and I also see what happens next—Danny's surprised enough that he trips over his own feet and goes down the four steps to the bottom. He catches his fall with one of his hands, flat on the ground, but the other's holding Pumpkin, and despite everything Pumpkin has done to us, Danny is much too nice to smoosh him.

"Oh my God," I shriek. "Are you okay?"

There's no question—I have to go to him. I have no further thoughts about dignity as I lower down onto my butt, the crutches slung over my lap, and descend the rest of the way on my ass.

Panic pounds through me when I see the look on Danny's face —his eyes are cinched shut, and there are lines at the corners of his mouth.

"Did you break yourself?" I blurt as I plop down beside him with zero grace.

"No," he says, his body heaving, and that's when I realize...

"You're laughing?"

He opens his eyes, and they're glassy with unshed tears.

"Can't...stop," he says through gusts of laughter. The hamster looks almost tranquil in his other hand, but maybe that's because he gets his kicks tormenting people, and we've given him plenty of opportunity.

I start laughing too as he sits up. Because it's funny, the two of us being nearly incapacitated because of a hamster. Me going down the stairs on my butt like I'm a little kid.

I hold my hand out for Pumpkin, but Danny shakes his head.

"Don't be a martyr," I say. "You need to check out your wrist. Do you think it's broken?"

"Want a little company?" he asks, giving my pink cast a pointed look.

"Nah, I'd worry about us being too matchy-matchy. You'd have to get yellow or something. Say, what's your favorite color?"

"Orange."

I purse my lips. "Orange and pink. I think I like that."

"I almost regret that it's not broken," he says, still ignoring my outstretched hand.

Inspiration strikes, and I lean against the wall for support and then pull off my flower-patterned shoulder bag. "Put him in there."

"Won't you need your..." he trails off, eyeing the bag with wariness. "I have no idea what women carry in those things."

"A wallet, a phone, and a ton of shit I don't need." I take out the things I do need and stuff them into my coat pockets. Then I hand the bag over, and Danny dumps Pumpkin in before zipping it up. He gives me the nod of a co-conspirator, and when I hand him the bag, he takes it without any passive aggressive-murmuring about holding something with flowers on it.

I'll bet Daphne didn't appreciate that about him.

It's a dumb thought, and I push it down. Clearing my throat, I say, "Ready?"

"As I'll ever be."

We slowly make our way down to the lobby. When we reach it, I can see Shauna and Delia waiting for me on the other side of the glass door, Delia eyeing the elevator at the end of the hall with suspicion it definitely deserves.

"Well," Danny says.

"Well," I say. "Enjoy the purse, it's treated me well. Obviously I'll have to burn it after you drop off our wily charge."

"Obviously." He nods toward my sister and our friend, then turns from me. I watch, my mouth slightly parted, as he makes his way across the lobby in a few strides with those long legs and stops in front of the fucking elevator.

He grins at me before he steps onto it, as if to say, here I am again, rolling the dice.

Or maybe he's telling you he likes the memory, the voice in my head whispers.

When I get outside, Delia asks, "Do you know Danny still has your purse?"

Shauna laughs. It's deep and hearty—the unselfconscious laugh of a person who enjoys laughing. "I'm more concerned about why it was wiggling."

"It's a long story," I tell them with a wave of my hand. "But we *did* capture a prisoner. It remains to be seen whether or not Pumpkin will fall in love with us. I'm guessing no, and also that Danny will return him for a very reasonable ransom."

"I understood very little of that," Shauna says, though her lips are still tipped upward. That's one of the things I like best about Shauna—she has this air of being perpetually amused by the world, and if possible, one should always be amused.

The three of us pile into the car—me in the backseat so I can prop my leg up. Several minutes later, Shauna turns into the parking lot of a strip mall that looks like it would have been solidly mediocre ten years ago. It's old and dilapidated now, the kind of place no one would break into, because people don't like stealing black mold.

"We're here," she announces as she parks.

I look at the store in front of us doubtfully. The handwritten sign taped to the top half of the door looks like one of the storefront signs I used to make with construction paper and crayons when I was seven or eight. Back then, I wanted to open a clothing store, not a bar. The name was the same, though. *Glitterati.* I'd decided on that by the time I was five.

Plenty of people tried to manage my expectations—school counselors, older relatives, and my mother most of all. They probably thought they were doing me a service because I wasn't a dedicated student, but that never crushed my spirit. I knew what I wanted, and I spent years fighting to get it.

"This woman has a business license?" I ask, whistling through my teeth. "I've been trying *way* too hard."

"You're assuming she's successful," Shauna says. She turns in her seat to smile at me before exiting through her door.

"Well, she did drag all three of us non-believers here," I mutter as I untangle myself from my belt.

"Speak for yourself," my sister says. She's all grace as she exits the front seat and, because she's Delia, comes around to help me. It'll make her feel better, so I allow it—not because I need it. That's my story, and I'm sticking to it.

"You believe this woman's really psychic?" I ask, lifting my eyebrows. Then, remembering what Danny said earlier, I ask, "Does Danny know her? He made some weird comment when I told him what I was doing."

Shauna and Delia exchange a look that fires up my curiosity.

"What do you know that I don't? Tell me quickly so I don't pop a blood vessel in my eye."

Shauna laughs. "Well, she ran into him a month or so back. She told him he'd already met his soulmate but didn't make a good impression on her, so Danny..."

"Oh," I say, trying to sound like I don't give a shit. There's a sick, sinking feeling in my stomach. "Huh. So he thinks it's Daphne, I suppose. Have you met her?"

"No," Shauna says, "but Leonard doesn't like her much."

"I get the sense Lucas feels the same way," Delia adds. She's the only one who calls her fiancé Lucas instead of Burke—but I guess it does it for both of them, because she doesn't seem in any hurry to change her mind.

"Yeah, I don't like her either." The words slip out before I can get the sense to shut the fuck up.

"But you've never met her," Shauna says.

I wave a hand. "She looks very serious and severe in her photos. Danny may seem like a wet blanket, but he's actually pretty cool."

"You looked up photos of her?" Delia asks, studying me with the intensity of a little sister who knows too much.

Shit. Mayday, mayday.

"I thought you wanted to give him a makeover so he'd have a better chance of winning her back?" Shauna adds.

"I did say that."

Before I moved in with him. I'd said it after hearing a bare-bones account of the story from her and Delia. All I knew was that my soon-to-be roommate was going to be working with the ex-girlfriend who'd rejected him.

Shauna has a raptor instinct my sister lacks, so I know I'm in trouble.

I push open the door to the shop to avoid more thoroughly addressing their questions.

There's a desk in front of us, and behind it, a dark-haired

woman in dark glasses and a man with curly hair are aggressively making out, their tongues visible, their hands sliding under each other's clothes. They're so close, I could probably reach out and touch them. The air inside the shop reeks of pot and something spicy. Patchouli, maybe. Or sandalwood.

I can't help myself, I say, "If you're really psychic, wouldn't you have known I was about to knock?"

Chapter Eleven

Mira

"You *didn't* knock," says the woman I presume to be Josie the Great. She sounds pretty high and mighty for a woman whose lipstick is smeared. "And the sight doesn't work that way."

"So how does it work?" I ask. The man with the curly hair sighs as if he's inconvenienced by my presence, which I suppose is true of his hard-on.

"You can't expect her to tell you that," he argues.

"Yeah, it's like asking about someone's cycle," Josie tells me with a hard look. "Do you want to tell me about *your* cycle, Mira?"

"Sure," I say. "The last time I got my period, it was super bloody, and my Moon Goddess cup leaked all over—"

"Jesus, I can't believe I quit the law for this," the guy says, but his expression is bemused, like he maybe doesn't mind. I guess he doesn't, because Josie the Great's lipstick's all over his mouth, and he's not running for a mirror.

"You were a lawyer?" I ask him.

"Sure," Josie answers for him. "We all make mistakes. Shauna tells me you're here to talk about yours."

I shoot Shauna an accusatory glance, and she shrugs. "Byron was a definite mistake."

Not going to argue with her there.

Josie gestures to a table set up in the back of her shop. There's a group of black candles in the center that're basically a pool of melted wax, and a crystal ball she probably brought from Party Depot. This is a racket, obviously, but I'm not above taking part in it.

Josie eyes my crutches as I make my way to the table. "You had an accident."

It's a statement of the obvious—people don't carry around crutches for fun—but goosebumps shiver up my arms nevertheless. Damn it, I really am getting suggestible.

"No shit," I say, taking a seat by the head of the table, balancing my crutches against the side.

The used-to-be-a lawyer sighs again from behind the front desk and pulls a book out of a leather satchel. I can't see the cover well from where I'm sitting, but judging from the self-important font, I'm guessing it's not a romance novel.

Shauna sits opposite me, Delia takes the chair next to mine, and Josie the Great takes the spot at the head of the table.

"So, Shauna said you might be able to tell me if I've been hexed," I say, since there's no point sitting around and singing kumbaya.

"Oh, you definitely were," Josie says.

I choke on nothing. It's not that I buy it, just that I didn't expect her to be so direct in her lies. "You can...see that?"

She shrugs. "Sure, but that's not why. Your ex-boyfriend came in here around Halloween."

Shauna gives Josie the Great a look that has claws. "Why the fuck didn't you say anything when I called you?"

"I figured you knew. You're the one who made the appointment with me."

It's coincidental, too coincidental, and I feel an uneasy shiver work down my back.

"How do you know it was him?" I ask.

Josie shrugs for a second time. "I could say it's because I'm psychic, but he also had a photo of you. So let's say it's both things."

That's creepy. Really fucking creepy. I've always been a fan of Halloween—of pretending to revel in darkness, but I'd prefer to keep it on a hypothetical level. Witchcraft is something that belongs in books and spooky stories told around campfires.

Delia pokes at the black wax on the table, and I notice her face has lost color. But then her lips tighten and she says, "You cursed my sister?"

Josie raises her hands, palms out. "I'm running a business here. What would you have me do?"

"Not put hexes on other women," I say, even though I don't truly believe she did any such thing. Sure, there's no denying that I broke my ankle and ill-advisedly made out with my roommate. But I've always been capable of making bad decisions on my own.

"Not to interrupt," says the used-to-be-a lawyer from behind his desk and book, "but hexes pay the most, and we needed to get our dishwasher fixed."

"You hexed me because you needed to get your dishwasher fixed?" I ask Josie.

"Poe says stupid people pay more," she says. "And I charged your ex double." I have to hand it to her, she's both confirming that she fucked me over and doing it in a way that butters me up.

"What hex did you put on me?"

She waves a hand, "Oh, you know, a simple hex. You're lucky he came to me. He wanted to dabble in some very dark magic, but I told him it was above his price range."

"Couldn't you have just pretended to do it?" I ask, sounding as petulant as a child.

She gives me a high and mighty look, then pushes her glasses up her nose with her middle finger. "I have professional integrity, you know. Besides, Bryan told me you poured lemon juice into his milk. I'd want to hex someone if they did that to me."

Used-to-be-a-lawyer flinches behind his desk. "Yeah, that's cold. He said he poured himself a whole glass and got two sips in before he realized it. I had to wonder why he took that second sip, but hey..." He lifts his hands.

"Stupid people pay better," Josie repeats.

"His name's Byron," I say with a sigh.

Josie makes a pinched face, as if she drank that soured milk. "You're the one who slept with him, you know. We didn't force you to sleep with a man named Byron. That was your own doing."

"Let's move on from that part," Delia says, even though I'm pretty sure she agrees with ninety percent of what was just said. "What can she do to break the hex?"

Josie puffs her lips out. "Well...you could throw around some black salt or do a magic mirror spell."

"Would those things really work?" I ask, fascinated despite myself.

"I don't know. I saw them on Google. But they sound kind of cool."

"Cool?" I lift my busted ankle. "Does this look cool?"

Josie stares at it for a moment, seemingly transfixed, then turns to the used-to-be-a-lawyer with shining eyes. "It worked, Poe. I'm a golden god."

"You're a goddess," he says, giving her a look that says he'd enjoy it very much if they could finish what they started before I came in.

"Wow, thanks a lot," I say. "Can you be less successful the next time you hex an innocent woman?"

She lifts a finger. "I could have put a darker hex on you."

"Look," I say, "I'm not even sure why I'm so pissed. I don't believe in hexes."

Josie gives me a knowing look, then taps her fingers to the middle of her forehead.

"What is it?" Shauna asks, her tone bemused. "I can tell there's something you're dying to say."

"You don't need to believe in a hex in order for the hex to believe in you." There's a self-satisfied air to her, as if she just said something brilliant.

"Seriously?" I say. "That doesn't make sense."

"You need to open your mind," Josie says with another tap to her temple.

"I'm more alarmed by Byron going to such extremes to try to hurt me," I say. "Where'd he get the hair?"

The thought makes me shudder. Did he cut a lock of my hair at night? How fucked up is that? I can practically feel my sister freaking out, too, so I reach over and take her hand. Squeeze it. She squeezes back and doesn't let go.

Josie inclines her head to the side. "He said he snaked it out of the shower drain."

"Gross," Shauna says, making a face.

"So couldn't some of it have been his?" I ask.

"Huh," Josie says, pushing her lips out as if this thought had never occurred to her. "I guess you're right. We probably hexed him too."

I almost want to believe in hexes because I'd really like that asshole to have a string of bad luck. I want his guitar strings to snap, his hair to fall out, his—

"Can we hire you to undo the hex?" Delia asks.

My sweet sister actually believes this woman who hot-boxes pot and finds spells on Google has some sort of connection to the great beyond. Then again, she was six and a half when she realized unicorns weren't real—and she cried bitter tears into her pillow until her little cheeks were creased from the fabric. I'd pay for a "cure" just to ease her mind, but Josie shakes her head.

"It's our policy not to accept money to undo spells by anyone but the person who originated them."

Poe, the used-to-be-a lawyer, nods. "Sorry, no can do. A few incidents have gotten messy. People throwing hexes at each other left and right, escalating to physical violence, that kind of thing."

"Well, let's go," Shauna says, getting up. "We should tell the guys what's up so they know to look out for this asshole. I say we send them all to pay him a visit."

"Yeah..." Poe scratches the back of his neck. "That's exactly the kind of thing we'd like to avoid."

This situation certainly isn't helping my newfound paranoia. Still, I'd prefer to confront Byron myself. I don't want it to turn into a Sharks and Jets situation if Byron has his bandmates over. Admittedly, Danny, Burke, Leonard, and Shane could absolutely cream The Lizard's Gizzards since their only aerobic activity is walking to the bar or their weed dealer's house in between gigs, but it would be best for everyone to dial the situation down a notch. "*I'm* the one who's going to pay him a visit."

Delia squeezes my hand, and when I turn to look at her, she's even paler, which pisses me off more.

"I'll bring someone when I go," I tell her. Then, for reasons I don't care to explore, I add, "I'll bring Danny."

"He doesn't really have an I'll-kick-your-ass kind of energy," Shauna says. "Why don't I go with you? I really can kick your ex's ass."

She means it. In addition to being a clay artist, she used to be a personal trainer at a gym and is a black belt in taekwondo, something I've asked her to demonstrate when I was tipsy.

"Danny could kick his ass too, if he wanted to," I say.

It was the wrong thing to say, though, because fresh interest has sparked in Shauna's eyes. "Sure," I course-correct. "Whatever. You and I will go. Let's do it now."

"Danny, huh?" Josie says with a smug tone. I have the insane urge to ask her what she knows about him and Daphne. But then I'd be giving her what she wants, and marking myself as the kind of rube who believes she has a backstage pass to the other side.

"Yup," Shauna says. "Why are you so interested? Did you curse him too?"

"No," she replies primly, throwing a glance at Poe, who's still behind the desk. He's located some sort of crunchy snack and is loudly eating it. Maybe he used to be a lawyer, but Josie has clearly cured him of it and then some. "No, but something interesting is happening with him. I could see that very clearly."

I release Delia's hand and then use the crutches to lift to my foot, suddenly beyond annoyed with this scenario, this day, and most definitely this psychic. Balancing, I prepare to skedaddle—in as much as I am currently capable of it. "I'm not sure you could say anything vaguer or less helpful if you tried."

Poe gives a doubtful shrug, so clearly he's heard plenty of less helpful things said in this shop. I don't doubt him, actually.

Josie stands too, adjusting her glasses again with her middle finger. I wonder if she's doing it to spite me specifically, or if she always does it that way, to spite humanity. "You're going to want to listen to me, Mira. I know you're living with Danny."

I shoot an accusatory look at Shauna, who shakes her head, silently insisting she didn't pass along that information.

Oh...

"Byron told you," I say, glancing back at Josie. "It's hardly impressive that you know. He posted about it on Facebook." And acted like a man who'd been wronged, even though he'd started bringing other women back to his apartment while we were still sharing it.

She pouches her lips. "I would have known anyway. But, sure, he didn't seem pleased you were moving in with another man. Still...there's something you need to know. I can see that Thanksgiving is going to be *very* significant for you."

I let out a puff of air that's half laugh. "Thanksgiving isn't a significant day for anyone. It's a dumb holiday, especially for people who don't eat turkey or believe in colonialism. I resent having to close the bar for it every year."

"*Very* significant," Josie says, letting her voice trail off, like she thinks it'll be spookier that way. "You and Danny have to be together for Thanksgiving, I can see that clearly."

"Whoa-kay," I say, lifting my hands. I'm a little disarmed but trying not to show it. "My parents will be thrilled to hear it."

"It's no joke," she tells me, and I feel Delia taking my hand again. For some reason, I can't take my eyes off Josie. She has a surprisingly powerful presence. "And I think you'll find your parents both have other plans."

My dad does. A few very intelligent people choose to dine out on Thanksgiving rather than laboring for hours to produce food that's so unremarkable people choose to make it only once a year. Those people like to be entertained, hence my father's band always gets booked. But, again, that's a matter of public record, easily discoverable.

My mother, on the other hand, is both anal and determined to impress Delia's rich fiancé. There's no way she'll bow out of hosting Thanksgiving dinner—and there's no way I'm leaving Delia to deal with our mother by herself. Sure, Burke would protect her, but he hasn't been protecting her for as long as I have. She'd say she doesn't need protection anymore, and maybe she has a point, but even so...

Still, my family dynamics are none of Josie the Great's business.

"I'll bet Danny has plans too," I say. "It's in a week and a half. Everyone who wants plans has them."

"Not true," Josie says. "The ether tells me otherwise."

"Has it told you whether Danny's soulmate is going to be there?" I ask flippantly.

"Yes," Josie says with a sparkle in her eyes. "And so is yours."

For a split second, I feel myself quaking, as if this news actually means something. A *bad* something, if she's implying Danny's soulmate is Daphne and mine is some random dude I haven't met yet.

Then again, if *both* of our soulmates are supposed to be there, maybe...

It's this disarming thought, and the slightly gooey feeling it creates in my chest that activates my bullshit detector. This woman is messing with me.

I have no soulmate, and neither does Danny. Because soulmates don't exist.

All of these conflicting thoughts rip through my mind in an instant, before my sister blurts, "Please tell me it's not Byron."

"It's not," Josie insists before turning back toward me. "Just make sure you invite enough people. You're going to want a lot of people there."

"Because it'll up the chances of her soulmate being present?" Shauna asks through the kind of silent laughter that makes her look like she's suffering.

"It's always good to have a full table at Thanksgiving," Josie says. "It's a holiday for giving thanks." This is directed at me, and I'll be damned if she doesn't sound just like my mother. "You'll have regrets if you don't make the most of it. This year especially."

"You know what?" I say. "I have to give you credit for being creative. This is the most random fortune anyone's ever been given in the history of fortunes."

Poe coughs and nearly chokes on whatever he's eating.

"Well, it's the most random one I've ever heard," I mutter.

"Ignore me at your own peril," Josie says, and I can tell she's pretty proud of her turn of phrase. I have to admit it's a good one, as far as supernatural threats go. It helps that there's that black wax melted all over the table and also that it's started getting dark outside early now that November is nearly half complete.

"Where are we supposed to have this super-important Thanksgiving dinner?"

Her gaze lowers to my messed-up leg. "You don't look like you should travel far."

I can't tell whether she's being pragmatic, purposefully vague, or an asshole.

"So you're talking about my apartment."

She nods officiously. "You'll need to expand the table."

"We don't have the kind of table that expands. And I definitely don't have a soulmate."

She gives the kind of shrug that says nothing while saying more than I'd like to hear.

I turn to leave, but then look back and ask, "Is my neighbor across the alleyway up to some shady shit?"

"Keep watch," she says, and I'm embarrassed for having asked. Because, honestly, other than the very specific bit of advice about Thanksgiving and her upsetting news about Byron, this woman's prophecies are exactly as vague as you'd expect from a hack psychic.

"Thanks for the sage advice," I say. From the way she nods, I'm pretty sure the sarcasm flew over her head. Poe's watching me, though, and he obviously caught it.

"You should listen to her about Thanksgiving dinner," he says. "That part's true."

"So the rest isn't?" I ask, surprised by his honesty, more because he was almost a lawyer than because he's the right-hand man and paramour of a psychic.

"I don't know," he says, the corners of his mouth tipping up. "Sometimes Josie uses some creative license. It's one of the things I love about her."

She makes a sound like a cooing bird as she walks over and then slides in behind the desk with him. He shoves his snack aside and grabs her, and just like that, they're back where they started when they arrived—sucking face.

"Do you know how to roast a turkey?" I ask, turning to Shauna.

Chapter Twelve

Danny

When I knock on Big Mike's door, he opens it within two seconds—the timing suggesting he was either getting ready to leave or sprinted for the door.

"You decided to come for dinner?" he says with a wide grin. There's a funky smell in his place, and from what I can see through the doorway, there's no sign of any kid living there. It's clean and tidy, with a large leather sectional, a big plate glass coffee table, and nothing else that I can see from the doorway. The scene strikes me as strange for a guy with a young daughter. Ruthie's place is so full of kid shit, you can't walk from the door to the TV without tripping over a My Little Pony or a Lego. But his place looks spotless, like it's a model apartment.

If I hadn't seen the kid with my own two eyes, I'd question her existence. I guess he could have her just a couple of days a week, or even a couple of days a month, but that feeling of something's wrong doesn't lift. This guy's off. He's up to something, and I don't like it.

I also don't like it that he's leaning forward and checking out the empty stretch of hallway behind me—almost as if he's looking for

Mira. A protective feeling bristles inside of me, same as it did when she told me about those texts from Byron.

"I'm making tomato sauce," Big Mike announces. "I was hoping you'd change your mind."

For a second, I consider just turning around and leaving. I don't like this guy, or his weird, overly friendly schtick. But the rodent is still rustling around in Mira's bag, and despite what she said earlier, she might want it back someday.

Clearing my throat, I say, "No, sorry, man. I found your... Pumpkin down in the stairwell." I lift up the bag, then open it, and no shit—the hamster takes a flying leap at his face.

"Pumpkin!" he shouts as he reaches up and catches him, not that he'd need to, because the little animal's claws seem to be hooked into his large nose. The hamster doesn't seem overly fond of him, not that I blame him—it would be hard to forgive someone for a name like Pumpkin, but it's not my hamster, not my problem. My problem is figuring out how to launder the bag without ruining it, and also whether my left wrist is sprained. I didn't want to say so to Mira, but it *feels* sprained—or at least bruised in a way I'll be feeling for days. Then again, sometimes I feel things like pain more strongly than I should.

"Okay, then. Enjoy the reunion," I say, lifting my right hand to wave. I'm already turning.

"Wait!" the guy says. I pause, reluctantly.

"Maybe we could hang out sometime. Go to the Treasure Club. I'm new around here, and I—"

"That's not my thing, man. No judgment, but no thanks."

"Oh, because you got that pretty little piece at home," he says, nodding.

I have the sudden urge to punch him, but I grit my teeth and stay silent, hoping he'll do the smart thing and shut up.

"I got you," he says, even though he definitely doesn't. "My little lady doesn't mind much. She knows I go there for the spicy wings."

"Your daughter?" I ask, anger giving way to shock, because that's fucked up, isn't it? Not even my father would have the poor judgment to talk to my sister about hanging out with strippers.

"No," he says, looking at me like I'm the strange one. "My woman. My girl."

"Oh, okay," I say, ready to exit this conversation and never enter into another one with him. "Well. Cool. See you around."

Hopefully not. If I could rewind my life and make it so this conversation had never happened, I would be grateful.

I turn again, and this time he lets me leave, so hopefully I've gotten the message across. I need to get to a doctor's office so they can take a look at my wrist. It feels like it did that time I spent twenty-four hours trying to hack into a system.

But first I've got a stop to make. I consider calling in Leonard, who is the most physically intimidating of my friends, but something tells me Byron requires a different touch. Like the threat of legal recrimination. So I call Shane as I head down the stairs.

When he picks up on the fourth ring, I ask, "You busy?"

"Desperately. What's up?"

He's always busy these days, but credit where it's due—he answers my calls. My sister thinks he's a stuck-up prick. She always has, actually, but she says he's especially braggadocious now that he's a partner at Myles & Lee. Some days I think she might have a point. But he's still the guy who's always had my back—even when it was inconvenient or embarrassing to him.

"Mira's ex-boyfriend has been bothering her. Sending threatening texts. Telling her he's hexed her. I don't like it."

"Hexed her?" he asks incredulously. "Are we taking this as a serious threat?"

"I am. I don't like the thought of him escalating. She's already hurt, stuck at the apartment. If he knows where we live..."

"All right, I've got you," he says as I hurry down the steps toward the parking garage.

"Do you think we should get her to file a restraining order?" I ask.

"I can tell you right now that the judge will laugh us out of the courtroom if we go in there talking about hexes. They'll laugh at him too, obviously, but he's probably used to people thinking he's a dipshit."

The joke's funny, but I can't find it in myself to laugh. I've been on edge ever since Mira came into the apartment two weeks ago, dressed like a pirate. If I've slept more than an hour at a time since then, it's a miracle I can only credit to Benadryl and the restorative power of jerking off, because she's set up residence in my mind. The way she felt and tasted on that elevator, so open to me. The way she looked with that towel slung over her, her hips peeking out and making promises about what lay beneath. The sight of her curled up on the furniture like a cat, her leg stretched out in front of her. The drinks she makes for me, sweating out on the kitchen island. The notes in her cursive handwriting, hearts dotting all of the I's. The sound of her voice. Hell, even the sound of her name—*Mira*. She should have been dressed up like a witch instead of a pirate, because I feel like someone's bewitched me.

In my head, Leonard reminds me this is what happens when a man tries to make a monk of himself. I'm infatuated with this woman because she let me touch her.

But I know that's an oversimplification. I didn't expect to like Mira Evans, but I do. I feel an...understanding between us that is rare and...

Well, the guys would probably laugh at me, but it's fucking beautiful, like staring up at the sun for the fraction of a second it takes for your eyes to burn. It's not often that I feel a connection like that—which, in addition to my dislike of strangers and general unwillingness to put myself in uncomfortable situations, is why I spend most of my time with the four friends I've had for most of my life.

A voice in my head whispers that it's also why I was so interested in changing Daphne's view of me—because I already knew her. Because it seemed easier than finding someone else who interested me beyond the surface-level pull of scratching an itch.

Still, that doesn't mean I'm inclined to do anything about my pull to Mira—anything else, that is.

She hasn't given me any reason to think she wants a repeat of what happened on the elevator. I've noticed her watching me a few times, and the other night she sat close enough on the couch that her side was pressed to mine—but those things could be easily misinterpreted. The only sure indication of how she's feeling is what she tells me—and she's told me no.

Doesn't matter. I feel a certain...protectiveness toward her. I'm protective of all of my friends, and I have every intention of paying this Byron guy a visit he won't forget.

I pause on the first-floor landing, because my phone doesn't work well in the basement-level parking lot. "We can drop by his place and imply he's going to get himself into trouble if he keeps contacting her, can't we?"

"I'd be skirting a line, Danny," Shane says, but I know he's going to do it. I can tell from the way he says it, a little regretful but a little excited too, because part of him is bored as fuck in that high-brow, suit-wearing job he has. Sure enough, he adds, "You've got his address?"

"I do."

It was on about half of Mira's boxes, which I'd collapsed for her after Delia helped unpack them. Most of them were repurposed Amazon boxes, and she hadn't bothered to use permanent marker to cross out her identifying information. I'd told her she should probably get rid of the labels, but she gave me a look that suggested I was being anal and offered up the kind of platitude a person only gives you if they have no intention of listening.

"So...want me to pick you up?" I ask after giving Shane a couple of beats to think about it. "I'll buy you a coffee on the way home. Even one of those fancy lattes you like."

Sometimes he has me pick him up for outings so his car's still in the lot. It's a game he and the other partners like to play with each other—the person who stays in the office longest wins. They've got everything they need there, or so he says. A gym. Assistants to grab them food. Showers.

We used to go biking every morning—a pick-me-up before settling in for a long day at our desks—but now he only comes on Saturdays, and only then every other week or so. Before Drew left for Puerto Rico, Shane would also come to our Dungeons & Dragons game nights, a tradition we'd upheld since we were in middle school, adding Leonard's character when he was in town. We'd put those on hold, too, though—Shane's idea.

Something told me he wouldn't be first in line to pick them up again.

I don't need Ruthie to tell me he's leaving us behind. It's happening slowly, but my specialty is in finding patterns. This one's as obvious as code on a screen.

Still, I understand Shane in a way Ruthie didn't, and I don't blame him or hold it against him. He's done this before, and he's always come back. I know he'll come back again.

He pauses for a second, considering, then says, "Yeah, sure, what the hell."

"Thanks. See you soon." I consider telling him about my wrist, but he's already looking for an excuse to back out. If I say that, he'll insist the Byron mission can wait, and I won't be able to explain why it feels urgent without facing a lot of questioning.

I can stop at a pharmacy later and pick up a wrist guard—the kind of thing I've used before for protection against carpal tunnel.

Despite the uncomfortable ache in my wrist, I'm grinning as I make my way down to the basement. I knew Shane would come through for me—no matter how much his ambition tells him he'd be better off spending what little free time he has with people who can help him conquer the world. Not his nearly criminal buddy who's chained—almost literally—to his desk, and his other less-than-high-flying friends.

Of us all, Burke was the shiniest prize, but he's been tainted by his parents, Lucas and Melinda Burke, who are going on trial this spring for covering up their shitty business practices. Burke's the one who turned them in, because Burke is an all-around stand-up guy.

Leonard is what Shane calls an "alleged former criminal." Meaning he *was* a criminal, back when he was younger, having been raised to break the law from early childhood, but he didn't get caught for most of the things he did.

And then there's me...guilty because of what I can do with my computer.

———

SHANE AND I PARK IN FRONT OF THE BUILDING, AND FOR A second I just look up at it. It's part of a brick apartment complex in West Asheville, with plenty of parking around the buildings for residents and dirty signs advertising two swimming pools that won't be of use to anyone until May. There are a bunch of trees around us, the leaves that are still on them red and gold and faded green.

"You know," Shane says, then pauses for a few seconds, likely to build anticipation for his next words. It's a tactic designed for courtrooms, but I'm guessing he realizes it works just as well in daily life —for pissing people off.

"I know a lot of things," I say absently, my attention on the front door. "I also don't know a lot of things. I think that's probably true of most people."

"Very funny." He rolls his eyes, but he's snapped out of it a little —he's more Shane and less the suited lawyer.

"So what hallowed knowledge do you have for me this time?" I ask, glancing at him.

"It occurs to me that you're acting like a jealous boyfriend, showing up here. He might—"

"I'm not," I blurt. Shit, judging from the look of cunning in his eyes, I just gave him the kind of tell he's always looking for.

"Oh?"

"Oh. I'm just trying to be a friend. I can't be at the apartment all the time. I don't like the thought of him showing up there if I'm not around."

His raised eyebrows argue that I am always at the apartment—or almost always.

"I still go on my bike rides," I argue. "And to see Ruthie."

He angles his head. "How's my favorite hellcat doing?"

I shrug. "I haven't heard from her much lately. Which makes me think she's *definitely* wrapped up in one of her schemes. She never tells me beforehand."

He huffs laughter. "Yeah, because if she told us, we'd try to persuade her not to do it."

As if she'd tell him. Honestly, he's probably the reason she doesn't tell me—she knows he'd make fun of what she's doing. She doesn't care what most people think, but Shane has a special ability to scrape her nerves raw.

I'm proud of my sister's hustle, but it's hard to watch her burn through the money she makes at the diner on one of her money-making schemes. Growing up, our mother was always hawking some new MLM scheme—Tupperware, essential oils, bad makeup, that kind of junk—but Ruthie's more enterprising. She's got an old camper van called Vanny she keeps trying to turn into a mobile business—a pet clothes boutique, a store selling only unicorn toys and, for a hot minute, she thought about having it outfitted into a food truck before realizing how much money she'd have to spend on the required licenses. I help her as much as she'll allow, but sometimes I worry she's going to burn herself out. Between raising Izzy, her morning and lunch shifts at the diner, and her various business attempts, she's always taking on too much. But she acts as if the world will stop turning if she ever stops.

Maybe that's why Mira reminds me a little of her—because Mira's clearly having trouble in the liminal space she's in.

I feel privileged to be there with her.

Shane's looking at me expectantly, like he wants me to laugh with him. But my nerves are burned raw, and my wrist hurts like hell, and I'm confused on an almost cosmic level.

"Let's get this over with," I say.

"Tell me what's going on with Mira first."

I'd dared to hope he'd forgotten about his question.

"No," I say flatly.

He lifts his palms out. "Fine. I'm not going to ask what's going on with you and the hot bartender. I know you're still caught up in the whole Daphne thing, so I'm guessing you just want to bang her the same way you probably want to bang half the women you meet since becoming a monk. Although I still say you'd be better off entering the pact with me."

I'm pissed off by his condescension, and even more so by his attitude toward Mira. He's also dead wrong. I'm definitely *not* "caught up in the whole Daphne thing," and I don't want to bang half the women I meet. Then again, Shane isn't equipped to understand that. He thinks relationships are good for one thing—sex—and it's impossible to convince him otherwise.

But I don't feel like getting into an old argument, and I haven't forgotten he's here to help.

"Can't be a pact if you're the only person to have entered it," I say automatically. Shane's handled plenty of divorces, and one day, when drunk, he suggested that all of us enter a pact to never get married. Him, me, Burke, and Drew, because Leonard wasn't around then. No one took him up on it. "Care to enlighten me about what I should know, oh scholar of the law?"

"Struck a nerve, huh?" he asks, giving me a knowing look that instantly annoys me. My throbbing wrist isn't helping. I stopped by the store to get a wrist guard before picking Shane up, but I haven't put it on yet. I know he'd remark on it. And I also wouldn't look very intimidating if I showed up at this guy's door with my wrist trussed up.

"Not at all," I say. "I just want to get this over with so we can get that coffee."

Shane nods, but it's obvious he doesn't believe me. He does me the favor of not calling me on it, though.

"Okay, but what I was getting at is there's a chance that showing up like this might set the guy off."

I have to admit he's right, but I'm not ready to back down.

"You're good at reading people," I say. I almost laugh out loud when he sits up straighter in his seat, because I can hear Ruthie saying that he puffs up like one of her pastries every time he gets a compliment. "I want your read on this guy. I'm not going to feel comfortable until I get it."

"Okay," he says with a nod. "I can do that. But tone it down with the protective shit. We'll just tell him that we know about the messages, and we won't stand for him bothering her."

I nod in agreement, but as we leave the car, my whole body feels tense—same way it does on the days when nothing will do except for a long punishing ride up the mountain.

Chapter Thirteen

Mira

I nod to Shauna, and she knocks on the door of Byron's apartment with as much aggression as if it's his face. The hallway smells musty.

Delia's with us too, standing beside me. When I asked her to stay in the car, explaining that we want Byron to know we're angry and possibly dangerous, her expression hardened, and she insisted that she could do dangerous and, when it came to him, she very well might be dangerous. I'm proud, even though I know our mother would accuse me of corrupting my little sister. She always gets on Delia's case about not being focused or ambitious. That used to be her refrain for me, too, but now that the bar is doing well, I'm "overly focused on my career and not soft enough to attract any kind of man but a deadbeat." She's a real sweetheart, our mother.

Speaking of whom...

Josie the Great might be a hack of the highest order, but she's also in possession of good information, because when we got back into the car, Delia and I both had voice messages on our phones. *Delighted* voice messages from our mother, who said she was *so sorry* but she met a silver fox named Alberto at a wine tasting, and he was going to whisk her away for a European vacation spanning

Thanksgiving and Christmas. She apologized again, then slipped in a few barbs about how she deserved this because she's always the one who does everything for the holidays, and it's time for her to take some joy for herself. My message ended with an accusation that I'm selfish and a request for the recipe for the Old Fashioned we serve at the bar. Delia's ended with a request for her to ask Burke if he wants to invest in Alberto's dental instruments company.

Oh, and she offered to send me the menu plan for the Thanksgiving dinner she wanted to make and requested that I send her photos of the prepared food, proving she would still like to control us even though she's bowed out of our plans.

"You know what this means, right?" Delia asked me in the car on the way to Byron's. "Josie really *is* psychic."

"Let's not get hasty," I told her. "Maybe she's just nosy. Or good at making guesses."

Did Byron know about my mom?

I intend to find out before my sister becomes Josie the Great's first acolyte. It's obvious she believes everything the psychic said, and I have a feeling she's going to insist on doing every anti-hex cure she can find on the internet.

Given that I don't have much else to do this weekend, and am reluctantly freaked out, I won't deny her. Shauna seemed impressed too, and she more thoroughly messed with my head by telling us about another accurate reading Josie the Great did a couple of months ago.

It made me think about Danny and his supposed soulmate.

It can't be Daphne, can it?

Daphne, of the severe bun and wire glasses?

Daphne, who understood him so little she called him *basic*?

He deserves more.

There, I said it.

Shauna pounds on the door again, her mouth pinched. With her purple hair and all-black outfit, she looks badass, and I'm glad to have her by my side. Delia too. Because even though my little sister is the sweetest person I know, and usually looks it, no one would make the mistake of thinking she's here to sell cookies.

I hear movement behind the door, and I can imagine Byron peering through the peephole. He's probably wearing that scarlet silk robe he has, which he can fool himself into thinking makes him look like Lord Byron the poet.

"I hear you back there, you jerk," I shout before realizing it might not be him. The band guys hang out here a lot—too much, if you ask me—and he's had some women over since we broke up. I'd feel bad if I yelled at one of them. It's not their fault that they too fell for the charms of some guitar dick.

But the voice that shouts back is Byron's—"I'm not opening it. Just go away. Haven't you done enough?"

"Seriously?" Shauna growls, giving the door another bang. "You stole my friend's hair and her picture and brought it to a psychic, you little perv. You're going to face us like a man."

Damn, I'm not sure I'd open that door either. I give her slight nod, and she returns it.

There's a creak from behind us, and I turn and then nearly lose my balance, because what the actual fuck is *Danny* doing here? I'm getting cognitive dissonance from seeing him in this place, when he belongs in the clean and tidy apartment on Broadway Street.

My gaze flits to the guy who's with him, whom I recognize from photos as Shane, the lawyer pal he's known since childhood. He's good-looking, too, but in a hotshot way. My eyes bounce off him and stick to Danny, to the curl of his hair, to his deep, dark eyes, and his slight smile—always slightly sarcastic, like he's making a joke or feels like the punchline of one.

I clear my throat, trying to regain my grip on reality—and on this confrontation we're supposed to be having. It's not going according to plan. I figured Shauna, Delia, and I would storm over here, and our girl power would blow Byron over like he's a fall leaf. But I didn't account for Danny and Shane. Which is when it hits me that he must be here because of me. The knowing looks on Shauna's and Delia's faces suggest they know to.

Oh.

"Are you here to—"

"What the fuck?" Byron moans from behind the door. "Is that your boyfriend? Why would you bring your *boyfriend* to my apartment? You want to rub it in my face?"

Danny's friend mutters, "Told you," which means nothing to me other than that I've met someone else who enjoys saying *I told you so.*

Anger burns through me as quickly as it would a curl of paper. "Seriously? You've been bringing women home for weeks. Why the hell do you care what I do?"

"You're the one who chose this," he says sulkily.

"Because you're an asshole. Who steals people's hair, apparently. I shouldn't have to tell you how weird that is." When he doesn't respond, I add, "Didn't it occur to you that there was probably some of your hair mixed up in what you took from the drain?"

The door swings open, hitting one of my crutches.

I nearly fall over, but Danny's hand wraps around me from behind. I hear his intake of breath—and I realize it's the wrist he hurt in the stairwell. It's swollen, and I glance back at him with alarm. "Your wrist—"

"It's fine," he says through his teeth, but he releases me and holds it to his chest.

It's obviously not fine.

"I opened the door," Byron says flatly, clearly unconcerned that he almost knocked me over. "Now tell me why the fuck you're here with your boyfriend."

Turning to look at him, I frown. He has one of my old towels wrapped around his hair in a turban. He has medium-length chest-nut-brown hair, one of his best features, so it's not the first time I've seen him with a towel wrapped around it, but it's a weird way to answer the door in the middle of the afternoon. He looks like he's spent the day at the spa to try to combat a hangover.

"He's my roommate, not my boyfriend," I say. "I didn't ask him to be here, so I have to assume that you're so dislikable, he felt compelled to come on his own."

My tone darkens with every word, because I've decided I'm annoyed that Danny and Shane are here. They clearly came because I told Danny about those texts, and he figured he'd step in and handle the situation.

Part of me is...touched that he cared enough to bother, but I'm also kind of disappointed that he didn't wait to be asked. I didn't take him for the swinging dick type of guy. Then again, maybe all guys like to swing their dicks when given the opportunity. It might be a quality that's carried in the Y-chromosome.

I turn, looking over my shoulder, and aim a scowl at Danny. "I was handling this. You should have let me handle it."

"You're right," he says, looking away from me, at the door. "I just—"

Shane steps forward and clears his throat. "Mr...." He looks at me and lifts his eyebrows.

Sighing, I say, "Lord."

Yes, Byron's parents thought it would be classy as hell to name their child "Byron Lord." They have no one to blame but themselves for his decision to be in a band.

His lips twitch as he adds, "Mr. Lord. I'm Ms. Evans's lawyer, and you've been engaging in a disturbing pattern of behavior. Would your employers—"

"Your parents," I interrupt. Because no one in the band would care that he's harassing me. They liked me just fine when I used to give them free drinks every time they came around my bar, even if they weren't playing, but they all took Byron's side in our breakup.

His upper-crust parents would care, though. They might have thought their baby boy deserved better, but they like controversy even less than they do sassy bartenders.

Shane angles his head, his eyes on Byron's towel. I'm pretty sure he's doing it intentionally, as a power play. "Would your *parents* be impressed to learn you've been threatening her?"

Byron's gaze shifts to me. "You lawyered up all of the sudden? That's messed up, Mira. I figured we could settle all of this between us like adults."

"Is there anything adult about hexing someone?" Shauna says with a snort. "Or sending threatening texts to your ex-girlfriend? My ex-boyfriend is a real douche, but even he knew better."

Delia gives him a crestfallen look that would flay me if she ever sent it my way. "I'm disappointed in you, Byron. I thought you knew how to be a gentleman."

Maybe he's not immune to Delia's puppy dog eyes either, because he lifts his hands in a warding-off gesture. "It was an honest mistake." His gaze skates across my group of supporters. "And I regret it, okay? Of course, I do. I'm suffering more than you."

I can't help but point to my busted ankle. "How do you figure, jackass?"

I can feel Danny at my back again, actually *feel* him even though he's not touching me. I can tell he's furious on my behalf. Some of my annoyance with him fades, because I don't remember ever having someone stand up for me like this. I'm usually the one who takes stands. Now that I think about it, it must have cost him to be here. He's someone who doesn't like stepping out of his comfort zone—and showing up at my ex-boyfriend's doorstep while his wrist is hurt has to be very much out of his comfort zone. The rest of my annoyance fades, and I feel my throat clog. I step back slightly, not enough to run into him and further damage his wrist, but enough to show that...

Byron whips the towel off his head.

Half a dozen swears rip out of me, and Shauna takes up the chant. His hair is dyed a crispy peroxide blonde, and it looks patchy, as if some of it has fallen out.

"Look what I've done to myself!" he shouts, letting the towel fall onto the hardwood floor. Behind him I can see the familiar furniture that's still hunkering in the living room—the couch I've sat on hundreds or even thousands of times. It's humbling, seeing a glimpse of the life we used to share. I was crazy about this man once. Feral for him.

There is obviously something deeply wrong with my judgment, or at least there was.

"This is because of the curse?" Delia whispers in awe, her gaze whipping to my hair. It's a little greasy today, I'll be the first to admit, but it hasn't started falling out.

"Of course not," I say on reflex, although I have to admit the timing is pretty damn incredible. "Did you dye it at the roots with peroxide?" I press. "How long did you leave it in?"

He sniffs. "I fell asleep for a few hours."

"Well, that's obviously the problem, not Josie the Great, however much you or she would like to take credit for it. I'd say it serves you right, but I'm not a dick."

He sneers at me, his lip curling up. "You did just say it, you bitch."

I'm about to make a cutting comment about his boy-band hair, but Danny steps up next to me. "Don't call her that. Have some respect."

His words carry a threat I wouldn't have expected from him—with people he doesn't know, he usually comes off as quiet and accommodating. Flat. But he looks incensed, like he wants to do Byron some damage. I'd still prefer dealing with this situation myself, but I'm surprised to feel a little tingling between my thighs. It's turning me on that he showed up here, despite himself. It's turning me on that he's throwing out this Cro Magnon spiel that's clearly unnatural for him.

Looking from him to Byron, there's no question of which of them is the better man. It's laughable to compare them, really.

"Oh, fuck off," Byron says, but he's clearly intimidated. I see it in his eyes, and in the way he slams the door right in our faces and then turns over the lock. He must remember the presence of my supposed lawyer, though, because he calls through the closed door, "I'm going to leave her alone, Lawyer Guy, I swear. And if I can take the hex back, I will. Obviously. I can't even go outside. I'm going to have to wear a wig to our next show."

His hair doesn't look that bad—just positively fried—but he's obviously getting off on the drama, and I don't want to feed the monster.

I remember the voice message sitting on my phone and shout, "Did you know my mother met some rich European dude and cancelled our Thanksgiving plans?"

"Believe it or not, Mira, I don't give a fuck about your Thanksgiving plans.'

Huh. He seems to mean it, and honestly, I don't know why he'd know before me. He doesn't exactly keep the 4-1-1 on my mother.

"Good," I say. "Because you're not invited."

A door down the hall is flung open, revealing my former neighbor, a stout middle-aged woman named Linda. "What's all this fuss about?"

I shrug and step away from the door of my old apartment. "Byron has regrets about dying his hair platinum blond. We were trying to talk him through it."

She gives me a strange look, and Shane says, slick as can be, "Has he ever threatened you, ma'am?"

She snort-laughs. "The only threat that man poses is to the national level of intelligence."

Ain't that the truth.

"Let's go," I say to my crew.

We all head outside in silence, then converge outside the building as if in silent agreement.

Delia's the one who speaks first. "You *have* to host Thanksgiving dinner," she says to me. "Please, Mira. I'll help with all the food."

I still don't believe in psychics. I have a deep suspicion of Josie the Great. But there's that look in my sister's eyes. I can see her need to believe in a world where magic is real and anything is possible. I've always been the person who's made things magical for her, the person who's held her hand or hugged her when she needed it.

Don't get me wrong, our mother always did the things a mother needs to. She made our lunches and taught us how to launder clothes and clean the house and take out the trash. To cook serviceable meals and do our Geometry homework—I never did it, mind you, but that was my choice, not because no one explained why I should. But she didn't care about us beyond doing her duty—and although my father is a much warmer man, he's the kind of person who can only love people in fits and starts. He'll spend all day making you feel like you're the most special person in the world, only to disappear for four weeks without a word.

Delia needs to be loved better than that, and up until she met Burke, *I* was the one who did that. I made her a rainbow cake for every birthday and held her hand and told her it would be okay whenever there was an upsetting story on the news or someone she loved got hurt or she was exposed to the hard fucking truth that life is always, *always* as jagged and cruel as it is beautiful. That we only get the joy and the fun if we make the world give it to us—if we push back and refuse to be broken.

So that's why I find myself nodding. I turn to Danny and say, "Say, roomie. What do you think about hosting Thanksgiving dinner?"

Chapter Fourteen

Danny

I ignore Mira's question, because my mind is fixed on Byron Lord and his peroxide hair. He's hiding inside his apartment, and he should be, because I can't remember the last time I was this furious.

"That guy actually thinks he put a hex on you?" I ask through my clenched jaw. We're standing on the sidewalk outside of the apartment building, but Shane, Shauna, and Delia have congregated a slight distance away from us, closer to the parking lot, giving us space to talk.

Mira glances at them. "I guess he hired Josie to do it. So they both suck. She tells me that I have to host Thanksgiving dinner at the apartment, and on the off-chance she's right—"

"I don't believe in psychics," I say, mostly meaning it. "Or Thanksgiving dinner." I feel the persistent throb of my wrist and a growing ache in my temples. I'm drained. I'm burnt. I'm toast that was forgotten under the broiler.

I can exit my comfort zone, but there's always a cost, and I'm feeling it now. I'm also still tempted to burst back into the building and hammer on that asshole's door. To tell him that if he calls Mira a bitch ever again, even in his sleep, I'll make him answer for it.

I don't like confrontation, but I like it even less when someone messes with—

I rub my temples, but I do it with the wrong hand and flinch. Mira's still looking at me, so I admit, "I try to avoid the holidays."

"Do you celebrate when you can cross them off on the calendar?" she asks, and it feels like we're falling into our rhythm again.

"I'm happier when I have, yes. Cranberry sauce is an abomination. Watching my parents get drunk was worse. They're not together anymore, but I imagine their patterns haven't changed. They pull out the special sauce at this time of year. The last year I went home for Thanksgiving, someone called the cops on them. Both of them. My mother threw a ceramic turkey at my head."

Her eyes widen. "Why?"

"I don't remember."

I do. She did it because she was pissed that I might not be able to be their golden goose anymore.

"Did it hit you?"

I shove down the impulse to lift a hand to my forehead, to the small scar about my eyebrow. "No." I didn't lie for her, but because her sister and Shauna are likely close enough to hear.

The look of sympathy in her eyes tells me she knows. "You know, my mom and dad used to love fighting on the holidays, too," she says. "It's like they saved up all their shit for then. Why is that?"

"Some people find it more fun to be dysfunctional with an audience. They figure there's no fun in being miserable alone."

Her lips twitch into a smile. "Byron seemed to take particular joy in being miserable in front of an audience."

I run my fingers over the edge of my pocket, needing to settle myself. "Are you still mad at me for going there today? You're...my friend. I wanted him to know there are people looking out for you. People who have your best interest in mind."

"No," she says, glancing back at the others. They've drifted farther away and are standing in front of Shauna's car. Shane appears to be holding court, telling them a story. Shifting her attention back to me, Mira says in an undertone, "I think it's hard for me to accept help because I always felt like I had to be the strong one, you know? Delia's so sweet and sensitive, and it felt like that should be protected." She pauses, watching me, then adds, "Sounds like you're not close with your parents, so I'm guessing you won't be spending the holidays with them."

"I never do. Not since I was in my early twenties." Usually, what happens for Thanksgiving is that Shane and I go for a long bike ride, ending it with a sunset drink in the mountains, but he's already told me one of the other partners invited him over for the holiday. Ruthie and Izzy usually spend the day at a friend's house.

I guess I'll probably still go for the bike ride, but I have to admit the thought's a lonely one."

"We can talk about it later," I say, noncommittally.

Honestly, I wouldn't mind so much if she wanted to spend Thanksgiving with me in the apartment—or if she had a mind to invite Delia and Burke and Leonard and Shauna. But I'm not sure this woman is capable of doing anything in a small way. If I tell her yes, I'll probably have twenty people in my apartment, and the whole place will smell like turkey until the new year. That pink record table will be blasting Taylor Swift or Olivia Rodrigo, and people will be laughing and waving drinks around. I'll have to seclude myself out on the deck with a bottle of scotch and my laptop—same as I've done at every party that's ever been hosted there. Even the ones that include all of my friends.

"I'm going to persuade you," Mira says, poking a finger into my chest.

My sex-starved brain likes the idea of her trying—and the feeling of her finger drilling into me while she looks up at me, her eyes bright. Her lips painted red. They're a softer pink inside, and in that moment, I can't think of anything I'd rather do than suck on them.

She's not yours.

"I don't mind if you try," I admit. "But *why* do you want to host Thanksgiving dinner?"

Shauna laughs, cracking the realm we've built, just the two of us. I hadn't noticed her heading back toward us. Other things seep in—the sound of an Amazon delivery truck backing up, the squeaking of a bird, the rush-rush of the fall leaves in the cool breeze. The pain from my throbbing wrist. "Because Josie the Great told her she has to," Shauna answers. She waggles her eyebrows. "She also said both of your soulmates will be there."

It's another bizarre, cryptic statement from a woman full of them. But my first thought isn't to reject it because it's ridiculous—I want to reject it because the thought of either of us having a different soulmate is unacceptable.

I'm ridiculous.

Mira has told me nothing more can happen between us, and I need to accept her decision and thinking stupid, grandiose thoughts. So I say, "Okay, then my answer is a hard no."

"So what do you think?" I ask Shane after I pull to a stop in the parking lot of Myles & Lee.

He raises his eyebrows, which is enough to clue me in that I've done it again—presumed people can follow the network of my thoughts even though they are stuck in my head, visible only to me.

"Is this Byron guy a threat?" I clarify.

He snorts a laugh. "No. I agree with the neighbor. He's only a threat to the gene pool." His gaze sharpens. "I'll have to ask you again, Dan. Why do you care?"

I swear and run my good hand through my hair. The other one is now encased in the wrist protector. "I don't know."

"I do. You really do like her, huh?"

"This isn't part of the plan," I tell him. "I live with her. It's not a good idea to mess that up." I grip my hair. "Shit. I've already messed it up, haven't I?"

He doesn't know about the elevator, but based on his shrug, he probably knows *something* happened. "I'm not good with this stuff, but maybe you should talk to Drew. He lived with his fiancée before they got together."

"I think I'm mad at him," I say, realizing it's true as I say it. We've been talking online and playing the game together, sometimes with Mira, but I've avoided his calls even though I obviously have to talk to him before the meeting with Big Bear Games.

"For leaving?"

I nod.

"I get that," he says. "But before now, he's never done much for himself. You either. You might want to give it a try."

He gazes at the building, then tugs on his tie a little.

"You're not in your usual hurry to get back to your desk," I comment. He even insisted on going for drive-through coffee after leaving the apartment complex. Normally, he would have been sweating bullets until he got back to the office, Friday evening or not.

He shifts his gaze to me. "Something's going down. I don't know what it is, but it's big. Myles had an all-hands-on-deck meeting the other day, and he didn't include me."

"That why you're going to Thanksgiving at his house?"

His expression turns bemused. "When your boss invites you to Thanksgiving dinner, Danny, you don't make a bulleted yes or no list. You go."

"I thought you were a partner?"

"Sure, but some partners count more than others, if you know what I mean."

I don't need to tell him that I don't—I'm guessing from the bemused look on his face that he already knows.

"What are you going to do?"

Sighing, he adjusts his tie again and reaches for the door. "Keep playing the game, bud. That's all I can do." When he gets out, he leans in and says, "Hey, find out what Ruthie's up to this time, will you? I need a laugh."

I give him a hard look, because he might be my best friend, but she's my little sister. I don't laugh at her. Not even when she called me up one time saying she thought it would be a good business idea to sell sex toys that look like other things. Carrots. Churros. You name it, and it's still a no. "I won't help you laugh at her any more than I'd help her laugh at you."

He just smiles at me and taps the roof, shutting the door.

When I get home, I sit in the car for a minute, feeling uncertain about going upstairs. I want her to be there, and I don't.

Finally, I climb the steps.

Mira is stretched out on the couch, a blanket spread over her in a way the reveals her curved shape. She's watching something on the TV.

John Dies at the End.

My mouth lifts up of its own accord as she presses pause. "So you're one of those people who rents the movie the night before book club."

"We're having a book club?" she asks, sitting up and propping her cast on the coffee table. "You should have warned me. I make a mean cheese dip."

"Is that something you planned on putting together for our hypothetical Thanksgiving dinner?"

"I will if it'll convince you."

I set my keys on the side table by the door, think it over, and then sit in my chair rather than next to her on the couch.

"That's your favorite chair, isn't it?" she asks thoughtfully. "You always have your eyes on it."

Partly because she's taken to sitting there.

"I'm partial to it," I admit.

"I already read the book," she says, gesturing at the screen. "I'm pretty sure I wouldn't have the slightest idea what was happening in this movie if I hadn't."

It shouldn't matter. But there are billions of books out there, with several new ones out every day. I can't help but feel pleased she chose one I'd recommended to her. "You obviously hated it if you wanted to watch the movie too," I say, leaning back, my gaze hooked on her—the slightly wispier hair at the sides of her face, shorter, her big eyes with the cat-eye makeup. The tiny bump on the bridge of her nose.

"Obviously." Her gaze drops to my wrist guard. "Your wrist is fucked up, huh?"

"Only mildly. My psyche is in much worse shape."

Her laughter fills me. "You and me both, my friend." She pauses, scrutinizing me. "I've been wanting to know...Why'd your mother throw a ceramic turkey at your head?"

She surprises me by leaning over the arm of the couch and the chair and lifting a hand to my face, her fingers brushing over the scar. I've never liked touching it. Sometimes memories flash through me so vividly it's as if they're happening *now*. And I can see my mother's screaming face, smell her breath stinking of whiskey. But it doesn't feel like that when Mira touches it—it feels nice.

"How'd you know?" I ask, disarmed. I didn't tell her it had scarred me or where.

"I didn't, but that's what it's from, isn't it?"

I nod, my throat constricting as she pulls her fingers away.

"Why'd she do it?"

"You think she had a good reason?" I ask, deadpan.

"No, but I'll bet she had a bad one."

A smile sneaks up on me, because she's funny in a way I appreciate, and I nod. "She did. I did something illegal, and I got caught. She was worried the authorities would put me away. I'd been giving my parents money, and she didn't want the flow to be cut off. Neither of my parents did."

"*You* did something illegal?" she sputters, sitting up. "But you seem like such a rule follower."

"A nerd, you mean," I say. "I am. But it's a mistake to think nerds follow the rules."

"I want to know what you did, obviously." Her eyes are shining, and she's propped her elbow on the arm of the sofa closest to me. She's leaning against it, her lips parted slightly, and her shirt is gaping enough that I can see the lacy edge of her bra.

I'm less than a foot away. I want to push my chair forward and kiss her. I want—

"Obviously," I repeat. "But there's that NDA I mentioned."

Intelligence gleams in her eyes. "So, it has something to do with the place where you work."

"Yes, and I've said too much already."

She leans forward just a little more, and my eyes travel down the slope of her neck to her breasts, cupped in that insubstantial bit of lace, her flesh peeking through, warm and inviting and soft. I know because I touched it with my hands and mouth in that stolen moment. I'd be lying to myself if I pretended I didn't want to do it again. I swallow against my dry mouth, which becomes drier when she smirks at me. "You just got done telling me you aren't a rule follower."

My pulse quickens, because I can feel things changing. There's an invitation in her tone, and in the way she's leaning forward. I don't know where that invitation will bring me, but I'd like to tear open the envelope and find out. So I nod, just a slight movement, and say, "I'll tell you this much. Someone fucked with my sister, and I didn't like it. So I showed him that he wasn't as almighty powerful and untouchable as he thought. It worked."

"But you got caught?"

"I always intended to get caught. Not much of a message if he never found out who did it. I was a dumb kid, though. I didn't think much about the price I was going to have to pay for taking him down a peg."

She tilts her head, studying me, her lips still parted. "You've only made me more curious, you know."

"Good." I lean down and slide my shoes off with my good hand. "Maybe I like being a mystery to you. There's nothing boring about a mystery. That's why I can't stop listening to those damn podcasts."

She rolls her eyes. "I only thought you were boring before you broke your whole mild-mannered nice guy act."

"People *like* that act."

"No one likes that act. It makes you seem much more forget-table than you actually are."

"I don't set out to be noticed. If people notice you, they expect things from you. They try to put you in boxes."

She watches me for a long moment, her eyes intent, then says, "I'm starting to think there's not a single box that would fit you. You're too remarkable."

I let the compliment wrap around me, easing into the parts of me that still want to find that box or recipe that will make me feel like I fit somewhere, before I respond, "Tell that to the elevator."

She laughs, and I bask in it—and in the way it transforms all of her, her features tipping upward, her nose wrinkling, her breasts bobbing.

When her laughter dies, she says, "Speaking of the elevator..."

Blood drains down to my dick.

"Yes?"

She grabs the crutches lying across the floor and gets up. For a moment, I think she's going to come to me. That she's going to straddle me in this chair and make it my favorite for another reason, but then she makes her way to the open kitchen. She grabs something from the island, returning a moment later to hand me a little box.

"Your glasses have finally arrived," she tells me as I take the box —a case—from her. She looks as excited as if a pair of plastic shields might actually transform me.

"Ah," I say, "my Patrick Dozey glasses."

"You remember his name," she accuses without heat.

I incline my head. I do.

I open the box, revealing a pair of glasses with thin tortoise-shell frames. They're unremarkable, which is just as well, and I can't deny I like them better than the pair Ruthie chose for me.

"Are you going to put them on?" Mira asks in excitement.

"Why don't you do the honors?"

"Don't mind if I do." She surprises me by sitting on the arm of my chair, propping her crutches against the wall. Again, I feel the sense that things are changing—the ground shifting beneath me. I lift my face to her, and she gently slides the glasses on, letting her hands run through my hair after she finishes. Her eyes are on mine, and I'm riveted to her, unable to look away. Is she breathing faster than usual, or is that me?

"Well?" I ask after a moment, because the tension has wound so tightly around me I'm not sure I can take it anymore. "Have I been magically transformed?"

She leans a little to the right, then the left, studying my face in a way that makes me laugh. "They're good," she says. "Just right for you. Go look in the mirror so you can bask in my brilliance."

"And the brilliance of my own face, I suppose." I don't really care what the glasses look like, to be honest. If she likes them, that's good enough for me, but I go through the song and dance of walking to the mirror across from the entryway and looking.

"Well?" she asks, her face shining as she follows me on those crutches, her hot pink cast visible in the mirror.

"They're glasses," I pronounce, grinning when she scowls at me. "I like them." And I mean it. They're better than the others, and I appreciate the way she looks at me when I wear them. I definitely appreciate the way she put them on. I like the shirts she chose too, although I object to the money she must have spent. "My computer's going to be incredibly impressed by them. Now, what else do I need to do to be less objectionable for people to look at?"

"You've *never* been objectionable to look at."

I'm relieved she said it, but I say, "I'm going to write that one down for posterity."

Her lips twitch. "You know what I mean. It's just...you don't care about stuff like this, so you need someone to care for you."

Her words hit me in a way I didn't expect, maybe because there aren't a lot of people in my life who care to fill in the details my brain couldn't give a shit about. There's Ruthie, obviously, but she's spread so thin, between being Izzy's only parent and her attempts to find something for herself. My friends have always helped me too, when help is needed.

"Thank you," I say through my throat, which feels thick again. I'm emotional, I guess, but I can't parse what all of the emotions are or why they came to be.

"You're welcome."

Then, before I can tell myself no, or remember all the reasons I don't want to do it, I say, "I don't really get why you want to do it, but we can have Thanksgiving dinner here. I wasn't really planning on doing anything anyway."

Everything in her brightens. Using one hand to balance on the crutches, she reaches out the other to touch my chest, the warmth of her hand sending pulses of energy through me. Pulses of need. "You won't regret it."

"I disagree, but I'll do it."

Her hand pulses against my shirt. Black, chosen by her. "I want us to do this together, Danny. But I want it to be something we can both enjoy. I think we should get a space heater for the balcony so you can go out there to get away from everything. I thought about setting up one of the bedrooms as your quiet place, but I don't think the soundproofing is good enough because you always seem to hear me when I open the front door. The balcony is quiet, though, and you can go out there with one or two of the guys if you want to hang out but don't want to be bombarded with all of it at once."

For a moment, I'm speechless. Her words touch something deep inside of me—the part that's always thought that to be acceptable I have to pretend I'm someone I'm not. "You've given this a lot of thought," I finally say, when the words come to me. "Thank you, Mira."

"*Thank you,*" she says, so close, so achingly close. I don't think I've ever wanted anything as much as I want to touch her. "You're doing this for me, aren't you?"

"For my Pygmalion."

"I haven't changed you," she insists. "I don't want to change you. The clothes and the glasses are just window dressing."

Emotion lodges in my throat, threatening to choke me. So few people have ever offered me that kind of acceptance. The part of me that still wants to be different riles from it, and the rest of me is comforted in a way I can't put to words. She hasn't moved her hand, and the heat of it feels like a promise. A benediction. A trial by fire.

Looking into my eyes, she says, "I want to know you, Danny. All of you. I've been trying to piece together what you do all day. I know you work for the man who hurt your sister. You said you did something illegal that gave him some sort of hold over you, and you're on the computer all day. You're...you must be some kind of hacker."

It's like a bucket of water has been poured over my head. Maybe that's why she said it—to swerve the conversation away from a road that would lead somewhere she isn't yet prepared to go.

"Maybe," I say, looking down at her through the glasses she chose for me, "I can neither confirm nor deny that."

"Thank you for telling me," She says, even though I didn't say much. She seems to know it's more than I tell most people.

"I'd like to know more about you too," I admit. "Why aren't *you* going home for Thanksgiving? I figured you were going to your mother's place. Burke mentioned something about it the other week."

"My mother's going off to Europe with some guy she just met. It's a relief, honestly. There's nothing she loves better than pointing out other people's faults, and she's worse with Delia because she knows it hurts her more. Honestly, this rich European dude is a godsend." Her gaze sharpens on me. "I guess you understand all of that since you put yourself on the line for your sister."

I nod, because I do understand. The need to protect Ruthie is written into my DNA. I admire Mira's devotion to her sister—and did before I even knew her.

"Do you have any other siblings?" she asks.

"No, our parents decided not to bless anyone else with being their child."

It hits me that we're still standing. While I like the feeling of her hand on me and would prefer for her to continue to forget it's still there, she shouldn't be on her feet for this long.

"You look tired," I blurt.

Her eyes widen, and then there's a twitch of humor around her mouth. "You know you're not supposed to say that to a woman, right?"

Shit.

"This is where the nice, mild-mannered act comes in useful. I've never been very good at knowing what to say."

"I like a straight shooter." She surprises me by bunching my shirt into her hand for a squeeze. For a second, I think she's going to pull me to her for a kiss—but she releases it and nods back toward the couch. "Watch the movie with me? There's plenty of room on the couch for both of us."

She just got done saying she likes a straight shooter...

"Okay," I say, "but you should probably know that I'm deeply, painfully attracted to you. I have been all along. I'm going to sit in the chair because you made it clear that you don't think anything else should happen between us, and I'm not sure I can keep my hands to myself."

Chapter Fifteen

Danny

Mira's breath hitches, her eyes widen, and she searches my face. Or maybe she's just admiring those glasses she likes so much.

She opens her mouth, then closes it. Opens it again. "It's not often I'm at a loss for words."

"You're the one who said it, not me," I joke. I'm feeling awkward, exposed. Still, I'm not sorry I told her the truth. This draw I feel toward her is becoming harder to hide. Even though I'm someone who's accustomed to hiding things.

A smile flickers across her face, and then she bites her bottom lip, making me want to capture it in mine and soothe my tongue over it. "I'm attracted to you too," she says, and even though she doesn't throw herself at me, something inside of me eases. I'm not in this thing alone. "*Very* attracted to you. But we live together, Danny. You saw what it was like with Byron. I don't want to fall back into that. I can't. And after I go back to the bar...Our lives are so different."

"You're right," I say, because it's best to tell the truth whenever possible. "But I'm nothing like Byron."

"You're *nothing* like Byron," she agrees, biting her lip again. "But what about Daphne? You have feelings for her."

"Had," I correct, because it feels like an important point to establish. I'm a bit flabbergasted, honestly. She's mentioned Daphne several times, but I thought it was because she was trying to push me off on her. I didn't realize she was bothered by her, that she might even be a little jealous. "I haven't even seen her for eight years. I don't remember what she smells like."

"That's a weird thing to say."

I dip my head a little more. "I'm a weird guy. And I'm going to risk freaking you out by telling you that I can't get your scent out of my head."

She takes in a slow breath. "But before last week, you were looking forward to seeing her. You thought you might want to get back together with her. And she's obviously interested in you. She wants to meet you at a bar. *My* bar."

She's not wrong. That was a story I'd told myself. But I'm telling the truth when I say, "I haven't thought about her for weeks. To be honest, I'd prefer not to see her at all. It's just..." I pause, frustrated, because my mind isn't supplying me with what I have to say to convince her...

I'm not even sure what I want to convince her of, but it feels only right for her to know that I've been thinking about her, a lot. And that I want her desperately. There's something about her that fills me with raw need and makes me irrational.

I wasn't ever like that with Daphne. I respected her. I appreciated the way her brain worked. I was attracted to her, but it was always very logical.

I swallow, then admit, "I think the only reason I wanted to change Daphne's mind about me was because of what she said. She knew me as well as anyone, and she thought—"

Mira's hand is on my shirt again, squeezing, and when I look down into her eyes, there's ferocity in them. She lifts up as much as she probably can with the crutches and gives me a soft kiss on the chin. "You are not boring or simple, Danny Traeger. You're the very fucking opposite, and that's a good thing. The best."

Need roars through me until it's so loud it drowns out everything else. I wrap my arm around her back. Her crutches fall to the floor, and the loud smack of them doesn't make me flinch, because she's in my arms—and it's a wonder how much she seems to belong in them. Usually, I'm conscious of a million things—the sounds around me, the feeling of the air against my skin, the light—but it all temporarily goes quiet when I'm holding her, just like in that elevator. My head is bowed to hers, hers lifting up to me, and it's a moment that really does feel stolen from time. I see the glistening on her lip where she bit it, the tiny pinprick mole above her lip, the hazel galaxies in her eyes.

"I need to kiss you in the light," I say, and her lips fall open as she tips her head further up. Taking it for that invitation I wanted earlier, I lean in and claim her lips, sucking on the bottom one, because there's nothing I want so much as to kiss this woman. To mark her as mine. To bring us back to those hours when it was just us and the darkness. But it's so much better kissing her when I can see her, when she's substantial and whole and her lips are opening to me, her tongue twining with mine. She puts a hand in my hair, gripping tight, and the slight pain launches the pleasure to a higher level. The need I feel is unimaginable—and so powerful it may consume me alive.

I'm already hard. I feel like I've spent the last week and a half hard, off and on. Imagining her in that elevator, in her bath. Imagining us in endless positions together, exploring this ache I've been carrying around. I flex my arms around her, bringing her closer, and even though my wrist aches in the stupid plastic wrist guard, no ache could compel me to let her go right now.

My glasses press into her cheek, so I whip them off without thought and throw them in the direction of the side table.

In that moment, I feel like I'm exactly where I want to be, and I wouldn't change anything. She changes the angle of the kiss, bringing it deeper, and nips my lip, making me smile against her mouth even as I keep kissing her, because it seems terribly important to keep kissing her. Then she arcs closer to me, grinding against where I'm hard for her, and I'm worried I'll come on the spot, just from the feel of her through our clothes, from the promise of something more.

As our mouths move together, our bodies pressed close, my hand travels up the back of her sweater, feeling the soft expanse of skin there—soft and warm from lying on my couch, under my blanket, and I'm *glad*. I want her to enjoy these things that are mine. I want to ply her with lattes and show her fall leaves and bring her to the top of a mountain so we can watch the sun rise together in its ribbons of color and light. I want to make love to her until the dawn filters in through the windows of the apartment. I want—

She pulls away, panting, her hand falling from my hair, and the spell between us is cracked but not broken. My arm is still around her—not because I don't respect her need to restart the clock, but because her crutches are lying on the floor, and I won't allow anything to hurt or harm her. That's why I went to Byron's apartment today. I don't believe in hexes, but he clearly does, and he set one on her—that alone is enough of a reason for him to get a warning.

Keeping my head low, watching her, I say, "I think you're probably about to say that was a mistake, but I have to tell you it didn't feel like one."

"It didn't," she agrees, licking her lips. My eyes follow her tongue helplessly, like they don't know how to look at anything else, and truthfully, maybe they've forgotten. "But we can't do this. At least not yet. I won't...you need to go to that meeting with Daphne before we decide whether..." She lifts a shaky hand and gestures between us. "Because if you went, and—"

"I *never* felt this way with her," I tell her. "I never felt like I was in danger of getting carried away and forgetting my name and my social security number."

"You remember your social security number?"

I start reciting it, and she puts a finger over my lips. "You're not supposed to tell anyone that."

"I'm showing you I trust you, because I want *you* to trust *me*."

"Wednesday," she says. "Go meet her at the bar."

"I'll cancel that," I say. "I want to cancel it. I'll just go to the meeting on Friday. The one at Big Bear Games."

"No." She lifts her hand and runs her fingers across my cheek, sending sparks of longing through me. "No. Go to it and see what she wants to say. Then...Then maybe we can figure this out." She shakes her head as if she can't believe what she's saying, but I *need* her to believe it.

I didn't expect any of this. But when one of life's essential truths slaps you in the face, you listen.

"Wednesday feels very far way," I say, swallowing against my dry throat. Feeling blood pounding in my dick. "But I understand your point. And I want *you* to understand that nothing is going to change for me. I'll hear Daphne out, but the only thing I'm interested in from her anymore is selling the game."

"But what about...I don't think we should live together if we..."

"I could move. Find a studio or go stay with Shane." I doubt he'd roll out the red carpet, particularly if he's worried about this work bullshit, but I'll figure something out if there's a need.

"This is your home," she says, her eyes wide. "You'd leave it for me?"

"So we can figure out what this means? Yes."

She studies me, her one hand behind my neck, the fingers cupping it and sending tingles of need down my spine and to my dick. The look in her eyes, as if she appreciates what she's seeing and would like to see more of it, is mesmerizing.

"What if it's just a sexual attraction?" she asks.

"Then we'll have a lot of really good sex, and it'll still be worth it."

She licks her lips like a woman who's trying to drive me crazy and succeeding. "Okay. Even so, I think we should wait."

"Even so," I say, swallowing, trying to ignore the uncomfortable press of my needy dick against my pants. "What do we do now?"

"Watch the movie?" she asks. She's still studying me, and it occurs to me that this must be some sort of a test. Byron the blond would have pushed her to forget her request. He would have taken a hammer to her boundaries. I can't do that if I want to explore our connection, and after what just happened, there's no uncertainty left in me.

I want Mira. I want her in a way that defies everything that's ruled my life...and the beauty and terror of it is that I don't care.

I sweep her up into my arms before she can tell me not to bother. My wrist protests but not enough to make me stop. I carry her to the couch, reaching down to move the blanket before I lower her onto the cushions. The blanket goes on top of her, the better to soak up her scent so I can have it with me if she's not here.

"Danny," she says softly, "you didn't need to do that. I have to get better at hopping around on one foot. Otherwise, all of my muscles will atrophy, and it won't be a good situation for anyone."

"I know," I say, "but it's been a long day for both of us, and they won't be doing much atrophying tonight."

She surprises me by leaning up to kiss my nose, her lips a soft, sweet press.

"I thought we weren't going to do that anymore."

"That was the last one. I like your nose."

"You may be demented," I tell her with a smile. I feel her lips there like a brand, but there's something unsettled in her eyes. "You're freaked out by all of this?"

"Aren't you?"

I search my mind, my body. I should be afraid, but I'm not. "No, surprisingly," I say. "But I don't mind that you are. You're right...this is a pretty unusual situation."

"And so are we, so I guess it fits."

I smooth her hair, then kiss her forehead. "Go ahead and turn on the movie, there's something I need to do."

Her eyes widen, and there's a spark of interest in them. "Are you going to go jerk off in the bathroom?"

"You seem very interested in my jerking-off habits," I comment. I'm not surprised that she knows what I'm after. My dick is so hard it's probably visible from space.

"I am," she says, eyes gleaming. "I like thinking about your hand wrapping around your dick, about you thinking about me while you pleasure yourself."

I groan, because if she intended to make me crazy, she's most definitely succeeding. "I'm going to do it in my bedroom. I'll be back soon."

"I'm going to be thinking about you doing it."

I think, again, about trying to convince her there's no reason to wait for Wednesday, but she threw down a gauntlet for me, and I'm not going to fail. I let my hand slide out of her hair and cup her cheek. "Good. Because I'll *definitely* be thinking about you."

Chapter Sixteen

Mira

When I wake up, he's gone.

The weird thing is that I know before I even leave my bedroom. There's a hollowness to the apartment, like the inside of an emptied shell. Last night was...unexpected.

Dear God was it unexpected. Danny is the sneaky kind of hot that's seeped into my bones, and I want to eat him like one of those pretty cakes displayed in the window of the bakery down the block from Glitterati. There's just this...*thing* between us. It's impossible to deny, even though I've been trying. It's desire, obviously, but it goes so much deeper.

Last night, we watched the rest of the movie together, even though I couldn't think about it because there was a constant pulsing between my legs—a knowledge that he'd fisted his dick, again, because he wants to fuck me with it. Because he wanted me so badly he couldn't take it anymore...

There's something powerful in knowing you can affect someone that way—especially a man like him, usually so guarded.

After we watched the movie, Danny consented to another round of mixology. I made both of us a drink this time, and we tapped the glasses together and took a sip.

He eyed me over the top of his glass, his lips lifting slightly, then said. "This one's my favorite yet."

"But?" I pressed, because I could tell there was one.

"But I still like beer better."

I tilted my head, studying him. "You might not be boring, but you have questionable taste."

"I like *you*," he said, his eyebrows lifting.

"Again, you have questionable taste."

"Before, perhaps. But not now."

I figured we'd go to our separate beds and attend to some self-care, but we sat up late and talked. About the murder podcast and our theories about whodunnit. About creepy Big Mike and his hamster. About his game. I asked him more about his job, about hacking, but he gave me the kind of answers that just gave way to more questions.

I could tell neither of us wanted to end the spell that had been cast—the same as on that elevator, when the only thing that existed, for those few hours, was each other.

When we finally admitted defeat, he carried me to my bedroom and then, no shit, he tucked me in. Part of me wanted to tell him no, that I was a grown-ass woman who didn't need someone to ply me with blankets and lattes and carry me around like I'm a princess, but it felt...nice. Because I might not need to be taken care of, but there's a part of me that wants it.

"You threw those glasses," I accused him through a thick throat.

"I'll go get them now," he said.

"What if they're broken?"

"I'll fix them with masking tape, and you can pretend I'm Harry Potter."

"You're too tall."

His mouth hitches up. "Can't do anything about that one, I'm afraid."

Then he kissed me on the forehead, soft and sweet, and left the room as if he hadn't just upended my world.

I'd promised myself that I wouldn't make the same mistakes I'd made before—moving too fast, living together too soon—but after seeing Byron and Danny side by side, I have to admit that they're nothing alike. The only similarity was the color of their hair, and now that Byron's gone patchy platinum blond, that one similarity has also been obliterated, thank God.

The truth is, Danny's different from anyone I've ever known, and if I refuse to fully explore our connection, something tells me I'm going to regret it. Like two years from now when Delia is showing me his wedding photos to Daphne.

Yes, my mind is an untidy place.

But it seems important for Danny to see Daphne first—for him to come to me after he closes that door. I spent a few sleepless hours last night asking myself why, especially since my body is burning for him, and I reached this conclusion—

I'm fucking intimidated by her.

I don't like being intimidated by another woman. I *love* women. Not as much as Azalea, but only because I have an unfortunate addiction to dick.

The thing is...

Daphne is brilliant. I wasn't ever any good at school. I did get an associate degree in business management—but it's not worth the paper it's printed on compared with her PhD from *Stanford*.

The solution is probably for me to stop Googling her, but I've already done the damage, and I know that Daphne is smarter than me.

There, I said it. She's smarter than me, and Danny is obviously a man who appreciates intelligence. So, I can't help but worry that he'll take one look at her, and the last eight years will melt away. She'll realize the truth—that she was crazy for thinking he's anything approaching boring. And, hell, his new glasses and shirts will probably cinch the deal, because I'm the idiot who's gift-wrapped the man I'm interested in before sending him off to another, more suitable woman.

Admittedly, they'll be meeting in the bar, surrounded by people, but in my head, it's just the two of them eye-fucking each other across the table before they for-real-fuck on the surface.

So...yeah...what's going on is that I'm jealous.

It's not a usual emotion for me, and I am one hundred percent sure I don't like it.

Sighing, I check my phone, and then sigh harder when I see a text from Byron, who apparently condescended to unblock me.

I'm not playing around, Mira. I know I fucked up this time.

There's a photo of him with the fried platinum hair, and I immediately save it as his contact photo on my phone before texting him back.

So tell Josie you changed your mind. I might not believe in hexes, but I'd prefer not to have a hypothetical hex on me.

I DID tell her. She said we both need to be present to lift it. Her first availability is on Wednesday afternoon.

I think back to the storefront with the crayon drawings on the sign. No fucking way is her first availability on Wednesday, unless she's spending the weekend at another dance festival. In fact, this whole thing stinks like the sardines my Sicilian grandfather used to eat.

Is this some messed up attempt to get me in the same room as you?

Not everything's about you, Mira.

I'd like to think the curse you put on me is.

Love is the curse.

Wait. That's fuckin sick. I can write a song about this.

Something like…I put a hex on my ex because love is a curse.

That's good, right?

Do you think the guys will like it?

I'm glad my broken ankle could serve some higher purpose. I'll think about Wednesday.

I already made the appointment.

Of course you did. If I'm not there, feel free to bring some more drain hair to stand in my place.

Maybe I'll go. Wednesday afternoon is when Danny's meeting Daphne, and I don't want to wait here at the apartment, thinking about the possibility of him and Daphne banging on a table at my bar.

When I get up, I make my way to the kitchen to prepare coffee, but there's a cold latte waiting for me on the counter. A maple leaf sits next to it—the colors a stunning blend of gold and red that makes me smile when I lift it up into the late morning sun beaming in through the picture window. Then I look at the note beneath the very-welcome coffee.

Sometimes being a leaf peeper has its benefits.
Wednesday feels very far away right now.

I press the leaf to my chest, feeling a little dizzied by the thought of him choosing it for me—before setting it back on the counter and nuking my coffee. Did he take his car up there? I know he usually bikes, but his wrist might still be bothering him. I like the image of him sitting up on some mountain ridge, or wherever he likes to go, drinking his coffee while he studies the leaves and the birds. Growing up here, the changing of the leaves never really meant much to me—it was one of those beauties of life that went unnoticed because it was always there, but looking at this leaf, this perfect leaf he found for me, I feel a tug of longing. I've never purposefully woken up before nine o'clock, but I don't hate the thought of going there with him sometime.

I sit on the couch with my coffee, and for a few minutes I sit there in dreamy silence, thinking about golden and red leaves and fall flavors and the look of admiration and warmth in Danny's eyes last night when he told me he was *very attracted* to me.

And then I see it. My "friend" is back in the apartment across the street. She's watching me again. I look her in the eye and wave, because she deserves to get called out on being a creeper. She doesn't wave back, but she also doesn't look away. She keeps staring at me like one of those weird kids in a horror movie, and I feel a prickle of unease skitter down my back. It's like she wants me to know she's watching, but why?

I give her the finger to see if that'll get me a reaction, and it freaks me out more when it doesn't—when she keeps standing in the window like a murderous doll, peering at my middle finger as if she'd like to break it with her mind. I'm very much inclined to close the blinds, but I don't want to lose the stare-off or indirectly admit that she's gotten under my skin. Because even though I don't under-stand why, she obviously *wants* to get under my skin.

Is she just bored or is this something else?

It kind of *feels* like something else, but I'm pretty sure I've never seen her before this week.

The buzzer rings, and I avert my gaze from the window for a

second. When I look back, she's gone, and I feel like James Bond's martini—shaken, not stirred.

I don't like the weird mystery woman, and now I feel absolutely justified by my obsession with Danny's binoculars. I will be taking a closer look at her apartment later, although I don't know what I could hope to find out.

Maybe there'll be a bloody murder weapon on the floor, conveniently visible from the window, and I can call in an anonymous tip and make her someone else's problem.

I answer the buzzer, because at least I know it can't be the weird blonde murder lady.

"It's me!" Delia says.

"And Shauna," Shauna says. "Tell me you have caffeine."

I buzz them up without responding, because I'm still shaken.

A few minutes later, I open the door and feel immediate regret for not asking more questions, because my sister is holding a huge cardboard box full of a bag of black salt, a hand-held mirror, a couple of fabric dolls, and a random assortment of other shit.

"We're here to break the hex!" she announces brightly.

"Is it too late to kick you out?" I ask with a groan.

"Yes," Shauna says. "Because I haven't had any caffeine, and Enchanted over here spent all night researching how to break hexes." Enchanted is her new nickname for Delia, because when they were at Glitterati one night, a drunk tourist asked for her autograph, convinced she was Amy Adams.

"You did?" I ask as Delia walks in with the monster-sized box. I want to take it from her, but there's the crutches to consider, and I have to stand by like the useless person I currently am while she carries it in, and Shauna closes the door behind her.

"Of course," Delia says as she settles it onto the kitchen island. Now that she's inside, I see the dark circles under her eyes. "You're my sister. I can't let you dye your hair with peroxide."

"I'm pretty sure Bryon's just stupid and the curse had nothing to do with it," I tell her. "Besides, it sounds like Josie agreed to break it herself if the two of us come by on Wednesday. I'm thinking I'll go. Just in case." I nod toward the enormous bag of salt she's pulling out of the box. "Maybe I'll throw some of that over my shoulder for good measure."

"Wednesday?" Delia asks in horror, pausing halfway in her efforts. "But *dozens* of things could go wrong before Wednesday." She lets the salt plop onto the table and grabs out a sprig of leaves. Sage.

I guess Josie really has her convinced that I'm metaphysically fucked.

Truthfully, I'm more concerned about the potential psychopath across the alley. My initial impulse was to tell them about her, but I can tell Delia really did stay up all night worried about me, and if she learns about the blonde lady, she'll probably think my weirdo neighbor has something to do with the hex.

Either that or she'll tell me I'm the one who's psycho, what with giving the finger to someone I've never met.

Shauna picks up my perfect leaf, and I feel something pulsing in my chest, almost like panic.

"Hey, that's mine."

Her lips twitch, but she sets it down on the island, which is of course when she sees the note. Looking up with a glint in her eyes, she says, "Don't hold out on us. What's happening on Wednesday?"

"I already told you, the anti-hex thing. Maybe Byron can bring a little doll of me, so I don't need to show up in person."

Shauna puts a hand on her hip. "That's not what Danny was talking about."

"He's meeting Daphne at a bar on Wednesday evening. My bar," I add as I swing my way over to the kitchen island. I want to put the leaf in my pocket, but I don't like the little knowing tilt of my friend's mouth. So I add, "He's *super* excited to see her, especially now that he has those new glasses I got for him."

I'm only saying it to put her off the scent, but there's some real bitterness behind the words. It's all that ill-advised Googling I've done about Daphne. Still. I'm pretty sure I did the right thing, telling him to take the meeting. If he doesn't, he'll always wonder what she would have said.

"You know, Leonard has this theory about you and Danny," Shauna says contemplatively, tapping her nail on the note.

Five seconds ago, I'd intended to keep my involvement with Danny a secret, but I'm nothing if not capricious, because I find myself saying, "Does it have something to do with him finger-banging me on the stalled elevator?"

I've never been good at hoarding secrets. Besides, I can't deny I want to talk to someone about all of this.

Delia drops the salt, and I can hear it spilling everywhere. Good luck getting that out of the cracks of the floor, Danny.

I've managed to surprise Shauna too, but there's just a slight widening of her eyes before she grins at me. "It was less graphic, but yeah, that was the general idea."

"*Mira*," Delia says, and there's something syrupy sweet in her voice but not saccharin.

I lift a hand. "Let's not get ahead of ourselves. He still has that private meet-up with Daphne, and I told him we couldn't explore whatever's going on between us until he goes. Plus, you have to admit our lives aren't compatible. He can't be around crowds or noise for long, and I basically thrive on them."

Shauna shrugs. "Who says you have to share everything? Isn't it better to keep some things for yourself?"

I shrug back. "Maybe, but there's no denying Danny and Daphne have a lot more in common. I mean, even their names sound compatible. They could get married and have lots of D-named children."

"Danielle...Dickface...Droopy, the possibilities are truly endless," Shauna says. "But I feel like you're evading the point.

Before last week, you couldn't even remember what Danny's face looked like from one meeting until the next. We need to know more about what happened on that elevator. You know, leading up to the fingerbanging. And over this last week."

I feel my sister watching me. "She got to know the real Danny," she says. "He's a wonderful man."

I nod, and my throat thickens, almost like I'm about to cry. "I did. But—"

Delia's lips firm, her eyes narrowing on me, like she knows I was about to spout off some bullshit self-conscious drivel about not feeling smart enough for Danny. We know each other's scars like they're our own. "Glitterati was rated the #1 new bar in Asheville in that *Mountain Express* poll."

"Yeah, maybe five people vote on that. Besides, women don't have to be in competition with each other." And, let's face it, if I was in anything but a drinking or mixology competition with Daphne, I would lose and lose badly.

"Don't forget that you're a businesswoman too," Delia insists. "A good one."

Time to change the subject. My chest feels suspiciously like a raw wound that someone's ladling salt into. It's not just Daphne...

The logical side of me that can't see this thing with Danny working beyond this liminal space—this apartment where each of us can be separated from the outside world.

I swing my way over to her and poke some of the salt on the counter. It is, as advertised, large-grain black salt.

"Delia," I say. "Josie's not psychic. Or capable of hexing people. I screwed up my ankle because I was being stupid. It was my own fault. And, as we've already established, Byron's an idiot who doesn't follow directions. So, we don't have to worry about any of this."

She's already shaking her head. "Josie knew about Mom. Plus, I talked to Mom last night, and she said she hadn't made the decision about going to Europe until yesterday afternoon. So there's no way Josie could have learned about it from someone else. She knows things she can't."

It's definitely a weird coincidence, and I have a feeling of uneasiness, even though it's only a pale reflection of the tingle down my spine from when that woman was watching me.

"So it was a lucky guess," I admit, leaning on the side of the island. "I don't like you worrying, Delia."

"So let me do this," she says, trying to corral the spilled salt. I'm still unclear on what she's setting up, but there's only one thing I can say.

"Hand me the salt, and let's get hexing."

"We're supposed to break the hex," she says, giving me a worried look.

"I've never been good at following directions."

Chapter Seventeen

Danny

"Well, what do you think?" Ruthie asks, her eyes bright. Her hair is styled in two braids, which makes her look like she did when she was seven or maybe eight. I can see little Ruthie in my mind's eye, looking up at me for approval after she finished some school project or other, because she could already tell that our parents didn't give a shit.

She asked me over to her apartment this morning, saying she had something to show me, and I'd braced myself for a reveal of the next incarnation of Vanny. What'd it be this time? Used shoes? Upmarket tampons? I said yes, of course, because I always say yes on the rare occasions when she asks me for something.

Even though what I really wanted to do was wait for Mira to wake up.

Ruthie arranged for Izzy to stay with a friend for an hour or two so she could do her grand unveiling, so it's just the two of us in the parking lot of her apartment building. Well, the two of us and an assortment of random strangers walking to and from their homes or messing with their cars.

Her van's been painted with a mural of books and baby animals. Someone's anchored shelves inside, and they're stacked with children's books. Hundreds of them. There are furry poofs and floor pillows and fairy lights anchored around the ceiling.

It's an improvement on the sex toys idea.

I know she mustn't have done the majority of the work out here. Her best friend Tank has an autoshop, and he usually lets her fix up Vanny in his garage, where there's also a lounge area for Izzy to hang out and do her art or watch TV.

"Where'd you get all the books?" I ask, because she didn't ask me for money or help. There's an ache in my chest, because we could have done this for her—me and Shane, Burke and Leonard. I would love to have done this for her.

"I've had this in the back of my mind for a while," she says excitedly. "I've been making a collection. Free libraries. The book bundler. That kind of thing. Plus, I went to this estate sale with Izzy last weekend, and they sold hundreds of them to me for less than a hundred bucks."

"I wish you'd asked me for help," I say. "The guys and I could have rigged up those shelves for you." I wave at the mural. "Leonard's girlfriend's an artist." I swallow the rest of what I want to say—*they wouldn't have charged you any money.*

Her lips are firm. "You think I'm going to ask you for any favors? You—"

"I'd do it again," I tell her. "I'd do anything for you and Izzy. You know that."

"Which is exactly why I need to protect you from yourself."

This again. She thinks I ruined my life for her, so now she won't even take a stick of gum from me, unless I give it to Izzy and encourage Izzy to give it to her.

"I'm an adult man, perfectly capable of making my own decisions. I was then too."

"And I am and was an adult woman, perfectly capable of making my own mistakes."

I could argue with her—she'd been eighteen, a teenager, and

he'd been thirty-seven and married. Jarrod Travis is a predator, a pest, and a loathsome human being. He's a man who deserves to face the great mysteries of life—the void—alone and with no love to cushion him.

He has also, for the last ten years, been my boss.

The day I get to quit Safe-T Net, I'll throw a party.

Metaphorically, of course.

But Ruthie and I have said all that, and then said it again. She knows my stance, and I know hers.

I've agreed I'm going to treat her like an adult, and run any big brother plans by her before rolling them out.

She's agreed she's going to avoid making mistakes that she knows are mistakes.

Of course, her definition of mistakes and mine aren't always the same. Jarrod wasn't the only piece of shit she invited into her life. I knew her ex-husband was worthless within ten minutes of meeting him, and Shane almost came to fists with him at least twice. But Ruthie was in love.

Maybe love is a state in which we're all rendered blind.

My mind shifts to Mira, to the feeling of her mouth on mine, to the need that kept me up half the night. Am I screwing everything up? I'm not particularly worried about the fact that she's Delia's sister and will thus be part of my circle of friends even if everything falls apart between us. If I have to miss a few gatherings, fine by me. It's more...

I'm a little thrown by what I heard myself saying last night. Maybe more so because I meant it. I'm prepared to give up the apartment for the possibility to be with this woman I've only known for weeks. For ten years, that apartment has been my home. My sanctuary.

My prison, a voice in my head whispers.

It comes as a surprise, and I feel my face twisting up from it. I've never thought of it as that—not consciously—but in some ways it's true.

"What is it?" Ruthie asks, nudging my shoulder. "You went far-off again."

"Oh, just thinking."

"No shit. I was asking what all that thinking was about."

A corner of my mouth lifts. "Maybe I have a rival book van, and I'm trying to think of a way to break the news to you."

She laughs and shakes her head. "As transparent as concrete, as always. Seriously, though, what do you think? I know I always say this, but I'm excited about this one."

She told me a little about her plan already. She'll partner with local events and breweries as a play and story station for kids—where they can read and color and choose a book to bring home. And she's talked to a couple of local shelters, including Dog is Love, from which Leonard, ironically enough, adopted a cat, about having them bring adoptable kittens and puppies for the children to read to.

I put an arm around her. "I'm proud of you. It's brilliant, Ruthie."

It's also extremely unlikely to bring in any kind of real money, but I don't feel the need to point that out. She doesn't do it for the money. Ruthie's chasing something that'll make her feel happy and fulfilled. She wants to make a difference in the world, or at least a small corner of it.

I understand. Growing up in our family, we always felt less valued than the dwindling supply of alcohol in the cabinet.

She wraps her arms around me, catching me off-guard, but it only takes me a second to hug her back. "I love you," she says softly in my ear.

"I love you too." I break away and say, "Hey, so for Thanksgiving—"

Her eyes widen. "What about Thanksgiving? Aren't you and Narcissus going on your usual ride?"

Narcissus is her nickname for Shane, who always argues that nicknames are supposed to be shorter than a person's actual name. She rebuts that he's the one who first started calling her Ruthie two decades ago, so it's his fault if she doesn't know how to nickname properly.

"No," I say, peering into the van, taking a closer look at the mechanics of the shelving. "Shane got invited to his boss's place for Thanksgiving, so—"

"So he dropped you like a hot potato," she asks, her lower lip jutting out. She looks like she's ready to hop into the book van and run him over.

"When your boss asks you to do something like that, you do it," I say, not necessarily because I believe it, but because that's what he said and I feel that I should offer up a token defense for him.

"If you say so." She blows her bangs off her face. "I don't like that he—"

"We're having Thanksgiving at the apartment," I blurt. "So obviously you and Izzy should come. If you want, I mean. I know you usually go to Tank's parents' place. Or Jacqueline's."

"Jamie," she says, rolling her eyes. "We've been friends since I was ten."

"Jamie," I correct. "Well. Anyway. It would be great if you came. And Shane won't be there, obviously, so hopefully you won't feel inclined to burn down the apartment."

She studies me for a second, then says, "This was your roommate's plan?"

I see no reason to say no. It obviously wasn't my idea. "Yes. But I think the other guys are coming with their girlfriends."

"You're in love with her!" Ruthie says, the idea seeming to excite her even more than Vanny's new incarnation. "There's literally no other reason you'd ever agree to that."

"I'm not in love with her," I say, feeling sweat bead on my upper lip. Suddenly, I'm a little overwhelmed. By my feelings for Mira, which are big and powerful. By Thanksgiving. By Ruthie's new scheme. By the past week and a half and everything it's done to shatter what came before it.

Some things need shattering, but it's still made me feel like the ground beneath my feet has turned into something unknowable, like the floor during an earthquake.

"I'm sorry," Ruthie says as she takes a small step back. "I shouldn't have jumped to love, but you like her, don't you? I could tell earlier, when you were talking about her broken ankle."

"Listen to yourself."

She laughs lightly, and I can't help but smile. "You're such a guy. Broken ankles can be extremely romantic. Like if you had to carry her everywhere."

"I have carried her a few places," I admit. She widens her eyes, and I shift a little on my feet, uncomfortable again. "That's as much as I'll be saying right now, but yeah, I like her. She's..."

She's something else. She's loud and brash, smart and funny, and there's a deep well of her that she doesn't let most people look down, but I've gotten a view.

I'd like to take a bath in it.

"I want to meet her," Ruthie insists.

"And you will. If you come to this horrible holiday dinner that's certain to be a disaster."

"Oh, I'll be there," she says with a grin.

"And don't think about stopping by unannounced before then. You know I prefer knowing what to expect."

She pokes a finger into my chest. "I also know it's good for you to learn to deal with interruptions to your plans."

"There've been plenty of those lately," I mutter.

"Speaking of plans. What's going on with your game? Are you selling it?"

I didn't tell her about Daphne working for Big Bear Games. I don't want to tell her now. She has an irrational hatred of Daphne that's on par, or possibly even stronger than, her irrational dislike for Shane.

"I hope so," I say. "They haven't given us an offer yet, but I did some research, so I know the ballpark range of what we'll be looking at."

"It's almost over," she tells me, giving me that look I hate seeing on her face. Guilt.

"It's almost over," I agree. "But it wasn't your fault, and I won't have you thinking it."

She lifts a hand and opens it to mimic a mouth. I close it with my hand.

"It wasn't your fault," I repeat. "Jarrod Travis is a predator. He's—"

"Danny," she hisses, glancing around the parking lot. No one's paying any attention to us unless someone's hidden beneath one of the poofs in Vanny. "You have to be more careful."

"I know," I admit, because she's right. I signed that NDA, after all. I won't ever be able to talk publicly about that prick, not unless I want to cough up more money than I could possibly make in a life-time. Even so, I'll still be making yearly payments to him for another five years, unless I manage to put together a lump sum big enough to cover what I owe.

And I can't professionally do what I do best for anyone but Safe-T Net. Not until the fifteen-year term is over.

The game is my best hope.

Ruthie hugs me and promises to bring pumpkin pie and not pop in without notice, but I know her well enough to expect she will be visiting soon. The most notice we're likely to get is a text message when she's already waiting at the door.

I drive home, my mind hung up on Ruthie and Mira. I was hesi-tant to introduce Daphne to Ruthie. The thought of them meeting had put an itch at the back of my mind—I'd known they weren't two people who would understand and like each other and the only thing they'd have in common was that I understood and liked both of them. But I don't feel any discomfort attached to the thought of Ruthie and Mira meeting.

If anything, they're likely to gang up on me, the same way Shane and Ruthie do on the rare occasions they have a ceasefire. The prospect makes me smile—a smile that fades when I reach a stoplight and notice the face of the driver behind me. Big Mike.

He's probably going the same place I am, so maybe it's not that big of a coincidence—this city isn't so big it's an impossibility. I've run into Burke and Leonard at the grocery store, and one time Shane and I both went for a bike ride without telling each other and ended up meeting on the trail. But this doesn't feel right.

Has Jarrod heard about my meeting, or maybe about my extra-curricular hacking, and paid this guy to keep an eye on me?

It would be ballsy as fuck, but Jarrod only cares about the rules if they're tilted in his favor.

Big Mike trails me right into the parking garage, then takes the space next to mine.

Another bit of weirdness.

I'm probably being paranoid, but this guy is either stalking me because he's hard up for friends or because he has a secondary reason for doing so. I'm guessing it's Door Number Two, since I'm not the kind of person who oozes friendly vibes. I'm unsettled by the possibility and also deeply pissed off. I mean...how deep do the lies go? I'm interested, but I also want to keep my contact with him to a minimum. If it's information he wants, he won't be getting it from me.

We exit our vehicles at the same time, and Big Mike calls out, "Hi, neighbor," the sound of his voice putting my teeth on edge.

"Hello."

I head for the elevator, then think twice because the big guy is trailing me. While I'd be utterly okay getting stuck in the elevator with Mira again, a couple of hours in the dark with him is significantly less appealing.

He follows me through the door. "What were you up to on this beautiful fall morning?"

"It's past noon," I intone, making my way up the steps.

"Ah, even better," he says, acting completely oblivious to my deep desire to get away from him. "Nothing better than a fall afternoon, some brewskies or ciders, and a bonfire. Say, what do you say we—"

"Nope." I up my speed.

Big Mike belches out laughter. "Little lady keeping you busy, huh? Bring her along too. I'll bet my girl would—"

We reach the second-floor landing, and I turn to face him. "I'm trying not to be rude, buddy, but I'm not interested in being your friend, or going to strip clubs with you, or babysitting your gerbil."

"Hamster," he says. His expression looks flat. Unsurprised.

"My mistake, but they're both rodents." I'm tempted to ask him about Jarrod straight out, but if this guy is in his pocket, then I don't want him to know I know. "I'm guessing you get the picture."

"Yeah, I do," he says slowly, lifting up his big meaty hands. "Just trying to be neighborly."

"No need. We're not neighbors. You live downstairs."

He gives me a slow smile I don't like one bit. "Sure. Because you're up there in Lucas Burke's penthouse."

So he knows Burke is the owner of the penthouse. That's an interesting piece of information, because I'd never had the misfortune of seeing this guy prior to a couple of weeks ago.

Did Burke's parents pay Big Mike to keep an eye on me? I can't understand why they'd bother. Sure, they're upset with Burke for tumbling their empire into the dust, but I had nothing to do with that—or with them. I've met them half a dozen times, maybe, and his mother still mistakes me for Drew.

Leonard, they have a grudge against. He used to work for Burke Enterprises and is the one who first realized they weren't on the up and up. But the only thing I could have done to piss them off is living in the unit upstairs, which they originally bought for Burke well over a decade ago. Sure, it must piss them off that a kid who grew up poor with a couple of alcoholics for parents ended up living in their penthouse, but they've got bigger problems than me.

I'll talk to the guys about it, obviously, but I'm guessing Big Mike is trying to get me off the scent, which only makes me more interested in why he's holed up downstairs. Not interested enough to have dinner with him, obviously, but interested all the same...

Big Mike's still staring at me, wanting that reaction, so I tell him, "Yes, I'm perfectly well aware of where I live. I hope you enjoy those *brewskies*."

And then I turn and keep walking up those stairs. I don't like giving my back to him, but if I refused to, it would be as good as saying I'm intimidated by him.

I feel him watching me as I go up, and when I reach the next landing, I can see him still standing there, probably figuring out what his next move will be. Hopefully getting some moving boxes because he's not going to make any inroads with me. Or Mira.

I'm relieved when I reach the fourth floor, but it only lasts until I open the front door, because Delia's waving around a mirror while Mira sways a smoking, stinking bundle of plant matter through the air. The ground looks like it's covered in fine gravel.

"Do I want to do know what's going on in here?"

Chapter Eighteen

Mira

"No, probably not," I tell Danny, trying not to laugh, even though I feel it bubbling up inside of me, impossible to resist. I grind the sage out onto a plate as if it's a cigar.

"We did a few rituals to try to break the hex," says Delia, sounding confident even though the only thing the rituals seemed to accomplish was to create this mess. There was no blinking of lights, no feeling of something breaking or changing. No sound. No... anything. I didn't expect anything to happen, but it would have been fun if it had.

"You're sure this didn't happen *because* of the hex?" Danny asks. It's a fair question—the kitchen area looks like a cyclone blew through it.

Delia's eyes widen. "You think it did?"

"On that note," Shauna says. "We should probably leave. I promised my grandmother I'd help her make soup." She eyes the condition of the kitchen, then says, "Do you need help cleaning?"

"I'll do it," Danny offers.

She mimes wiping sweat off her forehead. "I was hoping you'd say that."

I point at her. "Your job for Thanksgiving is to figure out how to roast a turkey." My finger swings toward Delia. "Yours is to make pies. You make good pies. The more pies, the better."

"What are we making?" Danny asks, and I feel an unexpected burst of pleasure from hearing him use that word. It's a dangerous way to feel, though, and I try to guard myself against it.

"We will be supplying the most important part of Thanksgiving dinner," I tell him.

"The booze," Delia finishes with a half-smile. "You always say that."

I do. But I suddenly wish we'd both shut our mouths, because I find myself remembering what Danny said about that ceramic turkey. It occurs to me that there's another reason why the two of us are mismatched. I sell alcohol, and he told me just last night that his parents are alcoholics. He drinks a little, but it must still be...well, loaded for him.

My brain thinks it's funny that getting loaded is loaded for him, but I don't want to smile or laugh, because my eyes find that little line above his eyebrow and linger there.

I don't like the woman who did that to him. When Delia was little, our mother seemed to love digging into our various faults. I told my sister that we didn't have to be like her. We could find something to like about everyone. Even our mother—her something-to-like was that if she said she was going to do something, she did it. She didn't do it with a lot of compassion or grace or warmth, but you could be assured it would get done. But I don't think I can find anything to like about a woman who'd hurt Danny.

I clear my throat and look away. "Beverages of all types. There may be children present."

Danny nods. "I was with Ruthie just now. She's going to come, and she's bringing Izzy." Turning toward Shauna and Delia, he says, "We'll make the mashed potatoes too. I make good mashed potatoes."

"I'll bet you have a food scale," I say. In my mind's eye, I can see him measuring the ingredients, meticulous as always. "You do, don't you?"

One of his eyebrows wings up. "Yes, but is it in grams or ounces?"

"Oh, definitely grams. You'd never condescend to measure things in ounces."

I'm blessed by the upward angle of his lips. "You'll have to wait to find out."

"Well, we've got a week and a half," I say, "so there's plenty of time for us to figure all this stuff out. We can start a group chat."

I burst out laughing at the immediate look of horror on Danny's face.

"What?" he asks.

"Your face," I say through laughter.

His lips twitch. "Yes, it's been known to throw women into fits of hysteria."

Shauna gives me a knowing look, then shifts said knowing look to Delia. My sister sighs and packs up her witchery box, except for all of the salt and whatnot that made its way into the cracks of the hardwood floor. "You need to go on Wednesday," she says. "Just in case. I know you think this is silly, and maybe you're right, but that woman knows things she shouldn't."

"You're talking about Josie," Danny says, his gaze darting from her face to the box and then to me.

"Yes."

Delia gives each of us a one-armed hug, making Danny look awkward, and it occurs to me that he's not comfortable with physical affection from people he doesn't know well. Then Shauna says her goodbyes, too. With another wave, they're gone, and it's just the two of us again. Maybe it should be awkward after last night, but this is our place out of time, and it's not. It feels right in a weird, delicate way—and I have to wonder, again, if it can ever be the same once my ankle's intact.

"What are you doing with Josie on Wednesday?" he asks.

I tell him about Byron and the anti-hexing.

His face creases into a frown.

"Yeah, yeah, I know it's bullshit," I say with a sigh, starting to half-heartedly clean up the kitchen island with a sponge. "I think it's just...I need a distraction, and there's no denying Josie is entertaining."

"The sponges for cleaning are under the sink," he says.

"Of course they are. They're next to impossible to reach down there."

"Sit down, Mira," he says, reaching over and touching my shoulder. His hand is so big, it easily wraps around it, and a hot and cold shiver passes through me. "I said I'd do it."

I reach up and touch his hand, layering mine over it. "Thank you for my leaf."

He looks into my eyes, and I'm swept away by his intense regard. "I'd like to take you up where I found it."

It echoes what I was thinking earlier—that I want to see the changing trees through his eyes and find the beauty I've been missing.

"I'd like that," I admit, my fingers moving over his because even now I can't be still. I want his hand to move too—to trace down my arm and pull me to him. To reach under my shirt, the way it did last night, his skin warm and hot against mine. But I already know he won't. Not unless I ask him to. I set a boundary, and he's made it clear that he respects that.

He respects *me*.

So I sit in one of the chairs at the counter and watch him take out the sponge and efficiently clean the kitchen island. It's the kind of thing that probably shouldn't be sexy, but he does it so efficiently, with such authority, that I feel myself leaning closer, wanting a better view.

He retrieves the broom from the closet where I didn't know it was kept and starts to sweep.

"Isn't your wrist still bothering you?"

He shrugs. "It felt mostly okay when I woke up this morning. I took a couple of Advil."

"Good. You know, you're like a sexy Cinderella."

His smile is so subtle most people would miss it, but I'm getting used to catching his smiles.

"Please never say that to any of my friends. I'd never hear the end of it. They already give me shit about the pumpkin spice thing."

"I make no promises."

His expression loses some of its humor and he sits at the chair across from me. "I've been trying to come up with a way to say this that won't piss you off, but I'm coming up empty. So I'm just going to stay it. I don't like the thought of you going to see Byron and Josie by yourself. Will you bring someone?"

"You really think they're dangerous?" I scoff.

"They believe they hexed you," he points out dryly. "That speaks of ill intentions. I'd feel better if you went with someone. If you want...I'll go with you."

Something catches in my throat, because we both know that's the evening he's supposed to "catch up" with Daphne.

"What about your ex-girlfriend?" I ask.

"I told you I'd cancel that. I want to."

"How important is it for you to sell your game?"

"Very. But we can sell it to someone else. I don't really want to work with Daphne on it anyway. It would be awkward and uncomfortable. I'm going to ask her if Big Bear can put someone else on the deal." He runs a hand through his hair, glances at the door. When he turns back to me, his expression is different—serious and grave. "There's something I need to talk to you about."

The way he says it reminds me of the blond- or maybe white-haired woman across the alley.

"Me too," I say. "I know it'll sound paranoid, but—"

He reaches his hand across the kitchen island, and I take it without thinking, liking the way his fingers wrap around mine. "Come with me."

Yes, please is the first thought that drifts through my head, even though it's obvious he's not going to throw me down on his bed.

Once I'm all set up with my crutches, he leads me toward the balcony, then mutters under his breath and says, "I think we should go for a walk, actually."

"I'm not much for walking these days," I say, swinging my right crutch into the air a little.

"A drive," he corrects. "We can go see those leaves."

"Didn't you already do that today?" I ask, baffled.

"They're still there."

There's something off about his tone, in his behavior. He's skittish, and nervous energy seems to be pumping off him. He keeps messing with his pocket even though there doesn't appear to be anything in it.

"What about lunch?" I ask. "Shouldn't we pack something?"

"We'll get something while we're out."

It's obvious he wants to leave, now, without talking this out in the apartment. My paranoid brain kicks in, reminding me about that woman across the way. Did he find out she's been watching us? Does she have a...a bug in the apartment?

I can't think why the mystery woman would have it in for us. I've seen Daphne's photo, so I know it's not her, and as far as I know, I haven't pissed anyone off enough for them to go to the trouble of renting a very expensive apartment just so they can watch me from it. But Danny...maybe she's there for him.

The thought puts a sick twist in my chest, so I don't say anything as we leave the apartment. I don't say anything as we put on our coats and walk down the stairs. We make it down without any further hamster incidents or run-ins with overly friendly and informative neighbors.

When we get settled inside his car, the passenger seat pushed all the way back so I can get my leg straight in front of me, I turn look at him. He gives his head a slight shake that tells me he's concerned there might be something in the car too. Well, fuck, that's not good.

"You're kind of freaking me out," I whisper through my teeth.

"I'm kind of freaking myself out," he replies in an undertone. But he buckles himself in and looks over to make sure I've done the same before backing out of the lot, so at least we're not dealing with a car chase scenario yet.

We make small talk as the car winds farther up the mountain. Okay, correction—I make small talk, asking him about his sister, my interest increasing when he tells me about her plans for "Vanny."

After several twists and turns, we turn onto the Blue Ridge parkway. The leaves are a canopy of red and gold around us, although several trees are already bare. The day is crisp but sunny— about as beautiful as a fall day in the mountains can get. If we were to open the window, I'll bet the air would smell of apple spice, with a hint of campfire on the backend, because people are making fires in their hearths and backyards at this time of year. Many of the old houses have oil heating, and fire is cheaper than oil. I may be a summer girl at heart, but I appreciate it. I'd appreciate it even more if we weren't potentially fleeing a...

A what?

A stalker?

An observer?

Finally, Danny pulls over and parks the car on the crispy grass, strewn with leaves. There are no other cars around, no people.

He helps me out of the car, and I feel utterly ridiculous to be up here, on a mountain, with crutches.

"We're not going far." He points toward a patch of trees that looks exactly like all of the others. "There's a bench hidden in there. You can leave the crutches. I'll carry you."

Two weeks ago, I would have insisted on making my own way.

Two weeks ago, I broke my ankle because I was being stubborn.

"Okay."

He sweeps me up off my feet for what feels like the hundredth time recently, holding me against his chest as he easily moves through the trees and brush. Although he said it "wasn't far," he walks for at least six or seven minutes. His outdoor competence is sexy, particularly because I couldn't navigate my way out of a paper bag, and I'm calmed by the steady but rapid beating of his heart. By his clean scent, engulfing me and promising that we're in this together.

We reach a hidden break in the trees, and sure enough, there's a little wooden bench, green with age. There are initials carved all over it—Minnie loves Mickey; R and S, in a heart; Maya hearts Tom. Danny lowers me down before sitting next to me, his thigh pressed to mine, and even though I'm keyed up and worried, I can't deny I'm aware of every place where we're touching, as if the skin has become a thousand times more sensitive—capable of feeling him between multiple layers of fabric. There's a little opening in front of the bench, through which we can see the rolling blue mountains, and all around us the remaining leaves are a sea of colors.

"Whoa," I say, leaning into his shoulder. He puts an arm around me, bringing me closer, then looks at me as if to ask if it's all right. I respond by leaning in. "This is where you found my leaf? Suddenly, I feel less special."

He angles his head to look at me—his lips dangerously close. "There are a lot of leaves out here, sure. But there was only one perfect leaf. It took me half an hour to find it."

Well, damn. The thought of him standing out there, looking for something to bring home to me like an offering lodges emotion firmly in my throat. The little things he does for me...they've built up into this powerful need for him. To make him happy. To know him. To be part of his life.

I shake it off, because I need to know why he brought me up here. "Danny, it's beautiful out here. But I'm guessing you didn't come here for the second time in one day just because you wanted to show it to me."

"I *did* want to show it to you. This is where I'd bring Ruthie when we were kids, when I had to get her away from the house. No one would ever come here to bother us."

No one except the children who apparently came here to make out, I think but don't say.

He squeezes me closer, "But no." Another glance. "I wonder if Big Mike even has a daughter."

"Excuse me?" I ask, completely thrown. I'd figured this was about the woman across the way. I definitely didn't foresee it might have something to do with Big Mike's status as a parent. "We saw her."

"We saw a little girl. We never saw the two of them together. What if he stole the hamster from her or bought it so he has an excuse to wander around the building?"

"What brought this on?"

He unfurls his arm from me and rubs his hands over his face, wincing a little, so apparently the left one isn't all-the-way better. "I sound crazy, don't I?"

"I have my own crazy to share with you, so let's start with yours. Why do you think Big Mike pretended to have a child and stole a little girl's hamster?"

His mouth lifts at the corners. "When you put it that way, I definitely sound nuts. He was following me this morning, I'm pretty sure of it. And when I brought the hamster home yesterday, he invited us over for dinner. He was being really weird about it. He also said he couldn't help going over the top for his little girl because he's a single dad, but there was no kid stuff in his apartment. My sister's place is like a minefield of toys."

"Okay, that's sort of weird," I acknowledge. "But not necessarily damning. What about the woman who lives across the alley."

"You've seen her again?" he asks, rubbing his jaw.

I tell him about what happened earlier and the weird vibe it gave me. Saying it, I feel a little ridiculous, too, especially since I'm the one who escalated things, but there was something strange about the interaction. Sinister, even.

"I'll find out who owns or rents both units," he says with a nod when I'm finished.

"You believe me?" I ask, relieved.

He takes my hands, sending a sizzle through me, and looks into my eyes with that intense gaze of his. "This is all my fault."

"While it's novel to hear a man admit to that, I'm going to have to ask what you mean. Do you think this has something to do with your job?"

He nods, glances around us as if he's worried Big Mike and his hamster might have sidled up behind a tree, and then says, "Big Mike implied he's interested in me because we live in Burke's apartment, like maybe he's working for the Burkes."

A gasp escapes me. I know all about the Burkes, given my sister's about to marry one of them. Burke's parents, Lucas the second and Melinda, are despicable people, so I wouldn't put it past them to try to intimidate us just because we're Burke's chosen family. But it feels like a lot of effort for them to put in, especially since they don't have a particular reason to dislike Danny, as far as I know.

"It felt like he was trying to send me down the wrong path," Danny continues. "I think my boss caught on that I'm planning to quit. Big Mike's trying to pump me for information. That's why he's always being overly friendly, trying to get me to go to strip clubs, and—"

"Seriously? He asked you to the Treasure Club?"

"Seriously."

"Maybe you should have gone to get information from him," I say, mostly because it's funny to think of Danny sitting on a stool next to Big Mike.

He looks at me for a long moment, his eyes moving over my face as if he thinks it's worth remembering, then says, "I'm doing a bad job of showing I'm interested in you if you think I want someone else's boobs in my face."

Emotion scratches at my throat. I take his hand, weaving our fingers together. "I'm glad you don't. Will you tell me why you think they're following you? I know there's an NDA, but there must be—"

He squeezes my hand. "I don't care about that right now. My boss, Jarrod Travis, runs a huge web security company, Safe-T Net."

"I've heard of them," I say. "I get those pop-up ads."

He laughs humorlessly. "They make damn well sure everyone knows about them. He and my sister were...involved for a few months, about ten years ago now. She didn't know he was married. She thought she was pregnant, so she told him, and he insisted that she get an abortion because he'd never let a little slumming ruin his life. Turns out she wasn't pregnant, thank God. But she was upset he'd treated her that way, and she told me everything." He works his jaw, his eyes flinty and hard. "She was eighteen, and he was thirty-seven."

"Asshole," I say, squeezing his hand.

"Asshole," he agrees. "I decided I was going to teach him a lesson. I worked in web security, but I also did some unpaid work on the side. I like...testing systems. Finding their weaknesses. I'd send companies the information so they could make sure they were protected. They called me—"

"Robin Hood?" I interrupt, getting excited.

He laughs. "No. The Reaper."

"Wow, that's way cooler. So you fucked with Safe-T Net's system."

"I did," he says. "They were down for almost a week. Then I posted about what I'd done online so everyone would know what a joke Jarrod was. What I did was illegal, obviously. Jarrod said he was going to press charges at first, and my little sister had to watch me be walked away in handcuffs."

"Shit."

"Shit," he repeats, his mouth in a flat line. "Shane wasn't a lawyer back then, obviously, so I had to go with a public defender. Nice guy, but he was overworked and in over his head. He wasn't going to do shit for me, especially not against Jarrod's lawyers. I was looking at five to ten years in jail. Millions of dollars in fines."

I feel like my mouth's going to drop open like some cartoon character's. I've learned that Danny is a thoughtful, introspective, cinnamon roll of a man, but all this time, he's secretly been a badass too. He's so complicated, and every new layer I uncover makes him more appealing to me. "What'd you do?"

"Jarrod offered me a deal," he says tightly. "To work for him and help fix the safety flaws so I could pay off my debt. I'm paid what they pay their other techs, but I have to reimburse them $35,000 a year for fifteen years in restitution. That comes out of my salary, but if I leave, I need to pay it out of my pocket. I also had to agree not to work anywhere else in web security for fifteen years. I wouldn't have taken the deal," he adds, his jaw working again. "I would have risked it. But Ruthie begged me not to leave her alone. The only reason I was in that mess was because I hadn't listened to her when she'd asked me to stand down, so I couldn't say no. It's been ten years, so I've got five left."

"So he took away the main way you can earn money because he wants you to stay."

"He *needs* me to stay," he says, "but it also gives him satisfaction to know that I fucking hate him, and I have to contribute to his success. There's nothing he loves better. I work remotely, but he makes me meet with him four times a year, just so he can look me in the face and tell me what to do. The next time is coming up this week. Thursday. And I already feel the rage pounding in my gut. It's like he's daring me to do something—to punch him or..." He sighs and runs a hand over his hair. "That's why I've spent so much time working on the game. It has nothing to do with web security, so it's an out. If it does well, I can pay him off in a lump sum. I can be done with him."

He still won't be able to do what he likes doing, what he does best, but he won't be trapped anymore. I've only been trapped by my physical limitations for a couple of weeks, and it already has me convinced that every paranoid theory I've ever had has merit. What would it be like to be trapped for ten years? Fifteen?

"Do the guys all know?" I ask, shocked. His hand is still wrapped around mine, and he turns it over and traces my palm.

"They know the general story. It's why Burke invited me to live with him. I'd been staying with my parents, because Ruthie was still there, but neither of us wanted to stay after..."

I lift my fingers to his face and trace the scar. His pupils dilate as he watches me, his face serious, and then I tip my head up and kiss where my fingers just traced. "You're nothing like I thought you'd be."

"Basic?"

"Of course you seek out comfortable things. No one ever gave you the chance to be comfortable or safe. You've given all your safety up for other people."

"I want *you* to be safe," he says, serious again. "I think—"

I lift a finger to his lips, like silencing someone in a library. He's about to tell me that I should leave the apartment, and I'm going to refuse, of course, and then we'll have to have an argument about it. It's going to happen, inevitably, but I don't want it to happen right now.

I trace his lips with my finger while he watches me, his eyes dark as coal and as deep as the center of the earth—molten inside, because there's always heat between us, banked or burning. Then I lean in and kiss him, softly this time, my way of showing him that I see him now—all of him—and I very much like what I see. He kisses me back the same way—gently, like he's worried I'm going to break, which simply won't do. So I take his lower lip between my teeth and nip him. The groan I get in return feels like a reward I didn't know I needed. Leaning in, he weaves his hand through my hair and pulls me closer, kissing me hard now, like he knows I'm not going to break —or if I do, it'll be because we broke each other.

I pull back and say a truth that's been growing inside of me, a truth that doesn't much care how fast it's been, or that my life has been turned upside down and topsy turvy. "I think I'm in serious danger of falling for you."

"Good," he says. There's a spark of humor in his eyes—and plenty of heat. "Does this mean I get to touch you again, or does the Wednesday Rule still hold?"

"Dear God, Danny," I say. "This is no time to be a gentleman."

Chapter Nineteen

Danny

Every thought in my head has been obliterated. Every thought except that I want her. I want her *now*. Each day, it's been building—this molten need, and now I'm more need than man. My brain certainly isn't firing the way it should be, because I should be panicked, I should be pissed, I should be scraping over every inch of the apartment to see if Mike or the mystery woman planted a bug to watch me. To watch *us*. I should be hiding Mira somewhere she'll be safe from their notice. But the only thing I can think about is Mira, and how she just told me she's in danger of falling for me. I'd told myself not to hope for it, but I did, of course. And now that she's opened the door, I never want it closed. I'm hungry for the slope of her neck, the press of her breasts against her shirt, and the way she quaked when she came on the elevator. I'd like her to quake that way around my cock—I'd like to feel her fall apart with my name on her lips, so we could help put each other back together.

It's been so long, so miserably fucking long. And even longer since going through the motions of sex was anything but the expression of a physical need.

I want her right here, tucked into the trees with the scent of autumn all around us, the red and gold and green and the mountains that have always calmed me.

This is no time to be a gentleman.

I lift her up on my lap, feeling only a slight twinge in my wrist, careful not to jar her cast. She gives a little breathy sigh that I breathe in because I want her sighs. I want her exhalations. I want everything she's willing to offer me.

"You're beautiful," I say, tracing my fingers along her hairline and tucking some stray hair behind her ear. The way she leans into my touch makes me glow inside, because for some reason she trusts me. "I wanted to bring you up here to see the leaves because this is a special place to me, somewhere I've always gone to remind myself that even though there are terrible things in this world, there's also great beauty. There's *wonder*. But I don't need to go up here to remind myself of that anymore. All I need to do is look at you. When I look at you, I feel like everything's going to be okay, even if I don't know how."

She swears under her breath, and I'd laugh if she weren't on my lap, if her lips weren't tipped up to me, her legs spread around my waist, bringing the part of her I want to claim so close to me. We've barely even touched, and we're both still in our winter coats, but I'm hard for her. I'm so hard I feel like I might actually lose all my blood to my dick and die if I can't lose myself inside her.

"You have a way with words," she says, rocking against me. "I used to think quiet people didn't have much to say."

"Sometimes we have too much to say, and that's why we're quiet." I lean down and kiss her forehead, then her cheek, then slowly move my mouth down to hers, learning the feel of her face beneath my lips. I'd like to learn every part of her with my mouth, my hands, my dick. I'd like to know her body like I'm getting to know her mind.

It starts as a soft kiss, a learning kiss, but I'm too fired up for that to last. She feels incredible against me—as if all my life I've been searching for the one person who was meant to fit with me, and I've finally found her. Our mouths part, our tongues dance. My hand lifts to her hair and gathers it, bringing her in closer, and she writhes in my lap, driving that deep, thumping need in my dick.

Take, take, take, it tells me. But I don't want to take with her. Or at least I don't want to take what I don't first give. Her arms grab that back of the bench, providing her with better leverage as she grinds against me, a little breathy moan escaping her. I swallow it, claiming that too, my hands leaving her hair so they can tuck under her coat, her sweater, and find the warm soft flesh there. It's not enough. It can't be. Not until I'm buried inside of her, not until her taste has filled my mouth—and even then I know it won't be.

I deepen the kiss, my hands palming her back and dipping beneath the band of her skirt to grab the perfect curve of her ass and guide her as she moves against me. Then I break the kiss so I can look her in the eyes.

"I need to be inside of you. I need to feel you clench around me. I need it like I've never needed anything."

Her mouth opens slightly, and I capture her bottom lip in my mouth.

"Don't be all talk, Danny," she says when I release it. "I can't abide a man who's all talk."

I squeeze her ass. She's still moving against me, and I'm so hard I'm in danger of embarrassing myself.

A burst of conscience compels me to say, "We probably shouldn't—"

"I'm pretty sure we're not the only people who have come here for that reason. The bench is covered with initials of other people who could."

"Kids who went here to make out," I say. "Not fuck."

The word seems to unleash something in her, and she moves harder against my dick, setting that need to boiling. "Well, we have better ideas."

It's all the invitation I need, until I remember there's a crucial problem with this plan...

"I don't have any protection," I say, my jaw flexing, because I'm on the cusp of losing control entirely. *So long. So long.*

"I'm on birth control, and I got tested after Byron and I broke up. For obvious reasons. You said it's been more than a few months for you?" She lifts her eyebrows, and I can tell she's wanted to ask me this. She's always so eager for information about people, collecting it like she's saving it up for winter. I like that about her, too, even if I've only ever been like that with different kinds of information.

"Almost two years," I say.

"Really?"

"Yes, that's something a man remembers."

Her eyes glimmer. "Is it weird that I think that's hot? It's like you've been saving yourself for me."

I almost laugh, but my laughter has been dried up the by the heat boiling inside of me. Insisting that I *do* something about it. "It's to my benefit, so why would I care if it's weird?"

"We don't need a condom. I want to ride you on this bench, Danny."

I swear, then say, "It wouldn't be good if we got caught."

"If anyone gets close, we'll know. The leaves will crackle. It's like nature's warning system for letting people have some fun."

I do some mental calculations. The trees still have plenty of leaves on them, enough to cover us from sight from the road, and no one is likely to see us. It's a risk, but not a huge one. I've come up here hundreds of times, and only on a few occasions has anyone else been here.

"It's cold out here," I make myself say. "I don't want you to be uncomfortable."

"We'll keep our coats and my leg warmers on, and if I notice I'm cold, you're not doing your job right."

My mouth is dry. Every bit of my existence—of who I am and who I've been, who I will be—is living in my dick. "You *did* promise that if you were riding me, I'd know."

"You've been thinking about that, have you?" she asks in a husky voice, giving a little rock of her body, because apparently she hasn't driven me crazy enough for her satisfaction.

"I haven't been able to stop thinking about it."

"Is it what you imagine when you touch yourself?" she asks. Her cheeks are pink, her eyes bright, and she's like a brilliant star, fallen to earth. One I've been lucky enough to find and collect, but part of me wonders if I'll ever be able to keep her. Or if she'll burn me up to ash. My dick is impartial to my potential future suffering. It knows what it wants and won't waver.

"That," I say, lifting up the bottom of her skirt. I know I should tell her we should wait, but in the back of my mind I'm aware that it would be a long wait. I need to search the apartment for bugs. The car. It would be hours. It's selfish, but I can't delay that long.

She helps me, shifting so she can get her skirt up and her panties down. I kiss the side of her face.

"I think of that, and the way you felt," I continue, "clenching around my fingers in the dark, the feeling of touching you, of tasting you, when I couldn't see anything—when the only thing I could focus on was you and how you felt and how I could *make* you feel. I fucking love that elevator. I want to build it a shrine and worship it."

She laughs, but it becomes husky and deep as I touch her, running my fingers over the soft, trimmed curls to find where she's wet for me. This view—of Mira on my lap with her skirt shoved up, her coat still on, her hair a mess from my hands—is the best view I've seen in my whole life. But I can think of one better.

"I'm going to set you down on the leaves," I tell her.

"But I want to ride you," she says, nearly pouting about it. And I can't remember the last time a woman's ever pouted because I haven't given her my dick fast enough.

"Mira, it's been so long…I'm probably going to come the instant I'm inside you. I need you to come too. I won't accept anything less."

"Oh, I'm going to come," she says, reaching down for the button of my pants, then the zipper. It feels like an impossible, blessed relief, because my dick has been digging into them for hours, it feels like. "Can't you feel how wet I am?"

Her hands wraps around me through my boxer briefs, tracing my dick through the fabric.

"I can do better." I pick her up, earning a delighted squeal, and set her down carefully in the leaves. "I want you to come twice. Once for my mouth, and once for my dick." More. But twice is the bare minimum I'll accept from myself.

I shove my underwear down, and wrap a hand around my dick, giving it a pass with my palm, because she looks so goddamn delicious lying in that bed of leaves, surrounded by red and gold and green, and waiting for me to put my mouth on her. It reminds me of when she was lying on that bed last week, covered by nothing but a towel. My mind kept telling me how easy it would be to pull it off. To ask for the right to make her feel good.

"*This* is what I've been imagining," she says, watching me, her pupils dilated. You with your hand around your dick. Thinking about me and making yourself come."

"I'd prefer to give you other things to imagine."

She's up an incline, so I kneel farther down the slope, the leaves crackling around us, and bend to her. I push her underwear down further, past her knees, and prop her legs up on my shoulders, careful with her cast. Her skirt is hiked up at her waist. "Is this okay?" I ask, looking up at her from between her legs.

"Better than okay." She runs a hand through my hair and grips. "You're doing the gentleman thing again."

"Would a gentleman do this?" I ask, then I do what I've been wanting to do since even before the elevator. Since, let's be honest, the first time I met her and heard her smart mouth, saw her curvy ass and twinkling eyes, her *everything*. I kiss my way up her inner thigh, and then I put my mouth to where she is, indeed, very wet for me.

I start out slow, learning her with my tongue and my lips, feeling what makes her moan and what makes her squirm. Listening to the sounds she makes and the little movements that show when she likes something or is neutral toward it. Adapting my motions to give her what makes her feel best. I'm in no hurry, because I would honestly prefer for this moment to stretch out forever.

"Don't be a tease, Danny," she moans, lifting her hips to me, and I'm smiling as I circle her clit with my tongue then take it into my mouth, sucking and flicking. I lift my fingers up, because I need to feel her again like this. I've dreamed of it. I've thought of it every single night as I went to bed alone and needy, my mind full of Mira. My whole body shakes with anticipation and need as I start fucking her with one finger, two, my mouth still working her, and she's making a sound deep in her throat, her hips lifting to me. I know she's going to come, and I do everything I can to absorb the moment. To save it for later.

When she whispers my name, the word strangled, I feel a moment of incredible satisfaction, of joy. Her body trembles beneath me, and she makes a sound I'm certain I'll never forget, her body going rigid and then limp. I kiss her clit one last time, then the flesh just above her legs.

"How'd you learn to do that?" she asks, her eyes wide as I lower her legs to get a better look at her. "That was..."

I don't say anything yet. I can't. I lift her into my arms and carry her back to the bench, sitting and helping her straddle me, my straining dick captured between us.

I swallow, trying to regain composure. "Sometimes I fall down a rabbit hole, I guess you could say. When I was younger, I decided I was going to learn how to pleasure a woman. So I did my research."

"With women?" she asks. Maybe I'm imagining it, maybe I only want it to be there, but I think there's a hint of jealousy.

"Sometimes," I admit. "Sometimes by reading."

"And watching porn," she says with a laugh, her eyes twinkling. She seems delighted by this, by *me*.

"Certain types. Most of it isn't very informative."

"Look at you, searching for informative porn. Why am I not surprised?" She rocks against me, her wet core an unendurable tease.

"I need you to take my dick now," I say, my voice sounding like someone else's.

A gasp escapes her lips, and she grips the back of the bench again, lifting. I guide her with my hands on her hips, my whole being concentrated on the movement and the knowledge that her sweet slickness is about to grip my cock and end the torture. Then she's lowering onto me, and the pleasure of feeling her all around me is all-consuming. Almost immediately I feel a tingling at my lower back, but I think of horrible things—of Big Mike and climate change and the likely disastrous state of Mira's computer security— to keep from coming too soon. She takes hold of the back of the bench for leverage again and tips her head back as she rides me hard, grinding into me each time she comes down. I lean forward to kiss the soft slope of skin, to bite it, to mark her as mine, my hands gripping her hips as if they're afraid someone will take her away. Or this moment will dissipate into mist and reveal itself as one of my dreams.

I dip my head to keep kissing along her collar bone, then use one hand to push down her sweater, her bra, so I can get my mouth on her nipple. The little sound of pleasure that issues from the back of her throat stokes the fire in my chest. I thrust up harder, but I'm maddened by the need to get closer to her, to feel her fully pressed against me. Then my gaze hits the huge tree beside our bench.

There are no branches around the trunk. I don't think, I just stand up and lift Mira, still buried inside of her.

"Danny?" she says, her voice breathy, her good leg wrapping around my waist as I carry her. The movement changes the angle, and I lift her and sink her back down, needing the friction, needing the feeling of her from every possible angle, every possible way.

"I want to fuck you against that tree."

"Yes, *please*."

I press her back into it, and stroke in deep, one hand braced against the bark, the other supporting her, and it feels so fucking good it quakes through me. There's a slight twinge from my wrist, but I could give a shit about my wrist, or about anything other than the sensations roiling through us. I kiss her neck, her face. I want to kiss all of her. I know I don't have much time left. I've put off the inevitable as much as I can. I'm going to come inside of her—and that thought drives me wild too, enough that I feel the tingling at the bottom of my spine. I grit my teeth and pause, because I'm not done. I haven't done my job fully, and I refuse, I refuse, to come before she does too.

Then I feel her clenching around me, hear her sharp inhale, followed by "*Danny*." And I decide the sound of this woman saying my name like that, when she's coming, is my favorite sound in the world. I thrust in once more, and I come so hard I'm surprised my eyes don't roll back in my head—that the world doesn't pause and take notice.

She kisses my neck and grips her hand in my hair. I know it's time to let go. To leave this place where my cock would very much like to stay, but I can't move yet. I need one more moment. I need...

There's the telltale scratch of leaves, but I don't even process it —my attention is on Mira.

"Oh shit," I hear someone say, every protective impulse in my body firing off, because we're not alone out here, and I'm still inside her. Then, words I'd hoped never to hear again, "You're under arrest."

Chapter Twenty

Mira

"Do you mind if I ask why you were out there, Officer?" I ask as Officer Dunkins, an apple dumpling of a man with red cheeks and wispy orange hair on his head, leads us to his squad car. Danny's still carrying me, because of my ankle, but at least the good officer turned his back to us at the tree so we could make ourselves decent.

He clears his throat. "Ah, I was driving around on my lunch break to get a look-see at the leaves, and I needed to take a leak."

"I'm starting to think the hex is real," I mutter to Danny in an undertone. "I mean, really, what are the odds?"

"Hex, huh?" Dunkins says. Really, the man has preternaturally good hearing when he wants to. "You been messing around with that pentagram stuff?" He shakes his head in a classic *kids these days* pose, as if he hasn't noticed we're both past thirty.

"No pentagrams for us, sir," I say. "Someone else put the hex on me."

"It was a punk kid, wasn't it?" he asks. "Damn kids, messing with forces they don't understand."

I glance at Danny. His jaw is set, and he looks like his face was carved out of stone, but I know his mind is probably whirring. I take a second to feel really sorry for myself, because *goddamn*, the most pleasurable moments of a person's life should *not* be bookended by getting arrested. Then again, maybe the most pleasurable moments of anyone's life are when they're doing things that could potentially get them arrested.

Danny's been pretty quiet, but suddenly he asks, "Weren't you also guilty of indecent exposure?" His dark gaze on the trees instead of Dunkins.

It's a good point, but Dunkins's brow furrows. "Two wrongs don't make a right, son. Those trees have seen enough today to turn them scarlet. Me too."

I'm tempted to point out that the leaves change every year, and if it's because of people having sex in the woods, then *a lot* of people are having sex in the woods. I keep my mouth shut.

We trek along in silence for a while before we reach the side of the road. Officer Dunkins gestures to his squad car, parked behind Danny's Outback, as if he's our host and we're lucky enough to have been invited to a party. "Come on in. Don't mind the smell none, I have lactose intolerance, but I can't help myself. Those pumpkin spice lattes get me every time."

Part of me wants to laugh hysterically, although it occurs to me that Danny should try to bond with him over their mutual love of basic lattes. Maybe then we can get out of here without asking our friends to bail us out of an indecent exposure charge.

Danny still has on his stoic look, though, and it only falters slightly when Dunkins opens his car door and a waft of stench emerges.

Dunkins rolls a little on his feet, like he's mildly self-conscious about his car smelling like microwaved roadkill. "Not a long ride down to the station," he says. "Sorry, but the back windows don't roll down. Security risk, you know."

"Definitely hexed," I repeat. I'm glad Byron's hair got fried. I hope it feels as dry as it looks. I hope it falls out in clumps and grows in grey. I hope his vocal cords wither, so he sounds like an old rooster. No one with such a crappy personality should have such a honeyed voice.

Danny lowers me onto the backseat, gives my shoulder a squeeze that radiates through me, then straightens up.

"Can I get her crutches, Officer? They're in my car."

"Don't try any funny business," Dunkins says, doing that foot roll thing again. "I've seen your license plate, now. Wouldn't be a hard thing to get you stopped and sorted."

Danny gives him an incredulous look. "You think I'd leave my girlfriend in your car so I can make a break for it?"

"I've seen stranger things, son," he says. "Why, the stories I could tell you would make your hair curl…"

A weird feeling unfurls in me as I watch them. I can't tell whether I'm freaked out or pleased that Danny called me that. *My girlfriend*. He said it so easily, without hesitation. Danny's like that, though—when he decides on something, he's resolute. Thorough.

Just like the way he thoroughly made me come on that bed of leaves…and against that tree…and in that elevator.

I'm both freaked out *and* pleased that he called me that, I decide. I….

Danny gets the crutches and lays them across the floor at my feet. Then he climbs in next to me, his nose twitching. With a deep sigh, he closes the door. Our thighs are pressed together, and I'm surprised by a sudden burst of happiness, which has no place in the back of a squad car that smells like death after my arrest for indecent exposure.

"I have an excellent sense of smell," he mutters for my ears only. Laughter bubbles out of me, but I'm able to disguise it as a cough by the time Dunkins gets in.

"You don't have a cold, do you?" Dunkins asks with concern. "I don't want to get sick."

"If I say yes, will you let us go with a warning?"

He laughs as if I made a joke, then says, "Buckle up, my friends, it's the law."

We do, and he starts the car, the radio blasting a Top 40 song written and sung by a teenage pop star.

Danny has a pained expression, as if the music and the smell are pushing him over the edge.

"So, tell us some of those stories, officer," I say. "You'll be saving me the money for a perm."

He laughs and starts chattering away happily as he weaves his way down the mountain. He's not as good of a driver as Danny, and it feels like I'm in the back of a Mario cart car being directed by a toddler jamming the keys on a controller. Danny doesn't say a word, but he lowers his big hand to my leg, and the feeling of it there grounds me.

If I was hoping befriending Dunkins would get him to go easy on us, I was wrong, because twenty minutes later, he parks in a space behind the station. As soon as I get my crutches sorted, he leads us inside, chipper as could fucking be, and says, "Now, let's get you booked, my friends. Don't worry. Might be we'll let you go with a warning, but we've been trying to crack down on this sort of thing. Not great metrics for tourism if we have people fornicating everywhere, left, right, and center. Did you know they've already taken to calling Asheville the city of sin?"

"Cesspool of sin," I correct.

"Quite right, quite right," Dunkins says. "You know, we've got some people here that take pride in that distinction, can you imagine?"

I have a bumper sticker on my car saying that very thing, but it doesn't seem prudent to tell him so.

"I'd like to call my lawyer," Danny says.

Dunkins rests a hand on his belly, frowning. "Always with the lawyers. What have you done wrong that you got yourself a stand-by lawyer, son?"

"He's my best friend," he says.

Dunkins whistles. "You see him enough that he's your best friend?"

As Danny patiently explains that he and Shane have known each other since childhood, and he is not, in fact, a serial wrongdoer or woods fornicator, I look around. There's a bunch of cubicles, and the whole place smells like stale coffee, which is a big improvement on Dunkins's squad car. Uniformed cops are sitting at their desks, most of them looking bored. One of them is openly playing Minesweeper, which is impressive because I wasn't aware computers were programmed with it anymore.

"Can I use the bathroom?" I ask.

Dunkins shifts his gaze to me, and his cheeks turn a brighter shade of red.

"Oh, of course. You'll need to clean up. Very important. Yes, my—"

"Where is it?" I ask, to put Danny out of his misery. He looks like he'd like to burrow into the floor and disappear.

I half expect Dunkins to insist on escorting me, or to say he'll only send me in if I consent to handcuffs, but he settles for giving me instructions. I use the bathroom, then stare at myself in the mirror for a moment. My eye makeup is smudged, and there's a leaf in my hair. Laughter gushes out of me as I clean up—laughter with an edge of hysteria because, honestly, we've gotten ourselves into quite the situation.

It's when I'm leaving that I see him.

Big Mike, clear as day, wearing a blue polo shirt with a popped collar and khaki pants. I'd know that ruddy complexion anywhere. He's not looking at me, so I follow his gaze to a cubicle across the way, where Dunkins is sitting in a desk chair, Danny seated across from him. Big Mike mutters something under his breath, then slips into an office. What the...

If he were under arrest for hamster napping or making financial deals with small children, he wouldn't be allowed to wander around the station, would he? Then again, I'm a public fornicator, and I was allowed to use the restroom...

I make my way toward the cubicle, my mind a mess.

"Take a seat, take a seat," Dunkins says as I near the desk. He nods to the empty chair next to Danny's. I lower into it, watching him. Wondering about Big Mike.

There's a cup of coffee sitting on the cubicle desk, and I fight a cringe as Dunkins lifts it up for a sip. It's got be cold and stale, but he doesn't so much as flinch.

Someone needs to get this guy a good pumpkin spice latte, but I hope to Jesus they'll ask for oat milk.

Nodding at the phone, Dunkins says, "Go ahead. Make that call, son."

Danny doesn't hesitate, and he's clearly got a much better memory than I do, because he dials his friend's number from memory.

My gaze wanders back to the door I saw Big Mike slip into, but there's no sign of him.

I hear Danny murmuring to Shane. He doesn't tell him what happened, probably because that would be the same as admitting to it, and he spends enough time with a lawyer to know better. Dunkins is looking at his screen, and he clicks through to something and then straightens in his seat as if he downed a gallon of milk and it just caught up with his digestive system. The second after he reads whatever it is, he minimizes the window.

Danny returns the phone to its cradle. "He's coming," he tells Dunkins.

"No need, no need," Dunkins says, leaping up from his chair with more oomph than I thought him capable of. "Chief says I can let you go with a warning." He waves a finger at us, and adds, "No more fornicating outside. You might think only the trees see you, but the man upstairs knows. And so do I." He taps his fingers to his eyes, accidentally touches his eyeball and flinches as he shifts the fingers to point at us.

Danny's brow furrows, because this is quite the turnaround. My mind jumps back to Big Mike, ducking into that room.

He did this. I'm not sure why, or how, but he's the reason why we're walking free.

Danny gets to his feet in a quick, fluid movement, not about to let this reprieve go. It's obvious he wants to get out of here as badly as I do. Or maybe more. He's been for-real arrested, so this must be bringing up memories for him.

I want to ask him more about that. I want to know everything about him, but I also want to get the hell out of here.

He helps me with my crutches, and not five minutes after we entered the pen, we're leaving through the door we used to enter it.

"Now, no more screwing around, kids," Dunkins says. "But you have yourselves a blessed holiday. You can tell everyone at the Thanksgiving table that you're grateful for law and order."

"Will do," Danny says, "and we'll say we're grateful for *you*, Officer Dunkins." Although I know he's being sarcastic, Dunkins grins as if he's just saved the world from a couple of delinquents. He shuts the door after us, so any thought of him driving us back to our car flies out the window.

Danny puts his arms around me. "I am so fucking sorry," he says in a whisper that finds my ear.

As if it's his fault.

As if I didn't twist his arm to take me out there in the leaves, with the view of the mountains spread out before us like a buffet.

"Do I smell?" he mutters. "I don't know if it's my paranoia kicking in, or what, but I think I smell like that car. I'm worried I'm always going to smell like that car."

Laughter rumbles through me. "You don't. But let's put a plastic bag over my boot and take a shower when we get back. A long one. There's something I have to tell you first though."

Big Mike, slipping into that room.

Big Mike, at the station but not in uniform.

"Come around to the front of the building," he says, giving me a squeeze. "There's a bench we can sit on across the street while we wait for Shane."

We make our way there, slowly, and even though it's afternoon by now, it's not much warmer than it was this morning. The fall is deepening, getting ready to give way to winter. Maybe that's a good thing: winter isn't the kind of season that lends itself to hexes. I'd like to think it doesn't, at least.

When we're settled on the creaky wooden bench, Danny leans my crutches up against one side. After he texts Shane an update, he puts his arm around me again. I let myself settle into him, then lean into his ear. I need to tell him about Big Mike, but what comes out first is, "You called me your girlfriend."

He edges away slightly so he can look at me. "I didn't want Dunkers to think you were—"

I give his arm a shove. "A prostitute? Why would he think I'm a prostitute? Why not you?"

His lips tip up. "You think someone would pay to fuck me?"

Yes. I think if women knew what he could do, they'd be lining up outside of the apartment. Truthfully, they'd probably do it just for his almost smiles and the little offerings he leaves out on the kitchen island. For his notes and his company and his ability to cook recipes exactly as they're intended to be made and served. For his secret badassery. For a few hours with the real Danny, the one he doesn't let everyone see. I settle for nodding.

"I consider that a compliment," he says. "And no, not a prostitute. I wanted him to know that I care about you. I was hoping he'd go easy on us."

I puff out air. "Not Dunkins."

"He definitely didn't go easy on the lactose."

I'm surprised into laughter, but the memory of Big Mike

intrudes. I squeeze Danny's hand. "Danny, Big Mike was in the station. And I don't think he got arrested for hamster-napping. He ducked into one of the offices after he saw us."

His eyes widen, and I can see him putting together the pieces that have started to form a picture in my mind. If Big Mike wasn't there because he was under arrest, then he must work for the department or be affiliated with it in some way. That's also the only way he'd have the power to get us sprung. And he'd only ask for our release if he didn't want us to see him in the building, because...

"He's an undercover cop." Danny rubs a hand across his jaw. "On the upside, this means he probably didn't steal that kid's gerbil."

"Do you think he's been trying to buddy up to you because he wants insider information on the Burkes?"

He stares at the building. "Maybe. But Burke's told them everything he knows. Why would I know something he doesn't?"

"Corroboration?" I ask, even though what he's saying makes sense.

"I think it's something else," he adds, his tone dark.

He's thinking about something in particular. I can tell because of the way he's tapping his bottom lip with his fingers, something he does often when he's deep in thought.

"What is it, Danny?"

His gaze shifts to me. For a second, I just bask in him. Because he looks unreasonably gorgeous with the low sun playing in his hair, illuminating his dark, long-lashed eyes, the edge of his jaw, his unruly hair. "You have to get out of the apartment. It's not safe."

Well, shit. Here's that argument I knew was coming.

Chapter Twenty-One

Danny

"That's not happening."

"Mira," I say, trying not to sound frustrated. I knew she was going to say no. It's not in her to stand down. It's one of the things I like about her, though that list is getting so long, it could give Santa's Naughty List a run for its money. I even like the things I was sure would drive me batshit crazy—like the way that SAD lamp illuminates her face, even though she's started blinking it off the second I enter the room, or how she always gets up at least three hours after me, her hair rumpled and pillow creases on her face. Each time I see her like that, my fingers want to trace them. I'm clearly not well. "There's something you don't know."

"That's obvious from your reaction," she says, opening her eyes wider. "Care to enlighten me?"

No, but there's no point in hiding it, probably. She already knows more than almost anyone else, other than Ruthie and Shane. I glance around, seeing no one suspicious. Well, there is a guy dressed as a clown, making balloon animals that have funhouse dimensions, and an elderly woman dressed up like Alice in Wonderland, but this is Asheville, after all. It's a regular day.

"I haven't stopped," I admit in an undertone. "I was supposed to stop acting as The Reaper. It was in my agreement with Safe-T Net," I remind her. "Fifteen years. No official web security work. No unofficial poking around as The Reaper." I swallow. "I don't use that name anymore. I do it as Bo Peep, which sounds much less manly, but I've still been testing systems for their weaknesses and sending along the information."

"*Danny*," she says. It's not a condemnation, but she looks... scared, and I'm the asshole who scared her. If Ruthie knew, she'd be scared too. Especially if she found out that Big Mike the undercover detective has been hanging out one floor below us, with a hard-on for chatting us up every chance he gets.

"If Jarrod finds out..." Mira continues, trailing off.

"It wouldn't be good," I admit. I flex my jaw, thinking about that prick Jarrod in his nice suits. I'm a good four inches taller, and whenever I go to a meeting with him, he makes damn sure I'm sitting and he's standing so he doesn't have to look up at me.

I couldn't let him keep me from helping people, from doing what I love. I couldn't give him that victory when he's already taken so much. When he's the first in a line of assholes who've hurt my little sister—the one who set the precedent, if you will.

It's felt damn good going behind his back, helping other businesses so they don't need to shell out for his shitty company's services. Admittedly, it's a whole lot less shitty than it used to be, because they have me—and I'll always have to live with the fact that I helped that sanctimonious prick. I did it for Ruthie, because she insisted she couldn't bear it if I went to jail, especially if it was because of something I'd done for her. I did it because she would have been left with no one to take care of her except for our parents.

But I'll admit that I also didn't want to go to jail.

No one wants to go to jail. I may like my life to follow a predictable routine, one that stops me from feeling everything is spinning out of control, but that doesn't mean I want to experience life only in single-size helpings. The way I'm drawn to Mira—who feels like life itself, like fire wrapped in flesh, like a revelation that dawns on me every time I see her—is proof of that.

Mira squeezes my hand, and I make a note to myself to get her some gloves. I haven't seen any sitting around the apartment, and her hands are cold. I layer my other hand over hers, trying to give her my heat.

"What are we going to do?" she asks.

The way she says it, so easily, as if it's a given we'll be dealing with this together, warms something inside of me. I wasn't totally honest with her earlier. While I did tell Dunkins that she was my girlfriend because I was hoping he'd lay off, I also did it because I wanted to say the word, to let it flow out of my mouth and enter the world. Like a wish I was freeing. Like a balloon flying out of a child's hand—although this wish will hopefully not strangle a marine animal.

Maybe I'm a sentimental fool, an idiot, no good with women, but I'd like to be a 'we' with her. It's felt like we were one over the past couple of weeks. Spending time with her is more sustaining to me than food. Than water. Than work. And being inside of her, claiming her...it felt right in a deep, aching way. I know, in a way that guarantees I'm a sentimental fool, that she was right. I *was* waiting for her. If she were to leave—

The void would feel like a gaping black hole, the quiet, deafening.

But I don't want her to stay, or to help me, if she's going to get pulled into trouble on my account. I've knowingly done something that could get me into deep shit. She doesn't have to get caught up in that. She shouldn't.

And if the woman across the way really is watching us, then there are two people who have me on their radar. Two people who could hurt Mira. If Big Mike's a cop, interested in me because of the Burkes or maybe because I'm Bo Peep, then who the fuck is the woman across the street?"

Her lips firm. "You can stop looking at me like that because I'm not going anywhere. Not happening."

My heart beats faster, because I want her to stay...even if it's the last thing she should do. "What about the blonde woman?"

"What about her? We still haven't established which one of us is actually the weirdo pervert. I've used those binoculars you let me borrow *very* liberally. Most of the time she's just knitting."

"What color yarn?"

She gives me a weird look. "White, I think."

Bo Peep. Sheep. It's a stretch, but it could be a message. I say as much, and her lips firm.

"You said there was only a folding chair and desk in there. Is that still true?"

"Yes."

"You were right. It is weird." Another puzzle to be solved. I have to find out who rents or owns that unit. "Did Big Mike notice you noticing him at the station?"

"I don't think so," she says, her brow furrowed. "He ducked into that office pretty quickly. If he knew he'd been seen, it seems like he would have handled it differently."

She's right, which is a relief. I can try dealing with him differently now that I know. Maybe I'll have to make an invitation of my own.

"Your friend," Mira says, and I stir, glancing in front of us. Shane is striding up the green in big steps, a smirk on his face as he takes us in on the bench. It's Saturday, a day off, but I'm not surprised to see him in his suit, as if he just headed over from the office. As always, he seems to notice everything—my hand covering hers, the way we're sitting close together.

I lift Mira up, then help her with her crutches. We're standing by the time Shane reaches us.

"They sprung you?" he asks. "Do I even want to know what you were doing? I figured it might have something to do with that peroxide guy."

Knowing Mira, I'm not surprised when she says, "Indecent exposure, but there's something else we need to talk to you about. In private. While you drive us back to Danny's car." She pauses a second before adding, "Please."

He gives me an 'are you serious about this' look, and I nod, because yes, it's a serious situation, and yes, I *am* serious about her.

"Okay," he says, nodding slowly. "I'll need to make some calls if I'm not going back in today."

He does that as we walk back to his car. Once we're inside and on our way up to the mountain spot, which he knows as well as I do, I tell him everything. When I get to the part about working under the name Bo Peep, he squeezes the wheel hard. I don't have to ask whether he's pissed. I know he is. He's mad that I didn't tell him—and madder that I did something stupid that could get me into the kind of trouble he might not be able to pull me back from. We'll be talking about that later, I'm sure, and not in front of Mira. Then I tell him about Big Mike's weird behavior and how Mira saw him at the station. I also tell him about the mystery woman in the apartment across the way.

"You were watching her with binoculars?" Shane asks, glancing at Mira in the rearview mirror.

"Binoculars aren't illegal," she insists.

"Depends on what you're watching," he says with an almost smile.

"I didn't see anything fun, just an empty apartment with a folding chair and table. She's always by the table, sometimes knitting, sometimes not. We figured that could be a sign. The wool. Bo Peep."

He takes that in, nods, then gives me a sidelong glance after he takes a turn in the road. "Seems to me you're mixed up in some shit, my friend. We've got to search that apartment."

I nod, grateful he's taking this seriously. "I figured as much. We can get Leonard and Burke to help us."

"I'll call in the P.I. I work with—Deacon Montgomery. Burke knows the guy. He'll have a better idea of what to look for."

I know Mira will glare at me for saying this next part, but I go ahead and say it anyway. "We need to get Mira out."

"Excuse me?" she squawks from the backseat. "I already told you I'm not going anywhere."

To my surprise, Shane shakes his head. "No, man. You've got an undercover cop watching you. You can't change your routine just after you were brought into the station. He'll know he's been made. We have to find out what he wants, and make sure it's not you behind bars."

"I won't let anything happen to her," I say.

"Excuse me," Mira says, obviously pissed. "I'm here, and I have a right to have a say in this conversation and not be treated like furniture."

I turn in my seat and glance back at her. She looks like she wants to immolate me with the fire of a thousand suns. I'd let her. It's a stupid thought, but I'm having a stupid day—might as well be consistent. "Okay. I won't let anything happen to *you*."

"So don't," she says. "But it'll be within the framework of me staying in the apartment, because I'm not leaving."

She looks like she'd stomp her foot if we were standing...and if she had a foot to spare.

I'm tempted to remind her about what she said last night—if we're going to explore what's between us, one of us needs to move. Obviously, I'm not going anywhere if I'm at the center of this shit hurricane. The last thing I want is for Big Mike or the wool lady to pay a visit while Mira is alone in the apartment. That's un-fucking-acceptable, obviously.

But if I tell her that, she might say I'm the one who said I'd go. So I decide to shut my mouth, for now.

I look out the windshield. The glimmer of my car is just up ahead, so at least no one's stolen it. After parking behind it, Shane squints at it for a moment. "You think there's some kind of tracker on it? Could Dunkins have come looking for you?"

Mira surprises me by bursting out laughing. "No way," she says. "I'm pretty sure there would be no manufacturing that look of surprise."

Shane gives me another sidelong glance, his hand lifting to his chin. In my head, I can hear Ruthie telling me this is his ambulance chaser pose, the one he'll get put on billboards someday. She even came up with a slogan for him: *Got in an accident? Call Shane, he'll make it rain.*

"What the fuck happened out there, anyway?" he says, snapping me out of the memory.

"You already know more than I'd like you to," I mutter. "And I'm sure you can guess the rest. I agree that the officer was surprised. Besides, I don't know why they'd send him looking for us if Big Mike didn't want us to see him at the station."

Is Big Mike even his name?

Probably not, which means he chose to call himself Big Mike. It's a funny thought, and I find myself smiling, even though this is not a smiling situation.

Shane nods thoughtfully. "Yeah, but I'd still like to have Deacon take a look at the car and the apartment."

"Me too."

"And you need to fill the guys in. I agree that it's unlikely this has anything to do with the Burkes, but Big Mike referred to them by name."

"Does this mean we're having a party?" Mira asks, sounding much too happy about it.

"If you consider it a celebratory occasion that our friends are coming over to make sure we're not being spied on by Big Brother, sure," I say, opening my door so I can help her out.

"Oh, Danny," she says with a smile that lights something up inside of me. "If you know what you're doing, you can make anything a party."

She probably didn't mean for it to sound like a threat.

Chapter Twenty-Two

Danny

A couple of hours later, Mira and I are hanging out at the kitchen island while Shane's P.I. searches the apartment. He's already checked the car and declared it free of tracking devices, which is a relief for both me and whoever would have been given the tedious job of tracking me. Now, he's in my bedroom, where he's spent at least fifteen minutes, making me worry that someone has been watching or listening to all of the jerking off I've been doing since Mira moved in.

Shane had to return to the office briefly, but he's coming back with Burke and Leonard—and presumably Delia and Shauna. I don't know what Mira's said to her sister, but I've seen her bent over her phone, so I'm guessing she's said something.

Hopefully Delia and Shauna will leave the rest of their salt at home. I keep finding grains of it everywhere.

My mind flickers from the ever-present salt to what's on my computer screen. I've been doing searches on my laptop while Mira makes us drinks. Mostly, I've come up empty, but I've just found something interesting.

I glance at Mira, intent on giving her an update, but I'm riveted by what she's doing.

I love watching her make drinks. It's methodical, but there's artistry to it. A pinch of this, a dash of that. I watch her until she looks up, her brow furrowed as if she's a little annoyed with me for interrupting the process. I lift my hands. "I found something, but I don't want to freak you out."

"Not a propitious start," she says, shoving the cocktail stirrer aside. "But you *are* wearing your glasses, so I'm more inclined to listen to whatever you have to say." She swings over on her crutches, moving closer until her side is pressed against me, her scent cocooning me. I feel an instant unwinding of some of the stress that has held my shoulders rigid, and also a pounding sense of need. It wasn't enough earlier, not nearly. I want her naked and spread out on my bed. I want to spend all weekend, and possibly the rest of my life, alone with her so I can explore every last inch.

I look at her. Swallow. "The apartment across the way is unoccupied. It's going up for sale next spring."

"How do you know?" she asks, cocking her head.

"I'd rather not say."

Plausible deniability and all that.

Fear flashes through her eyes, before she says, "Could I have been spying on the real estate agent?"

"It's possible," I say, but I don't believe it. What real estate agent would stage an apartment with a folding chair and table? And why spend hours in the place if it's not going up until spring? Why would she, of all things, knit there?

"So that woman really is spying on us," Mira says flatly.

"I'm going to ask Deacon to look into it." I run a hand over her back, her hair, remembering the leaf that was tucked into it earlier, when we were hauled into the station. I knew I should pluck it out, but she looked beautiful in such an unearthly way with that leaf tucked into her hair—yellow and red and orange—almost like she was a fae creature.

It's a fanciful thought, but then again, my whole life I've been accused of being stuck in my head—of going in so far it's hard to pull myself out.

"Okay," she says with a nod.

"I still think you should leave," I say. "You can stay with Burke and Delia, or even—"

She reaches for my chin, turning it up to her. Fire pulses through me from her touch, as if it's yanking me up out of the ether and tethering me to this existence. Her eyes are resolute but warm. "I am *not* leaving."

"I'm the one who did this. I'm—"

Her hand tightens around my chin, sending that buzzing fire feeling all over my body. She needs to be safe, but at the same time, I feel impossibly grateful to have earned this woman's devotion.

"All you're guilty of is helping people," she insists. "Because you couldn't help yourself. Because you didn't want to give in to a bully with a shit-eating grin, an ego complex, bad taste in ties, and really, really off-color teeth."

"You looked him up," I say, smiling despite myself.

"Of course I did. I'm an incurable gossip. You should know that about me."

I lean up, my chin still captured in her hand, and kiss her. Then I do it again, because I can't get enough of her lips. Soft and slightly swollen, bold, like she is about everything.

She watches me for a moment, her eyes shining and vulnerable. "I don't know what I'm doing with you, Danny. I feel like I should be worried about it."

"I don't know what's going on in general," I say. "The world felt very predictable a couple of weeks ago, but now, I have no idea what's going to happen next. Yesterday, we agreed to host Thanksgiving dinner here. I hate Thanksgiving dinner."

"So do I," she says with a hint of a smile. She runs her fingers across my scar again. It feels like she's helping me reset a memory.

Which is why her next words send a jolt through me: "Maybe Josie's right and we need to reclaim it."

I hold her hand there. "At least you haven't started in about Christmas trees yet."

Her eyes light up. "I may not be a fan of Thanksgiving, but I love Christmas. I love it *hard*. This place is begging for a seven-foot tree. With glitter garland, obviously."

"Let's get through Thanksgiving first." But I like the bright glimmer in her eyes. I don't feel much excitement about Christmas, other than for Izzy, who is at an age where she talks about Santa Claus as if an old, bearded man is her close, personal friend, but I want to bask in Mira's excitement. If she's here for Christmas, and by God I want her to be, I have a feeling I'm going to be lugging an eight foot tree up those stairs. Because I want to give her more than she asks for.

"Why am I not surprised that you're a hardliner about not having a tree before Thanksgiving?" she asks.

"Why confuse people? You invite them over for Thanksgiving, and there's a tree out, they might think they've lost their minds. Just like we've probably lost ours." I lift my eyebrows. "You did just finish saying Josie might be right about something."

Her smile widens. "Except we're not paranoid. The woman across the street really has been watching us, and you were right about Big Mike. I doubt that little girl's his kid. An undercover cop wouldn't bring their real kid to work with them."

I bring her hand to my lips and kiss it. Her skin is soft and still a little cold against my lips. I already ordered those gloves for her. In three different bright designs, because if she gets to go overboard and buy a whole damn wardrobe of shirts for me, then I get to do the same. In twenty-four hours, they'll be here. I want to be around when they come so I can see her face.

"No, not unless it was Take Your Daughter to Work Day." I

scrunch my mouth to the side. "Do I actually need to hang out with that asshole to try to get information from him?"

"Probably," she says. She's trying to sound amused, but I see the worry in her face.

"If I'm in trouble, it's my own damn fault," I insist. "This doesn't have to involve you. You barely even knew I existed a month ago."

"I knew you existed," she says, "but I didn't know you were *you*. There's a big difference."

"Yes, you thought I was a nice guy," I say dryly. "The horror."

"You *are* a nice guy. A nice, complicated, super-intelligent, and perverted weirdo badass, and I am honored to be your—"

Girlfriend.

"Plaything."

"Just for now?" I ask.

"Let's see where things go. I'm still confused about all of this. About life. And crutches. And major holidays."

It's not the answer I want, but I can't begrudge her for stalling for time.

"Am I supposed to pretend we're only roommates around everyone else?" I ask. Because I'm a man who likes to have boundaries clearly established and explained.

Her lips twitch. "Don't you think that ship has sailed? I get that Shane's a lawyer, but I'm sure all the guys know about our arrest for indecent exposure by now."

She's wrong. Shane can keep secrets. But I don't feel inclined to correct her. I don't want to pretend she doesn't matter to me—I loathe pretending. I have to do enough of it every day. I have to pretend not to be overwhelmed by simple things, not to be annoyed when people ask inane questions or offer up conversation that is ninety percent nonsense. And, most of all, I have to pretend whenever I speak to that prick Jarrod.

"You're okay with me being confused?" Mira asks. "You seem like you want to know the answers about everything."

I run my hand over her hair again, needing the silky feel of it, as my mind works that one over. "You know, there's this book where people finally get the definitive answer to life, the universe, and everything."

"Do tell," she says. "That's not the kind of thing you should hold out on."

"It's forty-two."

"The number?" she asks, her lips tipping up as if she's amused just in anticipation of the joke.

"The number. So obviously the answer left them with more questions than ever. I think that's a pretty good allegory for life, don't you?"

"Okay, Reaper," she says, giving her head a shake. Probably a *Danny you're so strange* shake, but I don't mind. I don't think she does either. And hearing her call me that feels strangely grounding, like two sides of myself are finally being joined. "I'm going to finish those drinks. Should I make a drink for Deacon? Would that be weird?"

"Probably," I say. "He's on the job."

"Wouldn't it be weird if I didn't make one for him, though?" she asks, her gaze darting in the direction of the bedroom. "I don't want him to feel left out."

"I don't want him to stick around," I say in a lowered voice.

She rolls her eyes at me. "You're such a people hater. What's the word for that?"

"Misanthrope. And I'm not being a misanthrope." In response to her raised eyebrows, I amend, "I'm not being a misanthrope *now*. I was hoping for a little time alone with you before everyone else comes over. We got interrupted earlier."

"It was a rude awakening," she says, her lips lifting. "You know, there was a leaf in my hair at the station. The gentlemanly thing to do would have been to pluck it out for me."

"I liked the way it looked," I admit.

She leans down to me, her red lips against my ear, and I feel my cock stirring before she even speaks. "Like I just got fucked against a tree?" she whispers. Then she leans in and bites the lobe, making me instantly hard.

This woman will be the death of me, but it will be a good death, the kind of death Medieval poets would write songs about.

Still, I'd be a fool to forget that she's confused. She's been plucked out of her life for a month, or however long it takes her ankle to heal, and once it's restored to her, she might want nothing more to do with this apartment, or the misanthrope who's willingly imprisoned himself inside of it.

Chapter Twenty-Three

Mira

No bugs in the apartment, thank bejesus. I didn't like the thought of someone watching me hop around on one foot, spy on my neighbors, and touch myself while thinking about touching my roommate. I'm so relieved to hear the good detective's all-clear that I offer to make him a drink on the spot. I want to be alone with Danny, too, for obvious reasons—but I also don't.

Because...

I'm scared, and not just of the hex, or the robot woman across the way, or the detective downstairs who is possibly trying to put the guy I like behind bars. I'm scared of the way I feel about him. I'm scared that it might change once my life goes back to normal, and also that it *won't* change. I'm scared of what my new normal might look like at the end of all of this. I'm scared of the multitude of questions that might end with forty-two.

So I hand over the detective's Old Fashioned, and the three of us sit down in the living room to wait for the others—him on our favorite chair, and us on the couch. I know they're coming because Delia has been sending me stream-of-consciousness texts and requests to leave the apartment. She doesn't seem to know about our near arrest, so I guess Shane has more self-control than I do, but she knows there's an undercover cop watching us, and also that the unidentified creepy woman has been upgraded to probably creepy.

Turns out, Deacon Montgomery, who seemed fastidious and to the point when he came into the apartment, is quite the talker when he's on the sauce. He's now on his second drink, and the dry looks Danny keeps throwing my way are giving me quite the core work out as I struggle to keep from laughing.

"You know," Deacon says, rubbing a hand over his salt-and-pepper stubbled jaw. "I remember a case of a woman watching a guy like that, apartment across the alley, from my days on the force. No one took him seriously. They thought he was a nut."

"Yeah?" I ask, feeling Danny silently begging me not to ask follow-up questions. "What happened?"

"Killed him," Deacon says bluntly, leaning back in the chair and making himself comfortable, as if he weren't delivering alarming news. He shakes his nearly empty drink at us. "Mind you, he went over there to confront her. Drank something she made for him, which was a big mistake. Don't do that. If he'd waited for *her* to try to break in, he could have had a chance."

"I'd prefer if there were no breaking in of any kind," Danny says hoarsely. "I've already asked my buddies to put a padlock in."

"You have?" I mouth, looking at him.

He nods, and a feeling of warmth comes over me, one that's only partially caused by the *very good* whiskey in our drinks.

Danny is serious about protecting me.

Deacon nods his head four times. I know when someone's had too much to drink, and I'm starting to think I made his second pour too strong. "That Burke's a good kid. Shame about those parents of his."

"You don't think this woman who's watching us could have anything to do with them, huh?" I ask, thinking about what Big Mike said to Danny about the Burkes.

He laughs and runs his fingers across his beard. "No. The kid hasn't lived here in weeks. She's interested in you." He points at Danny, then shifts the finger to me. "Or *you*."

Well, shit. I hadn't really considered that possibility.

Danny gets up and paces toward the window, then pulls the blinds down. I know without asking that we'll keep them that way until we've figured out who she is and how to make her go away.

"I've never seen her before moving here," I object. "She's a complete stranger to me."

"I've never seen her," Danny adds as he settles back next to me, "but her description doesn't sound familiar to me either."

"You don't need to notice someone for them to notice you," Deacon says, then shrugs a shoulder. "Just ask that dead guy."

"You're kind of freaking me out," I say.

"Maybe I'm trying to." Deacon sets his drink on a side table and hunches forward, putting his elbows on his knees. "Better to be careful than pay the price. That's what I always tell clients. Someone acts irrationally, you should expect them to continue acting irrationally."

A knock lands on the door, and I flinch, because the buzzer didn't go off. Doesn't the buzzer always go off? Then again, if it's someone who wants to kills us, they probably wouldn't bother knocking.

Danny gets up and looks through the spyglass, then opens the door. I can see Burke and Delia, Leonard and Shauna, and Shane in that slick suit of his.

"Sorry," Burke says. "I realize I should have used the buzzer, but I still have my key."

"Come in," Danny tells him, glancing back at me. "Mira's been making drinks for everyone, and she's threatened to order pizza."

"I don't make empty threats," I say as I grab my crutches and slowly get vertical. Delia comes running toward me as if I'm a character on the Oregon Trail who just contracted cholera and has thirty seconds to live.

"I'm okay, I'm okay," I say, laughing as she wraps her arms around me.

I don't mind much, to be honest. Usually I don't like to be fussed over, but the day has rattled me. This talk of dead people and stalkers and undercover police officers.

"I'm worried about the hex," she says in an undertone as if she doesn't want the others to hear her. She looks small and innocent, and I have a flash of memory of her as a kid. I wasn't much older, but I always felt older. Like I needed to protect her from the world.

"You shouldn't be," I say, even as I think, *me too*. "We did the whole salt thing. Evil couldn't survive such a thorough salting."

"You think I'm being silly."

"No. Never."

She pulls away, smiling. "Now, I know you're lying."

"But I *am* okay," I insist. "Danny said we're putting another deadbolt in."

Leonard, who's still standing between us and the door, lifts up a bag, creating a loud metallic clang. "No time like the present, am I right?"

"Don't we have to run that by the building management?" I ask, glancing at Danny, who's still standing by the door, his hand wrapped around its width—almost like he's testing it to see what kind of barrier it would serve should someone choose to test it.

"Probably," he says firmly. "But we're not going to."

Leonard grins at him. "My man."

Then Burke, who just got done greeting Deacon, introduces him to the people he doesn't already know.

"What do you say we get this party started?" Leonard asks.

I turn to look at Danny, who's watching me. The way his lips are upturned at the corners tells me he already knows what I'm going to say. "I told you it was going to be a party."

———

THE GUYS ARE ALL GATHERED AROUND THE DOOR, DEACON included, as if changing a lock is an operation that requires four adult males rather than one. It looks like Leonard's the one doing the actual work, but Burke, Shane, and Deacon are watching and messing around with different parts. It's like another one of those dick-measuring contests—you either laugh or you cry, there's no in-between.

Danny's standing a bit to the side, watching the charade but not participating in it. Although he's messing with the ridge of his jeans pocket, I can tell his resources haven't been totally drained yet.

In a mimicry of their setup, Delia and Shauna are with me in the kitchen area, where I'm the one doing the work of making cocktails while they watch.

"You know, Deacon is kind of a silver fox," Shauna says contemplatively, watching the guys.

"Are you *interested* in him?" my sister asks with such shock and horror that I almost laugh. "I thought you and Leonard—"

"He's got to be in his seventies, Delia," Shauna says dryly. "I'm a very satisfied woman, but Leonard and I want to find someone for my grandmother. We think it might be fun for her if she has someone to..." She shrugs. "Date. Fornicate with. You know."

I burst out laughing at her use of "fornicate," because I will never be able to hear that word without thinking about Officer Dunkins. Never. I will hear it in forty years, and still be transported back to the back of his smelly car.

"What?" Shauna says. "Old people still fornicate. I'm not going to stop having sex just because I reach a certain age. Where's the fun in that?"

Delia shrugs, watching as I add different ingredients to my cocktail shaker. "You're right. I work with a lot of elderly people, and the ones who are happiest have active sex lives." She scrunches her nose. "Except for Mr. Kortya. I think he's had chlamydia four times. He keeps asking me to pick up his prescription."

"Exactly," Shauna says, waving a hand at her. "So..."

"So you want to get your nana laid," I say. "Got it. I don't know much about Deacon, but he's very chatty when he's on the sauce, and he enjoys telling dark stories."

"Well, that's two ticks in his column," she says, nodding. "What do you say we invite him to Thanksgiving dinner? See if we can make this thing happen? We're going to make an online dating profile for her too, but I figure our best bet is diversifying."

"Sure," I say, very free-wheeling about inviting people to this dinner. It occurs to me for the first time that I have no idea where we're going to put everyone and don't even remember who's been invited. We'll have to make a spreadsheet so we can be sure we have enough food for everyone and places to sit.

Danny will need to make it, obviously.

I'm putting another ingredient into the shaker, when Delia's face scrunches again. Then she brushes some hair away from my neck and gasps. "Is that a hickey?" she whisper-screams.

"Keep it down," I hiss, glancing at the door. They're all staring at what Leonard's doing as if it's the most interesting thing in the world, offering advice that he probably doesn't need. Well, all except for Danny. He meets my gaze—his eyes filled with that usual hint of humor, like he knows exactly what I'm thinking about. Probably he does.

Glancing back, I shrug. "I like him. And sure, we had a little fun in the woods, and a police officer *may* have arrested us for indecent exposure, and yeah, we *may* have been brought to the station...and that *may* be how we found out about Big Mike. This is all theoretical, of course."

"This story is much more interesting than we were led to believe," Shauna says with a grin.

Delia looks like she's about to ask me if we can have the double wedding she used to dream about when she was a kid, so I lift my hands and say, "I don't know what I'm doing." I fight the urge to look at him again. It's like I can feel his gaze pouring into me. It makes me itch to go over there, to touch him, to prove to myself that he's real.

I don't like it one bit.

I like it too much.

"I'm in over my head," I admit.

Delia takes my hand. Looking into my eyes, she says, "You've always avoided getting involved with men you might actually fall for."

"You think I did that on purpose?" I ask with a snort. "I'm pretty sure I just have shit taste in men. Usually."

Because Danny's a good guy. Maybe the best guy.

"She's right," Shauna says thoughtfully, messing with one of the bottles on the counter. "I used to date a man who was the human personification of the color beige. I didn't want to take risks. Maybe you didn't want to get involved with anyone who'd distract you."

"From what?" I ask with a laugh. "The slow march toward death?"

Delia frowns. "Dark. No, from the bar."

I tap on the kitchen island, uncomfortable. I don't want them to have a point. "Danny would hate the bar," I say finally, then let my gaze find him again. There's that amused tilt to his lips as he listens to Deacon give a treatise on a locks. My heart starts pounding. I don't want him to hate the thing I've poured so much of myself into. But he will, won't he?

"The bar is the only thing you've ever let yourself have," Delia says quietly, "but it's not the only thing you deserve."

My heart pounds harder. Look at my little sister, being all wise.

"What do you say we get drunk?" I ask, loud enough for the group at the door to hear me.

"I'll have another," Deacon says from his supervisory spot at the door.

I glance at Shauna, who shrugs and says in an undertone, "It's another point in his favor. My grandmother's a lush. Don't tell Leonard I said so, because he'd take it as a challenge, but she could probably drink him under the table."

Chapter Twenty-Four

Danny

The lock has been changed. The apartment is safe...or as safe as it's going to get for the time being. I'm outside on the balcony, alone with my beer. It's cold out here, but a crisp kind of cold—the sort that keeps you awake. Mira's inside, holding court, making drinks and handing out pizza and getting our friends to sign up to make Thanksgiving dishes. I made a spreadsheet for that before I came out here so I could breathe again. After the day we had, there are too many people, even though they're all people I care about, with the exception of Deacon—although I suppose I do care about him if he's going to help keep me out of a prison cell. Still. It's too loud. Too much.

Shane left a few hours ago, saying he had to get back to the office, for which Leonard gave him plenty of crap.

I didn't. I'm worried about Shane, to be honest. Something's not right. He's been on edge lately, more touchy than usual about work.

A voice in my head says I have to get my shit together and get back in there. It insists Mira might say she wants me, but she'd prefer to be with someone who can sit up until one in the morning with a roomful of people without needing time alone to recharge. A feeling of loneliness, of being *other* pounds into me, and I lower my elbows to my knees, my head to my hands.

It's also been hitting me that I'll have to give up what I've been doing.

I won't be able to keep acting as Bo Peep, which is as much a part of my identity as being a shut-in who has a problem with eighty percent of people. Maybe ninety.

I should have already stopped, and then we wouldn't be stuck in this fucking mess of my own making.

Still, it's a depressing thought.

I hear the door open, and something inside of me lifts, because I'm expecting Mira with a smart word and maybe a drink. But it's Burke. He closes the door behind him and sits in the chair next to mine, a glass of straight whiskey in his hand that clearly didn't get the Mira treatment.

"You're upset with me," I say, feeling pretty damn upset with myself. "I was supposed to take care of Mira, and I fucked up."

"No," he says. "I'm glad you're into her. I...It's like one of my brothers getting with Delia's sister. She and I have been hoping this would happen. Leonard too."

I feel choked up. *Brother*. He's always taken care of me like I'm his little brother, even though he's only a year older than me. He let me live here in this apartment, and insisted on getting me braces when I was in college because he knew I was self-conscious about my teeth being crooked. I let him. I feel guilty for that, and for living here for all these years, for taking so much. I've given him things too, but if there's some celestial book chronicling giving and taking, I know that I'm in his debt to an amount that can never be repaid. I'm aware of it. I'm grateful for it. I'm fucking sorry for it too.

"I should have told you," I say, my throat raw and sore. "I should have told you that I was still doing Black Hat shit. I should have told all of you. I just..."

"You couldn't stop," he says, rotating the glass of whiskey. "It's part of who you are. It's not a bad part of you, Danny. Some people wield it like a weapon, but I know you were just trying to help people."

"We need to keep Mira safe. She shouldn't be here."

"You're in love with her," he says. "You fit together, man."

Even though I balked at the same accusation from Ruthie this morning, I'm not balking now, however ridiculous it may be for me to have fallen in love with a woman in two weeks. As for his second statement...

There's no denying I want it to be true—and there's nothing so easy to believe in as the things you want to be true. My mother is the best example of that. She's spent half her life living at the bottom of a bottle and ignoring my sister and me, the other half raging at us, and now that she's found Jesus, she calls up Ruthie every few months asking to see Izzy.

I've never gotten a call.

Half the time, Ruthie says she's slurring her words in her voice messages, so even if she loves Jesus, it's obvious she loves the bottle more. I haven't told Ruthie not to answer, but I don't think she does. She cares more about that scar on my forehead than I do—and I don't blame her. You don't take chances with the people who are precious to you, or at least you shouldn't.

"Yeah...yeah, I think I am," I finally say. "Mira has to be safe. I want her out of here."

He shrugs. "You heard what Deacon said. It's not a good time to change the routine. Besides, I'm having a new security system put in tomorrow."

Tomorrow's a Sunday, but I don't doubt him. He's a determined man with deep pockets.

"Thanks. But I still think it would be better if she stayed somewhere else. Somewhere..."

He gives me a wry look. "She's not going anywhere. I think you know that. Delia wouldn't leave either."

He's right, dammit.

"I've fucked everything up," I say, and return my head to my hands, needing pressure on my temples.

He doesn't try to touch me. He just says, "We all feel like that at times, bud, but that doesn't mean it's true. If you're worried about fucking things up—all it means is that you have things in your life you care enough about that you don't want to lose."

The door opens again. This time it's Leonard who comes through. I hear Mira's laugh through the open doorway before he shuts the sliding glass door behind him, sealing her off. There's a moment of panic, as if she'll be separated from me forever, but logic chases it away. She's not going anywhere, although it would be better if she did leave.

"You reading him the riot act?" he asks with a grin. "Because ain't no way I want to miss that."

"I don't think he needs it," Burke says, his gaze still on me. I can feel it more than see it.

"You tell him what I said to you earlier about Josie?" Leonard asks as he lowers into the third chair. He whistles. "Goddamn, it's colder than a witch's titties out here."

My gaze swerves to him. "You want to talk about *Josie*?"

"Damn straight, I do."

"What about?" I'm tired of Josie's prognostications and hexes. It seems to me we'd all be better off if she'd stop running her mouth. Still, I'm interested despite myself.

"She said you'd already met your soulmate and made a bad impression on her," Leonard points out.

"Yes," I say dryly. "I haven't forgotten."

"You assumed she was talking about Phoebe."

"Daphne," I correct.

He waves a hand as if it was an honest mistake. "Daphne. But what if she was talking about Mira?"

I'll be damned if he hasn't raised an interesting point—one that's been itching at the back of my head but refusing to make itself known. But I don't want him to know I find it interesting. Leonard requires no encouragement.

"Mira didn't seem too into you before she moved in here," he continues. "But she's been looking at you all night like you're the last cookie in the pack. Something's going on between you two, not that I'm surprised."

"You're not?" I ask because *I'm* fucking surprised. I ask myself why, and the answer's something like this—if she hadn't been stuck in that elevator and now this apartment with me, I doubt she would ever have given me a second look.

"No, she's a tiger. That's exactly what a man like you needs."

I feel a little crestfallen, maybe because I already know she's exactly what I need, but I'm still unclear on whether I'm exactly what she needs.

Boring. Basic. It's hard to explain how deeply those words have been burned into my brain. Maybe it's because I've always had the sense that I didn't belong, and Daphne was only telling me what I already knew, deep down. That even when I try to fit in I do it wrong.

Burke seems to know what I'm thinking, because he says, "And you're exactly what she needs."

"An anchor?" I ask, lifting my eyebrows.

"A lighthouse."

Leonard snaps his fingers. "What he said."

Chapter Twenty-Five

Mira

Everyone just left, and Danny and I are standing next to each other in front of the closed door. I feel an aching awareness of him. I realize I'm still holding the doorknob, like maybe I'm about to run—or hobble—out, so I release it and turn toward him. I feel overwhelmed by the day, and by the feelings that are beating through me like a second heart. I've been wanting to talk everything through with him, to touch him, but now I don't know what to do. "Is this awkward? It feels awkward."

"I'm sorry I had to go outside for a while. It was..."

"Too much," I blurt. "It was the Charades, wasn't it? I knew you wouldn't be into Charades, but I'll be honest, I really wanted to see how Deacon would do. You know, because of all the undercover work he probably wasn't supposed to tell us about."

He takes my hand—and it's trembling, fucking trembling—and squeezes it. "It wasn't the Charades so much as it was me. It's like I have this meter, and when it's full...it's full. Once that happens, I need to be by myself for a while, somewhere quiet." His lips lift slightly. "But the Charades didn't help."

Laughter bursts from me, even though I know he's telling me

something important. Something I need to listen to. "He was really good, though. You should have heard this voice he did for Macaulay Culkin."

"I wouldn't call myself an expert at party games, but I thought you weren't supposed to talk during Charades," he says, his hand still holding mine.

"He was *very* drunk." My whole body is aware of where we're touching, even though it's such a small surface area compared to the skin of my body, which is aching. Full of need for him to touch and stroke it.

"I'm sorry about all of this, Mira," he says, squeezing my hand. "I don't like having you in the middle of this situation."

"Deacon said it would be a bad idea to change things up now."

"He also thinks Charades is a talking game. I'm not convinced he's the best judge."

"You know he's right about this," I say, frustrated. "Besides, Big Mike's an undercover cop, Danny. He's not a danger to me."

His hand starts moving against mine, tracing shapes into it, like he's never content just to touch something—he needs to know it. It's wonderful and also distracting.

"Maybe not," he admits. "He might only be a danger to that hamster. But—"

"I'm staying."

"Why do you want to stay, Mira?" He looks into my face as he says it, his eyes probing and deep-seeing and so very fucking beautiful. He took his glasses off earlier, after doing his research on the apartment across the way.

Why didn't I see it instantly, how beautiful his eyes are? They're deep and dark and surrounded by long lashes, and they probably contain all the answers to...everything.

"Forty-two," I tell him, finally answering his question.

"You want to stay because of the number forty-two?" he asks, still rubbing my hand.

"None of us understand the answer to life, the universe, and everything. Maybe I don't understand why I have to stay, but I do. Can you accept that?"

"Do I have a choice?" he asks. He surprises me by lifting my hand to his chest, pressing it there. I can feel the thumping of his heart, the way it's speeding up.

Because you're touching him.

I can still feel his mouth between my legs, my back pressed up against the tree while he thrust in deep. The thought makes my knees weak.

"No, you don't," I say, my voice coming out breathy and strange.

"Do you still feel awkward?"

"Fuck, yes. Don't you?"

"No, not anymore. Not when I'm just with you. Maybe we can take a ride in the elevator," he adds, his heart thump-thumping against my hand. "We seem to do okay in there."

"We do okay in here, too," I say. Because it's true. I don't feel awkward because of him, but because of my head, which is frightened by the knowledge that these deep feelings have grown so quickly, so wildly, in such a short time.

I need to stay here. I need him to be inside of me. I need him to show me that he wasn't walking away from me earlier. That he was just taking a break, making sure he met his needs without kicking us all out.

He smells of the outdoors—of fallen leaves and cool winds and cider. I want to wrap myself up in that smell. In him.

I want to run away.

"Would it help if I put on those glasses?" he asks with a smirk. Then nods back at the kitchen island.

"It wouldn't hurt." My heart is beating as fast as his now. I can feel it in my chest. "I like basking in my own brilliance."

"Is that why you got me all these shirts?" he asks, pulling at the one he has on today. "So you can bask in your brilliance?" I think he's amused, but I can't tell, not totally.

"I like seeing you in them, sure," I admit. "Maybe I'll get you more. Forty-two of them. Just in case." What I don't add is that it adds a little something to my morning. Or that I run bets with myself about which one it will be. I swallow, then add, "I'd like looking at you without any of them on too."

I haven't gotten to see him naked, which seems absurd.

"Okay," he says, and before I can process what he's doing, he grabs the bottom of the shirt and pulls it off over his head, letting it fall onto the floor.

I suck in a breath. He's beautiful, lean and muscular from all of his outdoor recreation. I want to touch him, to trace my lips over him from head to toe. I want to mark him the way he marked me before I send him off to Daphne on Wednesday. I want her to know that someone else sees what she didn't—that this man is one of a kind.

My hand trembles as I reach out to touch him, pressing my palm flat against his warm skin. "Yes," I say, my voice quiet to my ears. "I think I like this look best of all. I could get used to it."

"Good," he says, sliding his hand over mine. I feel the crutch digging into my armpit, and I have a feeling of *I'm not enough.* He looks like some sort of Roman God, with his dark eyes, curling hair, and that torso of lean, layered muscle, and here I am, dragging myself around on crutches because I couldn't climb the stairs right. Danny's so smart and good and handsome, and I'm so scared that I'll lose him because I don't know how to keep him. How to have this and also my other life.

I let my hand trail up, learning more of him, claiming him with my hand. He leans down and kisses my forehead, the same way he did the other night, and then finds my mouth. He kisses me softly but passionately, like he'd prefer for the kiss to go on forever—and I let the crutches fall and wrap my arms around his neck, needing to feel his warm chest against me and make him warm with mine. He laughs deep in his throat, then wraps his hand through my hair and deepens the kiss, owning it and me and making me desperate for more—for closer, for deeper. He picks me up, and carries me to the kitchen island, sets me down on top of it. Then he reaches for the hem of my shirt.

"I need to see you too," he says. "I need to see all of you."

"Yes," I say, because that's the only word left in my head. *Yes, yes, yes.* My blood is beating hotter as he pulls it off over my head. His head instantly bows to the lace of my bra, and he runs his mouth over it reverently, as if he's worshiping me. His hands reach around and loosen it, and then his mouth is where I need it, sending sparks of pleasure down to my toes and pooling between my legs, and I need him, I need *this...*

I need to think it's all going to work out okay—that the sky will clear, and there'll be a double rainbow instead of another storm.

There are tears in my eyes and a moan in my throat, and I can't remember when I last felt so many things at once. It's as if I've been saving them up all year, or maybe all my life.

His mouth moves from my nipple to my throat, kissing me in a spot that makes my need flare. I shift, my legs opening as if he just pressed a button—and nearly knock over the drinks I made us.

"Oh," I say in surprise. "I made you a drink before they left."

"I'm otherwise occupied," he says, dropping another kiss on my neck and then grazing it with his teeth. He's standing in between my legs, his bare chest spot lit by the kitchen lights. One of his big hands is wrapped around my hip. He looks delicious. Positively edible.

"But I think this is the one, Danny."

He stops what he's doing—and I instantly regret it, but I also don't, because no one's ever looked at me this way. So enraptured, as if what I'm about to say is more interesting than anything that's ever been said in the world.

"The better-than-beer drink?" he asks, lifting his eyebrows. My eyes dart to that tiny scar, and there's a tightening in my throat.

I clear my throat. "*Yes.*"

"Even if it is, I'm not convinced it's worth the interruption," he says, leaning in to suck my nipple again. I bury my hand in his thick hair, and when he pulls away, his lips slightly shiny, I can only kiss them. He's smiling when I edge back.

"You must really want me to try this, huh?"

Yes. No.

I do want him to try it, but I also want his hands and teeth on me. His cock inside of me.

I'm going to miss him, when I'm back at the bar.

I'm going to miss these nights together.

When I get home, he'll be asleep. When I wake up, he'll be working.

My throat suddenly feels like it has a grapefruit lodged inside it, choking me, but I clear it and grab the glass closest to my spread legs. "Bottoms up."

He takes the glass with the hand that was on my face, his other hand still wrapped around my hip like he doesn't want to let me go. "Moment of truth."

It feels like one. I realize I'm holding my breath as he lifts the glass to his lips. My entire being is focused on it, on his reaction, on my ability to make this man a drink that will impress him. I feel pathetic for caring about that, for wanting to impress him, but there it is...

I care what he thinks.

I value his judgement.

I value him.

I...

He watches me over the rim of the glass and takes a sip.

I'm frozen. Everything in me is waiting, hushed in anticipation, like a child who gets up too early on Christmas morning.

He gives me a slow smile I feel down to my marrow. "What's in it?"

"It's a twist on an Old Fashioned. I figured we could make it a whole thing for our new menu—twists on classics. Sometimes people don't realize the classics are popular for a reason."

"It's good," he says, his hand caressing my hip, moving in little rhythmic circles that are making my desire for him into a pulsing, living thing. A kind of thing that has teeth. But I still need his answer. My nipples are cold, wet from his mouth, but *I still need his answer*.

"Better than beer?"

He pauses for a moment, and my heart nearly thumps out of my chest.

"What kind of beer?" he asks enigmatically. His fingers slide beneath the band of my skirt, warm and seeking, and I want him. And I want his answer.

"Your favorite beer. The pinnacle of beer. The Mona Lisa of beer."

"The Mona Lisa of beer, huh?" he asks with a wider smile. "You're assuming I see value in the Mona Lisa."

"Don't toy with me."

"I enjoy toying with you." He lowers his head and nuzzles my tits, making me squeal. "I was hoping you might let me toy with you some more."

"*Danny.*"

Looking up at me, he grins. "Yes, Mira. It's better than Mona Lisa beer."

I squeeze him with my legs and wrap my hands in his hair. I kiss his mouth, his cheek, and his neck, laughing. "Victory!" I crow.

He grins at me, sliding his hand deeper into my skirt to cup my ass.

"Is it the best thing you've ever tasted?" I ask. "It is, isn't it? This is going to be the toast of our fall menu. I'm calling it the 'Moment of Truth.'"

"Not the better-than-Mona-Lisa-beer?" he asks, still smiling at me, his mouth only inches from mine. "Because that has a certain ring to it."

"So? Is it the best thing you've ever tasted?"

His expression turns smoldering. I feel it everywhere. My lips, my racing heart, my exposed tits, between my legs. "No. *You're* the best thing I ever tasted."

My lips part, and I unintentionally squeeze him with my legs again—as if my body is saying, *yes*, him, *get your act together, idiot.* "Did you practice that line in the mirror?" I ask. "Because it was a pretty slick delivery."

His smile widens. "Sometimes even a man without any natural charm gets lucky."

"You have plenty of natural charm, but I don't mind if I'm the only one who notices. In fact, I'd prefer it that way."

"I need another taste," he says.

I know what he means—I see it in his eyes, hear it in his deep, husky voice—but I tap the drink forward with one hand. "Go for it."

"You drink it," he tells me, tugging at my skirt. "There are other things I'd like to do with my mouth."

I help him take my skirt and panties off, and he delivers on his promise. God help me, he does.

I'm still gasping from the biggest, loudest, most bone-shattering orgasm I've ever had when he stands up. I can't summon any words, so I attack the band of his pants with my hands, getting his button unfastened, lowering the zipper. He shoves them down, and then he's bare for me, completely bare, and I only have a second to appreciate the view—better than the mountains or the very best of the fall foliage, better than the Mona Lisa by far—before he steps forward. I help guide him with my hand, and then he's sinking in deep, right where I need him, and even though I just came so hard I nearly cried, I feel on the verge of it again. I feel the fluttering, the tugging, and the need—so hot and pounding and there. Right there.

He's all the way in, and I wrap my legs around him harder, wanting to keep him there.

"Oh. My. God," I say into his neck, right before I bite it, and he laughs as he strokes out and then slowly in again, his hand on my ass.

"You left...a hickey on my neck earlier." I tell him as he kisses my neck.

"Good."

"It's not...oh god—fair," I say.

He pulls his head back, even as he slams into me, making a guttural sound escape me. "You can mark me too," he says. "You want to show everyone I'm yours?"

When he angles his head, silently inviting me, my mouth decides for me, sucking and kissing and biting because I want him. And I want other people to know he's taken, that there's someone who lives in his heart. I don't know what it means or if it can work in the long term, but I know that much.

We come together, and he carries me to the bathroom, and, no shit, this man helps me take a bath.

————

"Danny, if this were a normal week, I'd be at work."

We're lying on the couch together, Danny's lying behind me with his arms around me, tracing those magical circles on my arms. We just watched an episode of *Bridgerton*, my choice, obviously, but he accepted it with good humor. We're both drinking a Moment of Truth. It's fucking delicious, if I do say so myself. I'm relaxed. I'm happy.

I don't want it to end.

He runs a hand over my hair, tucks it behind my ear. "I know."

"I'd be at work for another two hours."

"Yes, I've looked up the hours for your bar."

I look back at him, wanting to know what he's thinking, but his face is unreadable. "And?"

"You work late," he says flatly. "That's indisputable."

"Don't you think—"

He pulls me closer, speaks into my ear, his breath sending warm shivers through me. "I'm going to sell this game, Mira. Then I can finally quit my job."

"Are you going to do it in person?"

I can feel him smiling more than see it.

"Of course. I'd punch Jarrod in the jaw after I deliver my resignation, but I don't actually want to end up in jail."

I'm tempted to remind him that we don't know why Big Mike is interested in him or what the weird lady across the alleyway wants, and either or both of them could disrupt our plans—could disrupt *us* —but I know he remembers. Danny isn't the sort of man who forgets important things.

"When that happens, I can set my own hours," he adds.

"You like mornings," I object weakly, because I can *see* it— Danny and me, sharing a life together. Listening to our podcasts and making lunch. Driving up the mountain to see the leaves. Hanging out with our friends, even if that means he needs to spend part of the night out on the balcony.

He presses a kiss to my cheek, his lips warm and firm. "I like *you*. I'd like you to meet my sister."

I feel tears pressing against my eyes. They're happy tears. He thinks it can work. He's thought through possible solutions. He wants me to meet his sister, who is obviously the single most important person in his life. Maybe it's okay to hope. "Good. I can already tell we're going to have a lot to talk about."

He grins at me. "I can take it. I'm used to both of you giving me shit. Might as well do it together."

Ruthie's taste in glasses aside, I know I'm going to like her.

Still, I'm worried life will pull Danny and me apart. I'm worried the dream will end, and I'll be alone again, holding up the mountain I put on my own shoulders.

Chapter Twenty-Six

Danny

Ruthie responded to my invitation so quickly I'm convinced she would have shown up this morning whether I asked her to or not. If anything, I'm surprised she didn't swing by yesterday, while we were busy installing the new lock. I'm glad she didn't. Whenever possible, I'd prefer for my little sister not to worry about me.

Mira's asleep in my bed—and the sight of her in there, tucked up beneath my brown duvet fills my heart with joy. After we finished watching *Bridgerton* last night, I wasn't ready to let her go, even if it was only down the hall to her own bedroom. So I asked her to stay with me. She yawned and said, "I can't believe I'm saying this, but I don't think I can have another orgasm today. It might tear apart either me or the space time continuum."

"I wouldn't want to be responsible for something like that," I said. "But I was thinking we could just sleep in the same bed. I want to be close to you."

The second the words left my mouth, I was convinced I'd said something stupid; the kind of thing people aren't supposed to say— as if there's an international accord about what can and can't be said and everyone has access to the master document except for me. Then she smiled at me and said, "Look at you, saying the perfect thing."

I wasn't inclined to argue, especially since it sounded a lot like she was agreeing. Earlier, it had felt like she was going to run from me, even as she refused to leave the apartment, so I was inclined to take what I could get, for as long as I could get it.

I got to sleep enveloped by her scent, by the feeling of her soft skin against mine. Usually, I'm restless because it feels like something is wrong—the sheets, the heat level in the apartment, the work I was supposed to do but didn't. The ignored calls on my phone. Last night, I was restless because I wanted to absorb every bit of the night as it defied me by passing by.

I don't really want us to leave the apartment. It's stupid, but it feels like the spell will end if we do. It feels like Mira might wake up and realize that I'm not what she wants. At the same time, I don't want Ruthie coming here until we have a better idea of what's going on. So I text my sister back.

> Why don't we meet for brunch. 11:00, Corner Kitchen? Mira's used to her hours at the bar, so she sleeps late.

> Ah, to be able to sleep in again. God bless.

Her answer makes me smile as I get ready for the day, putting on the red checkered shirt from Mira's shopping spree.

Ruthie always bemoans the fact that Izzy's like me—an early riser. She's never once slept past seven, even though my sister encourages her to sleep in. I've brought Izzy on early morning bike rides before—I have a special seat for her—but I'd never bring her on the Blue Ridge Parkway. Too dangerous. I may be willing to risk my own life, but not hers.

I clean up the living room and make coffee. Then—because I'm buzzing inside, full of energy, I tuck back the curtain and look at the apartment across the way. It's empty again, no folding table, no folding chair, no woman, which sends a chill through me. Did she clear out because she noticed we'd closed the blinds? If so, what will she try next?

I text Deacon the news, such as it is.

I'm looking out the window again, seeing a whole lot of nothing, when Mira emerges from the bedroom on her crutches. Her hair is rumpled, and I smile at the memory of yesterday's leaf. Her lips part when she notices where I'm standing.

My smile falls. "It's empty."

She swings forward, and we lift the blinds and look at the same empty window.

"I don't like this," she says.

Neither do I, but I don't want her worrying, so I say, "This is good. Maybe she got scared off. Or hell, she really could have been with the realtors after all."

She doesn't seem convinced, but then again, it's not easy to be convincing when you don't believe a thing yourself. I relay the plans, and then we spend the rest of the morning drinking coffee and doing a crossword puzzle together.

It's probably a pretty basic thing to do.

It's fun. I feel a deep sense of contentment, like I'm exactly where I'm supposed to be, with exactly who I'm supposed to be with, doing exactly what I was meant to do. It's...nice.

I help Mira shower, which makes it take twice as long, because I want to trace and taste every last inch of her, and then we do exercises for her ankle before heading out the door. We park near the restaurant, and when we get out of the car, I see Ruthie and Izzy waiting outside. My heart lifts.

"That's them, isn't it?" Mira says softly as we walk closer. They still haven't seen us yet. Izzy is searching the crowded sidewalks, but she's looking in the wrong direction.

"How do you know?" I ask, surprised. People don't usually pick up on that. Ruthie and I have the same thick, dark hair, but otherwise we don't look much alike. She has bright blue eyes, and so does Izzy.

"I just know," she says with a shrug. "Don't you dare tell my sister or Shauna I said this, but I can feel it."

She's looking at me like she expects me to tease her, but I like the thought. Maybe it's one of life's Big Unknowns, how the bonds people feel for each other can be so big they're seen and noticed.

Then Ruthie finally turns and sees us, her face brightening. She bends to say something to Izzy, and my niece comes hurtling in our direction.

"Uncle Danny!" she says as I sweep her up into my arms and whirl her around. Her little face is pink from the cold and maybe also excitement.

I set Izzy down and turn toward Mira, who's watching us with a grin. "This is my niece, Izzy," I say. "Izzy, this is my girlfriend, Mira."

I'm repeating the word from yesterday because I like the way it sounds. Because I want Mira to know I mean it.

I might not know how our future will look, but I want us to have one. I think she wants that too—and that's more than half the battle.

"Oh," Izzy says with wide eyes. "Mom said we weren't supposed to act like we knew about that." She grins up at Mira. "You're pretty."

"Thanks," she says, smiling at her. "So are you."

"Even your cast is pretty," Izzy says. "I broke my arm falling from a slide when I was three. I don't remember it, but Mom got me a white cast. Can you believe it? All of the colors in the world and she got white. Can I sign yours? I can write my name the right way, except sometimes my y goes in the wrong direction."

"You can sign it any way you like," Mira says, then glances at me and grins. "You know, your uncle hasn't written anything on it yet, and he's had plenty of opportunities."

"Uncle Danny needs people to tell him what to do sometimes."

It takes children to truly bite through to the heart of something. It's true. I should have signed it. I've seen other people do it. Leonard. Delia. Burke. A message from Azalea is on there, too, plus a few other people whose names I don't know. I've noticed the messages and drawings. But it never occurred to me that Mira might want me to write something—and she's never asked. This is probably one of those situations where *I* was supposed to ask.

Ruthie comes up to us and nudges me with her shoulder in greeting. I put my arm around her and squeeze.

"I'm glad you're here," I say, meaning it. Then I introduce her to Mira, who balances on her crutches to shake hands. My sister, the shorter of the two of them by far, pulls her in for a hug that nearly knocks her over.

"I like you already," Ruthie says into her shoulder. "You've lived with Danny for two weeks without killing or even maiming him. It's got to be some kind of record."

"Burke lived with me for ten years," I put in as she pulls away from Mira. "The only person I've ever lived with who's tried to kill me is our mother, and we can both agree it was a pretty half-hearted effort."

If Mira's surprised that I'd joke about such a thing, it doesn't show. She's studying me, though, like I'm a nut and she's holding a pair of pliers.

Ruthie frowns at me, reminding me about little pitchers and big ears—a reminder I seem to need every five minutes when I'm with my niece. It's hard for me to sanitize things for Izzy. But I do want her to keep her innocence. To see the world through a kaleidoscope that makes even bad things beautiful.

"She didn't really try to kill you, did she, Uncle Danny?" Izzy asks, peering up at me with her fathomless eyes.

"No, honey," I say, lifting her up and hoisting her up on my shoulders. It earns me a tirade of giggles. Today, I barely feel any pain in my wrist, just a twinge that reminds me of Pumpkin. "She wasn't trying to kill me. But it's best not to throw around things that could hurt people—even if you're just trying to get their attention. Let's try and remember that."

Ruthie gives me a shrug-nod combo, as if to say it's a fairly good save but I probably shouldn't have made the mistake in the first place.

"Why does he drive you crazy?" Mira asks, amused, as we walk toward the restaurant, Izzy hanging onto my head as if she thinks there's a reality that exists in which I'd let her fall.

"He's so overprotective," Ruthie says with an eyeroll. "My parents couldn't care less who I dated, but he practically gave every guy I brought home a quiz. Short answer, not multiple choice."

"It's easier to cheat on multiple choice," I grumble as we make for the door.

"Who says I wanted a good boyfriend?"

The big brother in me wants to point out that it's not what she wanted that interested me—more like what she deserved, but then I'd just be proving her point, I suppose. And I appreciate that she's being so warm and friendly with Mira.

Mira snort-laughs. "We've all been there."

I think about the guy with the platinum hair. I think about her seeing him on Wednesday. I scowl as I tell Izzy to duck. Laughing, she grips my head and bows low over it so she can make it through the door.

We're directed to our table, and as we sit, Ruthie looks at Mira and says, "I hear we're all having Thanksgiving together. You know,

I thought it would take an act of God to get Danny to celebrate again."

"I prefer the term goddess," Mira corrects, making me grin. Look at me, grinning at the thought of doing anything other than hiking and drinking on Thanksgiving. I guess I never thought I'd see the day either.

"So noted," Ruthie replies with a grin.

"Watch, someone's going to throw the Cranberry sauce at me this time," I say. "Then it'll be another ten years before I celebrate."

"I thought you said we shouldn't throw anything at anyone, Uncle Danny?" Izzy asks, her lips pushed out.

"Exactly," I say. "You remember that if you feel the urge to toss the cranberry sauce. It's disgusting, but it won't be any less disgusting if it's in someone's hair."

My gaze darts to Mira, and I catch her smiling at me. I'd let someone throw cranberry sauce in my hair to earn another smile like that again. I'd let someone rub the whole can of it down to my roots. Let's hope it doesn't come to that, of course.

We order our food, and even though the restaurant is loud and there are dozens of smells at war with one another, I'm happy because I'm here with *them*. We talk about Thanksgiving, and Vanny, and True Colors. Ruthie doesn't know about the meeting with Daphne, and I'm grateful that Mira doesn't feel the need to bring it up. Because that's a whole additional conversation I'd rather not have with my sister. She may say I used to give her boyfriend's tests, but she's always done the same with the women in my life— only she's more subtle. I already know that Mira has passed what Daphne failed.

Then Ruthie glances at Mira over the rim of her juice glass and asks, "Danny says you run Glitterati? I've heard about it, obviously, but I haven't been there yet." She gives Izzy a fond glance, then says, "I hear it's frowned upon to take children into establishments that serve hard liquor. But one of these nights I'll get a sitter."

Mira's face lights up, as if the glow she always carries around just went up a few voltages, and I feel a glimmer of...

Well, it's almost panic.

I've been telling myself not to borrow trouble. But there's no denying that Mira loves her job. Based on what Burke has previously told me, she's usually there around the clock. If she still wants me to move out after all of this is over, we'll be seeing a lot less of each other.

I can and will change my schedule, but will she be willing to make adjustments too?

It's occurred to me that she'll probably want me to hang out at the bar with her, and doing so might be the only way I get to see her most nights.

Will I be able to?

I excuse myself to the bathroom, but on the way there I pass a private room. I hear a voice I recognize, a clinking of glasses. Something tugs at my brain, and I glance inside. The door is only an inch or two open, which is enough for me to see.

Shane's partners are in there, instantly recognizable from the framed photo they gave Shane upon making him partner. They're in suits, of course, as is their guest. He's a man who probably couldn't pick me out of a line up, but I'd know him anywhere.

They're having lunch with Lucas Burke Senior.

Chapter Twenty-Seven

Danny

Well, fuck, this surely isn't good.

Better than if Shane were with them, obviously, because his absence suggests he doesn't know what they're up to. Please God, let him not know. He told me something was up at work, and I'm guessing this is the *something* he's been sensing. His partners would know about his friendship with Burke—they'd also know that he served as Leonard's lawyer a couple of months back, when someone set him up for those burglaries he didn't commit. Someone likely being the man who's sitting in there chatting with them.

I maintain that I'm not someone they'd remember, but Shane, with his multiple-hundred-dollar suits, probably is. If they've decided to use his law firm, I suspect it's as yet another FU to the son who turned them in.

I tuck into the hallway next to the bathroom and shoot off a text to Shane.

> Your partners are having brunch with Lucas Burke at Corner Kitchen. Did you know about this?

> Not our Lucas Burke, obviously. The asshole one.

Fuck

Fuck

Fuck

I'm guessing you didn't know.

FUCK

I'm coming

Is that a good idea?

Don't care

I head back out to the dining room. Mira gives me a searching look. "What happened? Why do you look like that?"

I'm not sure what I look like, but it can't be good because Ruthie nods instantly. "Yes, something happened."

I glance around, but no one else is paying attention to us. Their focus is on their eggs and pancakes, and in one person's case, a salad they probably regret ordering.

"Shane's partners are in the private room," I say quietly. "They're meeting with Burke's father."

Ruthie narrows her gaze and sits back. "That ass—" Her gaze shifts to Izzy, —"jerk."

"Already said the bad part," I mutter. Then, louder, "He didn't know about it, but he's on his way here."

"Uncle Shane is coming?" Izzy asks with the excitement of a child who's innocent of all the multiple layers of bullshit and red tape that come with being an adult.

"He's not your uncle," Ruthie insists.

I glower at her.

She lifts her hands in a proclamation of innocence. "What? It's true. My friends don't go around asking her to call them uncle."

"Uncle Tank does," Izzy corrects her. "And Shane says I can

call him uncle too. I don't want to stop. I've only got one real uncle, Mom. Most people have at least a few and some aunts too."

"Fine," Ruthie mutters, even though it obviously costs her.

"You don't like Shane?" Mira asks. I'm guessing she knows as much and is more interested in Ruthie's reasons.

"They've always been like that," I say. "I can't remember them ever getting along. Even when Ruthie could barely talk. She used to pretend she was a dog and bite him."

"Danny," Ruthie growls. If she wanted to protest that she's never pretended to be a dog, she didn't pick a good way to do it.

I go ahead and point that out, and her response is to bare her teeth at me and snap. I grin, even if it feels like my stomach is full of snakes.

Burke. Shane. Lawyers.

"I don't think Mom and Uncle Shane like sharing Uncle Danny," Izzy says. "They always like to tell him what's best for him, but sometimes they don't agree."

"That's not it," Ruthie says quickly. "I'm fine with sharing him, obviously. And he's a grown man and can do what he likes. It's just...Shane is infuriatingly full of himself. I mean, you've seen the way he wears suits every day, even on the weekends."

"He works most weekends," I point out.

"Oh, and you don't think he'd wear them anyway?"

I shrug, because it's an old argument, and I don't particularly care why Shane enjoys wearing suits. I only know that I don't. If there's any practical use for a tie, I've yet to hear a good argument for it. I feel strangled enough by normal shirts, thank you very much.

"Mom, you're not being nice," Izzy says. "You always tell me people can wear whatever they like when I say someone has an ugly dress on. Or that Uncle Danny wears boring shirts."

"You think this one's boring?" I ask, raising my eyebrows at Mira.

"No, that's the best shirt I've ever seen you wear," Izzy says.

Mira's lips twitch. I'm fine with giving her the win.

The waiter comes by with our food, which no one but Izzy seems to care much about just now. My mind is busy with Shane and Lucas Burke Senior, and also with Glitterati, which looms like a circus funhouse in my mind. I've never been there, but I've seen the photos. They look loud in a way a photo shouldn't be able to.

Mira hasn't said this, but I know another of her worries is that I'm not going to like her bar—that I'm going to reject this thing that's a part of her. In all honesty, I'm concerned she's right. There are very few bars that I actually like, and most of them have outdoor seating and three different beers on tap. The bars I like have an unfortunate habit of closing down, probably because I'm one of a handful of people who actually seeks these qualities out and finds them desirable.

But the one thing all those other bars didn't have was her.

Wednesday.

I'm going Wednesday. When I get back from Glitterati, I expect she'll have a quiz for me—short answer, because karma bites back and hard—and I can only hope I pass.

That's what's going through my mind when Shane bursts in through the door, wearing a suit, of course.

Ruthie waves a hand at him as if to say, "See? I told you. It's Sunday morning, for goodness' sake."

"What if he was at church?" I mutter for the sake of argument.

She just gives me a flat look. Fair enough.

"Uncle Shane!" Izzy shouts.

His grin belongs on those ambulance chaser posters Ruthie's envisioned. Fake as fuck.

"Hi, sweetheart."

I get up, because he's practically humming with rage and nervous energy. He's obviously not here to sit down and join us for a laidback brunch.

"I'll be right back," I tell my girls.

"We're doing just fine," Mira says.

I lead my friend to the private room, then stand back and to the side, watching as Shane stiffens his back and enters.

"Sorry I'm late," he says, smooth as hell. "Got stuck in traffic on Patton."

From the grim expressions of his partners, they know they've been called out, but they also know not to call him out in front of Lucas Burke Senior.

"I'm fucked," Shane says, taking the whiskey I just poured for him and adding a good inch. We're back at my apartment, sitting at the kitchen island. Mira went to a playground with Ruthie and Izzy—her suggestion, probably because she knows I don't want my sister here, and I especially don't want her here when I'm trying to have a serious talk with Shane.

"I take it your firm's looking to defend the Burkes?" I ask my friend, because I can't think of another reason for that meeting.

"They are," he confirms. "Either I'm on board, or I'm out."

"Did you tell them to go fuck themselves?" I ask, even though I can tell from his hangdog expression that he's not sure what he's going to do. I guess that's why we're here, just the two of us, and haven't called in the other guys.

"No," he says as he lowers his head into his hands.

"But you know they're guilty. Doesn't that automatically disqualify you from working with them?"

He snorts and gives me a *Danny, you don't know shit* look. "If being innocent were a prerequisite for working with us, we wouldn't have very many clients. Everyone deserves good counsel. It's one of the tenets of—"

"Burke is one of your best friends," I interrupt, because I don't need to hear a commercial for his law firm. Even if I find myself in dire need of legal help, I won't be hiring them. Not now. "His parents are terrible people, and you know it. First hand."

"I wouldn't be working on the case directly."

"You know what you have to do," I say. Because he does. I can see it in his eyes. In the level of the whiskey in his glass. I can see it in the way he keeps twisting his tie even though it's probably made of some expensive silk from hard-working worms.

If only knowing what to do made it easier to do it. I know from personal experience that it doesn't. I didn't want to work with Jarrod Travis. It was the last thing I wanted, lower on the list than prison, or at least on par with it. But sometimes the right answer is to pick the lesser of a lot of wrong ones.

Sometimes the right answer leaves you feeling like you're all wrong, even if you're the one who picked out and decorated the prison you put yourself in.

"It's not that easy," he says, his voice razor-edged. "You know how hard I've worked…"

"You have," I agree. "But maybe it was never the right job. Maybe it was wrong from the start. You're not like them. You're not an asshole."

He laughs without any humor. "Danny, sometimes you have to be an asshole to work among them."

"You know what you need to do," I say, because I believe it. I believe in *him*. He may have strayed from the person he was—but he hasn't left that boy behind entirely. He has a moral code. A compass that still knows true north even if he's not ready to see and follow it.

"Fuck you, Danny. It's easy for you to say, locked up here like you're in some hermetically sealed box. You can be a vigilante from your computer, and it doesn't cost you anything. It—"

"It could cost me everything," I say quietly. "Maybe it already has."

He swears, taps his hand against the kitchen island like he wishes it were someone's face.

"Want a ceramic turkey?" I ask, apropos of nothing.

He understands, of course, and half his mouth lifts, the other staying determinedly down. "I shouldn't be here right now. I'm not myself."

I nod to the whiskey. "You shouldn't drive."

He laughs through his nose—an inelegance he wouldn't normally allow himself. "I haven't drunk any of it yet. I need to go somewhere I can think."

"What about the bench?" I ask.

Vague, obviously, but he knows what I mean. After all, that bench on the mountain used to be one of Shane's spots too—a place to get away from it all. A place where you could sit with your thoughts and just be.

He shakes his head, smiling slightly. "I'm never going to be able to go up there anymore without thinking of you with your ass out."

"Very funny."

"You've got it bad for Mira, huh?"

"I do."

"You still going to see Daphne this week?"

"Yeah. I'm going to ask her if Big Bear Games can assign someone else to us...if they want the game."

"You *do* have it bad," he comments, studying me.

"Yes," I say flatly. "I just admitted I do. And I'm not at all sorry about it."

"Well, good luck with that." He gets to his feet, sighing, and then heads over to the blinds, lifting them. Looks across the alley. "Shit. She cleared out?"

"Looks like," I say, getting an uncomfortable feeling. A prickle of something, intuition or maybe just the feeling that I'd like some intuition to kick in, if it could be bothered. It feels like all of this should be connecting together in some way it isn't—the Burkes meeting with Shane's partners; Big Mike hanging out downstairs; the woman across the alleyway. If it were one of those podcasts that Mira and I like listening to, there'd be red yarn connecting each of these strange things neatly and succinctly together.

Maybe we need a murder board.

"Make sure you keep Deacon in the loop about everything," Shane says, letting the blinds drop. "He's good."

"I already told him. Shane, Burke needs to know about this. *Now.* He's been paying Deacon to keep an eye on his parents. It's a conflict of interest if Deacon's working both sides." I work that over for a second, then add, "Hell, maybe that's why he hasn't found anything solid on them."

Or maybe he's actually a shit detective. After all, he came over here and got so tanked he forgot the rules of Charades.

Shane swears again. "Yeah, good point. Just...give me a few days, okay?" He pauses, looking at the counter as if it might reform its shape to show him what to do. Then he looks up, his eyes wide. Pleading. "Thanksgiving. Give me until Thanksgiving, Dan."

"Burke needs to know if Deacon is trustworthy."

I care less if he's just mediocre at his job. Plenty of people are mediocre at their jobs, and I don't want to get the man fired. He's lonely in a way that speaks to me.

"I'll find out, okay?" Shane insists. "Trust me."

I want to trust him. I really fucking want to. Shane's been there for me through everything. But so has Burke. It's impossible to choose one of them over the other—it defies every notion I have of what is right and just.

So I nod. "Thanksgiving. *If* you find out about Deacon. I'm going to take your word for it, man."

"Thank you." He pounds his chest. "You don't know how much this means to me."

He leaves to go do his soul searching. Maybe at the bench. Maybe somewhere else. I'm hit with the realization that there are plenty of things I don't know about Shane anymore—including where he'd go if he's feeling low.

It's not a comforting thought.

Chapter Twenty-Eight

Mira

"So what dirt do you want on my brother? Ask me anything. Seriously, anything. He owes me."

I'm standing next to Ruthie, watching as Izzy mows through the playground like she's practicing for a tough mudder. Who knew being a kid required such work?

Then again, I was the kid who'd attack my mother's *Vogue* magazines and then get yelled at for it. I never had much use for outdoor recreation, even when I had two working legs.

I watch Izzy pull off a flip worthy of an Olympic gymnast, then say, "He told me you thought he might...well, that he might be on the autism spectrum."

I hadn't planned on saying it. I haven't been thinking about it all that much, beyond the research I've done about what I can do to make him more comfortable.

Ruthie gives me a sharp look. "He said that to you?" Before I can answer the obvious, she waves a hand. "Sorry, that was rhetorical. Obviously, he must have. I'm just shocked. He doesn't usually talk about that. I don't even know if he's told all of his friends."

"Why not?" I ask, caught off guard. "From what admittedly minimal research I've done, it sounds like there are a lot of adults who think they would have been diagnosed if doctors looked for the same things when we were kids that they look for now. Back then, they only looked for more extreme cases, right?"

She nods slowly. "He's never gone through the diagnostic process. I don't think he ever will. But it makes sense to me...him too."

"He won't do it because he figures it doesn't matter?" I guess. "He is who he is?"

"Partly..." She pauses, watching Izzy, her bottom lip between her teeth. After a full thirty seconds, she says, "Our parents thought something was wrong with Danny. He wasn't anything like they are—he didn't like to play ball with the kids in the neighborhood. He wasn't any good at sports, really, until he started biking. And when he was little the noise from the vacuum cleaner made him run into his room and rock. So did the parties they used to hold. Loud and late. Lots of alcohol and pot." She glances at Izzy, decides she's fine, and turns back to me. "Our mother used to call him a pussy. She'd say he wasn't any kind of a man. Of course, my father was a guy who got drunk and liked to throw things—same as she did—so they're not authorities on what makes a man. They'd tell him he was wrong in the head, and it wasn't until he did IQ testing in school, at his teacher's request, that they found out he had an IQ of 155." Her face hardens. "Then they saw him as their gold mine. Their way out. And he let them take advantage of him because he wanted to take care of *me*."

I feel my heartbeat accelerating. It's beating in my ears. I want to hug that boy. I want to smother him with love. I want to run to Danny and hold him and tell him the truth—that he's the best man I've ever known, and I feel impossibly lucky to have him in my life.

I swallow against my dry throat. "I'm sorry, but your parents are assholes."

"You're telling me," She says with a snort. "Our father ran off years ago, and I guess our mother's found religion, but it doesn't seem to have changed her. People don't change at their core, if you ask me. If someone's rotten, they're rotten all the way through."

I think about her dislike for Shane—does she see him as rotten all the way through? I don't know him well, but he did go out of his way to help Danny and me. "Do they reach out to you?"

"She does, occasionally. Most of the time I don't answer her calls. Sometimes I feel sorry for her, and I'll talk for a little while, but I've never introduced Izzy to them. They weren't the ones who were there for me when life was tough. Danny was always there." Her mouth lifts again, though not enough to qualify as a smile. "Even when I didn't want him to be." I'm startled to realize there are tears in her eyes. Even more so because I can feel them in my eyes too.

"Fuck," I say, then flinch and glance around. No one's looking at me except for a squirrel. It definitely seems judgmental, but it's probably just pissed off because it lost its nuts. "Sorry." I take her hand and squeeze it. "When you offered to give me dirt on Danny, I'm sure this wasn't what you meant."

She laughs, then rubs at her eyes. She must be rocking some truly exceptional waterproof eyeliner because it doesn't smudge one bit. I make a mental note to ask her about it later. "I'm glad he felt he could tell you that much. Sometimes he's so closed up, like he's some treasure chest at the bottom of the ocean—only he's the one who put himself there."

I nod slowly, because I know what she means, and I reflect that he told me that information about himself when I barely knew him. When we were shut up in the elevator together with only each other to guard against the darkness.

"I probably shouldn't have said so much. Dammit. He wouldn't like that I did. But I always say too much, and I can tell you care about him. I'm so happy. He deserves to have someone special in his life. He was with this awful woman Daphne a while back—"

I try not to lean forward and show my interest, but I'm like a drunk person trying to hide a good hand at poker, because she cuts herself off with a nod. "So, you know about Daphne."

"A little. I wouldn't mind knowing more. Particularly if she has some fatal flaw that can't be discovered by a simple Google search."

She laughs and grins, so thankfully I sounded less of a psychopath out loud than I did in my head.

Then her smile slips away. "She saw him the same way they did," she tells me. "She saw someone who was smart enough to take her ideas and implement them."

"He did her work for her?" I ask, happy to fuel my kneejerk dislike.

"She'd make it sound like she was asking him to do little favors, no more, no less, but *yes*. And when he didn't fall into line, she found someone else who would."

"You mean when he wouldn't go to Europe with her?" He couldn't, because of his agreement with Jarrod Travis, but I'm not supposed to know that. I don't even know whether Daphne knew. Maybe she didn't. Danny's not a man who would burden other people with problems he sees as his own.

"I'm so grateful he said no. That woman had some weird kind of spell over him."

Not what I wanted to hear, especially since I know he couldn't have said yes. Based on how Ruthie phrased it, I'm guessing Danny didn't share the details of his agreement with Jarrod with her.

"Huh. Well, he's meeting with her this week about his game."

She swears. "He didn't tell me that."

No, and I can't imagine why not.

"He's not going to let her push him around this time," I say, wanting to believe it.

She regards me for a moment, then says, "I believe you're right about that. You care about my brother, don't you?"

"I *do* care about him," I say. That much is factual. These feelings that have been wrapping me up are like a strong tide. An undertow.

The other times I've fallen hard for someone, it always felt like I was really falling, like the pain of landing was coming. With Danny, it's different. I'm comfortable with him, and I feel...cherished. But there's a voice in my head that insists that'll only make the landing harder. That I might be about to learn that a broken heart is a much sharper pain than a bruised ego.

"Good," Ruthie says firmly. "But here's where I say it." She firms her lips. "If you hurt him, you hurt all of us, and I'm much less forgiving than my brother."

"I get it," I say. "I have a sister too."

And I read her fiancé the riot act, little does Delia know. He listened to it and then promised me that I could drown him in a vat of whiskey if he ever fucked up. We shook on it, and I made him a drink.

I take a second to think all of this over. Danny's parents made him feel like he was different, wrong. Which is probably another reason he seeks out things that are simple and predictable. Comforting.

I'm none of those things, though, am I?

I don't want to be one more person who makes him feel like he's not enough. Maybe I've already made him feel that way, unintentionally, with the stupid makeover stuff.

I don't know what'll happen next, but I know I don't want to hurt him.

So I say, "I would never intentionally hurt your brother."

"Good," she says. "Now that that's settled, I want to pick your brain about my new business."

I lift out my arms. "Pick away."

So for a while we talk business while offering occasional *you've got this* and *ten out of ten* type praise to Izzy.

About a half hour later, Ruthie drops me off at the apartment. She doesn't come inside because Izzy has a playdate.

I make my way upstairs, slowly, and who do I spy on the third floor landing but Big Mike? He's messing with a flyer on the bulletin board by the door, something about celebrating the connection between lunar energy and the menstrual cycle, but something tells me it's just an excuse to poke around. That, or he saw Ruthie's car.

"Looking for your hamster again?" I ask, raising my eyebrows.

He laughs. "Not today." He tears a number from the lunar cycle sheet. "Sounds interesting."

Man, he really is shit at being an undercover detective.

"It's a pity they don't microchip hamsters," I say, "but I guess if they did it would take up the whole hamster. It would be like a cyborg."

He continues laughing, much harder than the joke warranted. I start walking away. "Say," he starts. "Would you mind giving me Danny's number? I think we got off on the wrong foot, and I was hoping he'd let me buy him a beer."

"You sure you're not going to try to coerce him to get a lap dance again?" I ask, giving him a wink. This is actually a little fun— after listening to all those crime procedurals, I'm out here talking to a bonafide undercover detective.

"You heard about that, huh?" he asks, having the good grace to look embarrassed. Or maybe it's just his character of Big Mike who's embarrassed.

"I did, yes. I've never understood why men like to go to those places together. Bonding through blue balls, and all that."

He goes a deeper shade of red. "The wings—"

"Aren't even that good," I interject. "I went with one of my friends years ago to see what all the fuss was about. Because people are forever talking about the wings at strip joints. You know what? They were under-seasoned. *Criminally* under-seasoned."

"His number?" he asks hopefully.

We'd decided it would be best if Danny talks to him to get some sense of what he wants, so I give it to him, then wave goodbye and tell him to give some love to Pumpkin.

If that's even his name.

When I walk into the apartment, Danny's standing at the window, staring across the way, and something strange happens to me when I take in the long line of him, the mass of his hair.

I feel tears in my eyes, although I'm not altogether sure why, and the feeling inside of me is so warm, so fucking warm, it's going to burn me up to a cinder, and then I'll float away like ash—and I won't even mind.

It's a fancy that makes no sense, but I don't care, because he turns to me, and his whole face lights up and he says, "You're home."

And it feels right. It feels true.

If I could run to him, I would. I settle for hobbling.

Chapter Twenty-Nine

Danny

The rest of the day is a blur.

I'm happy—and I also feel like I'm about to take a tumble.

It's a familiar feeling, because when I was a kid, I was taught the other shoe would always drop. My mother would get sober for a few weeks, start taking care of herself and the house. Of Ruthie. Then she'd have a fight with my dad, or he'd come home with a six pack and offer her one, and the cycle would start again.

Or my dad...

He'd realize I knew how to do things that could be helpful to him, and for a while he'd lay off. Because I was the kid who could fix anything—the kid whose small fix-it business was keeping Hot Pockets on the table. But I'd always end up doing something to set him off... Always. I wasn't the son he'd wanted—the one who'd drink beers with him and tinker around with car parts, and he never let me forget it.

But I'm happy to be flying high while it lasts.

Mira and I play True Colors together. We watch a movie. We make plans for Thanksgiving. We read side by side. We make love in my bed. On the couch. Against the window.

Her gloves come, and she opens them with such appreciation, I instantly want to buy her a truckload of them.

We make a murder board, using the poster board, yarn, index cards, and pins I picked up at Target.

Both of us enjoy this activity more than we probably should, but it doesn't result in anything conclusive. We still don't know who the woman across the way is, and she hasn't made any reappearances. Neither have the table or chair.

Night turns to morning. More sand falls through the hourglass, and I try to tell myself I won't be buried in it.

Shane texts me mid-morning to say Deacon swung by the law firm and told them he wasn't going to work for them anymore if they were going to collude with white collar assholes like the Burkes. It turned into a big scene, apparently, so unless he's very committed to undercover work and the whole thing was masterminded by Shane's partners, he's in the clear.

Shane still hasn't decided what he's doing, or at least that's the message I take from his continued silence on the matter.

I'm worried he'll make the wrong decision.

I'm worried it's going to tear this family we've made for ourselves apart, because I know that Burke probably won't be able to forgive him for something like that.

On Monday afternoon, Mira leaves for a few hours at Glitterati, and even though I'm busy doing work for Jarrod, I feel her absence like a toothache. It's a festering worry.

Big Mike texts me that evening, asking if I can get that drink with him, but his earliest availability is on Wednesday, just before my appointment with Daphne. So I ask him to meet me at Glitterati an hour before I'm supposed to meet with her.

"Can you really do back-to-back drinks?" Mira asks me incredulously after I tell her my plan later that evening. We just finished dinner, and we're sitting on the couch in the living room, our thighs pressed together.

"People do it all the time," I say, tracing circles onto her leg through her dress.

"I'm asking if *you* can really do it. It sounds like a lot."

I don't like hearing her put it that way. She's right. It *is* a lot. I'm not looking forward to either appointment, for reasons that go above and beyond being in a bar for two hours, but I'm sick of feeling like someone who can't do normal things. I also suspect that my sister may have told Mira the kind of things I would have preferred for her to keep to herself. Things that make me seem fragile.

As for the meetings themselves—Big Mike's motives remain suspect, and I have no desire at all to see Daphne, other than that I'm hoping she'll reassign the game. I would much prefer to go to the anti-hexing meeting with Mira so I can scowl at Byron.

"I don't think I have a choice," I say, glancing at the murder board, which we unanimously decided to hang up in the living room. Lots of threads with nowhere to go. "Maybe we'll finally be able to make some more connections once I talk to Big Mike. Is our drink on the menu now?"

"Not yet," she says with a grin. "But Azalea'll make it special for you. Not Big Mike though." She pauses, then says, "Something's been bothering me."

"And you didn't tell me about it immediately? I don't believe it."

She shoves me with her shoulder, but her smile falls flat. "Do you care that I'm a bartender? I mean, because of your parents?"

I tuck a lock of hair behind her ear, giving the question its due. "No," I say after a moment. "What you do makes people happy. It's all about creating joy. Besides, if it wasn't alcohol for them, it would have been something else."

"Thank you for saying that," she says softly. "I was worried it might bring up bad memories."

"A lot of things do," I say. "If I look at it in the wrong light, a can of soda could bring up just as many bad memories. But there are plenty of good memories that involve some light drinking too."

"Like Wednesday night." Her tone is wry, and I'm glad for it.

"Obviously."

"You know, I feel like we should ask for proof of life for Pumpkin.'"

"You think Big Mike did her in, huh?" I ask, putting an arm around her. "Maybe you should stop listening to *The Murderer Next Door*."

"Not because of my ideations about the woman across the alley?"

My smile drops. "We don't know what was going on with her, but maybe Big Mike will."

"We can probably just start calling him Mike."

"No way. We should respect his carefully layered façade."

She leans in and kisses me. "I'd like to do away with your carefully layered façade."

"You already have," I say honestly, "you did it almost instantly. I should buy you a trophy."

"I'd put it over the fireplace." She points to the mantel, and I can see it there—an ugly silver cup, the kind I never got for anything, because they don't give them out to the kids who are good at math and coding.

"Are you trying to give me reasons not to get you one?" I ask.

"No, maybe I just want to make sure you choose a pretty one."

I kiss the top of her hair, her forehead, her mouth. I want to carve her likeness into my mind the way it's already carved into my soul. I want—

"Danny," she says, her tone uncharacteristically serious.

"What is it?" I ask.

"It's all going to change, isn't it?"

She looks scared as she says it, and I'd do anything to take that fear away from her, even though I'm carrying it myself.

"Yes," I admit. "It already has, though, and it's changed for the good." I smile, because it was a stupid thing to say to someone who's broken an ankle. I tap her cast with two fingers. "Other than this, but you'll be free of it soon."

"Speaking of which..." Her eyes studying me, the cat-eye makeup giving them a more playful tilt. "You still haven't signed it."

"I will," I tell her. "But I've decided it's going to mean something when I do, and the words haven't come to me yet."

"Now you're really building it up," she says with one of her biggest grins. "If you write something basic like *get well soon*, it's going to be a downer. I expect A-level material."

I laugh as I run my fingers along her jaw, cupping it. "Nothing but the best for you, boss." Then I kiss her, hard, because I can feel it too—the currents coming for us.

Chapter Thirty

Mira

You're coming this afternoon, right?

I almost fell into a manhole, yesterday. I could
have died, Mira. And I had to get my hair cut short.

Oh, the humanity

This is serious. I've learned not to mess around
with this Halloween black magic shit. Never again.
There are powerful forces in the universe.

Yes, they're called karma. And peroxide. But, fuck
it, yes, I'm coming.

You won't regret it.

Don't be late.

Seriously. She might curse us again if you're late.
She doesn't seem right in the head.

At least you'll have an easier time telling our hair
apart now that you're a blond

I want to be with Danny.

I want to show him Glitterati the way *I* see it.

It is, obviously, a bar. It smells terrible in the back alley, and there's no denying it is, first and foremost, a place people go to get plastered.

But I see it as more than that. I see it as a place where they can step away from the harsh realities of life and into a fantasy where everything glitters, names are fantastical, and everything is softer. I run my fingertips across the top of the resin bar, admiring the threads of glitter that run through it. I was here for a couple of hours last week, but I've missed it. I've even missed the broccoli stench of the back alley.

This place is my escape.

It's my sanctuary.

It's the one thing I've built.

It's my proof that while I might not have school smarts, I have a knowledge for what people need.

"You're going to be late, girl," Azalea says, gesturing to the clock on the wall, one of the melting Salvador Dali clocks, because people shouldn't have to worry about time while they're here. We just got done finalizing—and laminating—our updated menu. It won't be distributed tonight, but Azalea will roll it out this weekend.

She's right. Judging by the approximate position of the minute hand, I have to get going. At least I screwed up my left ankle and am thus capable of driving—uncomfortably—on my own.

"You'll tell me if…"

I trail off. I don't really know what I'm asking for. Whether Danny and Daphne start making out across the table? Or declare to the bar that they're getting married and moving to Europe to have genius babies?

Or if Big Mike puts Danny in handcuffs and leads him away before any of that can happen?

The feeling of pressure in my chest and head is almost painful.

"Maybe I don't need to go to this anti-hexing thing. I could stay..."

"You need all the luck you can get," she says pointedly. "Your sister is too nice to hold the fort down much longer. Last night, she gave away five drinks. *Five.* She said they all seemed depressed. I said, yes, you dear sweet soul, that's why they're at a bar."

"You're right," I say, but a part of me wonders if I'm agreeing so easily because I'm afraid of what I'd see if I stay. "Make Danny a Moment of Truth, okay? Whatever he wants is on the house."

"I look forward to meeting him," she says, giving me long look. "You've never fussed yourself over a guy like this. He must be something else."

I can see him the way she probably will—the way I did before I moved into the apartment. Quiet. Fastidious. *Agreeable.*

"He is," I agree, feeling a lump in my throat. "Can you keep the music lower tonight?"

She lifts her eyebrows. "You said it always has to be at ten. It's in the damn rule book. It's the only rule in the book."

"Seven," I say. I tap my chin, then point to a booth in the back corner, the farthest from any of the speakers. "And save that booth for him."

"It's the worst view in the house," she says pointedly. "You like this guy or not?"

I'm looking at that table. It's located at the back door leading to the alley that smells like broccoli, and an idea starts to poke at me. It's not ready to germinate quite yet, but I'll keep watering it and giving it sunlight. A back room at the bar where it's quieter, darker, calmer—a place where people who don't love the hustle can find some peace. A compromise that'll allow Danny to spend some time here.

Maybe the idea will be a weed, and maybe it'll be a flower, but there's only one way to find out.

Azalea repeats her question, and I murmur, "I think I'm in love with him."

She whistles, then grins at me. "This mean I'm free and clear to make a move on Daphne?"

"She's probably still straight," I comment.

"No one's perfect." She waggles her eyebrow, making the bright green jewel piercing it waggle too. "And who knows. Maybe she just hasn't met the right woman yet."

I grin at her. "You do you. I certainly wouldn't mind if she wanted to sleep with someone other than my boyfriend."

"Look at you, gone two weeks and you've already settled down."

An uncomfortable feeling stabs at me, but when I think of the apartment, of making drinks with Danny or taking a bath together or working on the murder board, I feel a gush of the warmth I've only ever gotten here before. Danny is making me hope for what seems impossible. Then again, lots of people are devoted to their jobs and their partners. Maybe I can be one of them.

"What can I say? Maybe I just needed to meet the right guy."

———

THE WRONG GUY IS WAITING FOR ME IN FRONT OF JOSIE'S crayon-drawn storefront. His hair is short and a crispy blond, and he's only wearing a thermal shirt despite the cold front that's working its way in, bringing down more leaves.

Really, the fact that he saw that sign and then proceeded to go in there to pay that woman money is all anyone needs to know about his character.

"You're three minutes late," he blusters.

"She's not here," I say, because the storefront is very clearly dark and also, judging by the fact that he's out here without a coat on, locked.

"But she still knows."

"Oh, come on, Byron, she's not actually psychic. And even if she were, she wouldn't know *everything*."

He shushes me and looks around with wild eyes, like he thinks the plants might be watching. Christ, what happened to him?

Josie, I guess.

Or his own hubris biting him in the ass.

We wait for a minute in uncomfortable silence, and then I text Shauna, asking for Josie's number.

"This is all because you were late," Byron says, sulking, his arms wrapped around his upper body.

I take off my scarf and throw it at him.

"Is that your boyfriend's scarf?"

"Oh, for God's sake. It's purple. Does he look like the kind of guy who'd wear a glittery purple scarf?"

"So he *is* your boyfriend," he says miserably, as if he has any room to care. He wraps the scarf around his neck and arms.

"Yes," I say for the second time that day. It's becoming a habit, I guess, claiming Danny. I don't regret it. I just...

I wonder what's happening at Glitterati, is all.

"What do you see in him that you didn't find in me?"

He says this with a completely straight face, even though we're waiting outside the office of a psychic because he tried to put a hex on me and inadvertently hexed both of us. In his mind anyway.

Things have definitely been a little strange for me over the past few weeks, but I wouldn't say I feel cursed anymore. True, I did break my ankle. Also true, I was caught publicly fornicating by a portly officer whose name lends itself naturally to cops-love-donuts jokes. And, yes, an undercover cop and as-yet-unidentified woman have been watching Danny and me...

But I've discovered that I don't need to step into Glitterati for life to become strange and magical. It can be weirdly beautiful in a perfectly normal looking apartment, with a man who seems perfectly normal on the surface but is a hidden pool with depths that could drown you.

"We weren't right for each other, Byron." He tightens the scarf, and I have to admit he looks good in it. "We were never right for each other. I need someone..."

"You need someone *exciting*," he says officiously, as if he can't imagine Danny could fit the bill.

"You're right, and I've found him. I need someone who's exciting *and* steady." I think about Danny and that damn tree. Danny, telling me about being the Reaper and Bo Peep. Danny, carrying his niece on his shoulders. Danny. My eyes feel hot. My heart feels full and heavy and...worried. "Maybe you need—"

"*You're* both of those things," he says.

"But you need someone who'll pay you more attention... Someone who'll—"

Keep you from doing dumbass shit like placing hexes on people or crisping your hair.

No, he wouldn't like it if I say that. And even if I don't believe in the hex, I don't want another one on my head.

"Someone who'll hold your hand through life's ups and downs," I settle for. I want to be that person for Danny, and for the first time, I want someone to be that person for me.

"Fuck, these are good lyrics," he says, and he pulls his phone out of his pocket feverishly, pulling up the voice recording app. "I want to hold your hand, whether we're going up and down, baby. It'll be you and me. On the seesaw." His mouth pulls to the side. "Wait. Does that make it sound like I'm after a teenager?"

"Yes," I say, giving a theatrical shudder.

"Nix on the seesaw," he says into the app. "No seesaw. Hm. Merry-go-round?" He looks at me in question.

"Worse. A lot worse."

"No rides," he says into the phone. Then he pockets it and gives me a quarter of his attention again. "I don't want to walk away from us for good, Meer. We're perfect for each other. We keep the same hours."

That's a sore subject for me, but I manage to keep my cool. "Not a great reason for being with someone. Vampires keep those hours too, but I don't want anyone to suck my blood."

I see the flashing in his eyes, and he turns his back to me, muttering into the phone. Maybe I have a future second career in unintentionally writing song lyrics. Then again, there's a very good chance that all of these songs will suck.

Turning back to me, Byron says, "But you're my inspiration, baby. I just wrote the best song I've ever written, and everything you're saying is lighting a fire inside of me." He reaches for my hands. I dodge him, putting them behind my back like I'm a kid playing keep away. They're just hands, and I touch plenty of people with them, but it would feel wrong to let him touch me like that. Even for a second.

He frowns, but he's not ready to give up. "The hand-holding crap is going to track well with our fans too. And that vampire thing." He shakes a finger. "People like vampires."

"That one's already been done," I tell him, neglecting to mention that all of it's been done, and probably better. "And it sounds like it was our breakup that inspired you more than I did. Maybe you just need to keep breaking up with people to write good music."

He brightens. "You think?"

I shrug. "Sure, look at Taylor Swift." His name and the queen's don't belong in the same paragraph, let alone the same sentence, but I don't mind buttering him up if it'll result in him leaving me alone.

I glance at my phone, which I still have out. We've been here for thirty minutes, and Josie still hasn't answered my text. Fabulous.

"I'm only waiting out here for another five minutes," I warn.

My chest constricts at the thought of leaving—not because I'm worried about Josie, who's given us further proof she's unreliable, but because I don't know what I should do next. I could get back to Glitterati in time for Danny's meeting with Daphne, although not Big Mike. But if I do that, it'd be like saying I don't trust Danny.

I *do* trust him.

It's just...

I hear his sister saying that Daphne used to have some weird power over him. I've seen it too, haven't I? Danny's thought about what she said to him for years. It's influenced his perception of himself...even though it seems to me it's his mask she was talking about. The part of himself he tries to present to the world because he was taught that the real him wasn't right.

Somehow, she wasn't able to see beyond it. Or maybe she thought it was his limitations that made him basic.

Either way, she's a fucking idiot, and I don't want her voice in his head, telling him he's not enough.

My phone buzzes, and I sigh as I lift it up for a look.

It's a message from Josie's number.

It's done. I can feel that the hex has been lifted.

Is this your way of saying you can't get back here within the next five minutes? Because that's what it sounds like.

"What are you writing?" Byron asks, trying to look over my shoulder. "Is it about me?"

"Sort of," I say, because I'm not beyond the point of wanting to cause him a little discomfort. After all, he's the reason we're out here, freezing our asses off in front of a crayon drawing made by a thirty-year-old woman.

No. You only needed to reach a resolution between yourselves. I figured thirty minutes of forced proximity would do the job. Either that, or it'd make everything worse. It was up to you. But my connection to the other side tells me it all worked out. There are no more ill feelings on either side, and the hex is dead.

Wait, are you in there? Are you watching us with a camera or something? Because I've had it with the whole being watched thing. It definitely doesn't do it for me anymore.

No, my third eye does the work for me.

Byron jostles closer, trying to see my phone. I poke at his leg with the crutch, but it occurs to me that I should relent on the off-chance Josie is right. So, I show him the phone.

"Oh, rad," he says. "That makes sense. She's right about the ill feelings thing. I don't want your hair to fall out anymore."

"You wanted my hair to fall out?" I ask, unable to keep the annoyance out of my voice. I don't bother adding that I still have a few ill feelings toward him, although no actual desire for revenge. "Why?"

He shrugs. "Because mine got fucked up. Girls are always going on about doing their hair to get over a breakup, so I figured I'd give it a try...and then this happened. I guess I felt bitter."

"I didn't realize this had hurt you so much," I say. "I figured you didn't care too much. I'm sorry."

I mean it. I'm very happy we're not together, and also that I hopefully won't have to see him again after this afternoon, but I didn't intend to cause him pain.

"Thank you for that." He taps the pocket he stuffed the phone into. "And for the sick lyrics." He nods, kisses two fingers, and taps them to my temple. "It was real while it was real."

His eyes flash again, and I can tell he's weighing whether or not it would ruin a theatrical moment if he took his phone out to record that line too. He holds back, though, and for that I can be grateful—and generous.

"Take care of yourself, Byron. The blond's not bad on you."

A lie, but a kind one.

He's humming as he turns to go to his car. It's not until he gets in that I remember the scarf, but I figure I'll let him have it. It looks better on a blond.

I pick up my phone again and see another message from Josie:

> How are the plans for Thanksgiving going? If you'd like to have some extra guests, Poe and I will be in town, and we would be willing to do readings for the whole group.

> I'm going to block you now. No offense, but friends don't hex friends.

> Not even if they're paid?

> Not even then. Take it easy.

> What if I said we need to be there?

> I'm ready to roll the dice.

I'm pretty sure I mean that.

Chapter Thirty-One

Danny

I'm already on edge as I walk into the bar. It's too early for it to be busy, but it's already loud and bright. It's a sensory assault, like if someone peeled my eyelids open and made me watch the cartoons Ruthie used to like when she was a kid. *The Powerpuff Girls*, specifically—all pink and purple and glitter. I wouldn't exactly call it pleasant, being in here, and yet...

I see touches of Mira everywhere. In my mind's eye, I can see her pouring the bar into resin molds, the way she told me she did. I can see her choosing the mismatched glassware with a mischievous grin, like she thought she was getting away with something, because her mother sounds like a woman who'd throw away a set just because one dish is missing. I can see Mira making the trays, all molded from records, and the decorations hanging from the walls. There's so much of her here, and even though it's overwhelming, I can't hate it.

It's a relief—an unexpected boon thrown to me by the universe.

I only make it a couple of steps before the bartender, a woman with a septum piercing and long, rainbow dyed hair, gestures for me to come over. I look behind me—nothing—and then back.

"Danny," she says, leaving no doubt, or at least very minimal doubt, about who she's talking to. "Mira asked me to set a booth aside for you."

"Oh. Great. Thank you," I say, the words stumbling over each other. "You must be Azalea."

She lifts her eyebrows. "How'd you guess?"

"No one else is working here," I say before realizing it's a dumb response. "Sorry," I add. "I'm a little...on edge."

She slides out from behind the counter, slinging a tie-dyed rag over her shoulder. "It's not every day you meet with an undercover detective who's been following you around."

"Jesus, how much did she tell you?" I say before I can moderate my reaction with a more polite response.

She grins. "Both more and less than I wanted to know." Then she leads me over to a booth in the back. It's quieter here. Darker.

Mira chose it for you because she knew being here would be a lot for you.

It's a thought that comforts me—and troubles me. I don't like having to be a person she makes accommodations for...but I also am that person.

"I'm going to go make you a Moment of Truth," Azalea says. "Unless you want something different."

"No, that seems pretty apropos right now."

Her lips twitch like she wants to smile. I feel like telling her to go for it—the world would be better if people smiled when they felt like it and didn't when they did not. "You're not much like Mira's other men."

"I hope there aren't too many of us," I say as I lower into the back of the booth, facing the front door. Better to see what's coming.

"What if I told you there was a whole army?" she asks, lifting her eyebrows.

"I'd have to figure out how to kill them all and make it look like an accident."

Azalea laughs and slaps the top of the booth next to her.

Which is of course when I register that Big Mike is approaching us. He probably didn't hear me, but it's definitely not the sort of thing you should be caught saying when an undercover detective who's taken an interest in you is in the vicinity.

"Would you like a drink?" I ask him. "Azalea here is getting me a Moment of Truth." He looks like he's having trouble parsing the sentence, so I lift up two fingers. "We'll have two."

"All right," she agrees, still grinning. "Two existential dilemmas coming right up."

"I feel like that would be a different drink," I say, maybe to myself, "more bitter."

She's laughing again as she walks away. Well, I suppose there are worse impressions a man could make.

Big Mike looks confused as hell, which doesn't feel like a bad thing. I want him to be off his game.

"Take a seat," I say.

He sits heavily across from me, then takes his coat off and slings it across his lap. Seeing him do it prompts me to do the same.

Big Mike studies me and folds his hands on the tabletop. "You're probably wondering why I've been wanting to meet with you."

I shrug, then figure fuck it. Maybe I'm about to get myself arrested, but there's been enough artifice going around. I'd prefer for us to be straight with each other. "I'm guessing you must be lonely if you've resorted to buying hamsters from little girls."

He clears his throat. I'm guessing he's panicked and trying to look confused, but the result is that his eyes are bulging. "Pumpkin is my daughter's hamster."

"But that little girl we saw in the stairwell a few weeks ago wasn't your daughter, was she?"

He swallows that for a second before hedging, "I never said she was."

"No, but you were happy to imply it. Why? We both know you don't want to spend time with me for the pleasure of my company."

"Your girlfriend saw me at the police station," he says flatly, watching me.

"Yes, but I knew there was something weird going on with you before that. If you're going to pretend to be a single dad again, you'll want to have some kid stuff around the apartment. Something other than a stolen hamster."

"I bought it from her." He makes a face. "Hamsters are more work than I thought."

"And don't tell me you're interested in me because of the Burkes. They don't give a shit about me, and I'm guessing neither of them could pick me out of a lineup."

"Okay, Reaper," he says pointedly, and my heart speeds up in my chest. Because this is it, isn't it? The moment of truth. Sink or swim.

I nod, owning it. Part of me wants to correct him, to tell him that's not what they're calling me these days, but it's possible he doesn't know about my Bo Peep persona. If he doesn't, I won't be the one to spoon feed it to him.

He flexes his jaw, getting ready to make some pronouncement, but I see Azalea coming with the drinks, so I hold out my palm.

"Two Moments of Truth," she says, serving one to each of us.

"Oh, it's a drink," he says, his relief obvious.

As she walks away, I find myself smiling, though maybe it's the smile of a prisoner on Death Row as he breaks open his pint of Ben & Jerry's. "What'd you think it was?"

He smiles back, and this time I'm pretty sure it's genuine. "I was having flashbacks to the *Godfather*. Leave the gun, take the cannoli."

He opens his mouth—hopefully to level with me about what he wants, but his phone chooses that moment to ring. He frowns as he pulls it out, then answers it, lifting a finger to me. He listens for a moment before saying, "Fuck. Okay. I'll be right there."

Looking across the table at me, he says, "We're going to have a conversation, Danny Traeger. And when that happens, it'll be to your benefit to listen to me. I know who you are, and I know what you've been doing."

My blood feels cold and sluggish in my veins, even as my heart speeds up. I think of Mira. Of Ruthie and Izzy. I think of how, for the first time in a long, long time, I really feel like I'm living my life —and now I might be torn away from it.

I nod. "When?"

"I'll be in touch."

Damn, leave it to Big Mike to follow me for the past three weeks like a dog after someone with bacon in his pockets, only to take off the second I turn in his direction.

"Okay."

He takes off and I slide his drink over to my side of the table, because why not? I could use both of them.

By the time Daphne shows up, Mike's drink is half empty, and I'm feeling a pleasant buzz that hasn't drowned out the knowledge that I've been caught doing something I shouldn't have been doing, and I may soon be asked to pay the price.

Daphne looks like she could have stepped out of the past. If age has touched her over the past eight years, it doesn't show. Her auburn hair is pulled back, and she's wearing a slate gray skirt suit. She's lovely in a way that I don't feel at all in my chest, which seems to develop a case of heartburn whenever Mira is near.

"Daniel," she says with a smile. "I'm so happy you came. You look...different."

From the way she says it, that's a good thing. But I feel uncomfortable as I get to my feet. How do you greet a woman who delivered you a putdown that lived with you for years?

I reach out my hand for a shake, but she pulls me into a hug. I pat her back before pulling away, awkward and very desirous of leaving. Tipsy.

Moment of truth.

We sit down, and I say, "Funny coincidence, you asking me to meet here. This happens to be my girlfriend's bar."

"Oh?" Daphne says, and her clipped tone tells me she isn't pleased. "Doesn't seem like your kind of place."

"Then why'd you ask to meet me here?"

She lifts her eyebrows. "I figured it would be best to discuss this somewhere loud, where we couldn't be overheard easily. I remembered this place as being aggressively loud." She tilts her head. "Although the music is a lot quieter than the last time I was here."

This is all news to me. I figured we were meeting to discuss the game and the possibility of the two of us working together—in which case silence would be a boon.

"Why?" I ask, going for the direct route again.

She stares at me across the table, her gaze intense. I used to like it when she looked at me that way. I used to think it meant she saw something that other people didn't see. That she thought I was special. But maybe all along, she was trying to see down to my soul and only saw the color brown. "You're Bo Peep."

Jesus, so much for being subtle. I've gotten ID'ed twice in one afternoon, this time for my more recent efforts.

I see no point in lying. "Yes."

"And before that you were The Reaper." She lifts her chin slightly. "Why didn't you tell me?"

"I'd already been caught," I say. "I made an agreement to stop. That's why I was working for Jarrod."

"But you didn't stop," she insists flatly.

I feel an itch behind my ears, and suddenly the music feels like it's pounding into my head. The lights, drilling into my eyes. The glitter...

I could be drowning in glitter.

"What's this all about? I thought you worked for Big Bear Games? You're supposed to my contact for them."

"I do work for Big Bear," she says primly, pushing forward in her chair. She's now sitting at the very end of it, back straight, and it can't possibly be comfortable. "And they *are* interested in buying your game. But I also work for RetCon, and they're interested in you for far more than a game, Danny. My colleague, Lina, was supposed to make contact with you, but she's had trouble finding you alone." Her lips purse, and I think of the woman in the apartment across the way, with her folding table and chair. Her knitting.

Lina showed up for the first time a few weeks ago, right around when Mira moved in. Right around when Daphne contacted me asking about this meeting.

Mira immediately found Lina suspicious, and I feel a pulse of being proud of her, even though the world as I know it has been upended.

Black Hats mostly work alone. Mostly. RetCon is the biggest international group of Black Hat hackers. They're the ones who end up in the headlines constantly for breaking into banks. Government files. For lifting people up and tearing them down.

"That's why you moved to Paris," I say flatly.

She nods. "You should have come with me."

"I didn't tell you at the time..." Because Ruthie was right, I realize—I'd never fully trusted her. "But I couldn't have. I had an agreement."

"With Jarrod Travis," she finishes, probably to show me that she knows more than I do now. Daphne always wanted to be the person in the room who knew the most—and I guess she's achieved that goal. I don't particularly feel like congratulating her. "We can handle that situation for you."

I don't know how they intend on 'handling' it, but I'm sure it would rip my life into shreds so small they could never be sewn back together. It would rip me from Mira. From Ruthie and Izzy. From the friends who are family to me.

"I don't want any part of that," I say flatly. I take another swig of the drink. "Besides, I think the cops are on to me. There's an under-cover cop living in the apartment beneath me."

"I know," she says, practically glowing because once again she has proven herself. "And we can take care of that problem for you too. You'll find there's *a lot* we can for you, Daniel." There's an insinuation running beneath the words, sinuous as a snake.

Darkness laps at me, trying to pull me under, even as the lights beat into me. "At what cost?"

"None whatsoever," she says, which only proves she doesn't understand me at all.

"You'd want me to leave."

"You just got finished saying the police are onto you. Seems to me you'll be going away anyway." She lifts her chin, watching me through her glasses. Her eyes are sparkling. She's enjoying herself, and in that moment, I can't understand why I ever saw anything in her.

"I'd like a different contact at Big Bear to discuss the game," I tell her.

Watching me, she nods. I can tell she feels she's already won. The game is superfluous to her. "Consider it done. The offer will be more than fair."

The *if you do as I ask* goes unsaid.

I wonder if she's the only one at the company who's working with Retcon, or if the connection goes deeper. We'll need to sell it to someone else.

"What'll you do if I don't agree?" I ask, even though I think I already know.

"We have a lot of information on you, Danny," she says, leaning forward slightly, her back still straight. "You might say it's become a special interest of mine. I underestimated you. I'm not wrong often."

I bite back the urge to tell her she's wrong more frequently than she might think—and that the first sign you might be a narcissist is if you have the urge to say *I'm not wrong often* within the first five minutes of a conversation.

"That sounds like a threat."

She shrugs. "Call it what you will. I personally see it as a statement of fact. We know things you don't want other people to know. We can offer you protections no one else can. You're not a stupid man."

"No." I lift my eyebrows. "Not stupid. Just *basic*."

She grins at me, showing her teeth. Her canines look like she took a file to them. I feel an unexpected shudder of revulsion, maybe because I remember what it was to look at her face and feel something so totally different from what I feel now. "I told you I underestimated you. Drastically, it turns out. I think I'm going to enjoy getting to know you again."

"Maybe not as much as you think," I say, getting up from my chair. I pull out a couple of twenties and slap them on the table.

While she may have underestimated me, I obviously overestimated her.

"Is our meeting over?" Daphne asks. She's giving me that look again, like she thinks she can slice through all my secrets.

"Yes. I look forward to meeting my new contact on Friday. We'll be dialing Drew into the meeting."

"I'll let them know," she says. "I require your answer to my other question by the end of next week."

"Don't I get extra time for the holidays?"

"You think I've forgotten? You don't celebrate them," she says crisply. "Neither do I."

"I celebrate them now."

I leave without looking back at her, and I can feel her gaze on my back, following me out as if it's the red dot from a gun. But I pretend not to notice or care. I throw a wave at Azalea, who's watching me with an intensity that suggests she's been ignoring everyone else at the bar, and start walking through downtown, making my way through the maze again and again, until I don't feel the buzz of the alcohol at all anymore and my head is clear enough for me to drive to that spot in the woods—the one where Mira gave herself to me. It was my place and is now forever ours.

It's dark out, completely dark. But it brings me no peace to be out here, where none of my senses are prickling, because the complete darkness only reminds me of that elevator, where Mira was my world.

I know what I have to do, but I also know that Daphne's right. No matter what I do, I'm toast.

Then, when I'm feeling as low as I can go, my phone buzzes with a text. I check it and see two threads. One of them has several texts from Shane:

> I'm sorry, man, but I don't know if I can quit my job.

> I know you won't understand.

> I fucking get it. But this is my life. I can't give it up. Not even for Burke.

> Not even for you.

Before my heart even has time to sink with a disappointment I feel down to my pores, I read the other one, from Jarrod.

> I'm unexpectedly out of town, so I'm going to have to delay our meeting. Next Thursday. 11 o'clock.

Thanksgiving Day. Figures.

I write:

> It's Thanksgiving. I'm having people over.

I think of the spreadsheet, and the little turkeys Mira started making out of construction paper this morning, because she's officially gotten to the level of boredom where she's making construction-paper turkeys. Then again, I've seen her bar. I imagine it's the kind of thing she'd do for fun anyway. I'll bet Izzy would enjoy crafting with her. Maybe we could—

My phone buzzes again.

Eat late.

It's the kind of message a man would only dare write his employee if he felt certain he owned that man's soul. It flares something inside of me—some buried sense of resentment, of the need for revenge against someone, something, because my existence is spinning so thoroughly out of my control.

So I send another message.

Then I sit on the bench where Mira rode me, numb, looking out and trying to find a glimmer of light.

All I see is darkness.

Chapter Thirty-Two

Mira

He's still not home.

It's two in the morning, and he's still not home.

I've sent him a few texts he hasn't answered. Called a couple of times. Nada. Zilch. Zero.

My worry escalated to panic hours ago.

I've already talked to Azalea, and she said he left the bar before Daphne did. According to her, he looked pissed. So at least his ex-girlfriend didn't drag him into the bathroom to have makeup sex.

Probably.

But what the hell happened? Where is he now?

My mind suggests a few options and then throws each of them out—he wouldn't bring his problems to Ruthie, and his friendship with Shane is probably too strained right now for him to have gone there. If he were holing up with either Burke or Leonard, my sister or Shauna would have let me know. I'm desperate enough that I fleetingly consider the possibility that he might be in the apartment downstairs, finishing up his meeting with Big Mike, which Azalea said got interrupted.

Then my anxious mind finally finds a groove that fits—a place off the Blue Ridge Parkway. A bench with little letters carved into it.

I know what my sister would say.

She'd very reasonably point out that it's two in the morning, probably not the best time to go out for a joy drive, and even if I manage to find the right spot, I'm just as likely to accidentally run Danny over as I am to help him. But I'm itching to do something. I've exercised my ankle and my arms and my good leg. I've made half a dozen fucking paper turkeys. I've even made a signature Thanksgiving sangria and sent a few group texts to the Thanksgiving crew.

I've acted like a woman obsessed with Thanksgiving, when the only thought I usually give it is as a stumbling block on the way to Christmas.

I'll go out of my skin if I don't *do* something. I'll probably dress up as a turkey and go around gobbling at people.

"I'm doing it," I say, grabbing my keys off the side table and starting toward the door with the crutches. "I'm fucking doing it."

The empty room doesn't respond to me, and there's a creepy fullness to its emptiness, almost as if it's a shadow creature that should have a name.

"The hex was broken," I tell the shadow creature. And it's official—I've gone around the bend into full madness.

I head down the stairs, shaking my head at myself, at the situation, and at Danny, because I wish he'd come to me.

I make it into the car, then drive out of the garage in a daze. I'm still stuck in paranoia mode, because for a while I think someone's following me, but it turns out I just got in the middle of two people who were following each other.

When I'm sure it's safe, I make my way to the Blue Ridge Parkway, to Danny's spot.

My breath catches in my chest when I see his car there, but I'm not comforted. Because what if someone followed him out here? What if someone hurt him, or he got lost, or a raccoon bit him?

It's not easy being on crutches in the woods. Less easy when it's full dark and the moon is just a sliver hanging low in the sky, but I make my way toward the bench.

There's a figure lying on it. Danny's figure. I'd recognize him anywhere—those long lanky legs, his wavy mop of hair. One of his arms is draped down, the fingertips skimming the tops of the leaves piled around him.

Oh my God, is he dead?

My mind, fed on a diet of *The Murderer Next Door* and those binoculars sitting beside the armchair, kicks into overdrive. My heart beats like a scared rabbit's, and my hands shake as I try to make the crutches do what I want them to on the uneven ground covered in leaves and sticks and probably twenty different kinds of animal shit. I feel like I live my whole life in that instant in which I'm seesawing—yes, fucking seesawing—between realities where Danny is alive and ones in which he's dead. It's then that I know, really know, exactly how I feel.

"Danny!" I shriek, and the reclined body on the bench sits bolt upright, making me shriek louder until I realize he's perfectly alive and also that he looks terrified.

"Mira?" he asks, his voice shocked and frightened. He jumps to his feet and comes to me and my eyes are accustomed enough to the dark that I can see him, or see him well enough. His eyes fixed on me, intense and alive, and full of worry. When he sees that I am also alive, some of it washes away. But only some of it. "Why are you here?" His hand finds my face, then weaves into my hair. "Why are you here?"

He sounds worried. Maybe even a little pissed off.

Suddenly *I'm* pissed. I'd push him if it wouldn't result in me completely losing my balance and falling into the wet leaves. "What am *I* doing here?" I ask, pushing one of my crutches at him. "What are *you* doing here? Do you have any idea how worried I've been? I thought something terrible might have happened to you. I thought you could be dead."

He's silent for a long time, so silent, and a dark foreboding falls over me. Finally, he swallows, his Adam's apple bobbing deliciously in his throat, and says, "I didn't think about worrying you. I should have. I'm bad about..." He waves his hand. "I should have called you back. I didn't know what to say yet. It takes me a while sometimes. I had to sit out here and think. I needed to be alone."

"What happened, Danny?" I ask. Then, because we need a moment of levity, even if it's fleeting, I add, "Did you really hate the bar that much?"

His hand flexes in my hair, and he laughs, but only for a half a second. Then he tugs my hair slightly and bends to me, kissing me so hard I can't breathe, and I kiss him back the same way, because I can tell that whatever happened he thinks I'm lost to him—and him to me. He sucks on my bottom lip, my tongue, he kisses the corner of my mouth, and I feel tears in my eyes, because I was so, so worried, and I'm not comforted by what I've found.

"I liked it in there," he finally says, pulling away slightly but keeping his hands on me. "It felt like you."

"Too loud and too much."

"But in exactly the right way."

My heart throbs in my chest, wanting to grow bigger, also on the verge of breaking. I can tell it was still overwhelming for him, but I believe him. I'm too much too, but he makes me feel like I'm just right. "What happened?"

Sighing, he says, "It's all catching up to me, Mira."

"What happened?"

He helps me over to the bench, and I sit next to him, our thighs pressing together, and it strikes me that this is a place of confession for us.

He tells me about Big Mike, and how he left before he could say anything useful or meaningful. Classic negging. The guy's been all over Danny for the last few weeks, and when Danny finally pays him attention, he acts like he has more important things to do.

Then Danny moves on to recounting his meeting with Daphne and her offer. Her *threat*...and who the woman across the street actually is.

"That bitch," I mutter to myself. "You can't give in to them."

His jaw flexes, and I see something I don't want to—part of him is tempted. Part of him would like nothing better than to be a member of this group that lets him do the thing he loves doing.

"You're not—"

He takes my hand and squeezes it. His eyes meet mine and hold them prisoner. "Of course not. I might have fallen for it before, but now... She was acting like she'd be setting me free, but it would be another trap. They'd be telling me what to do and how, and I'd be at their mercy, especially if they were hiding me. No. I'd never agree to that. I'd never let them take me away from everything that's important to me." He's looking at me when he's saying that, his eyes glittering in the slight glow of the stars, that sliver of a moon. His hand flexes around mine. "I've decided to tell Big Mike everything. I've already texted him asking for a meeting, but he says he had to leave town and won't be back until next week. I'm meeting with him on Monday."

Fear pulses through me, because if Big Mike has been spying on Danny because he wants to build a case against him, then Danny might really go to jail. "But Danny, what if—"

"Then I deserve it," he says, meeting my eyes. "I'm not going to let my ex-girlfriend hide me away in another country." He pauses, looking out into the night. Swallows. "I could be in big trouble, Mira. It's hard enough being with someone who has limitations like I do. I might appreciate your bar, but I don't fit in there. I don't fit in *anywhere*, not really. Even with the guys—my best friends—I have to go off to be by myself. You...you're so full of life. You deserve to be with someone else who's like that. Someone who can keep up." A humorless laugh escapes him. "I'm not even in the same race."

"Who says it's a race?" I ask as a different fear overcomes me. Those currents are pulling him away from me, and I'm not sure there's anything I can do to stop it from happening.

He waves a hand at the darkness in front of us. "They do. All of them. Everything in our society is set up as a race. Who can talk the best game. Who can make the most money. Who can *lie* the best. I'll never be able to keep up. I was born missing something. I'm still missing it. I'll *always* be missing it."

I tighten my hand around his so much it probably hurts. "Danny, you're not missing *anything*. The people who told you that were wrong. You're the best man I've ever known. So kind and smart and handsome, and it fucking sucks that you don't see yourself the way I do, the way Ruthie and your friends do."

I know immediately it was the wrong thing to say, because he snatches his hand back. His jaw tics. "What did Ruthie say about me?"

"She didn't say anything," I retort quickly, but it's a lie and it sounds like one. "She told me a bit more about your parents. About what it was like for you, growing up with them."

How they made you feel you weren't enough. How they used you.

He gets up, pacing a few steps in the dark, and even though I know he'd never do such a thing, I feel a pulse of worry that he'll walk away and leave me here with my crutches in the dark. But he turns back, his eyes shining. "You put me in the back booth at Glitterati because it was quieter and darker, didn't you? And the music...Daphne said she remembered it being louder."

"So what?" I ask, taken aback. "I wanted you to be comfortable there. I knew..."

"You know there's something wrong with me," he says. "You know I'm not the kind of guy who could go to a bar for a couple of hours without having to be alone for four afterward. That's exactly my point."

"So what?" I ask, fumbling with my crutches so I can stand too. "You have a problem with me trying to take care of you? You take care of me all the time. You think it's easy for me to let you? It's not. No one's *ever* taken care of me like that." As I say it, I feel tears welling in my eyes—angry tears—and I don't know who I'm mad at. Him. Me. His parents. The universe, maybe, for giving me this perplexing and intelligent and giving man and then tearing him away from me. For making someone so wonderful and skewing his perception of himself so much he can only see what he views as his flaws.

"You don't get it," he says, and there's such grief behind those words that they feel like a sucker punch to the chest.

"No, I really don't."

"You were doing those things for me because I'm not normal," he says, his voice rising. "I..."

"So the fuck what?" Even as I'm saying it, I remember what Ruthie told me. About the way his parents used to treat him. It must have slid under his skin and made him see himself this way—as someone who's other. "You're better than normal. Better than basic."

"You think that now, but..."

I reach forward and shove him. Not an easy feat right now, but desperate times and all that. "Don't you tell me what I think, Danny. You may be smarter than I could ever hope to be, but you don't get to tell me what I think or how I feel."

My hand is on his chest, and it occurs to me that it might be the last time I get to touch him there. I feel tears falling down my cheeks.

"It's better this way," he says, his tone softer now. "It was probably always going to happen like this, after you got better."

It's nothing I haven't feared, but I didn't want to hear it from him. He was the one who knew how to make things work. He was the one who was smart enough to figure it out.

I drop my hand as if the contact is burning me.

"You're a coward," I tell him, even though I know it's not really true. He's taught me that a person can be so many things at the same time—a coward and the bravest man I've ever known. The person who healed my heart and also broke it. Maybe I shouldn't have followed him out here. Maybe he needed more time to process the bullshit that was just heaped onto him. But I did come, and all of this did happen, and now I'm starting to think I need time too. Because I can feel myself on the verge of falling apart, of crying and huddling into a little ball that's not at all the strong woman I aspire to be. And I don't want him to see me like that. Not right now.

I didn't see our conversation ending this way. I wanted to tell him how I felt, and now I'm talking to a brick wall. "I'm going home now."

"It's probably better if you don't stay at the apartment," he starts. "They—"

"That woman left," I say. "She's gone, there's a new security system, and Big Mike is a fucking police detective. I can't think of a safer place for me. If *you* don't want to come home, you don't have to."

He watches me for a long moment, his gaze tortured, and I realize I'm taking his home from him. But I don't want to relent, not now. Because he's the one who's pulling away.

His throat bobs. "Okay. We can tell everyone we changed our mind about Thanksgiving. We can—"

"No," I say, the word coming out sharply. "I *will* be hosting Thanksgiving dinner. You can come if you'd like. Ruthie and Izzy too."

He watches me. Nods. "I'm going to follow you back to the apartment to make sure you get there safely."

"I can get back fine on my own," I say, swallowing the tears.

His hands reach forward before falling to his sides. He looks devastated, but he's not back-peddling. He's not telling me that any of this is going to be okay. "I need my computer and some things."

"Fine," I say flatly. I take a step toward where the cars are parked, and I stumble, nearly losing my balance. He immediately comes forward to help me, his hand on my arm, but I snap, "No, you don't get to help me if I don't get to help you. Don't you think that's fair?"

He doesn't release me for a second, and when he meets my eyes, his look like pools deeper than time. "Mira, I'm sorry."

So am I.

Chapter Thirty-Three

Danny

I don't know where to go, after I gather a few things from the apartment. Mira doesn't talk to me while I pack my bag. She doesn't talk to me as I walk out, moving past my armchair and the SAD lamp, past the pink record table...

This apartment was where I belonged for years, but it's not mine anymore—somewhere, in the last few weeks, it became ours. Now...I guess maybe it's hers.

I'm in a stupor as I leave, as I walk out on the life I want.

What the fuck am I doing?

I didn't intend for any of that to happen. I'd decided to give her a choice—to tell her we could hold off on whatever was happening between us until after I had answers about what Big Mike wanted. But it scared me that she'd come out there at two in the morning to find me. Something could have happened to her. Someone could have followed her. RetCon could try to use her to get me to comply with their demands. And then all of my fears and inadequacies seemed to recognize their opening and swallowed me up. Part of my meltdown was prompted by the realization that Ruthie must have told Mira about our parents. How I'd let them push me around for so long.

It made me feel like less of a man. Like the little boy who'd been told so many times that he was stupid and useless...and the teenager who'd carried the weight of his family's finances.

Still, even though this isn't what I wanted, a voice in my head insists it was always going to come to this, even if Big Mike and Daphne didn't exist. So, it's better if it happens now. And maybe Mira won't mind so much anymore if I do get arrested. Maybe I'm doing her a favor.

But another voice in my head, *her* voice, is calling me a coward.

I don't consciously plan to go there, but I find myself parking outside of Shane's little bungalow. I look at the dash. It's past three in the morning. I can't go in now. I can't...

My phone buzzes, and I take it out, the movements mechanical. I'm so tired. So completely exhausted and overwhelmed.

The message is from Shane.

> Are you going to come inside or are you going to wait out there like a creepy stalker.

> Undecided. I'm surprised you're still awake.

> I'm drinking whiskey. Want some?

> I need to sleep.

> That's what the whiskey's for.

> It's past 3, and you're still awake. I guess it's not working.

> It's easy to be a smartass when you're texting me from my driveway.

I get out with the bag, and when I reach the door, he's there in the opening. He looks like shit, and the first thing he says to me is, "You look like shit."

"Thank you," I say, because the rote response is the first thing that comes to mind. We both laugh humorlessly.

"Come inside and tell me what you did." He steps back, and I step in, lowering my bag to the floor.

"Would it be okay if I don't talk about it yet?"

He nods because he understands me. He knows I'm not ready, but I will be, and then he'll be there for me.

A voice in my head suggests that I'm letting him make accommodations for me, even though I snapped at Mira for it.

I'm too tired to do anything about that. To even give it the thought it probably deserves.

"Come sit for a minute," he says, and I nod, because I can tell he needs to talk.

We head into his kitchen, which has recently been redone in a modern style that seems like an unnecessary touch for a man who doesn't like to cook and has made a pledge to never get married.

I sit on one side of the butcher block table, and he sits on the other. There's a glass of whiskey in front of me, and I take a sip. It burns.

Shane pushes back in his chair and sighs. "I didn't wait for Thanksgiving. I talked to Burke."

"What'd he say?" I ask, even though it's obvious the news wouldn't have inspired him to throw a parade.

His hand clenches around the glass, then releases. "He told me he understands."

I know without asking that this is the one thing Burke could have told him that was guaranteed to fuck with his mind. Burke wouldn't have done it on purpose. It's the big brother in him. He's like the eldest sibling in our group, there for all of us. A strong shoulder.

And I've let him down too.

"I feel really fucked up," I admit.

He nods but doesn't ask me why. "So do I. I can't talk to Burke until the trial's over. My partners agreed on that."

"Shit."

"Shit," he agrees.

We sit there in mostly silence for the next fifteen minutes or so, slowly drinking our whiskey, before I say. "I'm never going to belong anywhere, Shane, am I?"

He snorts. "You belong with us, you dumbass. And as much as your sister irritates the shit out of me, you belong with her too." He squeezes that glass again, then looks at me and says, "From what I saw, I think you belong *with* her too."

He doesn't say her name, and he doesn't need to. We both know who he's talking about.

"How'd you know this was about Mira?"

His upper lip pushes down slightly, as if he's trying to press away a smile. "You're in a world of shit, but none of that would phase you like being on the outs with someone you care about."

"There's something missing from me," I tell him, my skin feeling itchy all over. "She deserves someone who's normal."

This time he laughs. "You've got to decide, Danny. Do you want to be basic or not? Daphne only saw what you showed her, and you got upset when she thought you were boring. From what you've told me, Mira's always seen you, and that upsets you too. Who are you going to be, brother?"

If that isn't the eternal question.

I lay in bed for an hour or maybe two without sleeping. I type out three or four texts to her, deleting each of them.

Finally, I write:

> I need to get all of this settled. So many things are up in the air right now, and it wasn't fair of me to put you in the middle of it.

She doesn't respond.

I wake up with my alarm at six and text Jarrod to say I have the flu. Then I sleep until four p.m.

When I get up, I feel a greater sense of purpose. Shane's gone, but he texted me.

> I'll be home at 6. Have dinner on the table and waiting, sweetheart.

He's probably joking, but the rhythm of cooking, of following specific directions and having an expected outcome is soothing. So I look through his cabinets and make a chicken casserole out of the ingredients he has on hand.

My mind is whirling the entire time.

It's full of Mira. Of her scent, of the sound she makes when she comes, and the little dance of excitement she manages to pull off even when she's on her crutches. And I can't stop thinking of the look in her eyes last night and the way she turned her back on me as I packed my bag in the apartment.

I know I've fucked up, yet I'm not ready to pull a 180. I still haven't talked to Mike, and Daphne and her people are circling me. It's safer for Mira if I keep my distance. Besides, the decision has already been made, might as well sit on it.

Coward.

The word keeps echoing through my head. Maybe I am a coward. Maybe Shane's one too. Maybe that's why we're holed up here together.

I'm about ready to pull the casserole out of the oven, when my phone buzzes with a call. It's Ruthie.

I swear, but I still pick it up, because I can't not answer it. She or Izzy might be having a problem.

"You're being an idiot," she says as soon as I pick up.

"Hello to you too," I mutter, sighing as I pull the casserole out and place it on the stovetop.

"I just talked to Mira." I feel a twist of resentment in my chest, because *I* want to talk to Mira. "She said you broke up with her, but she still wants Izzy and me to come to Thanksgiving dinner. Why would you do something so stupid, Danny? She's perfect for you."

Anger stokes in my chest. "You talked to her about *me*," I say heatedly. "You told her about what it was like, with Mom and Dad. It wasn't your place to say any of that."

"No," she says, sounding more sad than angry now. "It was yours."

It hits like a blow, but I say, "You don't know everything, Ruthie."

"No, but that never stopped you from stepping in when I was doing something stupid. I'm just doing you the same courtesy."

"Maybe I would have told her everything if you'd given me time."

"Would you have?"

Her question buries in my chest. I don't like to lie, but there are so many things I haven't told people. "Well, now we'll never know, will we?"

"I guess we won't," she says, sounding on the verge of tears.

Fabulous, I've made my sister cry now.

"Come to Thanksgiving, Danny. Don't do this. Don't burrow yourself away like you always do when you're upset about something."

"I'm doing the right thing," I say, the words hollow. "I'm protecting her."

Ruthie can't know what I'm talking about, but she says, "Maybe she doesn't want you to protect her, Danny. Maybe she just needs you to love her." And I hurt down to my soul because I know she's not only talking about Mira.

"I do love you." *And her.*

"Then you should know that one of the things I want most, one of the things I wish for every night, is for you to be happy. To let yourself by happy." She pauses and then adds, "I sure hope this doesn't have anything to do with Daphne. Mira told me that she works at Big Bear."

She says her name as if it's a disease. "Not in the way you're thinking," I say. "It's Mira..."

I trail off. Because I was about to say *it's Mira I love.* I shouldn't say it for the first time to my sister, though, and I shouldn't say it at all the way things stand.

"I'll think about Thanksgiving," I end. I don't tell her that I've been told to report to work on Thanksgiving Day, to the fucker who hurt her. Maybe I do need to share more of my life, but I'll never willingly hurt her.

I'm hanging up the phone when Shane walks in. He looks like hell—even worse than he did last night. He gives me a lopsided smile and says, "Honey, you cooked."

Chapter Thirty-Four

Mira

The last few days have not gone well, but at least I've managed to get to Sunday. Things can only go up from here, right?

I've cried, made a fuck-ton of cardboard turkeys and a full drink menu for the holiday dinner, cried some more, and then picked up the abandoned binocs to verify that my friend across the alley is still gone. The disappointment I felt says a lot about how lonely I am.

I didn't mean to spill everything to Ruthie, but as soon as I texted her about Thanksgiving plans, she called me back—and it didn't take long for the whole story to come gushing out. Probably not the best idea, given that Danny got so upset about what she told me before. But I needed a sympathetic ear, and she knows Danny better than anyone, I think. Better even than his friends. She was adamant that she was spending Thanksgiving with me and, if she had anything to do with it, Danny would be too.

"He does this, you know," she said, leading to the obvious question—

"Does what?"

"When everything gets too much for him, he buries himself... well, inside of himself. But it never lasts forever."

This would be a banner time for it to start.

"Thanks," I said, because I was pretty sure she'd said it to make me feel better. "Whatever happens, you're pretty great."

"So are you," she said sadly. "Do you know where he is now?"

"No," I admitted, not feeling great about that fact, even though I could have asked and didn't.

"I know." She sounded pissed about it, which confirmed a suspicion I'd already had.

"You think he's at Shane's."

"Of course, where else? They enable each other. They always have."

I wasn't sure I agreed. Considering what we now know about Daphne and Big Mike, a sharp-shooting lawyer is exactly the sort of person he should be spending time with right now. But I'm guessing Ruthie doesn't know about any of it, and Danny wouldn't thank me for telling her. I also wasn't about to disagree with someone who'd just offered to help me.

Ultimately, though, however much Danny loves Ruthie, she doesn't have a say in his decisions. He's a grown man, perfectly capable of deciding where he wants to live and who he wants to be with. The fact that he's decided to be an idiot is completely and one hundred percent under his control.

I'm pissed at him for giving up when he's the one who told me, more than once, that we'd work through our differences.

So a big part of me is running on *fuck you* energy.

But I'm also devastated for me—and for him. Because we did have something special, and he walked away from it, whatever his reasons.

I'm also scared that he's going to find himself in the kind of trouble that not even his slick-talking buddy can get him out of.

I am, in short, a mess. Which is why I'm grateful when Delia, Shauna, and Azalea agree to come over for an early afternoon drink and bitch session so I can complain to them. They file in, looking like people who have probably showered and preened at some point over the last few days, and the horror on Azalea's face tells me what I already know. The homemade face mask I put together after watching a YouTube short both smelled terrible and was completely ineffectual.

Complaining usually makes anyone feel better, but it doesn't do much for me this time. I'm feeling so wrung out and alone that when Delia makes her inevitable offer to *come stay with me, just for a little while,* I actually consider it for more than five seconds.

But I still have enough gumption left to turn her down.

Shauna, who's been suspiciously quiet, gulps down the rest of her drink. "I'm just going to come out and say it. I invited Josie and her boyfriend to Thanksgiving dinner. She called Leonard and me, and she was sounding super pathetic, like they had nowhere else to go, and..." She shrugs, her nose wrinkling slightly like she smells the remnants of the face mask. "One thing led to another. This happened before I knew what was going on with you and Danny, obviously, otherwise I probably would have shut her down."

"Probably?" Delia asks.

Shauna tilts her head slightly, lifting her shoulder toward her ear. "That woman has wiles I don't begin to understand."

"You are *dead* to me," I say with a groan. "Dead. They're sitting next to you. In fact, I might sit the two of them between you and Leonard for ultimate torture."

"I guess I deserve that," she says before lifting her empty glass back to her lips again, chasing that last micro-sip. "I'm good with it as long as you sit Nana next to the detective."

"Deacon?"

He and I are practically best friends now. After he accepted my invitation to Thanksgiving dinner, he called me up to ask my thoughts on mashed potatoes. I admitted that Danny was the one who knew how to mash a potato, and we ended up telling each other our life stories and crying over the phone. It was a very bonding experience, and now I feel responsible for his happiness and well-being.

"She better treat him right. That man has been through hell and back. His ex-girlfriend left him for a clown. Like, a legit clown. This guy had the face makeup and everything."

Shauna sets her empty glass down. "My grandfather left Nana for a water performer, so they potentially have the circus in common."

"I thought she was a water aerobics instructor?" Delia asks with a frown.

"Same difference," Shauna says. "Anyway, we should let you get back to..." She waves at the army of construction paper turkeys rampaging across the table, which—I'll hand it to Josie—is definitely too small for the number of the guests, especially now that the guests include Josie herself. I wish I did have a leaf to add to it.

"You think she was planning this all along?" I ask.

Surprisingly, Shauna picks up the loose thread of the conversation and answers, "I wouldn't be surprised, but why us?"

"Maybe she and Poe have tried to con all of their clients into inviting them, and we're the only one's stupid enough to fall for it."

Her lips are barely holding back laughter—the effort probably only made because she knows this is her fault. "On the plus side, she promised to read everyone's fortune for free."

"And you think that's a good thing?"

Shauna has the grace to look embarrassed this time. "No, probably not. I swear...I didn't intend to say yes, it's just that she has this..."

"Uncanny power," Delia says, nodding. I hold back a sigh. She's basically Josie's new disciple at this point. I caught her texting her a question about energy the other day.

"I need to meet this woman," Azalea adds.

"Come to Thanksgiving dinner," I say with a wave of my hand. "Apparently everyone in the greater Asheville area will be here."

Except for Danny.

The thought is razor-edged.

"I actually really want to," Azalea says, "but unfortunately my mother hasn't met a super-hot European billionaire who wants to whisk her off to Europe."

"If it makes you feel better, I'm pretty sure he's just the founder of one of those MLM schemes."

She pushes her lips out and nods. "Maybe I should get into that. Earn myself one of those Mary Kay cars."

They leave, and I make another paper turkey while I look, for the one thousandth time, at the perfectly unsatisfactory message that Danny left on my phone.

At the same time, I remember him telling me that he needs more time to process things sometimes. Maybe it really is time that he needs.

But I hope he doesn't take too much of it, because I can feel my walls lifting back up and my resentment growing. Because he made me want him, *need* him, when I've tried to live my life as an independent woman—and then he left.

I hope he comes back while there's still something to come back to.

Chapter Thirty-Five

Danny

"You ready for this?" Shane asks. It's Monday afternoon, and we're outside of Big Mike's apartment. The knowledge that Mira might be upstairs is pounding through me. It may have only been a few days since I last saw her, but time has a different meaning again—this time it's stretched out, longer than it should be, as if minutes are hours and hours are days. I miss the way she smells, the way she always stretches lazily like a cat after getting out of my favorite chair. I miss the notes we leave each other at the apartment. I miss the little signs of her that she leaves wherever she goes—a bracelet discarded here, some lipstick on a napkin there. A handwritten note with no obvious meaning on the coffee table, as if she had a brilliant idea in the middle of the night and wrote it down, only to forget its meaning in the morning. I miss *her*.

But something is still holding me back. Maybe it's all of the unknowns.

I've never been good at dealing with unknowns, and right now everything in my life has taken on the curve of a question mark. All of the things that were sturdy and capable of being relied on are tilted. My old reliables have been taken away slowly but surely. Drew moved to Puerto Rico, and while he's still available pretty much around the clock to talk to or play True Colors, it's not the same. After that, Burke met Delia and moved out of our apartment. Then Mira moved in, and everything I thought I knew was sandblasted until it looked like something different...

I miss her. I *love* her. I still don't know whether I can be any good for her, but I desperately want to try.

Now, I'm here in front of this apartment, preparing to put my fate in the hands of a man who bribed a small child into selling him her hamster because he figured it would make his cover story stronger. A man who genuinely believed I look like the kind of guy who'd spill important secrets while getting a lap dance.

It's logical to be worried. I'm probably fucked.

Big Bear Games gave me an offer for True Colors on Friday. It was generous—too generous—but I had a long talk with Drew, and we unanimously decided to turn it down.

It was hard to say no to the money, money that would have allowed me to walk into that meeting with Jarrod on Thursday and quit on the spot, but I didn't want to feel I owed any debts to Daphne or her friend across the street. We'll find someone else to distribute it. I already have a few meetings lined up for the week after Thanksgiving, and Drew plans on coming home for Christmas with his fiancé and future grandmother-in-law, Mrs. Ruiz. They made the move because Mrs. Ruiz had a terminal diagnosis and wanted to spend what little was left of her life in Puerto Rico, but apparently there's something to be said for living where your heart is—because she's already survived longer than they thought possible.

Daphne texted me after I turned the offer down, saying she hoped my final answer for her would be different. It won't be, but I sent an ambiguous answer.

"You ready?" Shane asks. It's the second time he's asked that, or maybe even the third, so I figure it's time for me to start pretending.

I nod.

He insisted on coming with me as my lawyer. But my sister's words didn't go on deaf ears—I told him I wanted him here as my friend instead. I'm not going to let other people fight my battles for me.

I take a deep breath, then I put my fist to the door.

Big Mike answers on the first knock, eager as ever. As before, the apartment looks so staged I'm surprised there's not a fake cookie smell wafting out.

"This is my friend, Shane," I tell him in response to the baffled look he's giving my friend.

Fair enough. I didn't warn him.

"I'm his lawyer," Shane adds—because I'm pretty sure he couldn't help himself.

"Oh," Big Mike says, lifting his hands. A smile flits across his face. "Guess you did warn me about your lawyer friend the first time we met, but there's no need for that."

I'd take comfort in his assurance, but I'm pretty sure that's the attitude of all cops everywhere when the word lawyer is spoken.

We step inside, and Shane closes the door behind us. The only slightly personal item is a huge hamster cage against the front wall, in which Pumpkin is aggressively running on a wheel. He stops what he's doing and stares me down, as if he blames me for curtailing his freedom.

"Come in, come in," Big Mike says. "I've got a couple of drinks waiting for us."

Sure enough, there are a couple of glasses sitting out on the coffee table—whiskey, it looks like.

"I'll pour another one for your buddy here."

"I'm not going to drink that," I blurt. After hearing Deacon's story, I'm never going to drink anything without knowing exactly where it's been and who's touched it.

"You're worried I may have poisoned you?" Big Mike asks, sounding bemused.

"Not really, but I'd rather not find out the hard way."

He nods, then heads over to the table and takes a sip from each glass. "How about now?"

"Now, I don't want to drink it because of the germs."

He glances at Shane, who shakes his head. "I'm on the clock."

He's not.

"Whoa-kay," Big Mike says, taking a seat on an armchair arranged next to the sofa. He gestures to the sofa, and we both take a seat—me on the square closer to Big Mike.

"So, looking forward to Thanksgiving?" he asks.

"If you've been keeping an eye on me, I'm guessing you know enough to guess the answer," I say. "How about you tell me why you left the bar so suddenly last Wednesday after making such a big deal of wanting to talk to me?"

Big Mike glances at Shane, then the door. Finally, he says, "A contact informed me that Daphne LaRue was on her way to the bar."

I lean back, shocked. "You're interested in Daphne?"

"I'm interested in RetCon, and they're interested in *you*."

Shane's been watching our exchange, and he says, "Why would an undercover detective at the local department be interested in RetCon?"

"I'm with the FBI," Big Mike says, which is mostly shocking because he's always come off as so inept. Then again, it can't be cheap to part a screaming child from her hamster.

"That's *very* interesting," Shane says. "Now why don't you get to the part where you tell us what you want from Danny?"

"They're trying to recruit you," Big Mike says. It's not a question. "Because of your past as The Reaper. Your work for Jarrod Travis."

He doesn't mention my work as Bo Peep, which is a relief, but not much of one. RetCon knows, and they've made it clear they're willing to talk if I don't fall in line.

"Maybe," I say. "I agree with my buddy the lawyer. I'd like to know what you want from me." A new fear blinks into being. "Wait...are you trying to get me to accept their offer and go undercover?"

Big Mike laughs as if I've said something hilarious. "No, my friend. We don't send out other people to do our job for us. You wouldn't know what to look for, or how to lie."

Little does he know, I've been wearing masks all my life. I've also listened to enough of *The Murderer Next Door* to have a pretty good idea of what's suspicious.

But I'm not going to try to convince him to give me a job I don't want.

"Okay, so what *do* you want?"

"We have it on good authority that they're working on a project that could be devastating to national security. We were hoping you might be willing to steer them toward someone else. Red Snake," he says, sounding almost proud about it.

"That's you," Shane says.

I wouldn't have taken him for a hacker, but Big Mike nods and grins.

I'm tempted to tell him that he probably shouldn't have called himself a snake if he's planning to fuck them over, but what do I know. Maybe it's better to call out the possibility, act like you're above suspicion.

"So I tell them I'm not interested but my buddy the Red Snake is all in? You don't think that's going to come off as suspicious?"

"Daphne used to be your woman, right?"

I feel a throb of pain in my chest—and a strange awareness of Mira upstairs, maybe even directly above my head. Listening to *The Murderer Next Door* maybe. "Yes," I say flatly.

"So she trusts you."

I consider this, then nod. "I guess she probably does. I'd be a dick to abuse that."

Shane gives a dry laugh. He probably didn't mean to, given he doesn't particularly like giving away information for free, but he's not quite himself lately. "And she didn't abuse your trust?"

I consider it for a moment, then say, "They know things about me that could be...inconvenient."

"The Reaper," Big Mike says. "We know about that." He smiles at me, and it strikes me that the Red Snake isn't such a bad name for him. "And we know about Bo Peep too. Interesting shift."

Before I can tell him that I figured it wasn't such a bad idea for people to assume Bo Peep was a woman, Shane lifts a hand. "My client admits to nothing. But we would be interested in whether the FBI or local law enforcement would feel the need to pursue such... allegations, baseless as they may be."

Big Mike gives him a shit-eating grin. "Not if we get what we want. We could offer certain protections."

Shane glances at me, then back at Big Mike. "What else can you do?"

The big man laughs. "You're implying you want a cessation of his agreement with Jarrod Travis."

"And if I am?"

My heart beats fast and hard in my chest while I wait for his answer.

"Then I'd have to inform you that we can't dismantle a private arrangement. However, we could put significant pressure on Mr. Travis not to file suit if your client reneged on certain aspects of the arrangement."

"You have dirt on him," I say, instantly hungry for it.

Big Mike gives me a pointed look. "If you break into our system, I'll know who did it."

So noted.

"What if I want you to expose the dirt, and I don't give a fuck about the arrangement?"

"We sometimes have greater aims that I'm not at liberty to share with you, Mr. Peep."

"Very funny," Shane says. He drums the table with one hand, then says, "So you're offering Mr. Peep immunity and a chance to break his ties with Jarrod Travis."

"If he gets me in," Big Mike says.

They both turn to stare at me.

"Are you any good?" I ask.

Shane rolls his eyes.

"What?" I ask. "They're going to know something's wrong if he can't break into systems."

"I'm good," he claims, although we'll see about that. "I'll send some information for you to review. You'll have to pretend we've known each other for a long time."

"I'll say we're neighbors."

He reaches out a big beefy hand, presumably for a shake. I glance at Shane, who gives the slightest nod, more an angling of his head, and I shake it. "You've got yourself a deal, Big Mike."

"Say..." he pauses, glancing at the cage. "Do you want a hamster? Turns out they're more work than I thought."

"You can't give it back to the kid?"

"Her parents were pretty eager to get rid of it."

"Not a great selling point. Say, what's your real name?"

I don't expect him to tell me, and I'm not disappointed. "Mike Hunt," he says with a wink. Then, "How about that whiskey?"

Shane seems inclined to stick around, but I feel a powerful urge to leave, now. "I've got to go," I tell him. "But send me that information, and I'll take a look."

If his portfolio isn't impressive enough, we might have enough time for me to make it look more impressive. I don't enjoy knowingly dissembling, especially to someone who used to be special to me, but Daphne didn't show any contrition about trying to manipulate me. And if they're not doing anything dangerous, then "Red Snake" will have nothing to find.

We head out the door, closing it behind us, and Shane makes for the stairs. Something compels me to hang back. I don't know what it is until I see it from the corner of my eye.

"I'm going to take the elevator," I tell him.

"Seriously? There're only two flights of stairs." Then he must remember the edited version of the elevator story I told him, because he smiles and shakes his head. "You could just go upstairs and knock instead of drowning yourself in nostalgia."

He's right. I could. But I feel this urge to do it anyway. No, it's more of a *need*.

He feigns tipping a hat to me. "You do you, buddy. I'll see you down below."

I walk to the elevator, feeling strange in my body, like my legs are too long, my feet un-sturdy. I press the button.

It glows, and I hear the old gears working.

Suddenly, I know, without knowing how I know.

Or maybe I just hope.

Then the doors slide open, and I step in—and there Mira is in front of me. She looks just like she did the day we were stuck on the elevator, although I'm sure she'd tell me she was wearing a different outfit entirely. Her hair is pulled back, several pieces escaping the small bun, and her eyes are done in that cat-eye look.

Her lips part in surprise or maybe displeasure as the doors close behind me. I feel the elevator start to descend, and then it suddenly jolts to a stop.

What are the odds?

Chapter Thirty-Six

Mira

"What the actual fuck?" I say, because sometimes those are the only words that will do. Most people don't get stuck on an elevator once—twice is really pushing it. Except it *is* the same elevator, and I'm betting we're the only two people stupid enough to give a malfunctioning elevator a second chance.

It's the first time I've taken it since that day. I was missing Danny, and I figured, what the hell? Might as well make myself feel worse. I felt pulled to take it down into the garage, and I didn't have the gumption to tell myself no, because it felt like I'd gotten enough no's lately.

Maybe I knew on some subconscious level that he would be here in the building. He'd said he was meeting with Big Mike today, although not where. That fact that he's here—that he boarded on the third floor—means that he was in there. He was beneath me while I was swinging around the apartment on my crutches, getting ready for an afternoon at work.

Now, he's here, standing in front of me in a blue-checkered shirt —a definite win on my part—and he's so damn adorable I hate him for it. I hate him and I want to kiss him, and I'm dying to tell him about Deacon and Josie and the construction paper turkeys. I got bored last night and started an Instagram account for the turkeys, and even though I only got seven pity likes, it was the most exciting thing that had happened to me since learning about Deacon and that clown.

"Did you do this?" I accuse, because I'd like to accuse him of something, and I'm not sure I want to come right out and tell him he's been breaking my heart.

"No," he says, but he's staring at me in that way of his—like he wants to eat me with his eyes. "But I've never been more grateful to this elevator."

"You want to hold me hostage?" I ask, my tone hostile even though my heart is beating hard. It's more him than the elevator. His clean, familiar smell, the look of him in that shirt I chose. His hair curling slightly. His eyes so familiar. The way he can be taller than most people in a room but never seem to loom over them.

"I've wanted to talk to you, more than anything," he tells me, "but I didn't know what to say. Now, maybe I'll have enough time to think of the words."

"Boredom does strange things to a person," I say, thinking of those turkeys.

"I've never been bored when I'm with you."

His words furrow into me because I feel that way about him too. So many times, I've brought men like Byron home because they were fun and loud. Because they were people who stood out in a crowded bar. I wouldn't have noticed Danny in a place like that. He'd have been sitting in a corner or outside, his mind in far-off places. But he's the only man I've ever been with who doesn't bore me in daily life. Who says something interesting almost every time he opens his mouth—even if it's about the weather.

"You went to see Big Mike," I say. There's a popping sound, and I flinch. I glance up at the light, which flickers but doesn't go out.

Danny takes a half-step toward me, as if to comfort me, but I give him a hard look and he stops, looking unsure. Maybe I'm a bad person for wanting him to feel that way, but I do. I've spent the last few days drowning in uncertainty. Feeling like an abandoned cat someone left in an apartment after moving out. Worse: I've been marooned with his stuff. With his smell. With everything but him and his laptop.

"Yes," he says. "And I have a lot to tell you about that. But right now, there's something else I want to say."

"So the words are coming?"

"They're starting to." He swallows, and I watch his throat, seeing a slight mark on it that I left there. I want to kiss it. I'd also like to bite it harder.

"So?" I say coolly, acting like nothing he could possibly say would surprise me.

"Do you have a pen?" he asks. "Or preferably a Sharpie?"

Okay, that *is* a little surprising. Without thinking, I lean against the side wall so I can rummage through my bag and find a black Sharpie. I was using it to make those damn turkeys, and I slid some supplies into my bag so I could make a few for the bar. Something for which Azalea will surely give me shit.

"Thank you," he says, taking it from my fingers, and the place where our fingers brushed feels more alive from the slight contact—as if my skin is inviting his home again.

"What are you going to do?" I ask, rubbing my hand against my shirt as if I can shake his effect on me. "Write a giant help sign? I know what Dunkins said, but I doubt the big man upstairs is watching us."

"Maybe not, but the big man downstairs from us was watching."

Us.

"I thought you didn't live here anymore," I snap. "They say possession is nine tenths of the law."

"Shane might have something to say about that once we get downstairs."

"*If* we get downstairs."

"We'll get downstairs," he says, and there's such confidence in his voice that I believe him. All in all, I'm not as scared as I should be. Confined spaces usually leave me breathless, but my attention is so totally focused on him that the whole stuck-on-an-elevator-again conundrum is like white noise. Except, no, that's not totally true—it's because he's with me that I'm not scared.

I feel shaky as he gets down on his knees with the Sharpie, because I'm reminded of the things he did to me the last time he got down on his knees. I'm not proud, but if he shoved my pants down and buried his face between my legs, I wouldn't push him away. I'd hold his head there and ask for more.

But that's not what he does. His brow furrowed, he takes the cap off the Sharpie and starts scrawling on my cast. I take in a deep breath, because I know he's found his words, his message, at last.

I desperately want to read it.

I want it to be enough.

I want both of us to be safe, and together.

It feels like I'm standing there for an eternity, looking down at his bowed head as he scrawls on my cast.

The light flickers again, and without planning to, I weave my hand into his hair, feeling the heat of him under my fingers. He looks up at me for an instant, his lips lifting into a tentative smile, and I feel that almost smile everywhere—in my heart, expanding and hurting, in my chest. In my throat. Between my legs.

Then he bows his head back to his task, writing a damn essay, it looks like, filling up all the space that had been left empty.

"You're writing like you're getting paid by the word," I comment.

He caps the Sharpie and tucks it into my purse, a thoughtful gesture that makes me feel on the verge of tears again—and I still haven't read the essay he wrote on my cast. I expect him to get up, but he stays on his knees, as if he's awaiting whatever fate I choose for him. I know without asking that he'll accept whatever it is without question.

I glance down at the cast, but it's hard to read it from this angle and the writing is tiny. All I can see is the headline—42 *reasons I love you.*

Emotion wants to strangle me, but I don't plan on letting it.

"You could only think of forty-two?" I ask, my voice thick, a stranger's voice.

His smile lights up his eyes. "I could think of more, but I liked the significance of the number." He's still there on his knees, looking up at me. "I think I fell a little bit in love with you the first time you called me a dick."

Tears burn behind my eyes. "Get up here," I say, "get up here and atone for your tiny handwriting by reading it to me. I...I want to hear you say them."

He grabs the handle that runs around the middle of the elevator, as if it's giving it a hug, and stands in front of me. "Can I touch you?" he asks. "It's enough to drive a man mad, to be stuck in a box with the woman he wants more than anything in the world and to not be able to touch her."

"Not yet."

"You want me to read you the list?"

"I changed my mind. You can do that later. I want you to tell me why you left me the other night, and why it's not going to happen again if I forgive you."

His throat works, his eyes move over my face. His hands flex as if they want to touch me.

"I was worried about you getting caught up in my mess," he says after a moment. "But it wasn't just that. I was...ashamed. It makes me feel weak when I can't do things that most people can. Like there's something wrong with me, even if I know on some level that's not true. I...I've decided that I'm going to go through the diagnostic process. I feel like if I know for sure, it might help me come to terms with it, you know? It'll help me accept that there's not something wrong with me. That I'm the way I am for a reason."

"I'm glad, Danny. I think that's great. But either way, there's nothing wrong with you. Those things are part of what makes you *you*. And I wouldn't change you for anything."

He gives me a wry look. "And here I thought I was going to be your Patrick Dempsey."

"I *knew* you remembered his name."

"And I know you were just trying to help me by putting me at that booth in the bar, the same way you did when you picked out those shirts, but I still wish I were the kind of person who didn't need the help."

I laugh, then worry he'll think I'm laughing at him. I lift a hand, pressing it to his chest without thought, and I keep it there because his chest is exactly where my hand wants to be. "You think *I* like letting other people help me?"

"I know you don't," he says with a slight smile. "You wouldn't even let me help with your boxes when you were moving in. I had to sit at my desk like some kind of asshole."

"You didn't want to help. You didn't want me there. I *knew* you didn't. You're not nearly as good at hiding your emotions as you think you are."

He laughs, and I feel the rumble of it against my hand. I want to capture it in my fist. "I could barely look at you without getting hard. Of course I didn't want you moving in."

"Really?" I ask, intrigued by this.

"Really."

"Because it had been so long?"

He lifts a tentative hand, and his fingers feather across my jaw before cupping it. "Because you are the most perplexing, maddening, and tempting woman I have ever met."

"Is that on your list?" I ask, my pulse pounding as he edges closer. "Because it should be. It's pretty good." His mouth is so close to mine. All it would take is an upward press of my toes...

"It's on there."

"What else is on this list?"

"Your perfect sense of balance and poise," he says, and I shove him with the hand still pressed to his shirt but hang on to it too because I don't want him going anywhere.

"There you go again, being a dick."

"I seem to remember you preferring me that way."

And then I can't wait anymore—I press up and kiss him. It feels familiar and dear, but the way he kisses me back is hot enough to leave me a trembling mass on the floor of this elevator. Surely, I wouldn't still be standing if the crutches weren't holding me up. He must hear my unspoken thought, because he says, "I'll hold you up," then props them in the corner of the small space.

He sucks in my bottom lip and kisses the corner of my mouth, the top, and the place where my jaw meets my neck. Everywhere his mouth lands, a blaze of fire follows, because this is right—this man, this place, this everything. If we were stuck in this elevator until the end of time it might not be long enough.

Okay, that's not entirely true—I still want to get out of the elevator.

One of his hands holds me steady at my hip and the other burrows into my hair as he pulls me closer, changing the angle of the kiss. Our teeth gnash because I'm attacking him too, and then I pull away, stayed by a sudden thought.

"Danny, what are the odds of us both getting on the elevator like that, at the same time? Of it getting stuck again?"

"Astronomical," he says, smiling down at me.

"It's almost as if..."

As if fate brought us there, I want to say but don't. Because if I talk like that, I might be tempted to join Delia in her Cult of Josie, and I already own the industrial-sized bag of black salt my sister left here.

He presses a soft kiss to the corner of my mouth, then kisses me harder again, as if he can't help himself. "I felt drawn to the elevator," he says, interrupting the words with another kiss. "I didn't know why, but I knew I had to get on it."

Then he pulls back slightly, putting a little distance between us. In response to my sound of protest, he says, "I need to say something, and I'm going to get distracted if you're too close."

"Because looking at me gives you a hard-on."

"Because even thinking of you gives me a hard-on. It's just... About a month before you moved in, Josie told me that I'd already met my soulmate but I'd made a bad impression on her."

"Yeah, I know all of that," I say, because even the thought of Daphne puts a bad taste in my mouth. And that was true before I knew what she was really up to.

"I know how it sounds," he says, his tone almost apologetic, "but I think she was talking about you, not Daphne. You'd already met me, and I know what you thought. You're not great at hiding your real feelings either."

I want to respond to that, to tell him that I only thought what he wanted me to think. But I'm hung up on the other part of what he said. "You think we're soulmates?"

My mind flickers back to the moment in this elevator weeks ago when I asked this man to touch me to make me feel something.

He's made me feel everything.

"Is it too much?" he asks, his tone worried. Like he thinks there's a chance in hell I'd walk out on him if it were physically possible.

I lift up and kiss him again, softly, and say, "I love you, Danny Traeger. I'm going to give you the benefit of the doubt and assume your forty-two reasons are all amazing and worthy of being on my cast. And I very much like the idea of being your soulmate."

"Oh, thank God," he says, bending his head to me and kissing my eyebrow, my nose, my mouth.

And then, I shit you not, the light does the freaky popping thing again, and the elevator starts moving. I laugh into his mouth, and he seems to swallow it. Then the doors are opening, and Shane is waiting opposite us with someone who has a tool belt they are not currently using. Shane's mouth drops open, and it's so comical to see a man like him so disarmed that I pull back from Danny slightly and burst out laughing.

I distantly register that Shane is saying something to the man, the super maybe, about the elevator being defective and a lawsuit risk since it's now broken twice. But I'm still laughing. I'm too dizzy with happiness, with love, to pay such things any attention.

Through my laughter, I look at Danny and say, "Since...we're both feeling charitable toward Josie right now...I guess I should mention she invited herself to Thanksgiving dinner."

He gives me a wry smile. "Can't I be charitable from afar?"

Epilogue

Danny

It's Thanksgiving Day, and I'm waiting on a chair outside Jarrod Travis's office. No one else is present, so presumably I'm the only employee who was expected to show up today.

I've already knocked and been told that I'll be summoned when he's ready for me. So here I am, sitting in the most uncomfortable chair in existence, chosen exactly for that reason, I'm sure, outside of his closed office door like I'm a kid waiting to be called into the principal's office.

He's keeping me waiting because I said I have plans, obviously, but I don't mind. Because I *do* have plans.

Project Red Snake, as Mira named it after I shared all of my updates about Big Mike, is a go, as they say.

Big Mike is better than I thought he'd be—but I've spent the last couple of days helping him build up his presence and credentials. He was impressed, impressed enough that he says they may have some work for me in the future.

It's the kind of work I'm not supposed to be doing, but he insists that's not going to matter anymore.

Yesterday, I called Daphne to tell her that I wasn't interested in her offer but had an acquaintance who might be.

I'm ninety percent sure she's going to take the bait.

That ten percent uncertainty is more than I'd usually be comfortable accepting, but I'm feeling better about taking chances these days. Which is why I decided to show up here, even though I gave serious thought to sending Jarrod the middle finger emoji, followed by a turkey.

The door opens, revealing his punchable face and receding hairline. The thought of this man ever touching my sister makes me nauseous. I feel a familiar need to pound my fist into his face, but that's not why I'm here today.

As Shane would tell me, an arrest for assault is the kind of thing that would ruin anyone's day.

"Come in, *Danny*," Jarrod says, using my nickname with a special kind of glee, because it's another way in which he can feel superior to me.

"There's no need for that." In fact, I wish a few more people were present as witnesses—although I wouldn't want anyone else's holiday ruined.

He frowns at me. The lines that pop up probably rarely crease his forehead since he's so used to his fortune paving the way.

"I quit," I say, immediately feeling a hundred and ninety pounds lighter. I guess that's what happens when you lose the boss who's been making your life a nightmare.

"What did you say?" he asks, his face turning pink and then red.

"You heard me. I never wanted this job. This is a shitty company and making it less shitty is not something I'll ever be proud of. I did what I had to do at the time...and you did your best to make sure I regretted it. But that's over now. I quit."

"The money," he sputters. "You still need to pay me the money."

"You don't need it," I say. "But yeah...I intend to do that, once I have it. I did sign the agreement."

"You'll make the payments on schedule, or you'll be prosecuted," he says, his voice rising with each word.

I rise to my feet and look down at him, something I typically try not to do with people, but I'm happy to make an exception for him. "Like I said, I'll pay you the money when I have it."

I'm not going to tell him about my connection to the Feds. I expect he'll find out soon enough.

"You're going to regret this," he snarls.

"No, probably not. But someday you're going to regret that you ever heard my name, or my sister's. And I hope to be there to see it. I have a feeling I'll be laughing."

And with that, I turn on my heels and leave. I'm not afraid he'll follow me or try to attack me. He's the coward that I don't want to be. Not anymore.

———

WHEN I GET BACK TO THE APARTMENT, IT'S LOUD CHAOS EVEN though most people aren't coming over until two. Ruthie's already there with Izzy, and Izzy's watching some kind of crafting show on YouTube while Ruthie and Mira make various side dishes no one else signed up to make and babysit my mashed potatoes.

The second I open the door, Ruthie's head whips up and she drops the pan lid she was holding. I can see the anxiety in her eyes, so I nod and smile.

"You did it?" she shrieks, piercing my eardrums.

"I did it."

She runs over and hugs me, and Izzy does the same, even though she probably doesn't know why her mother's so happy.

"There's no way I'm missing out on a group hug," Mira says, and she comes over and joins in too—Ruthie and I holding her up because she's swaying on her crutches—and it feels right in every single way.

"I can't believe you're finally free," Ruthie says.

She doesn't know everything, but she knows that I quit my job today because I was able to "work something out" with the Feds.

She's already insisted on sending Big Mike a gift. For his sake, I hope it's not one of her winter fruitcakes.

I spend the next hour helping them prepare the side dishes and decorate the table and kitchen island, both of which feature a long line of paper turkeys. Mira showed me how to make them the other night, during a break from my work for Big Mike, and we started giving them each different expressions. Quizzical Turkey. Existential Dread Turkey. Seen-it-all Turkey. Tofurkey.

The first people to show are Burke and Delia, followed quickly by Deacon, who tells me that I'm "one hell of a lucky man."

I can only agree with such an obvious statement.

We're all on our first round of drinks—Drunk Pilgrims for everyone but Izzy, who gets a Sober Pilgrim, when the buzzer sounds.

I answer it, expecting Leonard to say something dirty into the speaker, the way he always does when he comes to visit, but Shane says, "Let me up, man."

My gaze darts across the room to Burke, who's mid-conversation with Delia and hasn't noticed. I press the buzzer as Mira reaches the door on her crutches.

"What's going on?" she asks.

"Shane's here," I say in an undertone.

"Wasn't he supposed to have dinner at his boss's house?"

"At noon."

Her eyes widen. "Some shit went down."

"Maybe."

Definitely. I look around for Ruthie, because if Shane's had a shit day already, he probably won't want my sister sniping at him. But she's busy talking to Delia and Burke. Izzy's still glued to that show, watching some talking slime doll gesticulate while a woman pretends crafts that probably took hours to make can be produced within minutes.

Children's TV baffles me.

"Let's find out," I say as I open the door.

Shane's already on the other side, looking jumpy. He's wearing a suit, although if he had a tie on, he's already removed it. There's a bottle of scotch in his hands.

"That's the good stuff," Mira comments with a nod.

"Should be," he says, slapping it against his hand. "I took it on my way out of the old guy's house."

Well, then.

"Come on in," I say.

"There's plenty of food," Mira says, "although Shauna and Leonard are supposed to bring the turkey, and they're not here yet, so what we have is a lot of alcohol and pies and side dishes."

"Okay," he tells her, still radiating that nervous energy. "Thank you."

When he walks inside, Ruthie's the first one to notice him. Her expression darkens, and she says, "Look who's graced us with his presence. And I see you went for a casual look, too!"

I glance at Shane, wondering if I'll need to referee today, but he doesn't bite back, his expression almost gray. I look back and see Ruthie's obvious confusion. This isn't the game they usually play.

Burke's taken notice of Shane too now. He watches him for a moment before giving a slow nod.

Deacon the P.I. shoots Shane a dirty look and shakes his Dirty Pilgrim at him. "You're not supposed to be here," he accuses. "I know what Myles told me, and I'm guessing he said the same to everyone else at that confounded firm. If I wanted to do any more work for them, I wasn't allowed to even be in the same room as the kid."

Surprised laughter gusts out of Shane. "Well, I quit and stole the old man's booze on the way out of his kingdom, so I think I'm good."

Relief wraps itself around me. I'd thought so, but it's good to have the confirmation. To know that he's free too, even though he's probably feeling like a top that can't stop spinning.

"Allegedly stole," I say, because that's supposed to be Shane's line. Then I pat him on the back. "Why don't we go out on the balcony for a second. You can tell Burke and me what happened. If that's okay with everyone else..."

"Yes," Mira says, "by all means, separate the women and children from the men." She's smiling, though, and when Deacon points out that he wasn't invited onto the balcony either, she tells him it's for the best because she and Ruthie need to coach him before Shauna's grandmother shows up.

Before we head outside, she takes the Scotch from Shane and shoves a drink into his hand. "You look like you need it."

"Thank you," he says.

We head outside into the cool air, and we all sit there quietly for a good minute before Shane turns to Burke and says, "I let you down. The old man had your father over for Thanksgiving dinner. I...I should have left the firm the minute I found out they were thinking of working with your parents, but I've given up so much for this job. I knew if I quit I'd never...Anyway, I did what I had to do. But I did it too late. I'm really fucking sorry."

"What happened when you left?" Burke says, studying Shane. He must see what I do—it didn't go down smoothly.

"I told him I was done, and he said that if I walked out and embarrassed him in front of his guests, I'd never work in the law again in this town. I said we'd see if his dick was as big as he thought it was, then I grabbed the Scotch I'd brought and left."

"So, it was technically your Scotch you took," I say for no real reason than that it's what goes through my mind.

"It makes it sound cooler to say I took it from him." Shane's half-smiling as he says it, and even though he's obviously distressed, I can tell that he's feeling some relief of his own.

"So I'm not the only one who lost a hundred and ninety pounds today," I say. He already knew about my plan to leave Safe-T Net, so that'll be no surprise.

He snorts, then looks surprised by it. Glancing down into the drink Mira made, which he took but hasn't tried, he says, "Yeah, more like double that. They're both assholes. I just..."

"Hope his dick isn't as big as he thinks?" Burke asks with a smile.

"I didn't want to be the one who said it," Shane says.

"Thank you," Burke tells him, then leans over and gives him a one-armed hug. "But you need to know you still would have been my friend whatever you chose."

The door cracks open, and Mira says, "I don't want to interrupt this, but I feel that everyone in the apartment should be aware that Josie and Poe have just arrived. And Josie's offered to do readings for everyone, isn't that nice?"

I get what she's not saying—get back into this apartment as soon as it's feasible.

I nod to the guys. "Let's go." And we all get up and head inside. I stay back to close the door. Mira, who's still standing by it, leans her head against my shoulder. "Thank goodness you read my bat signal," she says in a whisper. "Did everything go okay?"

"I think it's going to." And I mean it. We all have plenty of stuff to slug through, but it feels like everything is unfolding as it should.

After Mira and I reconciled, I offered to continue staying with Shane, for a while, and eventually find a studio apartment. But she insisted that I belonged here, and I wasn't about to argue.

This apartment means so many things to me, not all good or bad. It's been my prison and my solace, and it brought into my life the greatest gift possible.

I look in the living room, and Izzy, who's been glued to the weird slime show, turns and grins at Shane. "Uncle Shane, when'd you get here?"

"It's about time you noticed," he says, managing a smile as she runs to him and hugs his legs.

I see Ruthie smiling, because even if she can't bring herself to see the good in Shane, she loves her daughter more than anything.

Delia's hugging Burke, who's whispering something in her ear, and Josie and her boyfriend have quickly made themselves at home and are setting up what looks like a crystal ball on the kitchen island. They had to shove aside the Existential Dilemma Turkey to make room, which seems appropriate for some reason.

Josie has on a black veil, and a colorful dress that might have been purchased in a sealed bag reading Fortune Teller at one of those Halloween tents. Her boyfriend looks like he might have raided my collection of brown shirts.

"Hey," I say to Mira under my breath as I slide an arm around her. I have this urge to always be touching her, reminding myself that she's here. "They're kind of like us."

She scowls at me. "If you're implying I'm the Josie in this equation, I'm not happy with you, and next time you piss me off, you have to one up yourself from the last time you groveled. So you'll need to come up with more than forty-two reasons why you love me."

"You act like that's a challenge."

Someone clears their throat loudly, in a way that's meant to make people listen, and of course it's Josie.

"Hi, Josie," I say, because presumably you're supposed to greet people who have come to your home to spend the holidays with you.

"Danny," she says with a nod.

"We've heard a lot about you," Shane says.

Izzy has already returned to the slime show, because apparently a psychic has nothing on the draw of a crafting slime.

"I haven't heard anything," Ruthie says, giving me a dirty look. She should know by now that I'm no good at gossip or remembering whom I've told what.

"I'm the one who knew your brother and his girlfriend were soulmates," Josie says. "I told him months ago, but it took him a while to listen."

I feel everyone looking at me, their attention like legs skittering across my skin. Mira pokes me in the ribs.

"What?" I say, dumbfounded. "That's not true. You were much vaguer than that implies."

Josie shrugs. "A woman needs to maintain some mystery, and the veil is rarely transparent." A triumphant expression crosses her face. "But I was right, wasn't I?"

Her boyfriend gives her a little nudge, and she sighs and announces, "This is Poe."

He lifts a hand. "Hi, everyone. We brought bean dip. Thanks for having us over."

No one who lives here invited them, but it would feel rude not to say anything, so I nod and say, "Of course," which is not really a rational response.

Mira kisses the side of my face, and I'm suddenly grinning.

"So, who will it be?" Josie asks, flipping the veil over so it covers her face. "Who's brave enough to face the future?"

I probably surprise everyone in the room by raising my hand, as if I'm a kid in class she can call on, not a man in the living room of his own home. But Josie shakes her head. "We already know enough about your future."

She puts out a finger and toggles it around before landing on Shane.

He looks surprised and then disinterested, shaking his head. "No, thank you. No offense, but I don't buy into that stuff."

"You don't need to," she says. "The future catches up with all of us."

"Sure," he says with a chuckle. "Of course."

Ruthie puts a hand on her hip as she turns toward Shane.

His eyebrows hike up. "What?" he asks.

"Are you afraid of having your fortune told, Shane?"

"Of course not," he scoffs. When Ruthie doesn't look away, he sighs and heads over to the kitchen island, where Poe's now snacking on some bread that had been set out for later.

Shane sits on the stool across from Josie. She hums under her breath, staring at him, then bows her head to look into the crystal ball.

"You think she's studying her own reflection?" I whisper to Mira.

"*Yes*," she whispers back.

Josie snaps her head up, so suddenly that everyone in the apartment flinches. Everyone except for Poe, who keeps eating the bread.

"You should order a wedding cake. *Every* wedding should have a cake."

Shane gives an uneasy laugh before looking at Burke. "I think Burke can get his own cake."

"And he'll get a really splendid one. Three tier. Lots of those embellishments people like. But this one's not for him," Josie says, victory ringing in her voice. "It's for *you*."

Shane's laughter is more genuine as he gets to his feet. "Now, I know you're messing with me. I'm never getting married."

This earns another snort from Ruthie. "*Of course* you're not."

He turns in her direction, shooting her an annoyed glare. "You were married for four months, Ruthie. You're not exactly the poster child for marriage."

"Shane," I say tightly, because I saw it—Ruthie looks pissed as hell now, but before she went into the red zone, there was real hurt in her eyes.

"Sorry," he says, contrite, and I can see the day hanging on him. Maybe she does too, because she just shrugs and says, "It's fine."

The buzzer goes off again.

"That'll be the turkey!" Mira says, and we both head over to answer it.

When I press the speaker button, Leonard says, "We've got something to stick into your oven," and Mira rolls her eyes as she buzzes him in and then unlocks the door.

"You think there's anything to it?" she asks me in a whisper.

I sneak a glance at Shane, who's talking to Burke now. Delia seems to be offering encouragement to Deacon, probably because Shauna's grandmother is about to show up. Ruthie is talking to Josie. Izzy is hanging on to every last word of the slime crafter.

I think about Josie, who's right more often than she's not, even if most of her "readings" are so vague it would be hard for her to be wrong.

I think about what I'd like to happen.

I would like Shane to find the kind of happiness and peace I have whenever I'm with Mira. Especially now that he's unmoored—lost from the life he thought he was going to have.

"I'd like to think so," I tell her. "I want him to have what we have. I think everyone should."

She smiles at me, her eyes bright with it. "I agree."

Then the door bursts open, and there's again a flurry of activity and noise as Leonard enters with a stack of boxes, followed by Shauna and her grandmother and the teenage kid they've adopted as family. I feel my internal input meter turning a little more toward the right, but I'm also happy they're here.

"So, the bad news is that the turkey burned," Leonard says, "but the good news is that there's a Chinese restaurant near our house, so what I'm saying is that we brought Chinese food."

It takes half a second for him to notice Josie, then Shane. He whistles. "Something tells me some shit went down, brother. Want to give me the ten second rundown?" The others are coming toward us, closing in. I'm going to need a break later, but Mira already told me that I am going to be exiled out to the balcony whenever she notices I look queasy.

She squeezes my hand, probably because she knows it's already a lot, and I say, "Shane quit his job, stole back some scotch he'd given to his boss, and apparently he's getting married soon."

"Well, shit," Leonard says with a big grin. "That's a lot to be thankful for. Let's break open that Scotch and celebrate."

They pile in, our friends converging on them. I hear Josie shouting out the offer to read someone else's fortune, but I pull Mira back on impulse, guiding her out of the door before shutting it. Here, the sounds inside the apartment are a murmur.

Smiling, she says, "Are we making a break for it?" But I can see the slight worry under her smile.

I wrap my hands around her upper arms. "Maybe we should, but I just wanted a second alone with you. I'd prefer to tell you what I'm grateful for out here rather than in front of everyone else."

"You're about to tell me you're grateful for Officer Dunkins and all the law and order he brings, aren't you?" she says, and I'm grateful to see the worry on her face is easing.

I squeeze her shoulders, then drop one of my hands to claim hers, lifting it on its usual place on my chest. "You know me so well. But I'm not just grateful for Dunkins. Pumpkin has a special place in my heart too."

"Oh?" She wraps her hand around the bit of my shirt she's holding. "Is it because she broke my ankle?"

"She really seemed to have a vested interest in making sure we were stuck together. So did the elevator. It's a shame they're replacing it. I'd buy it if I could."

Apparently, we weren't the only ones who'd gotten stuck—just the two people who'd gotten stuck for the longest.

She's beaming at me, making me feel like I'm on the top of the world. Like I'm a man who can do anything he sets his mind to. "What would we do with an elevator?"

"Sleep in it. We could put it in our bedroom."

"I think I'll pass, but I'm pretty damn grateful to it too. And when we go around the table later, I think I might have to give a special shout out to pumpkin spice lattes. You've really changed my mind about them."

I lift a hand to her cheek. "Look at you, getting all basic on me."

"You love it."

"I do. And I love you, Mira Evans."

"I love you too, Bo Peep."

I bend to her as she lifts to me, almost as if we choreographed it, and we're still kissing when the door swings open.

"Oh, sorry," Ruthie says, grinning in a way that says she's not. "But I was worried you'd abandoned us to Josie."

"We're coming in," I say.

She nods, and disappears back inside, leaving the door open a crack. I let my hand linger on Mira's cheek for a second.

"You ready for this?" she asks, smiling.

"Probably not, but I think I have a couple of hours left. If you start a game of Charades, all bets are off."

Her hand flexes on my shirt. "Agreed."

"Shall we go back in?"

"I guess we have to." She's being wry, but I know she wants to. She's got that parade of construction paper turkeys waiting for her, after all. I swing the door open.

It's loud inside, and full of scents that now include the dissonance of bean dip, Chinese food, and Thanksgiving sides and pies. But I have to be honest: I don't think there's ever been a better holiday.

Maybe Josie was right about another thing to—it's time to reclaim Thanksgiving.

We walk inside, my arm around Mira, to do just that.

———

What's up next?

Shane and Ruthie in the enemies-to-lovers, brother's best friend, marriage of convenience romcom *You're so Vain*.

About the Author

ANGELA CASELLA is a romcom fanatic. Writing them, reading them, watching them—she's greedy, and she does it all. In addition to her solo releases, she's lucky enough to collaborate with Denise Grover Swank. They have three complete series and more co-written projects to come.

She lives in Asheville, NC. Her hobbies include herding her daughter toward less dangerous activities, the aforementioned romcom addiction, and dreaming of having someone else clean her house.

Visit her website at www.angelacasella.com or Angela and Denise's shared website at www.arcdgs.com.